Praise for *NO LAW AGAINST LOVE,*
Highland Press' Premier Book.
Join the authors in their fight against breast cancer!
Order at Amazon worldwide or all online bookstores

The lucky reader of NO LAW AGAINST LOVE is hereby sentenced to laugh-out-loud hours of enjoyment!
Couldn't be better.
- *Bestselling Author, Maggie Davis*

Funny, sensual and delightful...all in the name of charity. Take 16 very talented authors; mix in some of the most arcane and ridiculous laws that ever existed (some still on the books today), mix them all up, and you are in for an unbelievably rollicking good time! Yet, the best and most important thing to remember is that these wonderful ladies are doing this all in the name of charity. All proceeds will be donated to breast cancer research and treatment.
- *Marilyn Rondeau, The Best Reviews*

If you have ever found yourself rolling your eyes at some of the more stupid laws, then you are going to adore this novel. A stellar anthology that had me laughing, sighing in pleasure, believing in magic, and left me begging for more! Will there be a second anthology someday? I sure hope so! This is one novel that will go directly to my 'Keeper' shelf, to be read over and ove
Very highly r
- *Detra Fitch, H*

You might forget Highland Press is donating all of the proceeds from NO LAW AGAINST LOVE to breast cancer research, but you will never forget the brilliant characters that come to life under the passionate pens of 16 romance authors. While reading this anthology, prepare to break out in a sweat, bust out laughing and break all of the molds as far as romantic short stories are concerned.

- Aysel Arwen, Author of 'Romancing the Stars'

This brilliant anthology has the unique ability to make you feel good. Firstly, the reader feels pleased that just by buying the book she is doing good, as all profits go to breast cancer research. Secondly, and more importantly, the reader is given a thoroughly diverse group of short stories to enjoy, all written by some talented authors! You will laugh, smile and nod your head in complete understanding as a whole bunch of true-to-life characters take you on some very crazy, but always entertaining journeys! Everyone should have a copy of this book!

- Anne Whitfield, Author of 'With Regards, Anne'

Romance lovers the world over can rejoice in this fantastic volume of short stories. Based on obscure and little known laws, each tale centers around one of the laws. It's a fascinating concept for an anthology and one guaranteed to spark imaginative scenarios! From Scottish mountain cats in eye patches to travel agent fairies and shady angels, this volume runs the gamut of romance reading fun. Whatever your romance style, it's all here waiting for you. Get a copy today and curl up on the couch with it. Read it at the gym or enjoy it on a sunny day at the park-however you like to read, just get it and prepare to enjoy! *- Kenda Montgomery*

Blue Moon Enchantment

Highland Press
High Springs, Florida 32655

Blue Moon Enchantment

For information, please contact Highland Press, PO Box 2292, High Springs, FL 32655.

All characters in this book have no existence outside the imagination of the author and have no relation whatsoever to anyone bearing the same name or names, save actual historical figures. They are not even distantly inspired by any individual known or unknown to the author, and all incidents are pure invention.

ISBN: 0-9746249-7-7

PUBLISHED BY HIGHLAND PRESS PUBLISHING

A Wee Dram Book

For Senior Editors, Monika Wolmarans
and Patty Howell.
We couldn't have done this
without your overwhelming dedication.

ACKNOWLEDGEMENTS

Grateful thanks to our editors, Patty Howell, Diane Davis White, and Kemberlee Shortland and Monika Wolmarans.

Once again, a special thank you to my co-publisher, DeborahAnne MacGillivray, for all her support and the beautiful book covers she creates. Not only is she an exceptional author, her talent as a cover artist—everything artist— is something we're extremely proud of and thankful for. Thanks for this cover and its companion cover on Blue Moon Magic!

~ LLB

Our Authors

Gerri Bowen

Ann Marie Bradley

Leanne Burroughs

Candace Gold

Sherrie Holmes

Victoria Houseman

Patty Howell

Jill and Julia

Judith Laik

Deborah Anne MacGillivray

Jacquie Rogers

Michelle Scaplen

Kemberlee Shortland

Dawn Thompson

Jeanne Van Arsdall

Table of Contents

Under a Faery Blue Moon

by Dawn Thompson

Tatiana traveled the length of the portal between the physical plane and the land of the fey. She had paced there beside the abyss so long she'd worn a trench in the sweet myrtle, and totally trampled the meadowsweet to pollen spores. What was keeping Puck and Oberon? They should have returned long ago. It could only mean trouble. It *always* meant trouble when those two went off together.

She should have gone with them, of course. But there were good reasons why she hadn't. For one thing, somebody had to keep an eye upon the forest. The mist faeries, dryads, red-caps, and tree spirits were the worst to control under a normal full moon, they were impossible when the *blue moon* wove its magic. For another thing, Oberon always behaved like a lovesick satyr under a blue moon—or any other kind of moon, for that matter. She was looking forward to a breather, until he took Robin Goodfellow, the inimitable Puck, along. That alone flagged danger. All they had to do was unite two soulmates, just as they had hundreds of times. Now they were behindhand. It did not bode well.

Should she go, or should she stay? Should she tell the others she was leaving or simply slip away letting them think she was hiding somewhere watching them? It was hard work being Queen of the Faeries, without all this drama. There was nothing for it. She would definitely go, and she would most definitely slip away. To announce her departure for however a brief length of time would only give the forest folk license to run amok engaging in all manner of mischief. That decided, she cast a quick glance over her shoulder, took a deep breath, and stepped into the abyss that folded a pleat in time to align the parallel worlds for thru traffic.

Tatiana appeared in the place Puck and Oberon had come to ground, the sculptured gardens of the Dowager Lady Raintree's Mayfair townhouse. Although there were plenty of people milling about, none could see her. Humans couldn't see the fey, unless, of course the fey wanted them to. These humans seemed drunk on something; men and women alike in their cups. While that would not have been amiss at a Blue Moon Ball, their behavior under the influence was quite shocking. Distinguished gentlemen were chasing chambermaids. Countesses and ladies young and old, were reveling with counts and earls and dukes whom Tatiana surmised were not their spouses. With unabashed abandon, the entire congregation—the Dowager Lady Raintree included—ran helter-skelter over the property rooting out the rhododendrons, and trampling primrose beds. It was passing strange, reminding Tatiana of the faery ring revels at home. The handiwork of Puck and Oberon, she had no doubt. She craned her neck in search of the mischievous pair, but there was no sign of them. Had they caused this chaos and fled? What other explanation could there be? She hadn't come a minute too soon.

Tatiana peeked in through the ballroom terrace doors. Aside from a rotund reveler, who had hefted the punchbowl and was draining it to the dregs, the room seemed empty, everyone having fled to the garden for their debauch pursuits. All except one, Tatiana discovered at a second glance, a pretty young thing with a cap of strawberry-blonde curls, hunched over hugging her knees on the second step of the sweeping ballroom staircase. She couldn't see the girl's face, but she appeared to be crying by the way her shoulders were shaking.

Across the way, the clang of the silver punch bowl hitting the banquet table turned Tatiana's head in time to see the fat man stagger out onto the terrace and reel off into the crowd of milling revelers. Padding toward the discarded bowl, for she was barefoot, Tatiana bent down and sniffed it. *It couldn't be*! But it was, she took a drop on her finger and tasted it...*heart's ease*!

Tatiana slapped the skirt of her gossamer spider silk gown with hands balled into fists. "Wild pansy in the claret cup and the humans have drunk from it!" she seethed under her breath, although no one would hear. Faery speech passed as naught but the sighing of the wind to mortal ears. "I knew it! What have those two halfwits done?"

The ideal thing would be to eavesdrop on a conversation amongst humans in order to get the drift of the situation. The girl in tears had been abandoned, and one glance toward the ninnyhammers—a literal blur of guests and servants alike—cavorting in the garden scotched that possibility also. Not one of them was sober, if that was the correct word for it. Tatiana only hoped Puck and Oberon had concocted a mild dose. Whatever possessed them to put the *heart's ease* nectar in the punch in the first place, she couldn't imagine. A scant drop in the eyes of the subject was enough to make a body fall hopelessly in love with the first person they sighted. There was no need to infect the whole population. But then, people hardly slept at a ball.

"Oh, pother!" she cried. "There is no sense to be made of it. The damage is done, and it's up to me to undo it...*again*!"

Floating to the crying girl's side, Tatiana hesitated. It wasn't usual for faeries, no matter the species, to show themselves in their faery form to mortals; it simply wasn't done. Spinning in place like a prima ballerina, she emerged in the form she always took when dealing directly with humans and tapped the girl on the shoulder.

"Is there anything I can do?" she said.

The girl looked up and took her measure. A pretty little thing if her eyes weren't nearly swollen shut from crying. They were blue, when they weren't red, Tatiana surmised, the most striking feature in a very pleasant countenance.

"Everything's ruined," the girl wailed. "My aunt brought me here to introduce me to the Dowager Lady Raintree's grandson, Viscount Barnaby Critchton, and now look!" She waved her hand toward the gardens.

"Umm," Tatiana hummed. Were there naught but desperate spinsters at the Blue Moon Ball? "My name is Tatiana, what are you called, child?"

"Lady Penelope Abbot," the girl said.

The name didn't ring a bell. It certainly wasn't the young lady Puck and Oberon had come to champion. "Well, Lady Penelope, which one is your aunt?"

"The one in bottle green, with the rose in her teeth riding on the footman's back," the girl wailed.

"Oh, dear," Tatiana said, observing the rather large woman with pendulous breasts perched precariously upon the spindly-legged servant's shoulders. "I see what you mean...Is the viscount among those...eh out there?"

The girl shook her head. "No, he hasn't come down yet. Who is to introduce us now? This ball was my last hope of escaping spinsterhood. Half the ladies here are in the same situation. That is why the Dowager Lady Raintree hosts the ball each year. Now, someone will surely introduce him to another. I can't very well introduce myself, can I?" She looked up then, her eyes flitting over Tatiana's attire. Her jaw dropped, and she gasped. "Was this supposed to be a costume ball?" she cried.

Tatiana glanced down at her whisper-thin frock. *Syl on his throne*! She'd changed incarnations so quickly she'd neglected to change her costume. Her form-fitting gossamer green gown of spider silk did little to conceal her charms. She rolled her eyes and sighed. Evoking the name of the great god *Syl* in vain would surely cause reprisals, but by the way things were going she was sure that had already begun.

"Oh...no," she gushed. "I've just come from another affair...a masked ball," she said, proud of her quick thinking.

"What are you supposed to be?" the girl asked her.

"A faery," Tatiana said, with not a little pride. Expanding her posture, she fluffed her long golden hair and preened before the girl.

"Oh no," Penelope said. "Faeries don't look like *that*."

"They don't? And what do they look like? Have you ever seen one?"

"Well, no, but everyone knows faeries have wings, and wands, and...well, I can see right through that dress." She said the last in a stage whisper. She giggled. "Why, you look more like a Whitechapel doxy in that rig than a faery."

Tatiana backed up apace. Astonishment ruled her posture, and she was about to defend herself when a tall, impeccably dressed gentleman outfitted in Beau Brummel black and white came jogging down the stairs tugging on his spotless white gloves.

"*It's him*!" Penelope squealed, surging to her feet.

Tatiana stared. Never had she seen such a handsome figure of man from his dark wavy hair and smoldering blue eyes, to the tips of his fine leather dress shoes. Tight satin breeches left nothing to the imagination in the area of his well turned thighs, and the white silk hose accented perfectly formed calves. No padding needed here, or corset either, like so many of the men wore to mask their imperfections in view of the revealing fashions of the day.

Her heart was palpitating—fairly leaping from her breast. No man—human or fey, including Oberon—had ever affected her in such a way, so totally drenched her in fire from her bare feet to the crown of cobweb silk and dew pearls upon her head. It was as if her heart beat only for him. Longing overcame her. She was ablaze with a voluptuous swell of passion for him—a man she hadn't set eyes upon until a heartbeat ago. Madness!

But he looked right through her and passed by as though he hadn't even seen her standing there in her all-but-naked glory. Tatiana's heart sank. Well, why wouldn't he pass her by? He couldn't *see* her, could he? She hadn't made herself visible to anyone but Penelope, had she?

The viscount gave a polite albeit banal nod in Penelope's direction and strode to the banquet table. Tatiana followed him. What was wrong with her? She was acting like a peapod pixie foxed upon honeysuckle nectar, but she couldn't help herself. All she could think of was tearing off that tailcoat, then the white on white brocade waistcoat, Egyptian cotton shirt, and neckcloth. She wanted him naked in her arms that very moment. Nothing else would slake her insatiable hunger for him.

The rotund reveler earlier hadn't drained the claret cup after all. The viscount took up the ladle, tilted the bowl, and filled a punch cup. Turning, he raised it to his lips, but hesitated, his gaze meeting Penelope's across the way.

"Forgive me my want of conduct. Would you like a cup, my lady?"

"*No*!" Tatiana cried, bobbing up and down between them. "You don't want to give *her* a cup of that!" He couldn't hear her, of course, just as he couldn't see her.

Tatiana spun, and spun again in frantic circles, but nothing happened. Why couldn't she make herself visible to him? *Horrors*! He lifted the cup and drank, eyes riveted to Penelope's, and in the hazy stupor of enchantment, Tatiana knew. *Heart's ease* had strange effects upon the fey; all were susceptible; the higher their rank, the more severely, and she was Queen of the Fey. She had tasted the contents of the punch bowl. The only thing needed for the spell to work was one drop! The knowledge came and went in the space of time it takes to burst a bubble.

Viscount Barnaby Critchton, meanwhile, had eyes for no one but Lady Penelope Abbot, whose eyes were blue again and saw no one but him, although she hadn't touched a drop of the claret cup. Arm in arm, the two waltzed out into the garden; so much for formal introductions. What would the *ton* say? What did it matter? Half the *ton* was foxed on wild pansy, and had run amok in Mayfair, of all places!

Screaming like a banshee, Tatiana fled.

"We're in for it now," Oberon said from behind the potted palm in an alcove under the staircase where he and Puck had taken refuge. "She will never forgive us for this. If you'd caught a ride on that moonbeam instead of trying to shake that dryad out of the willow in the park down the lane, we would have been home in the forest by now, and Tatiana would never have come."

"You didn't have to stay with me, you know," Puck said. "You could have climbed right up that moonbeam and accessed the portal on your own. Why didn't you?"

Oberon scowled, taking his gossamer redingote back from the palm frond that had snagged it. "Let go, you miscreant reject from the tropics!" he railed at the plant, as he yanked it free. "Is everything in this god-awful place hostile to the fey?"

Puck leaked a lightheaded twitter. "You're just miffed because that dryad wouldn't give you a tumble," he said, patting the palm on its highest frond, as if he was soothing a child.

"That dryad had crossed over on the sly," Oberon grumbled. "She had no business being here."

"They all do it."

"Yes, well, that one won't do it again, I promise you."

Puck sighed. "You haven't been any fun for eons—not since you joined with Tatiana. Monogamy is boring. That's why you're so sour. Perhaps you ought to drink some of that punch. Methinks a little nip of *heart's ease* would do you a world of good."

"Never you mind about me," Oberon snapped. "What are we going to do about Tatiana?"

"It doesn't bother you that she is lusting after a total stranger—a mortal stranger at that—and if she could command her powers and materialize before him she'd cock a leg over that jumped-up popinjay faster than you could say *Will-o-the-wisp*?"

"That isn't her fault, it's your fault," Oberon sallied. "I don't know why I let you talk me into these escapades of yours. I do know you had better figure a way out of this one, or by Syl Almighty, you will rue the day you first laid eyes upon the King of the Fey, my goatish little meddler!"

"Oh, pish-posh, old friend," Puck scoffed. "Take ease. I have a plan, and you know plans are what I do best."

Oberon rolled his eyes. "Well, you need to be about it then," he said, pointing. "Do you see Tatiana making a total ass of herself out there? You had best set your 'plan' in motion before it is too late."

"My lord, you are too bold," Lady Penelope said, retrieving her hand from the viscount's amorous possession. It was stinging from his kisses. What had gotten into the man? His gaze all but froze her direct coming off that staircase. What turned him so quickly, she couldn't imagine. It quite took her breath away. And why was Tatiana bobbing about like that, waving her arms in the air. Why did he pay her no notice?

"I am foxed by your beauty," the viscount said, capturing her hand again. "Merely a taste of those luscious lips..."

"Remember yourself, my lord!" Penelope cried, ranging herself out of his reach on the stone bench they occupied beside the bower. "We haven't even been properly introduced, sir."

"A minor technicality," he chortled, waving his hand toward the cavorting guests. "Even Grandmama seems to have caught blue moon madness, and she did intend to introduce us, after all..."

"No! No kisses!" Tatiana twittered, forcing herself between them. "You're compromised as it is. Not one of these is a fit chaperon. You'll be ruined—you will!"

Penelope stared at her. Why was Tatiana pawing him like that? She had twined herself around him like a climbing vine. The viscount didn't seem to notice. How could he not? She was all over him. Why couldn't he feel her shocking advances upon his person? It was as if she were invisible to him.

Penelope scrunched back into the viscount's orbit. "Stop that!" she snapped, attempting to pry the faery's arms free. "Let go!"

"Well now," the viscount said, as Penelope's arms slipped around him accidentally in her attempt to loosen Tatiana's hold. "That is more like it!"

Penelope let him go and shoved him away as if she'd touched live coals. "You are mistaken, my lord," she said loftily. "You are most persuasive, but even though this lot has apparently run mad, I am still a lady. I would thank you to remember that, sir."

"But of course you are, Lady Penelope," the viscount murmured. "It must be the moon. The full moon is said to bring madness to those under its spell. It certainly seems to have done so here tonight." He drew her close again. How strong his warm arms were. The muscles rippling in his biceps and chest beneath the superfine frock coat riveted her alarmingly. "I will have that kiss, though," he whispered seductively, "...just one under that bewitching moon. It would be such a pity to waste it, and then I shall see you home, my lady, since none here are suited to the task..."

"No! No kiss!" Tatiana shrilled, attempting to force herself between them. Grunting and groaning, she tugged at the viscount's broad shoulders.

"Stop that, I say!" Penelope cried, shoving Tatiana away. "Who *are* you?"

"I am a man you have bewitched," the viscount crooned, evidently assuming she'd spoken to him. It was beyond bizarre.

Cupping Penelope's chin in his hand, he took her lips ever so gently at first. She stiffened as he deepened the kiss. His evocative male scent threaded through her nostrils, mixed with the ghost of his citrus shaving paste, and the claret he'd drunk, with odd top notes of...what was that...*wild pansy* of all things? It foxed her as if she'd drunk the wine herself, for she tasted it on his tongue as it probed deeper still. Warm and welcoming, it drew her nearer, and she melted against him, a captive of the enchantment that held them both enthralled.

Waves of enlightenment ignited Penelope's senses, as if she was seeing the viscount for the first time, viewing his attributes and failings as though through a kaleidoscope and loving him for—and in spite of—what she saw. It was as if she had come home. Crowding close in those strong arms was pure enchantment. Shocking though the strange sensations welling up at the epicenter of her existence were, she wanted more—wanted everything this man's volatile embrace promised.

It was a kiss like no other, not only a joining of the body, but of the soul, so all consuming a thing it diminished Tatiana's shrill banshee wail, as she spun waving her fists in the air, and finally spiraled off in the shimmering moonlight.

"There! You see?" Puck said. "I told you all would be well."

"Harumph!" Oberon snorted, waving a wild arm toward the two enchanted lovers in the midst of chaos in the Dowager Lady Raintree's sculptured gardens. "You call that 'well'? I haven't seen Tatiana hare off like that since I...ahem, well, never mind! Believe me this is far from over.

That stuff doesn't wear off, remember? The *heart's ease* enchantment is forever."

Puck gave a start. "Unless we work a spell to counter it," he said, discovery lifting his voice. "Oh! Let me!" Dancing about on the townhouse terrace, he leaped into the air and clicked his cloven hooves together. "You know spells are what I do best."

Oberon's winged eyebrow lifted. "I thought that was 'plans'."

"Oh, those, too, but *spells*. Now there's a noble calling for a nature spirit." He snapped his fingers calling his pan pipes to appear, and began to play a lively tune while tripping lightly about the terrace for one of such cumbersome proportions, Oberon thought.

"We don't have time for that!" the King of the Faeries snapped, snatching the flute. "I seem to recall Nero using his musical talents, at your encouragement, mind, while Rome went up in flames. Let us see if this occasion can be dealt with, with less inflammatory results, um?"

Tatiana resumed her natural diminutive state and made herself invisible for the ride through the all but empty streets of Mayfair, as the viscount's brougham tooled over the cobblestones in the moonlit darkness. Everything else having failed, it was best now that she work her wiles upon him unseen.

He was taking Lady Penelope home. Then, once shot of the competition, he would be hers. None were able to resist her charms—human or fey—when she set her mind to a conquest. She blasphemed under her breath. If she hadn't tasted that deuced concoction, she could resolve the situation in a trice—a snap of her fingers—a blink of her eye. Her magic was inscrutable and infallible. It simply *was*, or would have been if she hadn't drunk that claret. One drop and now look! That's all it took to render her practically powerless. What was she thinking? Everyone knew the spells of the fey turned back upon them could have disastrous results; a peapod pixy knew that, and she was Queen of the Fey! The deuced blue moon—that's what it was, and the meddling efforts of that goat-like little hairy-legged flute playing pain in the wings, Puck!

She perched upon the viscount's shoulder, what she could grab onto, since Lady Penelope was hogging it. The silly chit was hanging on like a dryad clinging to an oak branch in a stiff wind. Didn't she know the viscount was hers? She'd seen him first after tasting that punch. There was absolutely no honor in humans.

The isinglass coach window was rolled down letting in a breath of the sultry night air. Were those two going to sit there tangled together with their lips locked the whole distance to the girl's residence? Tatiana climbed over Lady Penelope's arm on the viscount's shoulder and grabbed onto a lock of mahogany hair curling about his earlobe. Resisting the urge to snarl that thick, wavy hair, as faeries are wont to do, she swung on it instead, meanwhile crooning one of the irresistibly haunting fey melodies known to turn even the most hard-hearted males to putty in a faery's hands. At least she hadn't lost that talent...But did he hear her? Evidently not! All at once, he flicked her away—right out through the open coach window with the back of his hand, as the coach rolled to a stop beside a stately townhouse across from the park.

"Eeeeeeeee!" Tatiana squealed as she sailed through the air, her opalescent crown of cobweb silk and dew pearls flying off her head.

"What was that?" Penelope said, breaking lip contact with the viscount at last.

He shrugged. "'Twas nothing," he returned, "merely a mosquito or some such bug buzzing in my ear. It's gone now."

Tatiana stood fuming on the cobblestone lane, her tiny hands balled into fists. "Bug? Did the clumsy lout say *bug*? I will show him 'bug'!"

The driver had set the steps and the viscount exited first. Handing Lady Penelope down, he led her along the well manicured walk to the front steps of the house and took her in his arms again. Now what were they doing? Did he just put his hand on her breast? What's more, did she just let him?

"What about *my* breast?" Tatiana shrilled at the moon—the deuced blue moon! "I saw you first, you bufflehead!"

Rubbing her behind, for that's what she had landed on, she limped along the path, but too late. Large feet all but kicked her to the curb.

"Until tomorrow, then," the viscount called over his shoulder sprinting down the walk, "...when I can begin to court you properly, my lady..."

Lady Penelope twittered a gushing "goodnight" and disappeared inside the townhouse. Finally! Still too stunned to fly, Tatiana watched the coach tool out of sight. It wasn't over. He'd be coming back tomorrow, like he'd said, and she would be waiting for him. The sun didn't rise upon the day Tatiana, Queen of the Fey, couldn't outsmart a mortal man. Still soothing her dignity, and her bottom, she limped toward the little park across the way; as good a place as any to pass the night, and the perfect vantage to watch for the viscount's return.

"Did you hear that?" Oberon said.

"Hear what?" Puck asked looking up from the book of spells he'd conjured as he had done the flute he was still piping on with his free hand.

"Give me that!" Oberon snapped at him, snatching the Pan pipes again. "You aren't getting this back until you set this nightmare to rights, Robin Goodfellow, you misnamed little imp! Be still! I thought I heard Tatiana scream."

Both faeries peeked around the edge of the carriage boot, where they'd been hiding having hitched a ride, in time to see Tatiana staggering toward the townhouse.

"Now what do we do?" Oberon said, jumping down from the coach.

"Not to worry," Puck tittered, hopping down alongside. "I have a plan, and you know plans are what I do best."

"Ummm," Oberon grunted. "Plans—spells, make up your mind! And what of those two lovers?"

Puck shrugged. "Oh, they're done. Their courtship has just begun. No worries there."

"And Tatiana?" Oberon waved his arm. "Look at her. She is positively enthralled! We will never get her through the portal like *that*!"

"Will you relax?" Puck drawled. "I think I've found the perfect spell...I just need something—" he searched the cobblestones "—that belongs to her..."

"What's this?" Oberon said, dislodging something sparkly of indeterminable origin that had come to rest against the carriage wheel.

Puck pounced upon it. "*That's it*!" he warbled, snatching the object off the cobblestones. "Tatiana's crown, somewhat out of round, but just the thing nonetheless." He raised it to his nose. "Ummm, primrose!" he crooned. "Her very essence still lingers—smell."

Oberon waved the crumpled crown away as Puck shoved it under his nose. "Enough! You'd best do whatever it is you're going to do, and be quick about it. She's coming back!"

Grabbing Puck's pointed ear, like the obstreperous child he was, Oberon blinked them into the little park not a minute too soon. If Tatiana hadn't been favoring her bruised body after the fall, they would have run right into each other, since they were heading in the same direction.

Squatting in a bed of flowering pinks, with the book of spells propped upon one shaggy knee, Puck leafed through the pages. Oberon looked on, his anxious eyes oscillating between the exasperating nature spirit at his side, and Tatiana, who had climbed up into the self-same willow he'd evicted the dryad from what seemed an eon ago for everything that had happened since.

"Will you hurry up?" he grumbled. "There are nettles in this stuff, and pinks make me sneeze!"

"Patience," Puck drawled. "Ah! Here it is!" He shoved the tome in Oberon's face. "We have to make a circle..."

"...out of what?" Oberon queried.

Puck stared at him with such an incredulous look, Oberon backed away. "It doesn't matter," Puck said, "as long as we create one, stay inside it, and either keep Tatiana, or one of her belongings inside it until the spell is cast." He waved the dented crown. "This will do nicely...Now for the ring..."

They both glanced about, but nothing met their eyes except the flowering pinks they squatted in.

"Here," Puck said, plucking a handful of the tiny pink blossoms, "grab some and do as I do. And don't sneeze! Cloak yourself. Who knows how many of her powers she still commands. We'd best be invisible for this."

Oberon did as Puck bade him. Sneezing, however, was inevitable, but if she could hear him, at least she couldn't see him as he helped Puck distribute the flowers.

"Now what?" Oberon asked once the ring was drawn.

"We dance, old friend, while I play my pipes, since we don't have a drum. Do you think you can manage that?"

"That is *all*?"

"That is much," Puck said with a wink. "We mark five places along the curve of the ring, and at these five spots, we dance and invite any fey that might be about and are brave enough to join us. When all five dances have been performed, we, with any and all who answer the call, dance randomly until dawn, at which time I evoke the incantation to break the spell, and she remembers nothing after she tasted that doctored claret...if we're lucky..."

"And if we are not?" Oberon persisted. Somebody had to think with a level head.

"Then I do believe she stays as she is!" Puck said, dismissing the spell book with flourish. "You really need to have more faith in me you know, Oberon," he said pouting. "But if you believe you can do better..."

"No, no—Syl, no! Please get on with it. Is there anything else I need know about before we begin this madness?"

"No—*yes*!" Puck quickly amended. "The dancing must be done *widdershins*, that is to say against the movements of the clock. 'Tis *deosil*, or with the clock, to cause an attraction, and *widdershins* to break the spell..."

"You lead," Oberon said. "You are by far the better dancer."

Wasting no more time, Robin Goodfellow, and Oberon, King of the Fey, began their counterclockwise revolutions, pausing at each of the five designated points to invite any others who might be near to come and join the dance, five being a magical number amongst the fey. Where they all came from, Oberon would never know, but come they did in droves—nymphs and dryads, brown men and pixies, red caps and gnomes to rally 'round their queen. And so it went until dawn, when the celebrants disappeared in the morning mist winding its lazy way through the little park—everyone except himself and Puck. Then they collapsed, exhausted to wait for Tatiana to wake and see if the spell had worked.

The sun had nearly reached the zenith when they stirred. Movement in the uppermost branches of the willow tree made Oberon's heart race.

He elbowed Puck, and pointed. "She wakes. Now we'll see," he whispered, suppressing a sneeze.

"Indeed we shall," Puck returned, nodding toward a familiar brougham rolling to a stop across the lane.

The viscount climbed down and strode up the walk with a definite spring in his step, thought Oberon, just as Tatiana yawned and stretched and flitted to the ground.

"Steady on," Puck said. Snatching up her crumpled crown, he dusted it off, and quit the circle of flowering pinks, with Oberon on his heels.

At first sighting, Tatiana snapped off a green willow branch from the tree she'd just vacated, and marched straight for them, loosing a string of oaths that disbursed the mist in her path like fleeing wraiths.

"Uh-oh!" Puck said, hiding behind Oberon's flowing redingote. The switch still beaned him nonetheless.

"And *you*," she said to Oberon, crowning him with the branch as well. "Could you not handle one simple request—to unite two lost soulmates at a foolish human ball? What have you two been up to? Do not presume to lie. Guilt is written all over your faces—both of you! Look at yourselves! You're castaway on human wine!"

Oberon opened his mouth to answer, but across the way, the viscount and his lady came tripping down the Abbot's townhouse walking arm in arm.

"Now, we'll see," Puck whispered in Oberon's pointed ear.

The lover's laughter turned Tatiana's head. "Where are we?" she said. "This isn't the townhouse I arrived at. Who are those shameless creatures, pawing and petting in the street at midday? And mortals say *we* are lustful creatures."

"You do not recognize them, your majesty?" Puck said, giving the willow switch a wide berth.

Tatiana studied the pair climbing into the brougham. "Now that you mention it, I think I do. The girl at least; we spoke, I think, not him, though. Syl, but mortal men are ugly." She spun back toward them. "Well? Did you accomplish your task?" she snapped.

"Y-yes, your majesty," they replied in unison.

"Good!" Tatiana said, prodding them with the willow branch. "Now, march! I'll deal with you back in the forest. Something untoward has gone on here, I can feel it in my bones; they're positively aching. You haven't fooled me, Oberon. You've been up to something, and you can bet it will be another blue moon before I let you share my bed and bower again. I said, *march*!"

The coach tooled off down the lane, as Tatiana herded them in the opposite direction with the switch.

"I told you, you worry too much," Puck whispered to Oberon as they hurried on, prodded by the willow branch. "I can't imagine why, when you know happy endings are what I do best."

If you'd like to read more of Puck's and Oberon's exploits,
we invite you to read
Belle of the Blue Moon Ball
in the *Blue Moon Magic* Anthology

Also available by Dawn Thompson:
The Ravencliffe Bride
The Waterlord
The Falcon's Bride

Visit Dawn's website at
http://www.dawnthompson.com

The Anti-Kissing League

by Leanne Burroughs

1909 Georgia

The bell over the door rang, signaling someone entered the store. Millicent Baker shook her head and sighed. She'd just climbed to the top of the ladder to restock the upper shelves and now someone had to come in. Typical.

Glancing over her shoulder, she saw a man tall and lean, his sandy hair the color of his plaid shirt, then stretched taut over broad shoulders and well-muscled arms as he reached up to take a large bag of flour from the shelf. He turned then and sauntered over and placed the sack cloth bag atop the counter. Her gaze took in the length of him, noted the firm thighs beneath what appeared to be new blue jeans. No one ever came to Napierville on purpose. Who was he? Why was he in her father's store?

Taking a deep, steadying breath, Millie climbed down the steps and turned to face the stranger, coming face to face with the most amazing pair of blue eyes. That he had one of the most handsome faces she'd ever seen didn't escape her notice either.

Then he smiled. Millie couldn't breathe.

She couldn't stop herself. Her eye swept over him from the tips of his shiny black shoes back up to his face. His lips were tipped in an amused smile – one light brown brow arched in speculation. Her hand flew to her cheek in embarrassment. Mercy! She'd been staring! A lady never stared. Well, all right, they did, but one certainly wasn't supposed to get caught doing it.

Warmth of a blush crept up her face. Why did she always have to do that? He'd think her a silly twit.

Regaining her manners, Millie approached the counter. "Hello. I haven't seen you here before. Are you new in town?"

What a stupid question to ask. It was obvious he was, because she knew everyone who lived in Napierville. The unexpected warmth that crept up her face had more to do with the handsome stranger than her obvious 'stupid' question. Didn't it?

His blue eyes sparkled and seemed to dance in merriment, but he lightly touched the brim of his fur blend hat in welcome. She noticed he didn't wear a plain straw farmer's hat like most local men wore to keep the sun from their eyes. She'd seen some like his in the catalogue her pa placed orders from. American bison fur with a twisted leather band around its crown. Those didn't come cheap.

Realizing he was speaking, Millie shook herself from her reverie.

"...three miles or so out of town."

"I'm sorry, where did you say you were staying?"

The stranger again cocked his brow.

"I said, my name is Geoffrey Standish. My aunt and uncle own a farm about three miles or so out of town."

"There's no one named Standish hereabouts."

"Nope, their name's Hooper."

"Ida Mae and Henry?"

"Yes, that's them. Uncle Henry's been ill, so Mother decided I needed to come here for the summer and help him on his farm."

Unable to stop herself, Millie grinned and choked back an amused chuckle. "You don't look like a farmer."

His smile was charming as he asked, "Is it that obvious I've never been on a farm before?"

Millie nodded, but said nothing.

"Actually, I'm from New York. And the fact I took Father's brand new Model 20 for a joy ride played heavily into her decision to send me."

Unable to tear her gaze away from his face, Millie just watched his expressive blue eyes. And his mouth. Oh yes, she did watch his mouth.

"So, am I to know your name as well or do locals hereabouts not practice proper manners?"

"Of course we practice *proper manners*, as you so indelicately put it. Northerners clearly aren't perfect either."

Geoffrey laughed, then cocked his head and stared without saying anything else.

"What?" Millie burst out in exasperation.

"You still haven't told me your name."

Drat and blast! She could feel the heat creeping up her cheeks again. "Millicent Baker," she stated formally, "but everyone calls me Millie."

"Well, it's nice to meet you Miss Millicent Baker. Now if you'll be so kind as to ring these items up, I'd best finish gathering what's on Aunt Ida's list." He gestured to the bags of flour and sugar on the counter. "I promised I'd return early." Chuckling, he added, "I think she was afraid I'd get lost."

Millie walked around the counter, following him. "If you'll show me Miz Ida's list, I'll help you fetch the items."

He shrugged and nodded his agreement. When he handed her the list, their hands brushed and Millie felt like a bolt of lightning shot through her. From his expression, he must've felt something too.

To cover her embarrassment, she headed toward the shelves stocked full of everything her pa thought people could possibly need. "If you'll follow me, I'll hand you the items and you can place them on the counter. It will be quicker that way."

The door opened and the bell jingled again. Millie glanced over her shoulder to see who it was as she reached to grab something off the shelf.

"Afternoon, Miz Esther. I'll be with you in a few minutes."

"Afternoon, Millie. No rush. I'll look around. I told my Homer I planned to get me a new length of material."

While gathering the items on Geoffrey Standish's list, Millie glanced at Esther Taylor. The woman hadn't moved the first step toward the material, but stood staring at Mr. Standish.

"Miz Esther, have you met Mr. Standish? He's here from New York. He's staying with his aunt and uncle, the Hooper's."

Material clearly forgotten, Esther Taylor approached them. "Ida Mae and Henry? Well, now, I didn't know they were expecting company. Thought I heard Henry's sick."

Tipping the brim of his hat in her direction, Standish said, "Yes, ma'am. That's why I'm here. When Mother received word Uncle Henry was ill, she decided I should come help this summer."

Giving an unladylike snort, Esther Taylor said, "Leila Hooper is your mother? No one's heard nary a word from her since she ran off with that Englishman and now she's sending you to help?"

Standish straightened his shoulders. "Yes, ma'am. Leila *Standish* is my mother, and *that Englishman* is my father." His hostility toward Esther Taylor's words showed clearly on his face.

To deflate the tension in the room, Millie handed him more items. "If you would place these on the counter, we'll have your order filled in no time."

She faced Mrs. Taylor. "You know where the material is Miz Taylor. If you see something there you like, I'll be with you as soon as I'm finished with Mr. Standish."

But the woman didn't move, just watched Standish walk toward the counter.

Hoping to draw the stubborn woman's attention away from Geoffrey, she asked, "Are you making a new dress for Sunday's social this week, Miz Taylor?"

Since the woman was not only the banker's wife, but the town gossip, Millie had no doubt that within the hour everyone in Napierville would know Leila Hooper's son was in own.

"Yes, dear, I am. You'll be there, too, won't you?"

"Yes, ma'am, wouldn't miss it."

Millie drew the ladder along the track and climbed up several rungs to reach for two bags of coffee beans. The weight of the second bag threw her slightly off balance.

Before she steadied herself, two strong hands grabbed her waist. As if she weighed no more than a feather, those same hands lifted her and placed her safely on the floor.

He turned her and peered deeply into her eyes. "You okay?"

Millie couldn't speak. Just nodded and stared up into those eyes. Eyes as blue as a Robin's egg.

Storming over, Mrs. Taylor pulled her away from Standish's grasp, then spun on him and wagged her finger in his face. "Young man, did your mother teach you no manners at all? It's not proper to touch a young woman you don't know. We're not some small backwards town. We have manners down here, unlike what I hear about people who live in large cities."

For several seconds Standish only stared at her. Then a smirk edged his lips. "I'd probably know her a lot better by now if some nosy busybody wasn't in the store with us."

"Well, I never!"

"No, ma'am, I imagine you haven't. I've been in town less than a week now and I've already heard about the ridiculous *Anti-Kissing League*. No wonder everyone's disposition is so sour in this one-horse town." He quirked a brow at the older woman. "Or are *y'all* always this rude to people?"

Mrs. Taylor sputtered. "Well I...I...I should have expected no less from Leila Hooper's young'un. Anyone that would run away with some foreign traveling salesman and leave her family without a word is no lady."

Standish's eyes narrowed, but his voice remained level. "Ma'am, I suggest you not say one more derogatory word about my mother. If you don't like my behavior now, you certainly won't like it if you continue."

He shifted to face Millie.

"Miss Millicent, I believe it's best I leave now." He reached for the bags of flour and sugar. "I'll take these for now, then be back tomorrow for the rest of the supplies and to settle Uncle Henry's account."

Without another word, he crossed the store and strode out the door.

Millie hurried to the window and watched the material pull taught across his thighs as he eased himself up to the seat on the wagon. Before he flicked the reins to start the horse in motion, Geoffrey Standish winked at her.

And then he was gone.

Brown eyes and brunette hair, tied back with a delicate blue bow. That's what teased Geoff's memory as the horse pulled the wagon down the rutted dirt road back to his uncle's farm. What a laugh. As if he gave a rat's ass about a delicate blue bow. What he did care about was the young woman wearing it. And he'd noticed every detail of her old-fashioned dress. Far from the up-to-the-minute fashions his mother received from London and Paris, this dress looked as if it had been around since the 1800s. But oh how it had fit her. From the small white standup collar to the pleating of the skirt as it flared over her hips, he'd noted everything. Made him want to know exactly what was beneath that tightly fitted blue bodice. Yet lust aside, it was her quick wit and smile that made him want to know more.

And that bothered him. She'd gotten under his skin. Oh yes, in those few short minutes together, Miss Millicent Baker—with her wide smile and dimples and the embarrassed flush to her cheeks—had definitely gotten under his skin. A woman was the last complication he'd planned on for this summer.

It was bad enough Mother had sent him off to this godforsaken place. He'd never even met Aunt Ida Mae and Uncle Henry and now Mother expected him to help on their farm? He didn't belong here. He belonged in Manhattan, working with Father at MetLife at One Madison Avenue, and driving Father's new Model 20. That was one fine vehicle, and Geoff was proud his Father owned one of the first few produced by the Hudson Corporation.

He wondered if his father's prosperity and wealth was why his mother's distant relatives had contacted them now.

Geoff's stomach knotted. Did they want money?

These people meant nothing to him and he wanted nothing to do with them. Hadn't they shunned his mother all these years? Now they expected him to help them?

No, he knew none of that was true. His aunt and uncle had been kind to him this past week.

What he hadn't counted on was a complication in the form of a pretty young woman who barely came to his shoulders. He'd felt the spark when their hands had first touched. And when he'd held her while helping her down from the ladder, Geoff acknowledged he'd felt things he'd never felt before. And certainly never thought to feel when told he was being banished to this place.

If not for that interfering biddy, he might even have been lucky enough to steal a kiss. Wouldn't that be funny? Kiss a beautiful young woman he didn't know in a town that currently had a ban on kissing?

The lunacy of it. Believing the future of their town's crops depended on men not kissing their wives. Wait until he was back home and told Brody and Rod about that!

"Why of course you'll attend the social with us after church today, Geoffrey," his aunt told him. "Everyone in town will be there. It was all we talked about at our quilting bee Friday afternoon."

Geoff rolled his eyes. How quaint! A quilting bee.

He'd been out in the yard, trying to repair the hinges that had torn off the chicken coop during the storm the night before, when Aunt Ida Mae had called out, "Geoffrey, dear, I'll be back later this afternoon. I'm heading to the quilting bee over at Clara Middleton's house. She's getting married soon. We have to finish her hope chest."

When she'd arrived home before supper, she'd been determined to tell him and Uncle Henry about her day as they sat down to eat.

"Geoffrey, dear, why didn't you tell me how rude Esther Taylor was to you the other day?"

He tried to talk around the mashed potatoes in his mouth. "Didn't matter. Just an old busybody."

"Yes, I heard."

He quirked a brow.

"Millie Baker told me," his aunt told him with a smile.

Ah yes, Millie. Beautiful Millie with the long dark hair and expressive brown eyes. He'd thought of her every day as he worked in the field, tilled the dirt. And he'd certainly thought of her every night as he tossed about in bed. He couldn't get her out of his mind.

He never should have gone back to town the second day to settle the bill. Although he had to, since he hadn't gotten all the supplies his aunt and uncle needed.

She'd been alone in the store then, too.

That day she'd had on a beige dress with a gingham checked apron over it. Not the best color on her, but his body had responded at the sight of her nevertheless. He'd had to shift uncomfortably as his pants had become considerably tighter.

She'd had everything boxed for him and she showed him where they were in the back of the store. He might have been okay if they hadn't touched again, but as he bent to pick up a box she'd done the same for the one beside it. Their shoulders had brushed and she'd jumped back like she'd been burned.

Burned? Hell, she'd practically singed him. He'd had to grab the supplies and get out of there before he did something he'd regret forever. Like kiss her.

And there was the crux of the problem. He wanted to kiss Millicent Baker. Wanted to do a whole lot more to her.

There was something about this simple young woman that made him feel like an untried schoolboy, and he didn't like that thought. Maybe he should just ignore her. Not talk to her the next time he saw her.

And today would be a good time for that. He would see her at church, then later at the social. He'd ignore her. Not be rude, of course, just make a point to stay away.

"Of course, Aunt Ida. I believe I've changed my mind. I'd be pleased to go to the social this afternoon."

Why is he ignoring me? Earlier this week I thought he might like me. Millie watched Geoff as he wandered around the churchyard, speaking to no one. The sight of him still took her breath away. His clothes were different from the men of Napierville. Theirs were functional. His the height of fashion. He wore a dark brown, three-button cutaway frock coat, which matched his brown pants that flared at the bottom. She'd seen the likes of his clothes in the Sears

Roebuck Catalog, but no one she knew wore such fancy clothes. His bowler hat was cocked to the side of his head and the sterling silver handle of his cane was hooked across his forearm. He could have posed for the catalog himself.

Her feelings hurt, Millie walked to the edge of the church yard. *Well, see if I care what that man does. If he wants to ignore me, that's fine. I'll ignore him, too*! Spreading out a blanket, she sat on it and leaned back against a tree.

A shadow falling over her made her glance up.

His arm outstretched against it, Geoff leaned indolently against the tree. A hint of a smile touched the corners of his mouth.

"Avoiding me, Miss Baker?"

"Avoiding you? You were...never mind. I just don't feel like being around people today."

Geoff inclined his head to watch her. "After telling my aunt how much you were anticipating this day?"

Not one to back down from a challenge, she met his eyes. "Then I was. This is now. Do you never change your mind about things, Mr. Standish?"

"Quite frequently, actually, but in New York we have far more to choose from. When very little goes on in a town, I would think you would wish to partake of every event that happens."

"Which goes to show you don't know me very well, sir," she said frostily.

While continuing to gaze down at her, he shifted position so his back rested against the tree.

"Actually, Millicent, I don't know you at all."

"I told you I hate the name Millicent. I prefer Millie. That's what everyone calls me."

"I'm not everyone."

"And clearly you do whatever you wish."

He smiled. "Usually."

"And what do you wish to do now, Mr. Standish?"

"Kiss you."

Startled, she jumped up and stared at him.

"K-kiss me? I...I...I have absolutely no intention of marrying you, sir. What made you say such a ridiculous thing?"

Eyes wide, Geoffrey looked at her like she'd lost her mind. "Marry you? I said—"

"You said you wanted to kiss me. Do you think so little of me that you think I'd allow you to kiss me if we weren't wed?"

"Kissing someone has nothing to do with getting married. It merely means I'm...slightly attracted to you."

"Slightly? Sir, when you were in Father's shop you hardly kept your hands off me. Ask Miz Taylor."

"I wouldn't ask that busybody the time of day. And if you're referring to me catching you before you fell, would you rather I had let you fall on your pretty ass?"

Millie spluttered, "How dare you speak to me like that? You...you...Ooooo...you should be shot!"

He chuckled. "And who do you plan to have shoot me?"

"If you keep aggravating me, I'll do it myself."

He moved away from the tree and stepped toward her. "A pretty little thing like you doesn't know how to shoot."

He ran his hand lightly up and down her arm.

Millie jerked her arm away. "Don't tell me what I do and don't know how to do. You don't know a thing about me."

"You already said that. But you're wrong. I do know some things about you. Your name is Millicent Baker, but you hate the name Millicent. However, since it suits you so well, that's what I shall call you." When she said nothing, but persisted to glare, he continued. "You try to make yourself invisible by wearing mousey beige, but you look prettier than some rich New York model when you wear blue. That's what you had on the first day I saw you, you know. A blue dress, with a blue ribbon pulling your hair back. It's an image I can't get out of my mind."

He reached behind her to untie the pink ribbon in her hair. "Until today. Now I shall forever think of you in pink. You should wear it more often."

"What I wear or don't wear is none of your business."

Something flashed in his eyes, but Millie wasn't certain what. She found out soon enough.

"Well now, that paints an interesting picture."

"What?"

"You wearing nothing at all. I do believe I can visualize that quite well. I—"

"Stop it," she shouted, then lowered her voice when several heads turned. "Are you trying to embarrass me? You can't say such lewd things to me."

"I can't?"

"No, you can't. You might talk like that to women in New York, but you can't say something like that here."

"And therein lies the crux of the matter, right?"

"I don't—"

"I'm from New York. An outsider. I don't belong here." He watched everyone mingling around the yard. "I've seen the way they've all watched me today. Like I'm some kind of freak. Ooooo, look. There's Leila Standish's son. What does he think he's doing here? No, sorry. Leila Hooper's son. They won't even acknowledge she married Father. That she *loved* him—loves him still. All they know is she had the audacity to leave."

Millie watched him a long time before saying anything, really seeing him this time. "That's a mighty big chip you carry on your shoulder." She gestured towards him. "Is that how you dress in New York?"

Geoff glanced down at his clothes. "Of course." He raised his eyes to lock on hers. "What's wrong with it?"

Millie laughed and placed her hand on his arm. She felt the surge of power and thought to pull her hand away, but kept it there purposefully. "Nothing's wrong. It's perfect. You look like you stepped straight out of The Sears Roebuck Catalog."

Again he looked down at his clothes.

"Sears Roebuck? These clothes are tailor made. I would never buy anything from—"

"Now look around you, Mr. Standish. Do you see anyone else wearing anything as fancy? No, of course, you don't," she answered for him, withdrawing her hand. "And you're well aware of that. Don't tell me you aren't."

"It's what I brought with me. Aunt Ida insisted I come to church and stay for the social." A wide grin crossed his face. "You would rather I had come naked?"

"Mr. Standish, you appear to spend a lot of time thinking about people naked.

"Not really. Only you."

She widened her eyes in exasperation.

"You're quite lovely when you're riled, you know." He reached out to lightly brush her hair. The corner of his lips curved up when she stepped back. "Sorry. Been wanting to do that all week. Ever since I held you in your pa's store."

"Mr. Standish, that's not—"

"Proper. I know." He moved to sit on the blanket and pulled her down with him. "What is proper around here, Millicent?"

"Talking."

"All right, I can do that. Tell me about the quilting bee. What do women really do at a quilting bee?"

She giggled. "Mean besides quilt?"

He rolled his eyes in response.

"We talk."

"About what?"

"A little bit of everything. Actually, this time the women were planning..." She stopped, her eyes flying to his face.

"Planning what?"

"Never mind. It was nothing really."

"Now, Millicent. Did your parents not tell you it's not polite to lie?" He hooked a thumb back toward the church. "Particularly at a church social?"

"Well, it wasn't a lie. It's simply that you wouldn't really want to hear it."

"Oh, but I would. Tell me, what the good Christian women of this town were talking about."

"You won't tell?"

"Now who would I tell anything to?"

"Your uncle."

A look of surprise crossed his face. "Uncle Henry? You were talking about Uncle Henry?"

Millie blushed. "Not him specifically."

He leaned closer. "Now I am interested. What do women talk about?"

"You promise you won't...tell?"

He nodded.

"They're planning a revolt."

"A revolt?"

"Shh, lower your voice. It wouldn't do for anyone to hear you."

"This I can't wait to hear. What are the women up to?" He stopped. "More importantly, what is my aunt up to?"

"They're forming a league of their own. To get their husband's to kiss them again."

He burst out laughing. "A league?"

"Yes, against the Anti-Kissing League. They're doing it for Clara. And for themselves, of course."

"Clara? The young woman Aunt Ida mentioned was getting married?"

"Yes." She nodded. "She's getting married soon, and her fiancé is so worried about the crops and what the men think, he won't kiss her. She says she's not going to marry him if he won't kiss her afterward. And the rest of the women are upset, too. Said if their husbands aren't going to kiss them anymore, they're going to stop doing things, too."

His eyes glinted with merriment. "Well, good for them. Whoever thought of the ridiculous notion in the first place?"

She lifted a shoulder. "I don't know. It kind of spread like a wildfire through a drought parched field."

"Do they really think it prudent to irritate their husbands?"

"You must know very little about married life, Mr. Standish. Sometimes it seems that all married folks do is irritate one another."

"Not all marriages are like that. My parents are very happy." His brows lifted. "They never sleep apart."

"There are other ways a woman could rebel against a husband. She could quit cooking or cleaning."

"Father hires a maid to do those things."

"We don't have maids, Mr. Standish. Women here take care of their homes themselves."

"Yes, I've seen how Aunt Ida cares for the house. She cooks and cleans from sunrise to sunset. Toils in her small herb garden, milks the cow, tends the horses. She never rests. It's no wonder the women of this town hate my mother. She left for a better life. They resent that."

She reached out to place her hand on his arm again. "Some of them do, yes. But people like Miz Taylor are bitter about everything."

"The banker's wife? Women like her want the things my mother has now. A fine home, a wealthy husband, the freedom to do anything she wants. Father even bought a new Model 20."

Millie's eyes widened. "You own an automobile? A real automobile?"

He chuckled. "Yes, it's why I'm here."

"What did you do? Smash it?"

"No, but I was a bit inebriated the last time I drove Father's new Model 20. My friends Brody and Rod were with me. How was I to know Brody was so drunk he'd fall out of the car when we rounded the corner? Guess I should have expected something like that since the car had no front doors."

"Your friend fell out of the car?"

He nodded.

"Was he hurt?"

"No, he was too drunk to be hurt. But simply because my friends and I were arrested for being drunk again was no reason to banish me to someplace in the middle of nowhere. So here I am. Twenty years old and banished for I have no idea how long. I would rather she sent me away to London, but she sent me here to punish me."

"You consider being in Napierville punishment?" She narrowed her eyes as she watched him. "Yes, I guess someone like you would."

"When she saw me off, she told me she hoped Aunt Ida would be able to instill some of the values in me she had failed at."

"She has a life like that and thinks she failed?"

He shook his head. "Not failed as you mean it. She just thinks I'm..."

"Incorrigible?" she added when he stopped.

He threw back his head and laughed. "Oh, that's good. Yes, in a way I guess I am. When I'm about town with my friends at least. We tend to..."

"Drink too much?"

He removed the hand she had on his arm. Held it between his. "Do you always finish other people's sentences?"

"Were my answers wrong?"

"No, I guess not. You seem to know me quite well. Is everyone in this town as observant as you?"

She shrugged, but said nothing.

"Is that what life here is really like, Millicent? Is that what a wife has to look forward to?"

"You don't know the half of it."

"What do you mean?"

"You mentioned cooking and cleaning. There's the sewing, washing, canning, and baking. Then you have mending, patching, ironing. Depending on how wealthy the family is, they might not be able to buy many of the things you're used to. Here a woman might have to make her carpet out of rags or fill her bedticks with oat straw. I imagine you bought such things from fancy stores."

He nodded, his eyes wide with surprise. "How do you do that?"

"I help Mother, but I don't do everything she does. I'm not married. Once I am, I'll have all that and more. You forgot the most important thing."

"And that would be?"

"Having children."

"And you want that?"

"Oh yes, Mr. Standish. I want *all* of that. As long as I have a man who loves me."

"Do you have that?"

She cocked her head in question.

"A man who loves you?" he added.

She shook her head. "Several men tried sparking me, but in the long run they're only friends. I don't know. Something's always been missing. Mother says I'm too fussy. What's really funny, although I'm sure you won't think it so, is that just the other night we had a full moon."

"Mean the Blue Moon?"

"Yes. You saw it?"

He nodded.

"Well, so did I. I was on our porch swing. Wanted to be by myself for a while. I glanced up at it and did something really childish." When he said nothing, she continued. "I made a wish on it."

"What did you wish for?"

"I can't tell you that, Mr. Standish, or it won't come true."

"But—"

She turned toward the gathered throng when sounds grew louder.

"Look," she told him, interrupting, "they're getting ready to eat." She drew her hand from his and stood. "Come, Mr. Standish, let's get some food. I'm starving."

Starving? Oh yes, that's exactly how Geoff felt. But it wasn't food he wanted. It was Millicent Baker. She'd be the main course and dessert all rolled into one.

When she'd laid her hand on his arm earlier, he'd thought it would brand him forever. If the entire congregation hadn't been milling about the churchyard, he surely would have taken her into his arms and kissed her – and the Anti-Kissing League be damned.

He thought back to her silly statement about having to marry him if he kissed her. Marry? Him? Not a chance. He still had too many wild oats to sow. He'd finish his time at his uncle's farm and then head home to New York. Surely his mother wouldn't insist he stay until his uncle was completely well. From something he'd heard Aunt Ida say, that could take *months*. Geoff had no intention of sticking around this one horse town that long.

Yet what had she meant about not being ready to marry him? Surely the prospect couldn't be that bad.

In truth, being here wasn't really all that bad. And he did get to tease Miss Millicent Baker in the process. But teasing her wasn't what he wanted to do.

He'd get his way. Always did. He couldn't remember a single girl in New York he hadn't bedded if he'd wanted to. Miss Baker might take a bit longer, but she'd give in. Geoff knew it.

For now he'd sit with her and eat if that's what she wanted to do. After all, a man did have to consider his stomach, didn't he? And Aunt Ida Mae had brought her fried chicken and peach cobbler. He'd had them both several times since he'd been here and had never tasted anything better. Not even at the fancy dinners his mother held for Father's bosses.

Millie grabbed Geoff's hand and pulled him along behind her. "Come on, Geoff, or the food's going to be gone before we get there."

"Fat chance of that," he said, hoping she'd never let go of his hand. "Those picnic tables are loaded with food."

After filling his plate to overflowing, Geoff headed toward where they'd been sitting earlier. "Hope you don't mind being over here alone. I don't feel comfortable being in the midst of so many strangers."

Sitting on the blanket, Millie spread her skirt around her before starting to eat. She gazed at him through those long lashes and Geoff wanted to lean forward to kiss her tempting lips. He knew he couldn't do that with everyone outside, though.

When she started to eat and a few crumbs of fried chicken stayed on her lips, Geoff had to fight off the urge to lick them away himself.

Too soon the day ended and Geoff walked Millie home. "Will I see you again?"

"Well of course you will. The next time you come in for supplies at the store." Something in his heart melted at the teasing lilt in her voice and mischievous glint in her eyes.

"Tomorrow morning?"

"I won't be there in the morning. I help over at the local institution three mornings a week."

Geoff frowned. "Why would you do something like that?"

Millie's eyes widened. "And why wouldn't I? They need my help even more than most of the people in this town. Someone has to help care for them."

"But they're...different."

"They're only a little slower than most people, that's all. Or their families don't want them around for some reason. Usually because they fear they'll be embarrassed if the person stays home. We got a new young woman in last week. Her family was able to raise the twenty-five dollars it costs to be admitted there."

"Is she...different, too?"

"Not really. It's such a sad situation. She's going to have a baby, and I guess her family's ashamed of her. Didn't want her around to be a daily reminder of her poor judgment. So they decided to put her in the institution. She seemed so lost when they left her there last week. I plan to spend most of my time with her this week so she won't feel so lonely."

"I never met anyone like you before. Most people I know only think of themselves and what they can do. You...you actually think of other people."

She nodded. "Is that really so unusual?"

"To me it is. You don't feel awkward being there?"

"No, not at all. The people there just want to be loved. Just like those of us outside the institution. The ones that break my heart are the children. I know times can be tough, but to just drop a child off and never see them again..." She broke off and peered up at the moon. "I couldn't do it. I want children so much, I can't understand how someone can leave them."

"I never thought about it before. Maybe they just can't...I don't know. Maybe they weren't meant to be parents and can't care for the child."

"So you drop it off? Discard it? Like some article of clothing you don't want?"

"I can't answer that question, Millicent. But look at you now. You're shaking. Are you cold? You can't be, it's warm out."

Her lips trembled. "No, I'm not cold, just sad."

Without thinking, Geoff wrapped his arms around her and pulled her close. He felt her shaking as she leaned her head against his chest. "You can't solve all the problems of the world, Millie, honey. But it's okay now. Just lean against me for a little while before you go inside." He brushed his lips over her hair.

They stood like that for quite a while before Millie finally pulled away and said goodnight.

After she closed the door behind her, Millie let out a whoosh of breath. He'd called her Millie. And he'd called her honey. Oh my!

The next morning after she finished volunteering at the institution, Millie walked outside and was surprised to find Geoff waiting on the steps.

"What are you doing here?"

"This isn't a very safe part of town. I didn't like the idea of you walking back to the shop all by yourself."

"Geoffrey Standish, I've walked this way by myself for over two years now. What makes you think I need your help now?"

"I wasn't here to protect you before. Now I am."

She sputtered. "Protect me? I don't need anyone to—"

He stopped her with a kiss.

Pulling her behind a nearby building so a passerby wouldn't see them, Geoff drew her into his arms and kissed her again.

"You can't do this," she said, barely able to breathe.

"I know. It's against the Anti-Kissing League. I don't care about that."

"Neither do I, but you can't kiss me. Mother said I'd..." Flustered, she stopped.

"Get pregnant? Do mothers still really tell girls that? Well, I can assure you that isn't true."

Lowering his mouth towards hers again, he ran his lips gently around her mouth, slipped the tip of his tongue along the seam of her pressed together lips. When she opened them on a sigh, his tongue plunged in, taking advantage of the opening. He gave her no quarter, but plundered her mouth until she tentatively answered his mating call.

What had she just done? He held her close after the kiss, but Millie feared her knees wouldn't hold her if he let her go. She'd never felt so weak before. Never felt such things in her womanhood before. He'd set her entire body aflame with that kiss.

Speaking of flames, would the town's crops die now? Would she be to blame for the shortage of food come the fall? Did she need to tell someone so they could do something to prevent it? No! She could tell no one. And she could never let this happen again.

She could never see Geoff Standish again.

What a ridiculous thing to think when his arms were wrapped around her. If she didn't see him again, she thought she'd die.

When they finally reached the store, she helped him fill the seed order his uncle had sent with him. Wasn't it too late in the year to still be planting crops? Why would his uncle want seeds now?

Wednesday and Friday Geoff stood waiting outside the institution for her.

"I told you I planned to walk you home, and I meant it."

He drew her arm within the crook of his as they walked down the lane toward town. Did her family really not care that she spent so much time in this part of town? It wasn't safe. Who knew what might happen to her. Geoff admitted he wasn't willing to risk that.

"And who's going to walk me home when you head back to New York?"

He stopped and pulled her behind a ramshackle building. "I don't know," he practically growled in her ear as he drew her close, "but while I'm here, it's going to be me."

"Aren't you supposed to be helping your uncle on the farm?"

"Everything's getting done. Don't worry about that." His lips brushed hers. "Worry about staying safe. If anything were to happen to you..."

"Geoff, the only person I'm not safe from is you. When I'm with you I feel—"

His lips claimed hers, ravished them as his tongue dipped inside her mouth. When he pulled her against him, he knew she felt his hardness. He wanted her to feel it. Wanted her to know he wanted her. Oh, how he wanted her. Needed her.

For weeks, he did the same thing three mornings a week. Every Monday, Wednesday and Friday he met her after she volunteered and walked her home. Every day he left a bit of his heart with her as she closed the door.

When he left her at the shop one Friday morning, she asked, “Are you coming to the dance tomorrow night?”

“Yes. It’s the only way I can hold you without the town gossips’ tongues wagging.”

Millie giggled. “I think they’re wagging anyhow. You had to expect they would with you walking me home each day. And your aunt and uncle never needed so many supplies before. You’re always in Pa’s shop.”

“Are you complaining about seeing me too much?”

She lowered her lashes. “No.”

“Good, then I’ll see you at the dance tomorrow night.”

Geoff rode his horse into town. Uncle Henry had been too sick to come and Aunt Ida refused to leave him. So Geoff didn’t need the wagon.

He slid off the horse and tethered him to a nearby watering trough before heading over to the large barn where the dance was being held.

His eyes scanned the room for Millie. His breath caught when he saw her. She had on the same light blue dress she’d worn the day he’d first seen her. Now she had a matching cape around her shoulders. She’d taken his breath away then and she still did now.

How was he going to return to New York? Never to see her again? Could he leave her? He didn’t think so. But could he live here? Give up everything he was used to in the city? Or would she go back with him like his mother had done?

And he couldn’t see Millie leaving town.

That left only one answer, but was he ready to make it? These people meant nothing to him. He sighed. No, that was no longer true. It had been when he first arrived here, but now Aunt Ida and Uncle Henry were family.

Walking closer, he pulled her into his arms as the music started. He saw busybody Mrs. Taylor watching him. He should have known she would. That woman had been the bane of his existence since coming to town.

He reached up and untied the ribbon at Millie’s neck and removed her cape, draped it over his arm as he whirled her around the dance floor.

Was that envy he saw in some of the other young men's eyes? Probably. His Millie was the most beautiful woman in the room. To him anyway.

"Did you have a busy day at the store today?"

"We did," she told him, peering up into his eyes. "This has been the oddest year. Pa keeps having to order plant seeds. We've never had such a run on them before. I don't understand it. I really thought it was too late in the year to plant anything."

Not knowing much about planting, Geoff just nodded.

An argument broke out in one corner of the barn. Mr. Taylor, the banker, was glaring out across the dance floor.

"I tell you, someone's been kissing, and I want to know who," he shouted. His eyes rested on Geoff and Millie as they twirled by.

"There's the answer to our crops dying, I tell you. Who knows what that young whippersnapper from New York has been doing to our Millie."

Everyone on the floor stopped dancing.

Drawing Millie to the side, Geoff pushed her behind him as he faced off with Mr. Taylor. He didn't have to see her face to know she was blushing. She always did.

Keeping his voice level, Geoff flicked his lashes at Taylor with disdain. "You can call me any names you want, sir, but when you start casting aspersions on my woman, I have to take offense."

"You saying you ain't kissed her?"

"I *ain't* saying anything one way or another. What I do is none of your business, and I don't appreciate you mouthing off about Millie in front of the whole town."

"Our crops are dying! Someone's gone and kissed someone!"

Geoff tensed, but tried to rein in his temper. "Sir, you may be my elder, but you don't know your ass from your foot."

A gasp went up around the room.

"Your plants are dying, sir, because it hasn't rained. Not because some man in this town had the level sense to kiss his wife."

"None of our men would have broken the League's rules," Taylor blustered.

"Then I misjudged them all. They're all just as foolish as you." He grabbed Millie's hand and pull her away from the accusing man.

Taylor called after them, "Well someone's done something they shouldn't, and I'll bet a day's wages it was you. The likes of you doesn't belong in this town."

Geoff stopped and Millie plowed into him.

Turning, his eyes narrowed as he stared at the elderly banker. "You want to say that again?"

"Geoff, please. Don't make a scene," Millie begged.

He didn't turn to face her. Kept his eyes on Taylor. "I repeat, you want to say that again?"

"I said you don't belong here," Taylor shouted again.

Geoff took one step toward Taylor when Millie's father placed a hand on his shoulder. "No, son, don't."

Geoff faced him. "He's slandering your daughter."

"And the young man my daughter loves."

A gasp went up around the room.

"You stay with Millie. I'll take care of this."

He approached the banker. "Ed, the next time you choose to say something about my daughter, maybe you'd best get your facts straight before you listen to your harpy of a wife."

"Well, I never!" Esther Taylor said, her voice rising.

"Well, now, ma'am," Joe Baker inclined his head toward her, "that just may be correct. You see, Ed here is the only man in this town that ain't been buying plant seeds from me here lately."

He eyed everyone in the barn.

"Now while I have to admit I'm pleased to be having such a run on them at this time of the year, it tells me one thing. *Every* man in this town has been kissing his wife and has been planting new seeds to replace any that might die."

Again his gaze swept the room.

"Am I wrong, men?"

Grumbles sounded throughout the room, but all the men nodded.

Baker told Taylor, "I believe you owe my daughter and young Standish an apology."

Ed Taylor mumbled something.

"What was that, Ed? Couldn't quite hear you."

"All right, said I'm sorry. But I'll bet—"

"Think I'd let that drop if I was you, Ed."

Joe Baker walked over to his daughter. Leaning down, he gently kissed her on the cheek and wiped away a tear with the pad of his thumb. He reached out the same hand to shake Geoff's.

As Millie's father walked away, Geoff watched Millie. She'd been shamed in front of all her friends and it had been his fault. Well, damn them all to Hell and back. He couldn't let it end here.

What was it her father had said? He'd called him the man his daughter loved.

Did she really? Did Millicent Baker love him enough to marry him? Well, there was only one way to find out.

Pulling her toward the center of the room, Geoff spoke loud enough so everyone could hear. "Millie Baker, you once told me I couldn't kiss you because you didn't love me enough to marry you."

He drew her into his arms.

"Well, I love you enough for both of us—and I want you to marry me. I'm asking you, Millie. In front of all of your friends. If I'm what you want, I'm here. Will you marry me?

In answer, Millie stood on tiptoe and threw her arms around his neck. The next thing he knew, her mouth was pressed to his.

He had his answer.

Ignoring all the hooting going on around them, Geoff placed his arms around Millie's neck and deepened the kiss.

Outside, a loud crash of thunder sounded.

Laughing, he pulled her behind him and headed outside for some solitude.

"Did you mean it, Geoff? You really want to marry me?"

"I wouldn't have asked you in front of the entire town if I didn't." He laughed.

"Then my wish came true," she whispered.

"What wish?" he asked, nuzzling her neck.

"My wish on the Blue Moon. I was so lonely. I wished for someone to love me—and two days later you walked into Pa's store. I hoped...but I didn't believe."

"And now you do?"

"Oh yes. I do. I really, really do."

Geoff lowered his head and kissed her again. New York or Georgia no longer mattered to him. The only thing that mattered was that he be with the woman who brought out the best in him. The woman he loved more than life itself.

While kissing her slowly, tenderly, a lightning bolt lit up the sky and mere seconds later thunder cracked.

The drought was over. It had ended with a kiss.

We invite you to read Leanne's story,
The Healer, in the companion book, *Blue Moon Magic*.

Also available from Leanne Burroughs:
Highland Wishes
(Winner – 2004 Readers' and Booksellers' Best
Winner – 2005 – RIO Award of Excellence)
Her Highland Rogue
(Winner – 2005 RIO Award of Excellence
Winner – 2005 National Readers' Choice Award)

Visit Leanne's website at
http://www.leanneburroughs.com

Leap of Faith

by Jill and Julia

June, 2006

Marcella Richards shut off her laptop, relieved to be done with her latest murder case. She'd won, again, freeing yet one more loser to roam the streets and do God only knows what. Marcella sighed and shook her head. She was good – the best Chicago attorney money could buy, and she understood all about the rights of the accused to adequate representation. But lately, she'd been bothered by the lack of humanity in some of her clients. Like the bastard she'd just represented, a lucky bastard who happened to be her annual pro bono case.

Having the air conditioning break down, trapping the jurors in a small, airless room to deliberate had worked to her advantage, but she didn't feel good about it – had no sense of elation. The twelve Chicago citizens wanted nothing more than to get out of the sweltering room. Reasonable doubt was very easy for them to agree on, that hot, late June afternoon.

Marcella closed the laptop, tossed her glasses on the desk and stood, reaching as far as she could to the ceiling, working the kinks from her neck and shoulders. Her penthouse apartment was quiet. Intent on getting the final documents prepared and sent off to her paralegal to be filed, she hadn't even bothered turning on the stereo. Verdict in, case closed, paperwork finished. Marcella smiled. She could leave for vacation with a clear head.

"Vacation," she said, thinking how foreign the word

sounded. How long had it been since she'd indulged in leisure time? Far too long. So long, in fact, she had no idea what to pack, where to go, what to do. She'd left those details up to her assistant, begging for a surprise trip somewhere, anywhere outside Illinois.

She kicked off her heels, pulled off her hose, and padded into the kitchen to get a glass of white wine. Glass and bottle in hand, she headed for the living room, with its massive windows and incredible view of the windy city. She flopped on the overstuffed suede sofa, propped her feet up and took in the sight of the buildings lighting up the endless night sky.

"Where are you now, Drew?"

She poured herself a full glass of wine, a feeling of melancholy seizing her, much as it always did between cases, when her mind could finally relax and focus once again on her personal life. Or lack of a personal life. After a sip of wine, she closed her eyes. What would she do in the days ahead with nothing but free time? Time to reminisce... think about the last real vacation she had.

The spring break spent in Cancun with Drew.

She'd expected a marriage proposal, but instead, she'd accepted her walking papers.

Eight years and hundreds of cases later, she still thought of him. Every day. No matter the season, no matter the circumstance, he was never far from her mind. "*How pathetic.*"

Loser at love that she was, she hadn't become involved with anyone else in all that time. Much easier to find fulfillment in work – she rarely lost cases – than to risk her heart at love. Heartache hurt more than lost legal battles.

She finished her glass of wine and poured another. This should be a celebration, she'd won another case, would be on the front page of the *Trib* again, have even more clients banging down her door. She'd be able to watch the zeros accumulate in her bank account. It no longer gave her any sense of satisfaction, It had become...boring. And lonely.

Standing, she walked to the windows overlooking the city she loved. She'd chosen this penthouse because of its view of the Sears Tower. She leaned into the glass and sipped more of the wine, enjoying the warmth that flooded her veins.

Who was she to ask for more? Blocks away from the best shopping in the world, no ties, no commitments, rich beyond her dreams, what more could she want?

"Drew." She drained her glass and grabbed the bottle to pour another. The one and only thing she didn't have that she wanted was the love of her life back in her life.

"What the...?" Marcella squinted out the window. She pressed her nose up against the glass, but nothing changed. There wasn't just one full moon in the sky anymore, but it was if it had suddenly broken in half, and now, staring at her were two brilliant, round orbs. She set down her wine glass and with a shaky hand, flipped off the light switch. Was it just a reflection?

Nope, the blasted things were still there.

She watched them, thinking they would merge together, or one would disappear as fast as it had appeared, but it didn't; the two moons just stared at her like yellow eyes, watching. Was that a blue moon, then? She'd heard the phrase before, but had never seen one — hadn't known they actually existed.

"Once in a blue moon..."

She whipped around, and flicked the light back on.

"Who's there?" She hadn't imagined the squeakily uttered words, no way. Too much wine, maybe, but that weird little voice hadn't come from inside her head.

"Look down, lovey."

"What the hell are you?" Marcella had to be imagining this. Had she fallen asleep? Was she dreaming? First a second moon in the sky, and now some freaky little creature...not two feet tall, wearing a purple cone-shaped hat, striped tights, glittery shoes with the points curled up...and a feathery red boa around her neck. Marcella blinked. "Oh my God, what was in that wine?"

"Now, now, no need to curse." The creature walked closer, forcing Marcella to back up against the window.

"Lola Lewinsky's my name, and I'm whatcha call a gnomette." The little person snapped her fingers and a cigarette, in an old-fashioned, long ivory holder appeared. She took a drag and blew the smoke right up in Marcella's face.

Marcella coughed lightly and shook her head, trying to get a grasp on the situation. "There is no such thing as a gnomette." Her analytical-lawyer-mind couldn't wrap itself around the thought.

"Well, what do I look like to you, then, lovey?"

"An intruder. Get out before I call the police." Marcella slid along the window until she reached the cell phone she'd left sitting on the table. Her eyes never left little Lola.

"Aren't you the tiniest bit–no pun intended–curious why I might be visiting you?"

"You have a reason?"

"Well, duh." Lola exhaled another puff of blue-grey smoke and then coughed like she was ready to hack up a lung.

"Talk fast little woman, or I'm dialing 911."

"Sure you will." Lola chuckled and plopped on the sofa, setting her tiny feet on the coffee table in front of her. "What would you say, exactly? There's this chick no bigger than a doll in my house and I can't get rid of her? Puleeze. You might be some smart lawyer girl, but you would sound a might bit, umm...loony." She emphasized her opinion by circling her ear with a finger.

"Why are you here? You know I'm an attorney. Are you in some kind of trouble? Do you want money?"

"So suspicious, so defensive!" Lola clucked her tongue. "Did that come from years defending crooks and killers?"

"How do you know who I am?" Marcella suppressed the urge to stomp her foot.

"Oh, Marcy, I know every little thing about you, lovey." She laughed.

"Marcy?"

"Yeppers. Ain't that what the studman used to call you? That special man a' yours?"

"Drew," Marcella whispered and sat on a chair across from the woman, certain she must be hallucinating, or at the very least, quite drunk.

"I'm here 'cause you asked for me, girl. You asked to have what you didn't have, but what you wanted. So here I am." She spread her arms wide and grinned like a Cheshire cat.

"I did *not* ask for some odd little creature to break into my house."

"Now, now, careful what you say. You're liable to hurt my sensitivities." Lola crossed her feet at the ankles and wiggled them side to side while taking a long drag off of her cigarette.

"Will you leave if I do?"

"Sure thing. Hate to be a burden, and all." She stood, started to walk toward the wall, but paused and looked back over her shoulder at Marcella. "'Course, won't you always wonder what I came here for?"

When she turned around and started her odd little swagger back to wherever she'd come from, Marcella heard herself say, "Wait!"

"Now you want me to stay?" Lola shook her head. "Make up your mind, already."

"Why did you come to me, Lola Lewinsky?"

"Well now, that's an easy one." She moved closer to Marcella, and stopped. "You saw the blue moon, and you made a wish, even though you may not realize it."

"Drew?"

"Yeppers." Lola nodded, somehow keeping the cone hat firmly over her grey-black hair. "You can have him if you want."

"How?"

"That is the question, isn't it?" Lola resumed her seat and rested her hands on her knees. Somehow the cigarette and its holder had disappeared. "You have to take a leap of faith, but I reckon you'll find it's worth it."

"Leap of faith?"

"If you choose to make that wish again, you'll be returned to the past, to a time when you had the chance to change the course of your history, to keep the man you love."

"What's the catch?" Marcella had been part of too many plea-bargain sessions to know people didn't give away anything unless they got something in return.

"You have to give up all this." She gestured broadly at the enormous penthouse. "Your fancy foreign car and your designer clothes. Your high dollar career. Everything you now know. Even your shoes." Lola glanced down at Marcella's bare feet. "Guess that won't be a problem for you." She cackled, which set off another coughing spell.

"I see." Marcella swallowed hard and nodded.

"Is he worth it?"

The Drew that Marcella once knew was more than worth it. But now, with so much time gone by? What a risk!

"*Is* he worth it?" Lola repeated.

The grandfather clock ticked one minute away, then another...then finally Marcella told the little gnome lady, "I won't know unless I try, will I?"

"Hot damn!" Lola jumped up. "Now we got ourselves a party!"

She spread her stubby legs and with both hands made a swirling, circular motion at the window. A ball of light, bright as any fire, flooded the room, and suddenly a hole opened where the window once was.

"Walk through, lovey. Confront your past...design your future. It's not often I'm able to give a person a second chance, but you got lucky."

Marcella walked slowly toward the hole. As she got closer, she craned her neck, looking ahead, but saw nothing save the street below, and knew she was crazy, totally out of her mind, to be doing this. But she squared her shoulders and took the leap, the adrenaline rushing through her veins propelled her forward, and suddenly there was nothing, but a black abyss...

March, 1998

Marcella awoke with a start. She sat up and brushed her long dark hair from her face and gazed, wide-eyed, around the room. Dawn's pale, pink light filtered in through the half-drawn curtains, barely illuminating the tiny apartment bedroom she'd been sharing with Drew for the last year. *A dream!* She had to have been dreaming. She fell back against the pillows with a sigh. But man, what a dream! Successfully practicing law, living in a ritzy Chicago penthouse, being visited by a little person in pointy shoes and a purple, cone-shaped hat...and no Drew.

Marcella yawned and stretched, snuggling back down beneath the covers. She closed her eyes, sleepily remembering and rehashing the details of her last murder case. The defendant, her client, never admitted to murdering his ex-wife, but Marcella sensed he was guilty. Still, thanks to her excellent trial skills and a broken-down air-conditioning unit, the man had walked. Marcella bolted upright again, suddenly wide awake.

Her last murder case! But, she hadn't even graduated college yet! How could she remember something that hadn't even happened?

"Oh, my God, it wasn't a dream." Somehow, someway, she'd traveled back in time.

"What wasn't a dream?"

Marcella turned, her jaw dropping. Drew stood in the doorway, the light from their tiny kitchenette illuminating his tall, leanly muscled body. He smiled and moved farther into the room.

"Uh, nothing. Good-morning." Marcella snapped her mouth closed and returned Drew's smile. "What are you doing up so early?"

"I have a class." He sat on the edge of the bed and leaned in, placing a light kiss on her nose.

"Then why aren't you gone? Sun's up, it's gotta be after six."

"My car won't start. The way I see it," Drew said, gathering her into his arms and nuzzling her neck, "we have two choices. Either you can get up and take me to class, or I can come back to bed and we can make love until your ten o'clock."

Marcella took a deep breath, drinking in Drew's freshly showered scent. "I don't have a ten o'clock."

"Mmm, all the better. I can come back to bed and we can make love until noon."

Drew pulled her down on the bed, rolling until she lay pinned beneath him. He cupped her face and kissed her, slow and deep.

Marcella pulled back with a sigh, draping her arms around his neck. She gazed into his eyes. "I'm afraid you're going to miss your class."

"Good." He moved off the bed and quickly undressed, leaving his clothing scattered on the floor.

Marcella watched him, her heart pounding. Eight long years. She hadn't made love in nearly a decade. And, knowing how splendid it would be – remembering his gentle skill and tenderness – only served to heighten Marcella's desire and anticipation.

Drew climbed onto the bed, slid beneath the covers and drew her into his arms.

"Mmm, you smell good," she said, breathing in the warm, slightly spicy smell of his cologne. "Good enough to eat."

Drew grinned and rubbed his hips against her suggestively. "Yeah? That sounds like a proposition, baby."

"Not a proposition, a promise." Marcella laughed and ducked down beneath the blankets.

"God, Marcy! That feels amazing." Drew reached down and stroked her hair.

Marcella continued her torment of him, until her own desires grew unbearable, and the air beneath the blankets grew too warm. She released him and shimmied up, capturing Drew's mouth with her own. She kissed him with all the pent-up passion she'd carried with her through time, telling him with her tongue and lips and body how much she'd missed him these past eight years and how sorry she was for leaving him behind.

Without breaking their kiss, Drew rolled on top of her, positioning himself between her outstretched thighs. He sank into her slowly, sliding deep inside, filling her completely. Marcella whimpered softly and lifted her hips, wrapping her legs around his waist and drawing him closer.

With infinite tenderness, Drew moved, withdrawing and then sliding back in. Slowly, passionately, he made love to her. Marcella's heart overflowed with love for him, with joy at being reunited with him, and her eyes filled with tears as she was swept away. Drew joined her, riding the wave and holding her close.

"Why are you crying, baby?" Drew asked moments later. He wiped a tear from her cheek, then kissed the wet spot left behind.

"Because I'm so happy," she said, offering him a watery smile. "And because I love you so much."

"Women," he said, but his crooked grin belied his teasing tone. "You always cry over the silliest things."

"We do, don't we?" Marcella nodded. "Good thing we have you big, strong men around to keep us grounded."

Drew laughed. "I love you too, Marcy. For always and forever."

"Careful, or you're going to get me going again," Marcella said, sniffling at his romantic words.

"Oh, I'm going to get you going again, all right." He cupped her breast, running his thumb over her hard, sensitive nipple. "You can bet on it."

Three weeks later, on the first day of spring break, Marcella joined Drew for a drive to the beach. She'd spent the whole morning remembering how this day had concluded the last time...the choice she'd made, the heartbreak she'd endured when she'd walked away, leaving him there and knowing they'd go their separate ways. This time, she'd make the right decision. This time, she'd put aside her high ambitions and figure out a way to keep him in her life, no matter what it took. She'd trust him with her life, with her future.

As they walked down the rocky hillside to the white sandy beach, Marcella held her breath, knowing the moment was near and anticipating the next few moments and the chance to make things right.

"Marcy, we need to talk." Drew dropped the cooler he was carrying onto the sand, freeing his hands to place them on her waist.

"I know," she said, her voice thick. "I've been waiting for you to say something."

"You have?" He cocked his head.

"Yes, I have." Marcy nodded. "We have some major decisions to make, Drew. I have only a couple weeks to let the law schools know. They've been holding a spot for me for quite awhile."

"Yeah, I know." He shifted, taking her face in his hands. "Listen, I can't tell you how proud I am of you for making it into Harvard and Stanford! My God! My girlfriend is brilliant!" He kissed her softly. "I feel guilty asking you to stick it out in Illinois with me, but I can't go with you. I don't wanna move to the coast, I'm a Midwest guy. I would feel like a foreigner out there. I want you to stay here with me." He grabbed her hand and squeezed it. "I don't want us to split up, and maintaining a long-distance relationship would be impossible. I know..."

"Drew, shut up." She leaned forward and kissed him hard on the lips, and they tumbled to the sand. This was the point that they fell apart the first time, when she let her selfishness and self-centeredness get in the way. Not this time. No way. Life without Drew hadn't been much of a life at all. "I've decided to go wherever you are. Find a closer law school..."

"You have?" Drew's mouth hung open, but then his astonished look slowly turned into a wide, happy grin. "You have? Damn, Marcy, why didn't you tell me? I've been worrying about this for weeks. God, I'm so glad. You won't be sorry, I promise. We'll make sure you get a great education, even if I have to get a second job to support us for a while. We'll figure something out, and..."

"Drew, what part of 'shut up' do you not understand?" Marcy softened her words with a grin. "I trust you, and I know if we're together, we'll be fine. Now kiss me again, you fool, and then get me a beer." She pulled him up against her. "This is our last spring break!"

"All done," Drew whispered out of the corner of his mouth.

Marcy looked his way and smiled. When he leaned over and kissed her, she felt butterflies in her stomach. Three years together and she still had the same reaction every time he touched her. Even in a classroom, with two hundred other seniors, taking the last final of their undergraduate career, he still managed to excite her. Every time he touched her, the rest of the world slipped away, and she'd find herself in all sorts of embarrassing positions. Like when they got caught making out on the beach two months earlier during spring break in Cancun.

As she followed his trip to the front of the room to hand in the blue book, she wondered, not for the first time, if she'd made the right decision. He was just a guy wasn't he? She could find another man. But no. She'd gone that route, and knowing what she did about the future, she doubted she would ever find a man that made her feel complete in the way Drew did.

They were headed to Northwestern University in the fall. Not the Harvard she'd really wanted, but still a terrific school. She'd still have her law degree, and he'd get his master's in journalism. If all went well, they would settle outside of Chicago, have two, point five children, she'd drive a mini-van and their weekends would be occupied with soccer tournaments.

A far cry from her single life.

She smiled and winked at him as he passed her to leave the classroom. Back to the exam at hand, if she could let her mind settle long enough to finish the essay.

"What are you doing?" Drew was standing in the doorway of their small one bedroom apartment, gawking at Marcy.

"What do you mean, what am I doing?" She straightened up from the open suitcase and walked toward him. "We're moving tomorrow, I was putting the last of our stuff in the suitcase."

"I mean, you were supposed to be dressed and ready to go to Vaco's." He glanced at his watch for emphasis. "Our reservation is in ten minutes."

It was then that Marcy noticed Drew was wearing a tie. He never wore a tie. She frowned at him. "Okay, so, I'll get dressed."

"Wait." He grabbed her arm as she brushed passed him. "I'm sorry. No biggie if we're a little late." He smiled and kissed her neck, and she left the room, hoping the outfit she planned to wear wasn't so wrinkled from being packed that she'd have to iron it. She hated to iron.

In four days she was to start law school. Again. Would it be as difficult the second time around as it had been the first? She hoped she remembered enough to get by without studying too much. She and Drew would both have to work part-time jobs to support themselves. What had she gotten herself into?

In the small bathroom, she donned a spaghetti-strapped tank top and fastened the tie on her long, chiffon, wrap-around pink and maroon skirt. A dab of make-up on her flawless, young face, and a comb through her hair, and she was ready to go. Now, where were her sandals?

She left the bathroom and bumped right into Drew. "Good thing the apartment in Evanston is bigger." He laughed. From behind his back, he produced a bouquet of red roses. "These are for you."

"They're beautiful! Thank you." She took them, holding them to her nose to breathe in their fresh scent. "What are they for?"

"Just because I love you, Marcy." He pulled her against him. "We've both been stressed about the move and starting a new school. But you'll see, it'll work out."

She started to cry again. Tears of happiness–Drew was all she could have hoped for and more.

"No tears, baby." He held her close, stroking her back, making her love him even more.

They left a few minutes later. Vaco's had terrific food, and it overlooked a huge lake. Drew had reserved their favorite table, the one with the best view. By the time the dessert came, Marcella was laughing, as Drew told a story about a reporter at the paper he'd worked at that summer. Marcella had clerked in a law office. The head partner had been impressed with how fast and how well she understood the intricacies of cases. She might have lost her Jaguar, but she'd not lost her knowledge of the law.

"So, anyway, I wanted to show you that last article I wrote for the newspaper."

He pulled the newspaper out from under the table somewhere and handed it to her.

"Where is it?"

"Front page." He took another sip of his beer. "Bottom."

"*Summer Intern Decides To Marry His True Love,*" she read the headline.

She looked up, a mixture of awe and thrill making her

feel numb, like jelly.

She looked back down, and continued to read:

> *She was the girl of my dreams the minute I laid eyes on her in my one and only Political Science class. She always had a clue, when I had none. She's beautiful, real and true, and gave up attending an Ivy League Law School to be with this schmuck of a guy who can't even fix a flat tire (she can do that too, by the way). The only question left as I finish my last article at the newspaper is, Marcy, baby, will you marry me?*

June, 2006

Marcella's head flopped to the right and jolted her awake.

She looked around the spacious penthouse. What the...? How had she ended up back here? She looked out the floor-to-ceiling windows at the Chicago skyline, confused, and then forlorn as she realized the truth. Nothing but a dream. No Lola Lewinsky. No second chances. No Drew.

Through tear-filled eyes, she continued to stare out the windows, noting the glittering lights...the single yellow moon. Her heart ached with the loss, and disappointment left a bitter taste in her mouth. She should have recognized it for a dream, should have realized – even in sleep – that it couldn't be real. A gnomette for heaven's sake!

Stiffness settled on her spine, and when she tried to get off the plush chair, she found herself struggling to get upright. She grabbed the arms of the chair and pulled herself up, and when she bent over to work out the kink, she realized she couldn't. In place of her flat stomach was a thick rounded bulge, protruding so far she couldn't even *see* her toes, much less *touch* them.

Marcella screamed.

She was pregnant, and couldn't even remember how it

had happened. She wracked her mind, feeling like the top of her head was about to explode. What the hell was happening to her?

Had Lola the gnomette let her get pregnant and then sent Marcella back to the future? How unfair.

She plopped back onto the chair.

"Marcy?"

She whipped her head to the right, and saw Drew. He was here! In her penthouse! How had that happened? But it wasn't a young immature Drew; lines crinkled at the edges of his eyes, and he'd filled out his tall form.

Suddenly all the memories of the past eight years came back to her. She had lived through them again, been given a second chance. At love...with Drew.

"Are you all right, sweetheart? I heard you scream..."

"I'm fine." She squeezed the hand he gave her, and smiled like her very life depended upon it. "Everything is fine now."

"Andy and Katie are sleeping, so no more practicing labor noises, okay?" He gave her an odd look and then kissed her cheek. "Do you need anything? I've gotta get that story about the Michigan Avenue renovations ready for print. It's the feature in the *Trib* Sunday." She glanced over her shoulder as he returned to their shared home-office.

They had made it. Andy and Katie were their two small children. She closed her eyes, blocking the tears that raw emotions and overactive hormones were creating. Marcy's leap of faith had made all the difference. One small decision had changed the course of their lives. Harvard and Stanford had wanted her, but Drew and the University of Chicago had gotten her instead. The memories all hit her again – from her eight years without Drew, and now the last eight years with him. Two point five kids, same penthouse in Chicago, two fancy cars. And love. Most importantly love.

A knock on the window made her eyes pop open. Lola, the sassy gnomette, wearing a black and white polka dot cone hat and matching glittery dress waved back at her. Marcy watched as the tiny woman scribbled something in bright, candy-red lipstick on the glass.

The squeaky voice yelled what she'd written. *Keep the*

faith. With a wave and snap of her fingers, Lola was gone, leaving a trail of smoke in her wake.

As the sound of Lola's husky chuckle faded away outside the window, Marcy knew she was right where she belonged all along.

We invite you to visit
Jill and Julia's upcoming website –
http://www.jillandjulia.com

When Mules Rush In

by Jacquie Rogers

Lander, Wyoming–July, 1882

I came into this plane of existence more than two millennia ago. You know me as Merlin, King Arthur's advisor and sorcerer. Those days changed into new days, and sorcerers fell out of favor when the Auld Ways were relegated to myth. But we are still here.

Since my unfortunate...er, retirement, I have roamed the earth as a wolf. But humans have a tendency to kill those magnificent beasts, especially in the British Isles, so I did what the Scots and later the Irish did–moved to America and migrated west. I have now assumed the shape of the most intelligent of all four-legged animals (and most of the two-legged ones I've met). A mule. I am still a sorcerer with a commitment to the Auld Ways: do no harm and mentor my human.

Luke Tyson is his name and money's his game. He's what's called a 'thoroughbred gambler' and he can charm the wings off a faery. He's been under more skirts than Amelia Bloomer's bloomers and has an uncanny ability to extract himself from the most dire of circumstances with a twinkle in his eye and a grin on his face.

My mission: to help him find happiness.

His mission: to avoid facing his true fear–that he'll die at the card table holding aces and eights. A friend of his, Bill Hickock, had that unfortunate bit of luck. Luke knows no other life, and humans have a tendency to stick with the familiar, even if it's killing them. That's what makes a sorcerer's job such a headache.

They say mules are stubborn. I think not. Mules simply refuse to do stupid and/or dangerous things. Humans, however, refuse to see what's good for them. To find happiness, Luke needs a home, a family, and a partner who loves him.

He needs love.

"Mighty fine garden you have there." The man sat back in the saddle, a dusty jacket covering his broad shoulders. Willow Jones swore she'd seen him somewhere before, but couldn't place him. Surely she would never have forgotten those strong hands and muscled thighs, let alone his twinkling, emerald eyes and slightly crooked, white-toothed grin.

Willow savored his velvety baritone voice as she wiped the sweat from her brow with her sleeve. No matter who he was or how handsome he looked, she didn't want him—or anyone else—on her farm. "Mighty fine mule you have there. Must be fifteen hands. Keep him away from the plants." She wiped the grime from her callused hands on her apron. "Are you here to buy some herbs?"

"No, ma'am." He pushed his black Stetson high on his forehead and rested his forearm on the saddle horn.

Her gaze lingered on his familiar body.

She knew him.

She'd dreamed him.

Every single night since the first full moon. The Farmer's Almanac said there'd be another full moon, a Blue Moon, this month and she'd wished for her dream man to come to her. He had.

Regrettably, she couldn't succumb to base desires because strangers posed a threat to exposing her identity. A threat to her very life, in fact. "Then I suggest you be on your way."

"This the Jones place? I was told I'd find Eleanor Winthrop-Douglas here."

Her stomach clenched. She gripped the hoe, steadying herself with it. "No one here by that name." She had grown up in Boston as Eleanor Winthrop-Douglas, but now she was Willow Jones, herb farmer. And so would she stay, no matter who came for her. "Get on with you now."

The stranger turned his mule away, but Willow had the strangest urge to call him back. "Wait!"

He looked over his shoulder at her.

"You must be thirsty. The well's on the other side of the barn – let me get you and your mule a drink."

Thank you, good lady.

She froze mid-stride and stared at the mule, then at his rider. "What did you say?"

"Not a thing, ma'am, but a long drink of cool water sounds fine to me." The stranger threw one leg over, then stopped. "Do you mind if I light a while? I'm getting a bit saddle-weary, if you know what I mean."

She knew what he meant. He meant to stay as long as he could and snoop around for Eleanor Winthrop-Douglas, runaway Boston debutante. Willow meant to send him on his way empty-handed. "Suit yourself. Follow me if you want some water, then you can ride out."

"Now why do I feel like you're rushing me on down the road?"

She didn't look back, but heard the clip-clop *of the mule's hooves. She dangled a bucket into the well and pulled the rope until the full bucket was a few inches higher than the side of the well, then poured the water into a trough. She patted the mule's butt. "There's your water, boy."*

I am not a *boy*. You may address me as 'Merlin.'

"What?"

The mule gazed at her innocently.

"Uh, well, have a nice drink, Merlin."

The man gripped the rope and dropped the bucket back into the well, then he raised an eyebrow. "I didn't tell you the mule's name."

A chill ran down Willow's spine. The stranger who stood before her was every girl's naughty dream. He'd certainly been in her dreams. Why, she'd just wished on a Blue Moon that a man like him would rescue her from her loneliness. But she wouldn't have a man who wanted to woo Eleanor so he could claim the Winthrop-Douglas inheritance. Besides, his mysterious mule gave her a bad case of the jitters.

"I think you'd better go."

He finished his drink and wiped his mouth on his sleeve. In no hurry, he pulled the rope up and perched the full bucket on the well's ledge. "Save you a little trouble for later." Then he took Merlin's reins, turned toward Willow and tipped his hat. "Thank you kindly for the water." He threw his muscular leg over the mule and mounted in one smooth movement.

She stood by the well and watched him ride away, his posture confident and his body supple. As he rode out of sight, she kicked a clod with her toe and cursed her lonesome existence.

The overly bright morning greeted Willow when she left the cabin to feed the chickens. One looked as bedraggled as she felt. "Did you have a restless night, DeborahAnne?"

The hen clucked and cooed.

Willow threw her an extra handful of grain. "Did you lie awake half the night thinking about a green-eyed rooster with broad shoulders who rides a mule?"

DeborahAnne walked away, clucking.

"I thought not." Willow finished feeding the chickens, gathered the eggs, tossed an armload of alfalfa hay to the Guernsey cow and milked her, then went into the cabin to cook breakfast.

As she stoked the fire in the cook stove, she heard the clip-clop *of a horse. She lifted a corner of the yellow-flowered curtain. Not a horse – a mule, and he carried the man with those dratted shoulders that kept her awake half the night. She ought to fill him with buckshot just on general principle. A night without sleep did not sweeten one's temperament.*

She stepped onto the newly swept porch and waited for the stranger to dismount.

Greetings, good lady.

She nodded but remained silent. Talking to a mule at six in the morning would confirm the townfolks' notion of her being a little tetched in the head. And her own notion, too. He couldn't have said anything, anyway.

Her gaze was drawn to the green eyes of the mule's rider, who stared back with equal intensity. Afraid he could see right through her, to the depths of her desire, she desperately wanted to break eye contact. She could not.

By the scent of the rose
May his true love be found
Golden-haired beauty
Her eyes of brown
To fill his heart's desire
With the Blue Moon's fire.

The mule tossed his head and danced about.

"Whoa!" his handsome rider yelled, tugging on the reins.

A sparkly feeling surrounded man, mule, and Willow. She could see it, but not see it. Hear it, but not hear it. Feel it, but not touch it. Her troubles disappeared and her heart found happiness.

Oh, but the drifter sat a fine seat.

"Would you like to have some breakfast? I have bacon and sourdough pancakes." She blinked, wondering what on earth had gotten into her. Not only had she invited a man to breakfast, she didn't even know his name. And no matter how free the sparkles made her feel, this man spelled trouble. He wanted Eleanor Winthrop-Douglas, and any man who

wanted her could only be described as greedy, despicable, or dangerous – or all three. Somehow, neither greedy nor despicable fit him. But dangerous...

"Did you see the shiny dust in the air?" he asked.

She really didn't want to answer that. "Yes, mister. Must be indicative of rain."

"Indicative? I'll bet you're the only person in fifty miles who knows that word."

She waved him off. "Do you want breakfast or not?" She made a quick pivot and escaped into her cabin. She had no answer for her unexpected invitation to him. No one except for her had ever eaten a meal in the cabin, and she preferred it that way. Or so she told herself.

If she kept herself busy enough, she believed that a lone existence was what she wanted. The problem was, at night she couldn't quite force herself to believe it.

The past few nights since the full moon had been unusually restless. She pictured the stranger coming to her, capturing her in his protective embrace, touching his lips to hers, then, overcome with blinding passion, begging her to make love to him. Oh, good grief, she had to quit thinking about that or she'd get hot all over again right in front of him.

He knocked on the door and she let him in. "Tyson's the name. Luke Tyson."

Willow offered her hand in the debutante way without thinking. "Willow Jones. Nice to meet you, Mr. Tyson." His bright emerald eyes enchanted her.

"Luke. It's just Luke." He removed his hat and hung it on the rack by the door. "I haven't had a home-cooked meal in quite a spell, so this will be a real treat."

She pulled her gaze away from him and picked up the knife to slice the bacon. "You don't even know if I can cook."

"You can cook. A woman like you, I'm expecting, can do anything she sets her mind to."

Willow thought the same thing about him. With that rich baritone of his, she'd bet he could charm the feathers off a peacock. "You can wash up out back. You know where the well is."

"I'll take that as a hint I don't smell too good."

He smelled fine, like soap and bay rum. In fact, he smelled too fine to be sitting in her kitchen waiting for a meal. "Take it any way you want, but no one eats at my table without washing up first."

Luke left the cabin and stayed out long enough for her to make coffee, put the bacon in the skillet to fry, and mix the sourdough pancake batter. She peeked out the window to see him striding toward the cabin, each pace displaying a cocky confidence. His damp, dark hair brushed his muscular shoulders. Willow shivered at the thought of gliding her hands up his strong arms, across his shoulders, and down his chest. Her palms tingled as if she'd really done so, and unrelenting need settled low in her belly.

She opened the door before he rounded to the front of the cabin so he wouldn't feel obliged to knock again. Merlin stood ground-tied, perusing her with an intensity she'd never seen from an animal—except for maybe her chicken, DeborahAnne. "Who are you?"

I told you—Merlin.

"I'm not sure I believe a mule can put thoughts in my head."

Ah, but maybe a sorcerer can.

"Sorcerer, my as—"

Careful.

"Pardon me. But I don't know why I'm talking to you."

Social repartee is appropriate, I would think, under the circumstances.

Luke stepped onto the porch and held out his hands. "Clean enough?" A wry grin settled on his sensual lips and the ornery twinkle in his eyes made her want to kiss him and *feel his arms holding her close to him, protecting her – but dangerous nonetheless.*

"Do you enjoy baiting me?" Willow charged back into the cabin, more frustrated with herself than angry at Luke. In fact, she couldn't find a single reason for her feelings about him. She needed to get rid of him. Soon. Before he found her out and dragged her back to Boston.

After she finished cooking breakfast and they'd sat at the table to eat, Luke asked, "How long have you lived here?"

Clearly, he was fishing for information on Eleanor Winthrop-Douglas. "Long enough."

"Seems like a hard life for a woman all alone."

"It's a hard life for anyone, and I'm as strong as the next person."

"If you mean strong as in 'obstinate,' then I expect you're right about that."

He had no idea how right. She would never return to Boston unless he took her back in a pine box, and she fully intended to prevent that from happening. And even if she did meet her demise, no greedy 'suitor' would ever get a nickel of her money. She had designated it all for charity, all except enough to buy the materials to build a house large enough for a family.

Maybe she'd even turn that last little bit over to the children's home. If she married, it would be because the man loved her, *not her money.*

This, Willow Jones swore.

Luke chose to draw back before he pressed his luck too far. He put the napkin on the table and stood. "Thank you kindly, Miss Jones. I'll be on my way now after I help with those dishes."

Visibly relieved, she said, "No. No, you don't need to help. There's only a few and I, uh, think...think while I'm washing dishes. For instance, I think about what I'm going to plant next year or – "

"Goodbye, Miss Jones." He brushed a kiss on her cheek as he edged past her. Her eyes rounded and she leaned into him. He gently pushed her back. "I'll see you on my way back."

She followed him out of the cabin. Merlin swished his tail and the almost imaginary shiny sprinkles 'happened' in the air again. Luke had a nearly overwhelming urge to crush Willow to his chest, protect her, and kiss her senseless. With all the willpower he could muster, he mounted the mule and gave him a nudge. Without guidance, Merlin seemed to know Luke intended to return to the campsite over the hill and a ways into the trees.

At camp, he dismounted and grabbed a few loose branches to break into firewood. "Willow Jones is definitely Eleanor Winthrop-Douglas."

Nate Worthington wanted his so-called fiancée returned to him in Boston no matter the cost. Luke had watched Willow for several days to make certain of her identity before approaching her. She had dead-panned him when he asked for Eleanor Winthrop-Douglas, but he knew for sure Willow and Eleanor were one and the same. Her city manners this morning confirmed it.

He did wonder, though, why a beautiful young woman would give up her millions to live on a remote farm in a hard-scrabble country, scratching a living from the dirt. She seemed happy doing it, too, and he'd bet his last marked card that she wouldn't be too cooperative about returning to Boston.

Nevertheless, he aimed to take her there and collect his fee. Nate Worthington had already deposited five thousand dollars in Luke's account, and another five thousand would be deposited as soon as he delivered Miss Winthrop-Douglas to Boston.

"Ten thousand dollars is a lot of money."

She's a fine woman. No wonder Worthington wants her.

"Ah, hell, Merlin. He doesn't want her. A man like that can't appreciate a real woman. All he wants is a sweet young thing to look good on his arm, and her hefty inheritance so no one finds out he's a lousy faro player."

Luke squatted by the fire pit, lit some dried leaves and waited until they took to flame, then added more leaves and some twigs. When the blaze grew stronger, he propped three logs against one another on end to give the fire lots of air and room to burn.

Willow Jones is your woman.

"Damn! She's sure – " Luke glared at Merlin. "Now I don't question that you put thoughts into my head and everyone thinks I'm a blithering fool because I talk to a mule. But you don't need to be getting ridiculous about things. Willow Jones is not my woman. She doesn't even like me much. She sure as hell doesn't trust me."

He filled the coffeepot with water and hung it on the tripod to boil. "As she shouldn't. It looks to me like the flighty Eleanor Winthrop-Douglas has changed herself into a hardworking herb farmer, and frankly, she seems quite happy."

And you thought...

"Don't get smart with me, Merlin. I don't know what I thought. I thought I wanted ten thousand dollars, that's what I thought." He'd never had even a passing notion that Miss Winthrop-Douglas wouldn't willingly return to Boston with him. Nate said she was fragile and biddable. Luke should have known something wasn't right when he offered enough money to live on for a lifetime. Ten thousand dollars would buy twenty men plenty willing to track down a 'fragile and biddable' woman.

Ah, but your charm is your ticket to prosperity.

"Huh. That's what I thought, too." Luke glared at the mule. "Are you gloating at me?"

All this thinking was for naught. He'd already used the five thousand to buy a ranch in Oregon, and he needed the other five thousand to buy stock and supplies, and hire a crew.

No matter what she called herself, Miss Winthrop-Douglas was going back to Boston.

"I am not *going back to Boston." Willow turned her back on Luke and whapped a clod with her hoe, hoping man and beast would just go away.*

"Sorry, Miss Winthrop-Douglas – "

"Do not ever call me that!"

"Er, Miss Jones, but I'm bound by honor to take you back."

"Ha." She wheeled around and glared at the man who'd haunted her dreams, not knowing he'd turn into a nightmare. But it appeared all men did that – when you had something they wanted. "Some nitwit paid you good money to abduct me and return me to that den of society snakes, I suppose."

"I wouldn't call him a nitwit – "

"So he did pay you. Who was it? Nate Worthington? He's unsavory enough to pull such an idiotic and dishonest stunt. I despise him."

"Your fiancé?"

"Never. Daddy didn't allow him to court me. Mr. Worthington staged a scene where I would be considered ruined, but all it did was give me an excuse to get away from the whole backbiting crowd and all their hurtful games. The only thing in Boston I liked was my garden. But I like this one better." She turned away and hacked out a healthy weed beside a pathetic excuse for a green bean bush. "Now, go away."

The mule acted up and spun in a circle. Sparkles flew from his tail and lay suspended in the air.

By the scent of the rose
May his true love be found
To fill his heart's desire
With the Blue Moon's fire.

Luke dismounted and took a couple of steps toward her, his eyes more enchanting than usual. "I would be obliged if you'd let me slay your dragons."

Willow stepped back, startled.

"Eh." He rubbed his temple. "What did I just say?"

Maybe I should adjust the charm to a more modern cant.

DeborahAnne pecked at Merlin's foot. He danced about a bit. Be patient, DeborahAnne.

Willow stared at the chicken. "Does that mule know you?" DeborahAnne strutted away and scratched the dirt, pecking for bugs. She'd always acted differently than the other chickens – observant and smart, and never one of the flock. At least she didn't talk. Well, neither did Merlin, but he definitely communicated. Then again, Willow had always felt compelled to speak to DeborahAnne even though she didn't return the favor.

Embarrassed to be caught talking to a chicken, Willow shrugged and avoided eye contact with Luke. "I think you and your mule need to leave now. I'm not going with you and that's the only reason you're here. So go."

Luke kneeled before her, took off his hat and held it over his heart. "My quest to find you brought me here, that's true, m'lady. But I stay because I long to caress your lovely skin, to kiss your upturned nose, to run my fingers through your long, brown tresses with strands of gold. I want to lay you gently on the grass and run my hands over your belly and touch your brea – "

"Enough!"

I may have overdone it.

Her skin heated and her breasts tightened at the very thought of doing or overdoing anything with Luke. But as enchanting as he seemed, she would never jeopardize her hard-won freedom. She licked her lips, then said, "Get on your mule. And. Get. Out."

"But m'lady – "

"Out!"

Luke pulled back on the reins as they approached his camp. He didn't know how he'd ever hold his head up as a man again. Men didn't go around talking like that to women they barely knew. Hell, men didn't say those things at all.

"Merlin, I don't know what you are or who you are, but you made me look like a damned fool back there. I need that other five thousand dollars. Besides, I can't give back the five thousand I took because it's already spent. So how am I supposed to drag that woman back to Boston if you have me on my knees describing her body parts?"

The mule plodded toward the campsite. I admit to some miscalculation.

"Some miscalculation. Huh. Try humiliation."

They rounded the bend to his campsite. Through the trees, he saw a couple of wagons and several horses. Luke whispered, "Whoa, Merlin."

Nate Worthington, dressed in a black frock coat, waved his arms about as he strutted around the men, hollering orders.

Merlin took a couple steps back before they could be seen. Worthington.

"Damn." Luke drew one of his Colts.

An impatient man.

"A dangerous man. " He spun the cylinder to make sure it was loaded. "Turn around quietly and let's head back to Willow's place."

Do you love her?

"Of course, not, you mangy beast. I just met her."

Then why are you warning her? Don't you want the other five thousand dollars?

Yes, he wanted the money, but not at the expense of the woman he . . .

He took off his Stetson and raked his fingers through his hair. Not at Willow's expense. "Ah, hellfire! She needs a man who'll give her whatever she wants, not some scoundrel who'll suck her dry and throw her to the wolves."

I presume you're not dragging her back to Boston.

"Yes, but don't presume I'm averse to strangling smart-aleck mules."

Let's not get snippy.

"Get a move on." Luke pressed his heels into Merlin's ribs.

Willow met them in the farmyard, shotgun in hand and the chicken by her side.

Luke tipped his hat. "Dinner on?"

She aimed the shotgun at his chest, but the look in her eye told him she wouldn't pull the trigger. "I told you to go."

"And if I don't, you gonna sic your attack chicken on me?" He dismounted and flipped the reins over the hitching post in front of the barn, but didn't wrap them.

"I might. I should. How much is he paying you to ruin my life?"

"Five thousand up front and five more when I deliver." The hurt in her eyes stabbed him in the heart, but this was no time to cave in to sentimentality.

"I should blow your brains out right here, right now, Luke Tyson."

"Better save it for your beau, sweetheart." The tear in her eye nearly undid him but he dusted off his bravado and charged ahead. "Worthington is at my campsite this very moment giving orders to his men. Their horses were saddled and ready so I expect you'll have company shortly."

"He's not my beau!" She took a step forward, the shotgun wavering. "And I'm not your sweetheart!"

"Either way, you're getting my help whether you want it or not." Luke took a quick glance around the barnyard to avoid looking at the woman who had every right to distrust him, to hate him, and whose luscious curves and callused hands drove him mad with wanting to kiss her all over. "Not much here to make a barricade. The cabin has no defense."

"How many?"

"Worthington, a couple of hired guns, and a servant—although he could be a gunman, too, for all we know. So four."

Merlin nudged Luke. And a scrawny fellow with a preacher's collar. Five.

"A preacher? Damn." He glanced at Willow. "Sorry, ma'am." He knew Worthington would stop at no less than a legal marriage to Willow, so Luke had to stop him. He could handle five ordinary men, but the two gunslingers could cause some minor difficulties. Luke's plans for the future didn't include his perforation.

Willow's eyes widened. "A preacher? Oh, my!" She leaned her shotgun against the porch. "DeborahAnne, bad men are coming. Will you please take the ladies into the coop?" The chicken clucked and flapped her wings. The other hens obeyed and ran into a chicken house attached to the side of the barn.

Luke couldn't believe what he saw. The scene looked entirely too Merlin-ish to him. "You trained a chicken?"

Willow shrugged. "Actually, I think she trained me." She grabbed her garden tools. "It's early, but I'm going to feed the animals in case we're, uh, detained."

"No, you're not. Worthington and his men will be here and I can protect you better in the cabin."

She balanced the shotgun on her left shoulder and picked up a bucket with her right hand. "Save your lecture, Mr.

Tyson. This farm and these animals are my life. I'm feeding them, and then I'll return to the cabin. And protect you."

"Fool woman." Luke followed her to the barn. "Hurry up, then." The tidy, clean barn had a stall for the Guernsey cow on the left side, with the grain and farm equipment on the right, and loose hay in the loft above. A kerosene lantern hung on a hook just inside the doorway.

She headed to the right and stashed her garden tools. "If you want to make yourself useful, climb up to the loft and throw some hay down to Cleopatra."

"Cleopatra?"

"The cow. She wants to rule the world, so I named her Cleopatra."

As he climbed the ladder to the loft, he half expected the danged cow to say something. He threw a couple armloads of hay to her. She shook her head and threatened him with her horns. "I see what you mean."

"Dust on the road!" Willow yelled. "Oh, dear."

"Oh, crap." Luke leapt the rest of the way to the floor and in three long strides stood by her side.

She cocked the shotgun. "It's gonna be a long afternoon."

"I expect so."

"DeborahAnne, go to the coop with the rest of the chickens." Willow almost laughed at the look of disgust on the hen's face. Who ever heard of a chicken with facial expressions? "Stay out of the way, girl. They'll be here in ten minutes and if you're underfoot, you'll be hurt or killed. These men won't care."

Luke walked up behind her and touched her arm. Warmth pooled there and beckoned her to lean into the security of his hard, lean chest. She resisted, of course. He needn't know how much Nate Worthington scared the beejeebies out of her. Luke's offer of protection gave her strength. He didn't need to know that, either.

"You'll be all right," Luke murmured in her ear.

She took tiny breaths to even her voice. "My shotgun holds two rounds. One has Nate's name written on it." She'd never marry that scoundrel, under any circumstances. And he would never, ever get her inheritance.

Luke tugged on her wrist and pulled her toward the cabin. "We'd best go inside. Better cover there."

"You won't get any of my inheritance, either." She didn't know why she said that, other than to see if he'd turn on her.

"Good. Looks to me as if your inheritance is the cause of more problems than it cures."

She would've been astonished if Luke had responded any other way. For some reason, she believed him. Trusted him, even, and his words made her happy.

He nodded toward the road. "They're almost here. Get in the house."

Glittery particles surrounded them. Willow glanced at Merlin – sure enough, he twirled his tail and it appeared as if sparkles came from the end of it. Her heart beat more slowly and she basked in the love that surrounded her. She had an overwhelming urge to touch Luke's lips. Taste them.

She let him lead her into the cabin. Once there, she swept her hands over his shoulders and chest. "Please kiss me." She tilted her head up and puckered her lips.

Luke lowered his lips close to hers. She could feel his breath and his heat, and craved his touch. But he pulled back. "It's Merlin," he growled. "Make no mistake about it, I want to kiss you. I want to kiss you so much I can hardly think straight. But I'm not going to kiss you or touch you unless it's of your own free will. "

Willow stepped back and smoothed her skirts. "Oh, my goodness." Her free will couldn't be trusted, because if she caved in to it, she'd beg him to kiss her again – a hundred times. To touch her all over, too. Oh, and she wanted to feel every inch of him.

Her fingers shaking, she managed to close the wooden shutters and direct her thoughts to more pressing business. "Each shutter has a removable corner. You can shoot through it."

"I mean it. I want to touch every part of you. Twice." His emerald eyes seemed glazed and she wondered if he knew what he was saying. "And taste you. All over."

Her body wanted him, sparkles or not. Need settled deep in her belly. "If they fire back, hold this cast iron skillet in front of your face."

"I can't aim through a skillet."

"I'll do the talking. Mr. Worthington is my problem, not yours."

"Darlin', you are my problem. I can't let you confront a man with two hired guns in front of him."

"Let?" She ought to bash him with the skillet herself. "You can't let *me? Mr. Tyson, you forget yourself. This is* my *farm and this is my problem."*

The five men rode in at a trot, and Luke drew both Colts. "Whatever you say." Somehow, Willow didn't believe him.

The two gunmen pulled to a stop first, then Nate, and behind him, the servant and the preacher. Nate had the look of a man who wanted to be top dog, but never would be. Luke, though...men would be proud to follow him, a real man, wherever, whenever he led them. He had a natural air of confidence, whereas Nate was just a little too loud, too reactive, too stiff. It was a subtle thing, but the difference was striking.

The men dismounted, dust swirling around them in an ominous cloud.

"Hold it right there, Mr. Worthington," she called. "I'm not going back with you. I'm not marrying you, and even if you fake a marriage, you wouldn't get any money. I've signed it all over to charity. So you might as well get back on

your horse and ride out."

Nate faltered, but climbed the steps to the porch anyway.

"Stop or I'll shoot!" She heard Luke move beside her, staying low.

Nate doffed his hat, then chuckled. Willow wanted to shove that chuckle down his throat with a shotgun blast, but she needed to keep her senses about her. He tilted his head toward the garden. "Take it out."

The man dressed in servant's clothing mounted and ran his horse back and forth over her herb garden time and time again, uprooting tender shoots she'd spent hours nurturing and trampling the life she'd worked so hard to build. Every hoof mark dug into her soul. Tears welled in her eyes but she blinked them away. Nathan Worthington would not get to her this easily. She could plant another garden next year.

"Are you ready to be my bride, Eleanor?"

"I am Willow, and I am quite happy as a spinster."

"Boys, I think she needs a little more convincing." He pointed his thumb at the barn. "Torch it. Maybe smoke will convince the little lady to welcome our upcoming wedded bliss."

"If they set fire to my barn, I'm going to pull this trigger, Mr. Worthington." She prayed they'd go away, but they didn't.

One of them took a safety match from his pocket and struck it on his boot, then lit the kerosene lantern. "Hell, boss, there ain't nothin' to light. This barn's so clean you could lick the damned floor."

Nate shrugged. "The hay will ignite nicely, then the rest of the barn will burn like it was kindling."

"Oh, no, Luke, he's really gonna do it."

Her hands shook and sweat beaded on her forehead. It was a good thing shotguns didn't require a lot of aiming. "He's going to burn my barn!"

She closed her eyes and pulled the trigger. The recoil

slammed the shotgun into her shoulder, knocking her back a few steps before she regained her balance.

Bullets splintered the logs all around the cabin. "Get down, Willow!" Luke grabbed her shotgun, then pushed her to the floor, covering her with his body.

"Oh my God, they're shooting at us!"

"That generally happens when you fire on professional killers." She looked dazed. "Willow, are you with me?"

"Yes," she squeaked. "What do we do?"

He rolled off her and handed her weapon back. "Take a long, slow, deep breath and then reload." Luke peered through a bullet hole in the wall, then another, until he spotted the positions of all five men. "Don't worry, I have a plan."

Luke knew he'd lost his mind, but he couldn't allow these men to ruin what Willow had worked so hard to build. He pressed his back against the wall beside the door and unholstered both Colts. "The two gunmen are on the east side of the house. Worthington and the other two are in the front. When I say the word, fire one barrel at your beau, then cock and fire the other as fast as you can. I'll roll out of the house firing while you reload. Do you understand?"

She gave a quick nod. She had to feel nervous – he was. "I'm taking the two gunmen out first. They're the most dangerous. You worry about Worthington." He paused to see if she was playing with a full deck, or whether she was still in shock. "Five against two, darlin'. Piece of cake."

"I'm all right. Let's do it."

"That's what I wanted to hear. I'll open the door on the count of one. Three...two...one!"

Willow fired like a trooper as he flung the door open. The ten-gauge was a more powerful shotgun than a woman her size could easily handle, but she braced herself and took the recoil without a flinch. She cocked and fired again. On the second shot, he rolled out the door, heart thumping and Colts blazing. He winged one of the gunmen and the servant. Couldn't find Worthington, though.

"Luke, the barn – it's on fire!" Willow blasted the shotgun again. "Reload, fast!"

She sure as hell wasn't in shock anymore. He rolled off the porch, leaned back against the cabin and reloaded both cylinders.

"Oh, no," Willow groaned. "Cleopatra will die in there."

"Find cover and keep firing."

Instead, the fool woman dashed across the barnyard toward the well. A bullet exploded into the wood right beside Luke's head. Splinters flew everywhere, some grazing his left ear and cheek. He wiped the blood from his face and took a quick survey – where were the shooters and how could he get to Willow without getting blown to smithereens himself?

Run. Stay low. *Merlin hunkered behind the well, taking cover.* The bucket is already in the water, full. I can pull the rope and bring it up. Douse yourself, then do your heroic deed—save the woman and her farm.

Luke wiped the blood from his left eye again, fired a couple of rounds in the general direction of Worthington's hired guns, then sprinted to the well and crouched beside Willow. Merlin had the bucket ready, but as soon as Luke reached over to get it, bullets sprayed everywhere, including through the bucket.

He was so happy to see her in one piece, he wanted to kiss her senseless. "I'm taking you back to the cabin."

"No, you're not!"

"You're gonna be hurt out here." Bullets tore into the ground all around and ricocheted off the stone well in front of them. He spun, grabbed his woman and yanked her to the ground. "Get down before they kill you, you crazy woman."

"I have to save Cleopatra. Nate's men won't kill me. I'm not any use to him if I'm dead."

"Don't fool yourself. I'll bet the preacher is getting paid enough to forge your signature on a marriage certificate. Now keep down."

"You're bloody!" she cried, then before he could stop her, sprinted for the barn, gunfire pitting the ground around her.

"You're bloody stubborn." He dashed after her.

DeborahAnne clucked and flapped her wings.

"Hey, boss, you wanna have chicken stew for supper?" one of the gunmen hollered.

Luke scooped her up and held her like a baby as he continued to run toward the barn.

She's trying to tell you to let the chickens out.

Luke dodged pistol shots, flipped the coop door open, and dropped the chicken as he went by. The outside air thickened with smoke. His eyes watered and his lungs labored, but he had to save Willow from herself. He only hoped she hadn't already succumbed to the smoke and heat.

Inside the barn, blackened by dark smoke, Luke felt his way to the left. The heat grew more intense and the sweat ran off his forehead and stung his eyes. He couldn't see a thing, but reckoned Willow would be at the cow's stall. Four or five more steps and he'd make it. He only hoped Willow was there and that Cleopatra wouldn't be wild with fear and put his woman in hazard's path. He made his way to the cow's desperate bawl.

"She's alive!" Willow croaked.

"I told you to stay put." Luke wanted to grab her and shake some sense into her pretty head. Instead, he felt around until he found her and pulled her close. "Put your apron over your nose, darlin'. I'll get you out of here."

"Cleopatra?"

"Her, too."

A beam crashed in front of them, and an ember seared his shoulder. He protected Willow with his body while he unhooked the stall gate. "Watch out, she might charge."

The cow didn't budge. Luke grabbed her halter and pulled with all his might. Finally she took a step, then another. He could see light and led her toward it. Then she did charge. Luke pulled Willow out of the way. Neither could talk for the smoke and heat.

Embers flew everywhere. One landed in Willow's hair and he crushed it out before it caught fire. He had to get her out safely. She was more important to him than anything in the world. He urged her, stumbling, toward the barn door. Once outside, they bent over, gulping fresh air, smoke billowing from their bodies.

At the crack of a rifle, Luke grabbed Willow and tossed her to the ground.

"Ah, my bride." Nate materialized out of the billowing smoke like the very devil himself. He grabbed Willow by the arm and dragged her toward the cabin. She had no fight left in her after the fire. Luke did, though, and was exchanging blows with Nate's henchmen.

She rooted for him as he threw a right jab into the jaw of the healthy gunman, who fell into the line of fire of the wounded gunman, taking a bullet in the chest.

The servant and the preacher apparently had all they wanted of Nate's scheme because they mounted up and rode off hell-bent for leather.

Nate jerked her arm. "I have our marriage certificate inside, Eleanor. You are now Mrs. Worthington."

DeborahAnne and her flock of chickens clucked and squawked as they surrounded Nate like a pack of hungry coyotes ready for the kill. "Get them away from me!" He took off running, tripped over the bullet-riddled water bucket, and fell face-first on the ground. The relentless hens surrounded him, pecking and scratching, clucking and clawing.

"Peck his eyeballs out, DeborahAnne!"

"I'd love to, but I've lost my pecker." DeborahAnne, a

lovely woman, flipped her black, knee-length hair around her shoulder and smiled. "I've waited fifteen hundred years for this day." A rope materialized in her hand and she tossed it to Willow. "You'll be safer if you tie his hands."

Maybe so, but Willow was so stunned at the woman who was a chicken that she stood frozen in place, staring.

Luke finally bested his last assailant. "Hand me the rope." But then he gawked at DeborahAnne, too. By the time Willow came to her senses and handed him the rope, Worthington's men had helped each other up and skedaddled for the hills.

"Get out of here and never show your faces in this country again," Luke hollered as he bound Nate's hands behind his back. "You might stop by the marshal's office and tell him to pick up your boss, though."

As the two gunmen galloped away, Luke grabbed Willow and crushed his mouth against hers, filling her with passion right down to her toes. She leaned into him, opening her mouth a bit to taste the tip of his tongue, caressing his back and hugging him with all the strength she had left. He pushed her back and gazed into her eyes. "Are you hurt?"

He had soot on half of his face and sported the beginnings of a black eye, but still, she'd never seen a more handsome man. "Only that you're not kissing me."

"Do you want to get married?"

"I don't know you." But she trusted him. She trusted him with her life and her heart—something she never thought she'd feel for any man. But Luke wasn't just any man.

He rubbed a smudge off her nose. "I didn't ask if you knew me. I asked if you wanted to marry me."

"Depends on how often you kiss me." She tilted her head up for another kiss.

"Every minute of every day." He obliged, gentler this time but no less urgent, and pulled her tight against him

until his hardness pressed demandingly against her belly. She could never get close enough to this man.

Tears sprang to Willow's eyes. "I loved you two weeks before you came to the farm. I dreamed about you. I thought about you day and night."

"And now that it's a Blue Moon – "

"I got my wish." She caressed the stubble on his sooty jaw. "If you really want to marry me, you'll kiss me again."

He smiled, his eyes twinkling. "I dreamed about you, too, and for the rest of my life, I want you by my side." He lowered his mouth to hers and kissed her until her knees melted.

So I'm still a mule. I'm deeply disappointed, although I'm quite delighted that my wife, DeborahAnne, has shifted back into the lovely woman I remember. Quite a shapely lady, she is. I rather like having her astride me, so to speak.

"Merlin, you're an ass. If you hadn't messed around with that hussy, Morgana, we wouldn't be in this mess right now."

One mistake, and you pay for it the rest of your life, which is the pits when you're immortal, I assure you. So I kept my counsel.

"You could have defended Luke and saved his life, you big lout. Why didn't you? It would have broken the curse and you'd be a man right now. I mean, what am I supposed to do for sex? The Catherine the Great thing? I don't think so."

If I had saved Luke's life, he wouldn't have been able to show Willow his true character, and since my first job was to help him find love, I couldn't protect him. Sorry, DeborahAnne.

"We'll just have to find you an opportunity to save someone's life soon, and you'd better not blow it or I'll give you back to Morgana. Maybe she deserves you."

But I knew she didn't mean those words. DeborahAnne has stayed by my side for millennia and she loves me as much as I love her.

I earnestly hoped the opportunity to save a life and turn back into a man would come soon, because my wife can be insufferable. But never has a man—or a mule—had a more intriguing mate.

Coming soon from Jacquie Rogers:
Faery Special Romances

Visit Jacquie's website at
http://www.jacquierogers.com

The Star Traveler

by Victoria Houseman

Isle of Palms, South Carolina
June 30, 2007

"We buried Mama today, Onyx," Hayley Stone said to her black Labrador Retriever. Her voice choked from shedding endless tears. Her furry companion replied with a soft whimper, putting her head in Hayley's lap. They sat together on a couch in the sunroom, watching the late afternoon waves of the Atlantic lap the shoreline.

Lillian Stone had been diagnosed with Alzheimer's five years earlier. Being the only unattached child of four siblings Hayley hadn't hesitated to move Miss Lillian in with her then. Besides, this home had been the family's summer house for the past forty years. It had weathered hurricanes, broken teenage summer romances, and been a part of birth and death. The family refuge from the hazy, high humidity days of summertime in Charleston. Mama loved nothing more than to see her babies – and then their babies – play in the sand and ocean.

No one in the family had minded when Hayley asked if she could live there full-time after her bitter divorce six years earlier. She hadn't thought twice when the devastating diagnosis had come, and issued the invitation to her mother. She felt it only fitting that Mama spend her last years with whatever she had left of her memories in the refuge she so loved.

Lillian had agreed without hesitation while decisions were still hers to make. She seemed pleased, though she knew that any of her four offspring would've been honored to take care of their mama in her time of need. And while she'd loved her children equally, Hayley had clearly been special. A change of life baby, born twelve years after what Lillian thought was her last child, Hayley had always marched to her own song.

After the death of their father, Lillian had held the family together the way she'd done everything in life – with the grace and dignity of a true Southern woman. She'd faced the heinous Alzheimer's with no less courage.

Hayley drew in a cleansing breath and let out a long, slow sigh. She had to let the memories of her mother emerge as they were ready, but just for today she'd force them back down in her soul. They were just too damn painful. She fingered the white gold locket she wore at her throat, a final gift from her mother, and surveyed the paper plates with half-eaten food and partially filled cups. She had to start cleaning now that all those who had come to pay their respects to Miss Lillian had gone.

"Five more minutes, girl, then we get to cleaning, okay?" She scratched the big head and closed her eyes, leaning her head against the blue ticking striped pillows.

"Woof." Onyx rolled her head into Hayley's hand.

"We've got to head back to Spartanburg, baby sis," James said in his soft drawl. He sat next to her on the floral chintz sofa and drew her head to his shoulder. "You were a wonderful daughter, Hayley. You took terrific care of Mama, especially these past six months, when the disease totally ravished her mind."

Gently winding her long, braid around his hand, he kissed the top of her head.

"I'm a doctor, James. Why couldn't I do more for her?" She looked at him and tears threatened to spill.

"You were a daughter, Hayley. First and foremost, you were her daughter. And, overachiever that you are," he said as he smiled, "you went above and beyond to make her last years comfortable." James chucked her under the chin with his thumb and forefinger, lifting her face to his. He met and held her gaze. "You want to honor Mama's memory?" At her nod, he continued, "You move on with your life."

"You're right." She gently moved the sleeping dog's head off her lap and onto the couch. Standing, she straightened her blouse. "I think I'll go back to work sooner than planned." Her mind made up, Hayley set about tidying the sunroom.

A soft, brown hand covered hers as she reached for plates on the coffee table. "I'll do it, child. You go on now and hug your brother goodbye."

Hayley walked her brother and his family to the front porch. She watched them drive away until she could no longer see their car. Then she returned to help Alice.

The petite woman had been with the Stone family since well before any of the children had been born. Steeped in Gullah heritage, she'd regale Hayley with stories of her youth as she braided Hayley's hair while helping her get ready for school. It had been part of their daily ritual when Hayley was younger. Often she spoke the native tongue and Hayley had exploded in peals of laughter. She didn't know Gullah, but had always loved the sound when Alice used it. Alice and her family were like extended family to the Stones. Through the decades, they'd shared in one another's happiness and tears.

Hayley attempted a feeble smile, but it felt forced. A lone tear rolled down her cheek. "I can't believe she's really gone, Alice."

"Baby girl, Miss Lillian left us a long time ago. These past six months she wasn't inside that shell of a breathin' body." Alice continued to put dirty paper plates into a garbage sack. "The Man Upstairs done called her soul home a long time ago. It just took some time for Miss Lillian to get the message and allow her body to follow."

Onyx let out a small 'woof' and stretched out to her full length on the sofa, causing Alice to raise an eyebrow in disapproval. "Humph. A dog on the furniture."

At that, Hayley had to smile. "She's my girl."

"She's a dog and a large one at that!"

Hayley put her hands over Onyx's ears in mock horror as a small giggle escaped.

"What I would love," Alice's tone turned serious, drawing Hayley's attention to her face, "is for you to have a *human* baby. You know it was your mama's fondest wish for you."

Bless Alice for her honesty. This woman was like a second mother to her. While it tore Hayley to her core to have it said, she knew the words were the truth. Her mother's last wish before the light left her eyes was to see Hayley settled. Wonderful husband, cherubic baby, a mother's dream for her young girl.

Dropping into her mama's favorite wingback chair, she buried her head into her hands. "It's not my dream, Alice. I have my dream. A thriving medical practice, a terrific beach house in the greatest place in the world, my Onyx."

"Uh-huh."

Hayley clasped her hands together, a pleading gesture. "I've done the marriage thing, Alice. You know, been there, done that, got the dang t-shirt. All I can say is I'm thankful there were no children because then I would've been tied to my creep of a husband forever."

"You're scared, Hayley. And yes, you have every right to be. Your first marriage was plain awful - but Stones don't quit."

Hayley rolled her eyes. "No really, Alice. Tell me what you really think. Don't hold back."

Alice drew herself up, fisted hands on hips. "I'll tell you this, Dr. Hayley Stone, you ain't too old to scold for gettin' sassy with me."

"I'm sorry, Alice, but it's just not in the cards for me. I've accepted that. Why can't everyone else stop pestering me about it and stop trying to match-make me?"

But deep in her soul, in that place that always holds the truth she often fought to deny, Hayley knew this wise old Gullah woman was right. She wouldn't risk her heart again only to have it trampled. Marriage to a fellow intern, a beau from medical school, had felt so right. They'd had the same goals, the same dreams. Coming home after a late shift to find him in bed with a nurse that looked to be barely out of puberty and then finding out that this hadn't been the first time or the first nurse, had sent Hayley retreating to the beach house.

"... maybe it's in the stars."

"Huh? I'm sorry, Alice, what were you saying?"

"I was sayin' that maybe your future isn't in the cards, as you done said, but it's in the stars. Tonight's the Blue Moon and you know what that means." Alice nodded knowingly while putting furniture back in place. After moving three chairs, the sofa and the coffee table back into place, Alice grumbled, "People come to pay their respect, but can't show enough to keep the furniture in place."

Hayley stretched, standing on her tiptoes while pushing her arms overhead to the ceiling. Suddenly the day's activities caught up with her and she felt weary. "Alice, you know that's just a myth." She began to recite the lore she'd heard since childhood, "*The night of the Blue Moon brings the Star Traveler, the one who grants wishes of true love to those who truly believe and deserve.* Or some such drivel. All it really means is that we are having two full moons in one month."

"Just 'cause you cain't put it in one of those tubes doesn't mean it cain't happen. You help families have babies that never thought they would be so blessed."

"That's different. I use methods that have been researched, studied for years. Nothing miraculous about fertility treatments." She continued to help Alice clean.

"I wonder what all those happy parents would have to say about that?"

Hayley shrugged, too bone-weary to argue the point.

An arm went around her waist and hugged. "Stop now, baby girl, you know I'm perfectly capable of finishing cleaning and setting the house to rights. Why don't you go and change your clothes and walk the beach. You know how much you love it and how it relaxes you." She turned to look at Onyx, snoring on the sofa. "And it would get that animal off the couch."

As usual, Alice was right. Hayley did love the beach. Looking out the window at the dusky sun casting a soft pink glow on the Atlantic, she couldn't believe how quickly the day had flown by. A walk on the beach at sunset would be the perfect way to stretch her tired muscles and chase her sadness away, if only for a short time. Spoken simply, yet direct, Alice's words cut straight to Hayley's heart. She needed to think on them while she re-evaluated her life.

Donovan de Lyon sighed – a heavy, tired sigh. He knew it was his duty in life to take over the family business when the time came. He'd been preparing for it for as long as he could remember. He had little choice, being a Star Traveler, from the de Lyon line of Star Travelers, the most respected and most revered in the galaxy. He would be Master Star Traveler, overseer of all, when his father stepped down. And, Donovan felt the time might be nearing. His father grew weary and wanted to spend his days with his mother. Donovan dreaded that day, but how could he tell his parents that he wanted no part of their family heritage? One that dated back thousands of years? It would break their hearts, but Donovan's heart just wasn't in it.

For now, though, while he puzzled over his future, he'd carry on his family's work - traveling from planet to planet, fulfilling wishes of happiness and true love and finding soul mates for those that deserved and believed in such things. While his parents had the best marriage he'd ever seen, and traveling the galaxy he'd seen plenty, he doubted true love was his destiny. Giving it to others was one thing; finding it himself proved to be an entirely different matter. The women of his world were only interested in him because he was a Star Traveler, a de Lyon Star Traveler, at that.

"Donovan?"

He turned to see his mother standing in the entrance of the family observatory, holding a tray with food and drink. She looked lovely in her flowing robes of rose and purple silk, embroidered with sparkling crystals.

"Good evening, mother. I'm going over the travel plans for this evening. Earth is having a Blue Moon and that always promises to be a busy night."

Rhea entered the room and set the tray on the worktable, careful not to upset the planetary charts. Peering through the high-powered telescope, she looked at Earth.

"It's a beautiful world. It is said our paths crossed long ago and that is why we are as human as they are and vice versa."

"Yes," Donovan agreed while finishing his flight plans. "They are the only species in the galaxy that match our genetic coding."

"I hear they have some very lovely women on Earth," Rhea ventured.

"Mother! Please..." He raised his head from his work and looked at her. "I know you mean well, but I just want everyone to leave me alone when it comes to my love life – or lack of it."

Seeing the crestfallen look on her face, Donovan stood and gave her a quick hug. "I'm sorry, Mother, I don't mean to sound cross, but everyone seems to feel it's open season on my love life. Everyone has someone that they want me to meet. I'm a grown man. I can find my own mate - if she exists." He was sorry he added that when he saw the distress it caused his mother.

"Your father and I only want you happy, darling."

"I appreciate the concern you and Father have for me. I really do, but I am happy. I have my family, my work..." he let the words trail off, as even he didn't believe them.

"Earth's Blue Moon is about to show itself and I have much to do before I depart." He hugged his mother and kissed her temple. "We'll talk when I return, Mother, I promise. Just, please, don't worry about me."

"It's what a parent does, no matter how grown her children."

Justus de Lyon entered the massive observatory, but had missed his son by moments. His eyes scanned the room until they rested on Rhea, his beloved wife. She stood on the deck of the observatory, looking out the wall-high glass windows. Constellations shone brilliantly. Coming up from behind, he wrapped his arms around her waist and bent to place a kiss on her cheek.

"Tears, my love?" He turned her toward him and stroked her cheeks with his thumbs.

"Oh, Justus, I wish for Donovan a love like ours, is that so much to ask?" Her eyes sought his and reflected concern for their inflexible son.

Justus sighed and hugged his wife to his chest. They turned to look out the window just as Donovan's starship ejected from the holding bay beneath them.

After a quick shower, Hayley donned denim shorts and a red t-shirt. She decided not to blow-dry her hair, but to let it dry naturally in the evening breezes from the ocean. It would be a mass of waist-length curls by the time it had finished drying, but she didn't care, she always felt free letting her hair dry naturally. Her mama had smiled and called her *The Bohemian.*

"Come on, Onyx. Let's go see if we can find that silly old blue moon."

Opening the door off the sunroom, Hayley took a deep breath and held it for a few beats before slowly exhaling. There was nothing quite like the scent of the June night air off the Atlantic; salty and fresh and warm. She jumped the three steps to the ground, having decided to forgo her sandals and feel the sand on her bare feet.

"Come on girl, let's run!" She took off at a moderate trot, Onyx on her heels. Running along the shoreline, her feet sank into damp sand, squishing between her toes. The heavenly feeling, along with waves around her ankles, helped raise her spirits.

She stopped short and stared at the night sky - at the most beautiful full moon she'd ever witnessed. Full and clear, she reached a hesitant hand skyward, as if to touch it. She knew ice crystals in the atmosphere caused the halo around the moon, still, there was something magical about it. Almost...ethereal.

Hayley moved away from the water, farther onto the beach. Sitting, she drew her knees to her chest and locked her arms around them. It was impossible to take her eyes off the glorious moon. Her furry companion sat beside her and both stared at the orb in companionable silence.

After a few moments, Hayley leaned close to Onyx and whispered into her ear. "What do you say, Onyx? Should we give it a shot?" At this point in her life, nothing could hurt, not even wishing on a moon.

Closing her eyes tightly, she intoned, "Star bright, star light...oops, wrong one!"

Onyx gave her a woeful look.

"Okay, okay." Hayley giggled. "I'll take it seriously." She kept her eyes open this time and stared at the moon. "Look, I'm not very good at this. I'm a scientist, you know? But, if there is anything, anything at all to this Blue Moon legend, I wouldn't mind a little love sent my way." She stopped, looked at Onyx, then back to the Blue Moon. "Okay. A lot of love."

A feeling washed over her that she couldn't explain. It was as if something inside her, something locked away for so long that she didn't know it existed, burst forth from its cavern. Now that she'd unleashed her feelings, she couldn't stop wishing.

"I'll make someone a great wife. I'm loyal and honest...and I'll love with everything I have inside me. All right, so I'm a lousy cook, but I'll make up for it in other areas." Pausing, she rested her head on Onyx's neck. "I can't believe I'm doing this, Onyx. Wishing on a moon based on some folklore. Yet, it feels, I don't know, right?"

Taking a deep breath, she continued as if the moon could really pass her message on to the Star Traveler. "I just don't want to be hurt anymore, you know? There has to be a good man out there - somewhere. Someone who'll accept what I have to give and want to give me the same love in return. It's not so much to ask, is it?"

Tears fell now. Tears for her mama, tears for her rotten marriage and tears for her loneliness. Hayley finally let the truth reveal itself to her. She wanted to love and be loved.

Onyx began dancing in circles, coming up on her hind legs every so often and letting out excited yelps.

"What is it, girl? Is something there?"

Hayley looked around the beach. Most of the tourists had gone in for the evening, but a few joggers still lined the shore. Mostly, though, the area was quiet. Even so, Onyx kept up her excited dance. Something caught Hayley's eye and she looked back in the direction of the moon. A bright streak of light flashed across the moon. A shooting star? Hayley stood and peered closer. Odd, but the light seemed to be getting brighter and gave off shimmers of heat. Frozen to the spot, her breath clogged in her throat. There was no way this was a shooting star because if it was, it was coming right toward her.

She opened her mouth to scream, but no sound emerged, not even a peep. Blackness rushed up and shrouded her. The last thing she remembered was staring into the greyest eyes she had ever seen, just as strong arms lifted her before she hit the ground.

Donovan checked the ship's systems three times, as per protocol. The ship had just come back from annual maintenance and everything green-lighted during the pre-flight check. So, what went wrong? As he passed Earth's Blue Moon, he felt a sharp pull to the left. The ship veered off course and no amount of trying to set her back on path worked.

"Correct the problem and put me back on course," he ordered Rachel, the ship's main computer.

To which she replied, "Trust me, Donovan."

Before he could argue, his seat's ejection panel engaged and he catapulted out of the ship on a crash course with the ground below. He vowed to get even with Rachel by trading her in for a new model once he returned home, after he found out what the hell she could've been thinking. His safety harness opened and he held on for the ride, all the while cursing Rachel under his breath.

Hard ground greeted his feet upon landing and he recognized the texture as sand. A small sound, almost inaudible, drew his attention to a woman not two feet away. Her huge violet eyes transfixed on him while her full mouth held an 'O' of surprise. Awash in moonlight, this creature was without a doubt the loveliest he'd ever seen, even with shock etched across her features. Long sable hair fell to a trim waist. Her body swayed and her eyelids fluttered. Donovan hurriedly released his safety harness and reached out just in time to catch the beauty into his arms before she hit the ground.

Searing pain shot through his shoulder. Donovan looked down and saw blood seeping through his shirt. The buckle on his harness must've cut him. He didn't want to drop the woman, so he sank to the sand while still holding her. Sitting, he cradled her to his chest. A black dog came over and sniffed him.

"Is this your mistress?"

The animal whimpered and nuzzled the woman's forehead.

"She'll be fine." He winced at the throbbing in his shoulder. "Though I'm not so sure about myself."

"Wh...what happened?" A soft voice asked.

"You fainted. I caught you." For the moment, Donovan felt it best to leave out the part about why she fainted, that he'd almost crashed into her because he'd traveled from another planet.

She looked into his face and their eyes held. Sparks of electrical currents ran the length of his arms and dove into his heart. By the stars, she was lovely.

"You're injured." The woman sat up slowly from his lap and peered at his bloody sleeve. Donovan's arms felt oddly empty when she no longer occupied them.

"I'm a physician. Let me have a look at that wound." Hayley leaned in to get a better look.

"I don't live too far from here," she added. "The light from the moon isn't enough for me to see your injury. We can go to my home so I can treat this for you."

Rising, she reached out to help the stranger to his feet. He placed his hand in hers. His rather large hand. Great strength emanated from him when he folded his hand into hers. She helped him stand.

"My, but you are a tall one, aren't you?" *He must be at least 6'4". Did I really just invite a total stranger into my home?*

Moonlight silhouetted him, making him look like a god and she thought she just might faint again, only this time from his beauty. Black hair cut close to his head framed impossibly high cheekbones. Grey eyes smoldered and Hayley jumped as she realized he watched her just as intently.

"Sorry, I didn't mean to stare." She did, actually, because he was so beautiful, but she wasn't about to admit that. "Come on. I live right up the beach." Realizing she still held his hand, she let it go, though it was the last thing she wanted to do.

As she led the way, Hayley saw him cradle his injured arm with his other hand. The smart thing would be to get her cell phone, call 911 and let them take him to the ER. While she didn't think his injury needed emergency care, he was a complete stranger. But for some reason she felt comfortable with him. Something about him told her he wouldn't hurt her.

"How did you hurt your arm?"

"My...um...seatbelt wasn't working properly."

"Here we are."

Hayley entered through the sunroom, the stranger followed, and she led him to the kitchen. She motioned for him to sit on one of the chairs at the kitchen table.

"I'll be right back. I need to get my medical bag. I'm Hayley, by the way. Hayley Stone."

"Donovan de Lyon."

As soon as Hayley had left the room, Donovan pulled out his communication device to contact home. He needed a ship sent to pick him up and he needed one of his brothers to finish his duties for the evening. Wishes still needed to be granted. Nothing but static emanated from the little machine. He continued to try different sequences of numbers, but nothing changed. The blasted thing wasn't working. Odd, it had never failed him before.

Footsteps sounded on the hardwood floor and Donovan shoved the device back into a pocket.

Hayley set her bag on the kitchen table. "Can you take off that t-shirt or do you need me to cut it off?" She proceeded to take out cotton balls, alcohol and gauze.

He pulled his good arm through the sleeve, then gingerly removed his shirt from the injured arm. Hayley didn't think she'd ever seen shoulders so broad and she wondered what it would feel like to rest her head against one of them. The thought startled her.

"Tell me about yourself, Hayley Stone."

"What? Oh..." Hayley began the task of cleaning and dressing his wound. "Not much to tell, really." Yet, once she began to talk, the words flowed. She told Donovan about her wonderful childhood and disastrous marriage, about fulfilling her dreams of becoming a doctor and helping others with the gift of life.

Donovan listened, never once taking his eyes off her. Kindness and understanding shone in his eyes. Oddly, she'd never felt so comfortable opening up to anyone in her entire life.

He watched her. "And what do you want, Hayley Stone? A child for you? A love for you?"

"Enough about me," she said, embarrassed she'd admitted so much. She finished dressing his shoulder wound and gave it a light pat. "There. All done. You'll be fine. It's just a flesh wound. Now, it's your turn to talk." She stepped to the stove to make hot tea. Grabbing two mugs, she set the tea on the table. Though a warm summer night, chamomile was perfect any evening of the year.

Donovan had a big decision to make. Did he tell her the truth now about his identity, that he was the Star Traveler, or did he continue to sit and talk with this enchanting woman who had just opened her entire world to him. Why couldn't she be of his world? He'd finally met a woman he wanted to love and honor forever. One he'd cherish and devote his life to. But her life belonged to her patients on Earth and he had a duty to rule in his world once his father retired.

Before he could change his mind, he blurted, "I am the Star Traveler." He hadn't meant to be so blunt, but there it was. The look of incomprehension and disbelief on Hayley's face would've been comical if it hadn't torn at his heart.

Replacing the cup in its saucer, Hayley stared at him for what seemed beyond an eternity. This beautiful man with the haunting grey eyes, who listened to her pour out her heart, was telling her he was the stuff of myth. Her heart sank. She quietly devised a plan to get to the phone and have the police take the crazy man in her house to the psychiatric ward.

"You don't believe me, Hayley, I see it in your eyes."

She tried to remember her psychiatric rotation, but her mind felt numb. Did she go along with him until she could slip away and get to the telephone?

"What's that like, being the St...Star Traveler?" she stammered. "It must be very interesting work."

"Don't do that, Hayley. Don't talk to me like I'm crazy. Star Travelers do exist and we have for centuries. We come to earth during the Blue Moon to grant happiness and love to those who truly believe. I wasn't supposed to be here until much later this evening, but my ship's computer, Rachel— "

"Your computer has a name?"

"...Rachel," he continued as if she hadn't interrupted, "changed course and literally threw me out of the ship. So, here I am. The gash you just tended to on my shoulder is from my safety harness, similar to what you would call a parachute."

Hayley rose and headed for the door. "I want to see this safety harness. I'll go find it."

She bolted out the door before Donovan could stop her. Running to the spot where they'd collided on the beach, Hayley stopped and looked around.

"I could've told you it wouldn't be here," he said, catching up to her. "Once worn, it gets absorbed into the atmosphere."

He placed his hands on her slender shoulders and turned her to face him. "Look at my wound, Hayley." Slowly, he took off the bandages she'd so gently placed on his shoulder a short time ago. Nothing. Not even a small scrape marred his beautiful flesh.

"I don't understand. The wound wasn't bad, but it couldn't have healed this quickly." She touched the spot where the skin had been torn and bloody not an hour before.

"My people are human, like you, but after many years of traveling to different worlds, our immune systems have evolved to heal quickly."

"You don't get sick or die?" The thought of him dying tore into her heart.

"Of course we do. We aren't immortal. We just have the ability to heal some minor injuries quickly."

He pulled out his useless communicator and held it out to her. Hayley turned it over and over in her hands, examining it. She'd never seen anything like it before, except maybe in science fiction movies.

"Why don't more people believe you exist?"

He laughed and the throaty sound washed over her in delicious waves.

"Could you imagine what our lives would be like if everyone believed we existed? We aren't a dating service. Besides, life is often the stuff of myth and legend. Makes things exciting."

"Okay, Mr. Donovan de Lyon, Star Traveler, time to tell me about your life. I certainly told you all about me."

Before she could protest, he lifted her easily into his arms and sat cross-legged on the sand. He cradled her in his arms. As she'd done with him, Donovan told her the story of his life.

"Ironic, don't you think? I am the Star Traveler, from a long line of Star Travelers, yet love has eluded me all my life."

The sad look in his eyes as he stared at the ocean made Hayley ache for him. She took his face in her hands and put her mouth on his. His lips tasted sweet from the tea and felt full and soft underneath hers. His arms tightened around her and brought her closer as he deepened the kiss. The promise in this couldn't be denied.

"I could love you, Hayley. Forever and completely. The way you've deserved." He pressed her head to his shoulder and it fit so perfectly, she knew she belonged.

"I never thought this would happen to me, Donovan. That a true love could be mine. Yet, here you are." His chest heaved and Hayley drew away to look into his eyes.

"What's wrong?"

"I said *could,* Hayley. I am the eldest and when my father retires, I am destined to take over as head of the family. I must return to my world. It's my duty." The anguish in those last words hung in the air like a wet blanket.

For hours, Hayley clung to Donovan. They sat on the beach in silence. No words were needed, just arms locking their bodies together.

Finally she spoke. "Is there no other way?" She doubted the feasibility of intergalactic long-distance dating. "I could..." she stopped and cleared her voice. "I could come with you, to your world."

"You could no more leave your world than I mine, my love. You have your patients and family."

The hand-held communication device crackled and sputtered. Donovan pulled it from his pants' pocket to see his parents' faces swim to life on the small viewing screen.

"Hello, my son."

"Father. Tonight's wish-granting didn't go exactly as planned. Rachel—"

"Did exactly as she was told," his father interjected.

Donovan stared at his parents' smiling faces. "I don't understand."

His mother continued, "You tried so hard to hide your sadness over your desire to find your heart's mate, Donovan. Yet, your father and I knew. We made up our minds that at earth's next Blue Moon, it would be your time for love."

"Why didn't you just tell me?"

His Mother chuckled. "Would you have gone along with our plan?"

"I suppose not." His heart swelled with love for these wonderful people. For them to do this for him. "What will happen when Father retires?"

"One of your brothers will take over," his father answered, placing a hand on his wife's shoulder. "You are our son and your happiness means everything to us. If we made one of our own children choose work over love, then we wouldn't be doing our jobs very well, now would we?"

They all laughed and smiled at one another across the galaxies.

"I love you all so very, very much." Donovan said to their images. With his arm across Hayley's shoulders, he drew her into his parents' view. "This is Hayley."

"Hello, dear." His mother's warm smile radiated off the screen. "We have done right by our son to send him to you. We know you will give each other years of happiness."

His father added with a sly grin, "And give us lots of grandchildren."

Hayley could barely speak, but there would be plenty of time to say all she wanted to these wonderful people. "Thank you. Both of you, so very, very much." These were the only words that would come, but for now, they were enough.

Donovan and his parents signed off with promises of a visit to introduce Hayley to his family.

The long day settled in Hayley's bones, yet she felt oddly light. A peace and contentment she'd never known before enveloped her.

"Come, love, let's go home. We have so many plans to make, but for tonight I want to hold you in my arms and watch you while you sleep." Donovan lifted her into his arms and carried her home. Onyx greeted them at the door, tail wagging.

"Come, hound, show the way to my lady's bedroom."

"Onyx." Hayley laughed for the first time in a long time and it felt wonderful. She placed a kiss to his neck. "Her name is Onyx."

They made it to the bedroom kissing and whispering words of love. Donovan kicked open the door and carried Hayley to the bed. He placed her in the center and followed her down, never letting go of her.

"Happy?" Donovan asked right before he trailed kisses down her neck.

She closed her eyes and snuggled close to him. "My mama's funeral was earlier today, but I know she's looking down from Heaven right now with a smile on her face. In fact..." Hayley stopped and brushed her hand over his cheek. "If I know my mama, she probably had a hand in this with Alice."

"Alice?"

"You'll meet Alice soon enough. She will absolutely adore you."

Donovan drew her close and held her.

"But to answer your question," she murmured against his chest, "yes, I am very happy. In fact, I want to take all night to show you."

The man in her arms completed her world. Though she'd only just met him, she had no doubt about that. And, she didn't need a medical textbook to confirm her happiness. Mama and Alice had been right. She just needed to find the right man. She wouldn't put it past her mother to wish on that same Blue Moon from her new home in Heaven.

Pulling Donovan's face to hers, she kissed him back with all the fervor and passion she'd held inside for so long, just waiting for her Star Traveler to awaken within her.

She'd taken a chance and wished on a Blue Moon. Alice would never let her hear the end of it!

Visit Victoria's website at
http://www.victoriahouseman.com

Sentimental Journey

by Judith Laik

Tacoma, Washington, March 1942

It was their last night together. Eve Larson stood in front of the romantic nightclub, the Spanish Castle, with its white crenellated turrets. She linked her arm through Howard Murphy's, their elbows cushioned by her wool coat and his uniform sleeve. With conscious effort she held lightly to her fiancé, not clinging, not begging him to stay with her.

She took a deep breath and renewed her vow to tuck her terror deep inside until after he had shipped out in the morning. Thoughts of what might happen to him in the midst of war wouldn't intrude into her mind. She'd show Howard the picture of gaiety and confidence so he could leave with no worries for her.

Howard purchased their admissions and they passed inside, engulfed in the happy, danceable music from the big band in the main room. Eve removed her coat and handed it to the coat check girl. She picked her way through the crowd at the Spanish Castle, leading her fiancé to the dance floor.

He took her hand and swung her into the Lindy. Frankie Roth's band played *Pennsylvania 6-5000*, an upbeat, loud Glenn Miller tune. Eve hoped the band played lighthearted songs all night. The cheery expression she plastered on her face would slip if they played a poignant ballad. Howard spun her around, flaring out the skirt of her teal rayon dress. She smiled each time he turned her to face him.

The band segued into *Tuxedo Junction*. Every twirl in Howie's arms carried the heavenly scent from the gardenia corsage he'd given her. When he pulled her close, she could smell his aftershave, cool and outdoorsy.

She intended to make the most of this magical evening, building special memories for them both to keep.

The song ended, and as Howard seated her, he asked, "Do you want something to drink?"

"I am a little thirsty," Eve declared.

He signaled to the waitress. "What do you want?" he asked Eve when the waitress arrived.

"Just a Coke." She refused to blur her memories of tonight with alcohol. Howard ordered a beer. They sipped their beverages. Eve couldn't take her eyes off Howie. His dark brown hair had grown since they'd buzz cut it for basic training, long enough for a curl to flip onto his forehead. Others might think his craggy features unhandsome. Eve didn't care about anyone's opinion. He was perfect to her.

Icicles stabbed her heart, making her shiver. She turned her head toward the dance floor so Howie wouldn't see the fear in her eyes.

Her foot tapped to the music. Frankie Roth's band played *Java Jive*. The air in the Spanish Castle was warm, close. The exotic exterior, in Moorish-castle style, wasn't repeated in the plainer interior. There were only the recessed dance floor, a shell for the band, and tables covered with white tablecloths arranged around the remainder of the indoor space.

The noise made conversation difficult. Eve sipped her Coke through the straw. Howard's nearness made her tingle. She reached over and put a hand on his arm, and he smiled at her.

The girl singer performed *Boogie Woogie Bugle Boy*, but if Eve hadn't already known the words, she'd never have distinguished them above the din. The crowd was boisterous—many of the men, and even a few of the women, in uniform.

With bases for three branches of the United States military close to Tacoma, a large percentage of the country's soldiers, sailors, and airmen inhabited the area. And a goodly number of them seemed as determined as she and Howie to banish thoughts of tomorrow. *How many of these young men will die in the next year?* A mist of tears blurred her vision.

"Let's dance," she said in an overly bright voice, pushing down her melancholy thoughts. She jumped up and tugged on Howie's hand. The band was playing Artie Shaw's *Frenesi*, the trumpet's notes soaring over the rest of the band.

"We'll have to leave soon." Howie stood, but didn't move toward the dance floor. "Your parents..."

"It's all right," Eve interrupted. "They know we won't see each other again," her throat closed painfully, and she forced the words out, "for a while. They told me not to worry about getting home on time."

She started toward the dance floor. Now she needed the strength and comfort of his arms around her and wished for some slow numbers. But the band still played boogie woogie. Maybe away from the crowd she could persuade him to hold her.

"Can we step outside for a little bit? I need some fresh air."

He nodded, led the way off the floor. "Do you want to leave?" he asked, stopping outside the coat check room.

"No, I want to stay until closing. I just need air." The attendant at the door stamped their hands and they walked outside.

It was a chilly evening, still winter this early in March. A light fog moistened the air. Eve said, "I shouldn't have left my bolero jacket at the table." She rubbed her arms, and Howie pulled her close, sheltering her within his warmth. This was what she really needed, more than air. She buried her face against his shoulder, hearing the steady dub-dub of his heart, reveling in the feel of the steely muscles under his jacket.

He was so strong, surely nothing could harm him. *Nothing can.* After a few minutes, she needed to dance some more, to keep the shadows at bay.

The band was taking a break, so Eve excused herself to go to the ladies' room. After using the facilities, she checked her appearance in the mirror, tucked some loose blonde strands into her up-do and applied a fresh coat of bright red lipstick.

When she returned to their table, Frankie, the bandleader, came back onto the bandstand. The musicians briefly tuned up and launched into a slower number. Eve grinned at Howie and said, "Ready to dance, soldier?"

In his arms again, she was determined to stop time. She concentrated on each impression that came to her senses: the warm air in the room brushing her face with the movements of their bodies and the swirling currents stirred by the other dancers around them; their scents as they passed by—perfume, shaving soap, sweat—exotic and musky; snippets of voices and laughter shifting in and out of her awareness in the general chaos of sound.

Eve's fingers on Howie's shoulder registered the rough texture of his uniform coat, while her right hand tingled at the warmth and vitality of his fingers wrapped in hers. As they went through the steps of the dance, their legs meshed, one of her legs between both of his, the contact muted by their clothing, yet stirring an erotic awareness in Eve.

Each place their bodies touched brought a pulsation that raced deep into her center. The rhythm of the music augmented the effect, its sensuous vibration shooting through her.

She sorted and saved each separate impression—even the onset of pain in her feet from hours of dancing in unfamiliar platform shoes.

The male singer, his voice like warm whiskey, crooned the words to *All the Things You Are*, and Eve hummed under her breath, "that moment divine, when all the things you are, are mine."

All the time, a black cloud gathered right at the center of her abdomen, coalescing and growing, threatening to dissolve her. *Go away*, she told it fiercely. *This night is to create good memories for Howie to carry into battle—no tears, no regrets.*

At last Frankie Roth announced closing time for the Spanish Castle. One final dance, the crowd thinning, and the last remaining patrons gathered their coats and hurried out to cars.

"Don't take me home yet," Eve pleaded once they were in Howie's car heading down Highway 99.

He cast a startled glance at her before returning his attention to the road. “But it’s so late, already past your curfew.”

“It’s only one night. I told you, Mom and Dad understand. Let’s go to our special place.”

“Okay, honey,” Howie said, a worried frown creasing his face. Eve reached for his hand and clasped it tightly, only releasing her hold when he needed to shift gears.

They reached the high bluff overlooking the Tacoma Narrows. The land was brush-covered, undeveloped, yet Howie’s 1939 Buick handled the ruts and potholes of the dirt track as gracefully as any car could. On this cloudy night, fog had settled deep in the gorge, obscuring its contours. Eve couldn’t see across the mile-wide channel of Puget Sound to the peninsula beyond.

The car radio played softly. For a few moments, they sat without speaking. What Howie was thinking, she could not guess. His expression was serious, almost forbidding.

They’d never had a problem finding words, but the feelings roiling inside Eve couldn’t be voiced, and she scrambled to think of a topic. “Remember our first date?” she asked.

His frown erased, and he turned to her with a chuckle. “I sure do. It has to be one of the more unforgettable first dates any two people have had.”

By what seemed like mutual agreement they both looked out at the foggy Narrows, once spanned by the unstable bridge known as Galloping Gertie. Soon after they had met in the fall of 1940, Howie brought her here to watch the third longest suspension span in the world give a crazy performance above the deep, swift channel, the ever-present wind causing the bridge to buck and twist like a wild bronco. A few days later, it had collapsed and plunged into Puget Sound.

Emboldened by Howie’s softer mood, Eve threw herself into his arms and they kissed hungrily. He locked her in his embrace as if he would never let go. She clung, twining her arms around his neck and melding her body against him. They shared desperate kisses that must last until he returned.

It wasn't enough—not nearly enough. It couldn't hold back the terror that coiled like a monster inside Eve. "Make love to me, Howie," she pleaded. Her words broke the spell.

Howie drew back, loosened his hold. "We can't do that."

"Why not? I love you. I want to be yours." After he enlisted in the army, Eve had tried to persuade him that they should marry right away, but he had refused to consider it.

"It wouldn't be right. Don't you think I want you, too? It almost kills me to wait. But when we make love the first time, I want everything to be perfect. The beautiful wedding you always wanted and the honeymoon. We'll go anywhere in the world you want to go. We'll have champagne and candlelight, and you'll wear a gorgeous negligee."

"None of that is important, Howie." The tears she had kept at bay came to the surface, and she blinked them back. "Not as important as us, loving each other."

"It has to be this way, sweetheart. Thinking about you, loving you, having you at last, are the things that will bring me back home."

What if you don't come back? Then I'll have nothing. Nothing to remember. Nothing to hold on to. Only she couldn't undermine his conviction. He was the one facing danger, possible death. She drew away. "I understand." She turned and looked at the Narrows again.

He ran his hand up her arm. "I'm sorry, Eve. I want to do what's best."

"I know." She tried not to cry, but the horrid dark thing that had been looming inside her all evening broke free. She stepped out of the car, walked toward the cliff. Howie went after her. "Eve?" His voice sounded tentative, worried.

Before she had a chance to think, she blurted, "Howie, don't come back dead."

She clapped her hand over her mouth, horrified. "No, that isn't what I mean at all. Just come back here, no matter what. Promise me you'll come back."

"I promise, I'll come back. When I do, we'll sit in the car right here and kiss, like I never left." His voice was thick with tears he manfully tried not to shed.

He took her hand, led her back to the Buick. On the way to her parents' house, the radio played *I'll Never Smile Again*. Once there, he took her in his arms for one last kiss.

When he drew back, Eve jumped out of the car before she broke down completely. She ran to the house. When she reached the porch, she turned to see him once more, but his car turned the corner and disappeared.

June, 1945

"Okay, children, line up at the door." With summer stretching ahead of Eve's kindergartners, utter chaos reigned in the schoolroom. She couldn't calm them.

She tried not to feel hurt that they showed no regret at leaving her. These were just her temporary children. She'd never have any of her own since Howard's plane went down during a bombing raid a few short months after he was shipped to England.

Even the children who returned to Central School in the fall would go to other classrooms. She would merely see them in the halls occasionally. And with so many military families in the area, many of them would have moved away by then. Still, she'd chosen this life, and it had its rewards.

"Marvin, stop pushing. Get in line." She smiled at the towheaded youngster with the impish grin.

The bell rang, releasing the entire school for summer vacation. "Goodbye, children," she called as a tidal wave surged out into the halls, masses of small bodies from every classroom making for the doors and freedom.

Eve caught the eye of Norma, who taught the first grade class next to her. "Want to meet for a cup of coffee?"

"Sure thing. I've got nothing to do for the next three months."

"Except date, go to the beach and work on your tan, and have a good time," Eve teased.

Norma's smile stilled. "It's what you need to do, too, Eve."

"Oh, I have my summer all planned."

Norma snorted. "What sort of plans do you have? Nothing involving a guy, I'm sure."

"Don't start," Eve warned.

"If you say so. I just want you to be happy. You can't mourn Howard the rest of your life."

"I'm not mourning," Eve lied. Mention of him still stabbed at her heart with a pain almost physical. "I don't want anybody else. Howard was the only man for me."

They left the school, Eve turning to look at the building one more time. Castles seemed to feature in her life, although Central's eight-story tower called to mind English Gothic rather than Spanish Moorish architecture.

At the little café, Norma brought up the subject again. "Eve, you shouldn't cut yourself off from life. You'd make a wonderful mother. You need to get out on some dates. You might even find somebody to love again."

Eve shook her head. She smiled, determined not to let Norma see how those words reopened the old wound. She and Howard had planned on four children. "I've dedicated my life to teaching. It satisfies my motherly instincts." She flipped open the menu. "Are you going to have pie with your coffee? A nice piece of apple with ice cream sounds good to me."

Norma dropped the subject, and the remainder of their coffee date passed pleasantly.

She wasn't the only one who'd hounded Eve to find someone new. Other friends didn't understand either. She couldn't give her heart to anyone else. Even her parents, though they never urged her to go out with another man, looked at her sadly and with puzzlement. "We want you to be happy," they said.

"I am happy. I have my career, helping children prepare for the years ahead. I have my gardening and canning. I have a wonderful family and friends. What more could I want?" If the words were hollow, she forced enough conviction into them to silence her doubters.

"Are you sure you don't want to come with us?" Dad asked, a week later. He and her mother prepared to visit Aunt Doris in Portland.

"No, thanks, Dad. I'll stay and look after things here. It's been so dry, the garden needs watering. Say hello for me—and to Cousin Mary, too." Mary had a new baby. Her husband was a sailor, stationed somewhere in the Pacific. She and Mary had grown up together, but it hurt too much to see her enjoying what Eve couldn't have.

Eve waved Mom and Dad off and then looked down at Mom's buff Cocker Spaniel, sitting at her feet with a dejected air. Aunt Doris was afraid of dogs, so Sandy couldn't accompany them. "And besides, you'd have to stay in a kennel if I went along."

Sandy looked up with a disdainful expression then returned his gaze to the corner where the car carrying his mistress had passed out of sight. He sighed heavily and allowed Eve to persuade him inside the house.

She met Norma for lunch at their favorite café. Over club sandwiches and iced tea, they caught up on the latest news. "I met him at the USO, Eve. I think he may be The One."

Eve smiled noncommittally. Norma had been on a search for a husband as long as she had known her, and each time Norma met someone new, she was filled with confidence that at last she had discovered the right man. Inevitably, however, within a few weeks she'd decide he had some major flaw that made him an impossible choice. He was too cheap, or didn't pick up after himself, or his mother was too possessive. And since most of the men who came to the USO were merely looking for temporary comfort before shipping out, Eve figured the odds weren't too favorable Norma would find true love there.

"It's a Blue Moon tonight," Norma confided.

"What?"

"You know, second full moon in a month. If you make a wish on a Blue Moon, it's bound to come true. I'm wishing for Jim to be the guy for me."

"I hope it works out," Eve said, picking up the check.

Pulling weeds from her vegetable garden a little later, Eve wiped sweat from her forehead and wondered what was wrong with her. She cast a glance at the unrelenting sun, and then bent to her job again.

The garden, an addition to the flowers Mom had always grown, was Eve's contribution to the family and to the war effort. With food severely rationed, every bit she contributed to their diet helped. She took pride in the colorful, delicious vegetables they ate fresh from the garden, and the jars of produce that had gotten them through the past two winters and would do so again this year.

Ordinarily, putting her hands into the soil gave her satisfaction. Today restlessness infected her, blighted her mood. She persisted until every last, straggly weed lay in a wilting pile in front of her. Yet it didn't bring her any triumph, only grim completion.

In the kitchen, she poured herself a glass of lemonade from the pitcher in the icebox. She sipped, looking out the window. The lemonade tasted flat, seeming to lack the tartness of the lemons and the sweetness of the sugar. The view out the window was equally flat. The sun's harsh brightness washed out the flowers and vegetables, the grass, the white-painted garage.

Howard hadn't only taken her heart; he took the colors, the tastes, the smells from the world. When did she last feel joy? But, her guilty mind protested, she wasn't supposed to feel joy. She'd lost the man she loved.

No joy? For the rest of her life? She was only twenty-six. She could easily live another fifty years. Was she really supposed to live all those years in a gray, unfeeling world?

She couldn't bear that thought. No, not having a husband or children didn't mean she couldn't find pleasures in small things. She loved her work. She vowed to make her life so full she didn't miss what it didn't contain.

It was time to push all her uncomfortable emotions—her grief, anger, loneliness—back into the far recesses of her mind. She couldn't lead the life Norma and her parents wanted for her, but she *would* find joy.

That night, she let Sandy out into the yard. The rising full moon winked at her. The Blue Moon. The dog came back in, and Eve checked that the doors and windows were locked, preparing to retire.

But she couldn't go to bed. Restless and aching, she paced for awhile, then suddenly dressed and went outside. Hopping into her '37 Chevy coupe, she backed out of the garage and gunned it down the street. She had no destination in mind. All she knew was that some force compelled her to go for a spin.

I Don't Want to Walk Without You played on her car radio, and she turned the volume higher, the sweet sound of Harry James' trumpet rending her heart. It was not so easy to put aside her grief. Perhaps with more time . . .

The streets of Tacoma were quiet, the radio her only companion. She wound past huge turn-of-the-century mansions in north Tacoma, steered by the fantastic turrets of Stadium High School, and then onto the downtown streets to the accompaniment of Bing Crosby crooning *I'll Be Seeing You*. The moon had risen higher. She caught glimpses of the blue-white globe through her windshield when she turned the car eastward.

Gasoline was rationed, and she shouldn't waste it aimlessly driving. Still, she felt jumpy. A reckless energy fizzed inside her like a giant Alka Seltzer tablet dropped in water.

With unconscious knowingness, Eve turned the car around and headed for Sixth Avenue. The street ran west, toward the Sound. She drove true and fast, in a fever of impatience.

She passed darkened businesses, an area of Craftsman-style homes, neatly maintained, and then finally reached the open land at the western edge of the city. Eve veered off Sixth onto the side streets, and then to unpaved roads, bearing toward Howard's and her favorite spot high above the Narrows. She listened to Benny Goodman's *Darn That Dream*.

She'd never thought to brave this place again. Memories assaulted her—the kisses, tender and passionate, they'd shared; hours of discussion, getting to know each other, exploring their dreams and plans for a future they couldn't know would never happen. Their final night together, and then a few months when they'd touched each other only in letters.

Letters that had stopped on a September night.

Eve navigated the familiar lane, unable to see through the tears that flowed from her eyes. Tears she hadn't cried since the day she received the news of Howard's death.

Her coupe, lower to the ground than Howard's Buick, scraped bottom on the deeper ruts in the lane. She should turn around and go home. No good purpose could be served by torturing herself like this. Still she pushed on as though guided by some unseen force.

She stopped the car in the same spot where Howard always parked, collapsed over the steering wheel, and sobbed. Tears were healing. Perhaps her compulsion to come here had served a purpose—crying and, finally, forgetting. No, never forgetting. She couldn't do that. But peace—she could find peace.

Eve rolled down her window and inhaled the spicy scent of flowering Scotch Broom. The last of the Broom—it was late blossoming this spring. The night was clear, warm, yet with a suggestion of something she couldn't put a name to—something weighty. Her heart beat faster, and her skin tingled. Lionel Hampton's mellow vibraphone pervaded the air with *Flying Home*.

If only you could, Howie. I'd give anything to have you here.

The moon was behind her, but its luminescence lit the area, shone off the water hundreds of feet below, creating a mystical mood. *That Old Black Magic* by Glenn Miller haunted the radio waves now. Eve shivered. She stepped out of the car, leaving the radio on. The night was never silent. Wind blew through the nearby Scotch Broom and other bushes and weeds. They rustled as if whispering to her. Crickets chirped, and though she couldn't hear the sounds of any other creatures, Eve sensed them around her. Even the lapping of waves far below traveled faintly to the heights where she stood.

She turned to face the moon, speaking through her tears, "Please, come back to me, Howie."

The breeze played upon her face like a caress. She trembled violently, afraid and yet eager. Night shadows shifted. Eve was suddenly breathless. There was something unfathomable in the air.

Her heart pounded a staccato drumbeat. She felt lightheaded, insubstantial, a being wrought of moonlight and tears.

"Howie?" she whispered. She mustn't be so foolish as to believe he could come back to her. The thought was madness, spawned by the moon and Norma's words earlier in the day...*bound to come true.* Maybe, if it weren't a wish outside the realm of possibility. She stood beside her car, ready to flee.

Another Harry James song began—*I Had the Craziest Dream.* A sob stuck in Eve's throat. Crazy, yes. She should run home, and then tomorrow check herself into Western State Hospital in Steilacoom.

You aren't crazy. It was like a whisper carried on the wind. The moon gazed back at her, a mysterious smile on its lopsided face. *Dreams do come true, and wishes, too.*

Jo Stafford sang *Long Ago and Far Away* in her pure contralto—singing about dreams that came true.

The moon shone down, bathing her in its cool, mystical light. A light that revealed a dark mass gathering at the far end of the field. The darkness resolved into human form and began to move toward her. Eve stood frozen in place, dizzy and disoriented. Terror and elation bubbled up in equal measure.

And then Howie was walking toward her. He was backlit by the moon—a silhouette—but there was no mistaking him. Was he real? A ghost? Eve couldn't tell.

It didn't matter. Apparition, ghost, or the real thing, she didn't care.

As he drew near, she rushed into his arms. Arms that were real and substantial. He held her tight. It was him, his scent, his voice. "Eve. You're here. I knew if I came, I'd find you."

His lips crushed down on hers, fierce and possessive. He pushed her back against the hood of her car, his lips moving over her face, her jaw. "I was wrong," he whispered. "We should have married before I left. I kept thinking about this, about what we missed. For a long time, I thought I would never get the chance to love you."

He frightened her a bit, but he seemed to sense it, for he drew back and gazed at her. The moon and the darkness leached the color from his eyes, but she could tell the expression in them, serious and a little doubtful. "Eve? I can hardly believe you waited for me all this time."

"Of course, I waited for you." Was that what she had done? Maybe so. Maybe even when she thought there was no hope, a part of her had still waited for his return. "Howie, when your plane went down—"

He put a finger to her lips. "I know, Eve, I know. There's so much to tell you. But not now." He pulled her close as though he could never hold her enough. "We'll be married right away. As soon as we can get the license and the blood tests, and make it through the three-day waiting period."

What happened to you? Where have you been? They would talk about it eventually, but for now it didn't matter. "Oh, Howie!"

"You don't care if we don't have the fancy wedding? The honeymoon we talked about? I don't even have a place for us to live yet."

"No, I don't care. I didn't think you'd come back. I just—I can still hardly believe it." She wrapped her arms about him, pulling him closer for another passionate kiss. Blood pounded through her veins. She was hot and shivering at the same time, and tears poured down her face.

He smoothed her hair, his lips pressing softly against her forehead. "Don't cry, love. I told you I'd come back. I gave my promise. It's the only thing that brought me back. I had to fulfill my promise to you."

"That and the Blue Moon. I made a wish."

He chuckled. "So did I." Then he kissed her again, their lips joined in passion and promise.

A Blue Vacation

by Michelle Scaplen

"I did not have sex with him!" Tori exclaimed as she walked into the office.

"Okay. " Nick followed closely behind. "Do you want to explain why he answered your phone when I called this morning?"

Brenda continued working at her computer and pretended she wasn't listening to her coworkers' latest argument. Not that it mattered what she did; Nick and Tori hardly paid any attention to her anyway. Of course, neither did Ray, Jack, Linda nor anyone else she worked with in the Action Mattress office.

"He...uh..." Tori tried to explain, then let out a heavy sigh. "Oh come on, Nick. When did we ever say we were an exclusive couple? "

Why anyone would want to be with any other man when they were dating the extremely gorgeous Nick Shelton, Brenda couldn't comprehend. She was merely a measly, data entry clerk and he was the company's head salesman, so their jobs never required them to work together. But that didn't stop her from fantasizing about him while she keyed in her entries every day.

"Forget it, forget everything," his voice was low but his tone was harsh.

Brenda looked up from her computer screen as curiosity got the best of her. She'd never seen Nick so angry—but angry was better than hurt. Tori Atkins was not worth getting your heart broken over. She was the office's self-centered, pencil thin, artificially-boobed secretary who treated men like dirt.

They both watched as Nick pulled an envelope from his jacket pocket and tossed it in the trash can next to Brenda's desk. "You can go to the Bahamas without me tomorrow."

"I'm not going by myself," Tori called after Nick as he stormed down the hall to his office. "I guess you've wasted all that money because my ticket is going into the trash, too."

Brenda blinked at the reverberations of Nick's office door slamming. It was unbelievable that they would throw airline tickets in the garbage when she hadn't had a vacation in over four years.

"What?" Tori asked her.

Great the one time Tori notices me is when I get caught staring.

She shook her head. "Umm, nothing I just..."

"Here." Tori dug through her purse, retrieved an envelope and tossed it on Brenda's desk. "You can go to the Bahamas."

"Oh no. I couldn't," Brenda stammered. But her heart, which was pounding like a jackhammer, screamed yes.

"Why not? Nick won't be going now. Why waste two tickets? Plus, the hotel is already paid for. The reservations are under my and Nick's name. Just tell the person at the desk you're me."

"Don't you want to go?" Brenda asked, looking at the ticket on her desk. A vacation, she thought, a real vacation!

"Nah, I'm a city girl. Now if that were a ticket to New York or LA, I'd be there in a heartbeat. I've already been to Bermuda. You see one island you've seen them all."

Somehow Brenda doubted it, but she wasn't about to argue. "Thanks Tori, this is really nice of you."

"Yeah, whatever." With a wave of her bejeweled hand, Tori walked—well, not quite—she *strutted* back to her desk.

This was unbelievable! Brenda felt like she'd just won the grand prize on a game show. What would happen next? Surely the sky must have turned purple, because something really had to be screwy with the universe. Nothing extraordinary ever happened to Brenda Blake.

For the past thirty-two years, she'd stood in the corner and watched life pass her by. The middle child, she'd always received average grades in school, and here she was in a dead end job. Nothing amazing ever happened to her because, truth be told, Brenda never *made* anything amazing happen. Face it—she was boring.

This had to stop! And the only way to accomplish that was to do it herself. “I'm taking my lunch break,” Brenda declared to everyone in the small office. Although it was almost two hours before noon, no one bothered to look at her. Brenda sighed and mumbled, “I might as well be invisible.” However, she wasn't going to let that discourage her. Grabbing her purse, she headed out the door.

As she walked downtown, Brenda tried to think of ways she could change her life. Passing a beauty salon, she realized it would be the perfect place to start. She could have a couple of inches cut off her mousy brown, poker straight hair, and give herself a new look to go with her new perspective on life.

She stepped up to the reception desk, relieved to hear they accepted walk-ins. After she'd been shampooed, she was directed to Candace's chair.

“How would you like your hair cut?” the hairdresser asked.

“I want something different,” Brenda said before she lost her nerve. “Take three inches off the back and add some layers.”

Candace smiled. “Something different is my specialty. Leave everything to me and you'll walk out of here a new woman.”

Those, of course, became the famous last words. Too distraught to return to work, Brenda stood in front of her bedroom mirror, mouth agape as she looked at her new do. Her previously shoulder length hair was now cropped to the back of her neck. And 'some layers' had turned into a head full of many, many short ones.

“I look like I just rolled out of bed,” Brenda said to her reflection. *Her reflection nodded in agreement.*

She called her boss to say she'd suddenly become ill and wouldn't be able to return to work for a couple of days. *Her boss didn't seem to care.* Fine with her, because now she was free to go to the Bahamas and enjoy herself despite her funky new haircut.

Fearing she'd procrastinate if she didn't take action, she dug a suitcase and an overnight bag out of the deepest recesses of her closet. Throwing them on her bed, she returned to the closet and searched for something suitable to pack. *Nothing!* All her clothes were plain and boring. *Is everything I own brown?* All in different shades, of course, but whether beige, tan, or taupe, it was all the same. Blah!

No wonder nobody noticed her at work. She blended perfectly with the drab wallpaper. She grabbed the few colorful short sets she owned and tossed them in the suitcase. Hopefully, the resort where she'd be staying would have some boutiques. She'd buy a new wardrobe on the island and for once in her life not care if she ended up maxing out her credit cards.

Brenda wasted no time after arriving at the resort. She checked in as Tori Atkins without any problem, put her bags in the corner of the room, and made a bee-line for the shops. Every garment in the store was bright and colorful. Funny, it seemed like the color brown didn't even exist on the island.

"Kon I help you, missy?" a beautiful saleswoman asked.

Charmed by the woman's thick Bahamian lilt, Brenda smiled. "Yes, please. In fact, I need a completely new wardrobe." It may have been a mistake, because she saw the same sparkle in the saleswoman's eyes as she'd seen in Candace's before the woman chopped away at her hair.

The salesclerk picked out hip hugging skirts the same shade as the azure sky. She found matching form-fitting tops in colors as vivid and dazzling as flowers indigenous to the island and brought them to Brenda with a flourish. Two sundresses in the store window caught Brenda's eye—one the same hue as the Caribbean, the other a yellow as bright as the sun. She had both in the fitting room. And to top it off, Brenda's face flushed when the clerk brought her a hot pink bikini consisting of so little material it would be illegal in some countries.

Maybe this is exactly what I need. Even though it would take years to pay off her credit card bill, for once Brenda wanted to live in the moment. Wanted to experience what everyone else she knew seemed to take for granted. After all, there was a beach and sunshine out there—and it was not only waiting for her, it was calling: "Come, enjoy."

"If it's all right, I'd like to wear the bikini out to the beach right now. Could you send the rest of the packages to my room?" At the clerk's nod Brenda grabbed a towel and sunscreen and headed straight for the door.

Outside, with the tropical sun warming her skin, Brenda found a lounge chair, poured on the sunscreen, and sat back to enjoy the peace and relaxation. She also checked out the male tourists as they walked past in their Speedos. After all, this was paradise and she intended to enjoy *all* the scenery.

She decided today would be her day of rest and she spent most of it poolside with an occasional dip in the warm water. She indulged in one of her favorite activities—people watching.

The sun's heat stirred her mind. Shy since childhood, she'd experienced life vicariously instead of living it herself. Sure, she had her own dreams, but never had the nerve to try and make them a reality. What if she failed? What if she asked for a promotion and her boss laughed in her face? What if she quit working for someone else and followed her desire of opening a children's dance school, but nobody signed up for classes? The thought of failure always kept her in check, and Brenda realized she was letting life pass her by. She didn't want to do that anymore.

After the sun had set and the moon shone brightly in the sky, Brenda went to the beach for an evening stroll. She was surprised to find the beach so crowded this late at night.

"Excuse me," she said to a woman who stood gazing up at the sky. "Is something wrong? What's going on?"

The woman smiled. "It's a Blue Moon. Make a wish."

Brenda almost laughed. She didn't believe in things like that. But what if...

Maybe Tori giving her the ticket was a sign, maybe it was a chance for her to make a new destiny. She wasn't quite sure she believed, but for once in her life she was willing to step out on faith. With that thought, she closed her eyes tightly: *I wish something happens on this vacation that will change my life forever.*

Suddenly, a cool breeze sent a tingle down her spine and she opened her eyes. The stars twinkled brighter in the sky, the full moon was now surrounded by a blue haze, and a shimmer of exhilaration swept through her. Was it her imagination? She didn't think so.

The island was full of dance clubs and casinos—parties, nightlife and excitement. It was time to start living. Brenda returned to her hotel to change into one of her new outfits. If her life was going to change forever, she'd have to go and make it happen. Behind her hotel room door there was nothing but loneliness. Brenda was tired of being lonely. Fiddling with the key card, she opened the door and stepped inside the room. She stopped cold when she saw a half naked man.

Nick tightened his grip around the towel covering the lower half of his body. "Shut the door!" he yelled.

After the obvious moment of shock wore off, the woman did as she was told.

"Who are you and what are you doing in my room?" he demanded.

The woman who was wearing a bikini that displayed long slender legs, and full, firm breasts shook her head and stared at him.

"Nick?"

He stepped closer to study her, and took great pleasure in doing so. When he'd called the airline the night before to arrange a later flight after his plans had abruptly changed, he hadn't expected to be greeted by such a beautiful vision.

"I...I thought you weren't coming...you told Tori..."

Her words brought him back to the moment. Refocusing his gaze on her face, it finally dawned on him he'd seen her before. Her hair was much shorter—sexy, with a just rolled out of bed look—and she was wearing something he wouldn't have expected the woman he knew from the office to wear. "Brenda?"

"Um...yeah, uh...Tori said I could have her ticket. She said I could go since you wouldn't be...but you're here." She backed away. "I'm sorry. I'll just pack up my things and..."

"No!" After getting dumped by the office slut, Nick had made some serious decisions. No more dating brainless, witless Barbie dolls. He was ready to settle down and find a woman who actually knew that five plus five equaled ten without using any fingers. And if she'd been hiding a fantastic body under a beige pantsuit, then all the better. "I didn't mean to frighten you. Let me get dressed and we'll figure something out."

Nick went back into the bathroom, where he'd just finished a hot shower, and threw on a pair of shorts and a t-shirt. He opened the door and found, to his dismay, Brenda had also covered up with an azure sundress that enhanced her blue eyes. Big, bright, beautiful eyes he could now see thanks to her sexy, shorter haircut.

"I'll check into getting an earlier flight home..." she said.

He detected despair, no, not despair...disappointment in her voice.

"Would you please sit down a minute?" She was wringing her hands like a guilty child and it was making him nervous. She pulled a chair from behind the small table and slowly sat. "You don't have to leave, we can share the room."

Brenda's eyes settled on the one bed. "But...but..."

The knock at the door interrupted the awkward moment. "That's room service. You hungry? I ordered plenty of food."

Am I hungry? She was starved, and for more than just food. She'd been invited to share a hotel room in paradise with a six-foot-two, blonde-haired, blue-eyed god. Could life get any better than this? Then it hit her—the wish had come true! If she could open up, break out of her shell, and show Nick the person she really was, she could do anything. Her life was about to change forever. *And if they ended up in that big bed over there having wild sex, all the better.*

"I'm a little hungry," she answered demurely.

Moments later, Nick placed the dishes on the table and sat next to her. He removed the covers and her mouth watered from the delicious aromas.

"There's enough food to feed an impoverished country," she laughed.

Nick stared at the pasta, chicken, vegetables, shrimp, and two large pieces of chocolate cake. "I told you I ordered plenty of food. I skipped lunch and they didn't serve any food on the plane. Help yourself."

She took a plate and added a small piece of chicken and some vegetables to it. Although she hadn't had much to eat at the poolside snack bar and should have been starving, running into Nick had diminished her appetite.

"Come on, you have to eat more than that," he said with a plate loaded to the brim in front of him. He reached over, grabbed the serving spoons, and added a hefty amount of pasta and shrimp to her plate.

What the hell. She was on vacation, she might as well live it up. "Thanks, Nick," she said after taking several bites. It tasted just as wonderful as it smelled. The angel hair pasta was covered with large shrimp and smothered in a buttery garlic sauce. "I've never had shrimp before. This is delicious."

"It's not bad. My mom's shrimp scampi is better though. She didn't make it that often. It gets kind of expensive when you're trying to feed five kids."

Brenda got a kick out of seeing Nick's face light up when he spoke of his mother. Any man who respected his mother had to be a good man in her book. "I'm one of five kids, too."

"I'm the middle one, two older sisters, two younger brothers. We didn't always have much, but we had a lot of fun. Got in a lot of trouble, too," he added with a grin. "So what was your house like?"

It wasn't easy for her to talk about herself, but with Nick's blue eyes focused so sincerely on hers, she relaxed. "Pretty boring," she confessed. "I'm the middle child, too. We were all very good little girls. Mom is a highschool principal, my dad's a cop." She smiled at the mock look of horror on his face. "Yeah, it explains a lot about me, huh?"

"Well, you are pretty quiet at work. Don't get me wrong, I'm not insulting you. Believe it or not, I'm not really crazy about women who come on too strong. I'm not much of a party animal, and I don't usually hang out at bars either. I love the outdoors, camping, fishing, that kind of thing."

"I've never been camping. My dad didn't think it was something girls would like to do. I think he always secretly wished he'd had at least one boy."

"I'll take you camping with me sometime. You'll love it."

"That would be nice." She smiled but thought he'd probably forget about his offer after they returned home. "What about Tori?"

"That was a mistake, it was over long before yesterday. I just had a bunch of frequent flyer miles piled up and had to use them before I lost them, so I asked her to go with me a month ago."

The way he looked at her with a sweet, dimpled smile made her heart skip a beat. "And now I'm glad she's not with me."

They chatted comfortably while they finished eating. They discovered other things they had in common. They agreed Columbo was the best detective show of all time, and they'd both learned how to play pinochle from their grandparents. Somehow he got her to talk about her dream of opening up a dance school one day. He'd been more supportive in this one evening than her parents had been her entire life.

While Nick placed the dishes outside the door for room service to pick up, Brenda paced the room. *Okay, now what?* Should she sit and act natural? Should she stand outside on the deck and wait for him to make a move? *Yeah, like that was going to happen.* Or maybe she should get naked and lie on the bed and see if he got the hint.

She was still pacing back and forth when he returned. He closed the door and she thought he looked as nervous as she felt. He took a step closer and his look turned into something more like shock.

"Oh my God, Brenda! Are you allergic to shrimp?"

Brenda ran for the mirror over the dresser. "Oh my God!" she cried in horror at her reflection. Her face was covered with a rash. "Oh my God!"

Nick followed her and put his arm around her waist. "Oh, sweetheart, it's not that bad." *Sweetheart?* Where had that come from? An hour or so with a beautiful woman who had a knowledge of things other than where to find brand name shoes for less and he's calling her sweetheart!

"It's not that bad!" She turned to him. "You can play connect the dots on my face."

Nick laughed, glad she had a sense of humor when other women would have melted into a puddle of tears. "I'll call down to the front desk and see if they can send something up for you."

"How about a paper bag I can put over my face?" Brenda rubbed at her cheeks in an effort to remove the little red spots.

He smiled as he walked to the phone. "Actually I was thinking about some Benadryl. Do they itch?"

Suddenly, Brenda began furiously scratching at her arms and then her face. "Dammit, why'd you have to ask that?"

She was absolutely adorable. Why hadn't he noticed her before? Because he was too busy lusting after a blonde bimbo who acted like he was the most exciting man in the world. *Well for three months at least.* If he'd looked two desks over, he'd have found that a quiet brunette was the woman for him. Maybe if he'd taken a moment to talk to Brenda, he would've noticed a sweet girl who had a great sense of humor. He'd been such a fool.

Well, so much for wishes, and my life changing forever, Brenda thought to herself an hour later as she sat at the edge of the bed. But then again, maybe her life had changed forever. She'd probably have to quit her job—maybe even move to a different city, all due to her embarrassment.

And everything had been going so well, too. She'd been able to overcome some of her shyness and have an intelligent conversation with Nick. He was easy to talk to—he listened, he asked questions, and he actually looked her in the eye when he spoke. Like he'd really been paying attention.

Now everything had gone down the dumps. Hives! It seemed so fitting once she thought about it. Just when everything was running smoothly, something had to go amuck. Feeling guilty for ruining his vacation, Brenda said, "Nick, it's only eleven o'clock, why don't you go out for awhile? I'll be fine."

Nick sat beside her on the bed. "I'm not leaving you alone. Besides, this whole fiasco is my fault. If I hadn't insisted you eat the shrimp, this wouldn't have happened."

She turned and saw the sincerity in his eyes. Giving him a half smile, she said, "You didn't exactly put a gun to my head. And I'm not even supposed to be here. This is your vacation."

He put his hand on her cheek. Such an innocent gesture, but it gave her goose bumps to go along with the hives. "I haven't asked you to leave have I?"

No, he hadn't and she still hadn't figured out why. "No, and for that I thank you, but I'm sure you would much rather be..."

"You're right," Nick said as he rose and took her hand in his "Let's go."

"What? I can't go anywhere looking like this."

He tugged her hand harder and pulled her off the bed. "Don't worry, it's dark outside, and we'll run through the lobby. You'll be fine."

A little while later she was walking hand in hand on the beach with Nick. The crowds had dwindled to just a few couples enjoying a late night stroll. Probably madly in love, unlike her and Nick. She was convinced he was only here because he felt sorry for her. Would a passerby consider them romantically involved–the thought sent a shiver of hope up her spine.

"Tonight's moon is a blue one you know," Nick said as he pointed toward the sky.

The moon was higher in the sky making it appear smaller than it had earlier. "I heard about that, but I'm not really sure what a Blue Moon means."

"Second full moon in a calendar month. It only happens every couple of years."

"There was a crowd of people out here earlier." She gave a short laugh. "They believed they could make a wish on it."

He turned to look at her. "Did you?"

For the first time tonight Brenda was happy she had hives. Maybe Nick wouldn't be able to see the rush of heat she felt on her cheeks. "Yeah," she admitted sheepishly.

"What did you wish for?"

"I can't tell you that," she said as they continued walking. "If I do, it won't come true." But it already had. *I just had to go and muck it up.* She closed her eyes and sighed, then turned to Nick. "So are you going to make a wish?"

They stopped again, and he looked up at the sky and stared at the full moon for a few moments. "Okay, done."

His arms were suddenly around her waist, his lips covering hers. Soft, gentle, and sweet. Fantasies were for losers. There was nothing in the world like reality. His hands ran up her back as he brought their bodies closer together, his tongue delicately meeting hers—but all too soon it ended.

"Wow, my wish came true! Huh, how do you like that?" Without another word, he took her hand and began to walk back up the beach toward the hotel.

Brenda was speechless. Nick grew silent, too, even as they entered their room. She wondered what he was thinking. Why hadn't he deepened the kiss? Why had he stopped it so abruptly? Well, why wouldn't he? It was probably just another kiss for him. Nothing special. She was just one in the long list of women he'd more than likely been able to charm. To him the kiss they'd shared probably meant nothing—but for her the moment he kissed her would be etched in her memory forever as the best in her life. She'd never tell him that, though. He'd probably laugh at her.

"It's late, you can have the bed. I'll be comfortable on the couch," Nick said as soon as they walked into the room.

"No, Nick, this is your room—for which I'm going to repay you, by the way..."

"You're not going to give me one penny. Take the bed. I'm tired and I'm going to sleep."

His abrupt tone hurt her. She turned away so he wouldn't see the tears that had rimmed her eyes. She'd been right after all. The kiss had meant nothing to him. Clearly he regretted ever having done it.

At eleven the next morning, regrets filled Nick's mind. He regretted having kissed her. He regretted not making love to her. God, he was such a mess, he wasn't even making sense!

She was like no other woman he'd ever known. Sweet, funny, and shy. Nothing like the usual hussies he dated. She could carry on an intelligent conversation. Throw in a killer body and a kisser beyond compare and she was everything he'd ever wanted. And that's why he hadn't made love to her last night. Sex would just have ruined everything—although he'd never wanted to make love to a woman more than he had Brenda. It would turn what he thought they could have together into just a summer fling—and he wanted so much more.

"I'm going to the beach, do you want to come with me?" he asked. He had to stop thinking about last night. Maybe leaving the room would help.

She'd just come out of the bathroom fresh from a shower and left a scent of wild berries in the air as she moved around the room. *God, she even smelled great*. He gaped at the colorful skirt and top she wore that accentuated every curve.

"I'm still covered in hives, I'm not going anywhere in the daylight."

"There are not that many left. Come on," he urged.

She shrugged. "Maybe later."

"Fine," he said gruffly to cover his discomfort. "Order whatever you want for breakfast and charge it to the room. I'll be back in a couple of hours." He wasn't about to fight with her, besides if she changed back into that tiny bikini, he didn't think he'd be able to overcome his lust, and they'd never leave the room.

Three hours later, Nick returned to the room, redder than a lobster. Dammit, he'd had such a restless night that he'd fallen asleep on the beach after applying only a light coat of sunscreen.

At least his dreams had been interesting. They'd been about Brenda being naked beneath him. Which was no surprise since that's all he'd thought of last night.

"Oh my God, Nick, you're sunburned!"

"I fell asleep." Now he was the sheepish one.

"I brought some aloe with me. Sit on the bed and I'll rub some on for you."

Great! Just what he needed, Brenda running her soft hands all over his body. But he was in a lot of pain and followed her advice.

It felt even better than he'd imagined. The gel cooled his skin, while her soft touch boiled his blood. He repressed the urge to pull her down beside him and kiss her until she saw stars. Heck not just stars—but moons...big, bright, blue moons.

"That's enough..." He shot off the bed. "I mean...it felt great. Thanks, Brenda." He crossed to the other side of the room, putting as much space between them as possible.

"What's wrong Nick? You've been acting strange. Is my being here ruining your vacation? I'll leave if you want me to...I told you I would. No hard feelings—I'll understand."

Of course she would—she was a kind and considerate person. "No, you don't understand." He ran his fingers through his hair. "Uh...Brenda, you didn't ruin my vacation. I ruined yours. Why don't you go out for a while? Go have some fun. Forget I'm even here."

She eyed him, but didn't move. Suddenly a slow smile crossed her face. "If I meet some handsome man on the beach, would you hide in the bathroom while we got it on?"

"What? No!" he said, shocked she would say such a thing.

She winked. "Never mind, I'll stay here then."

They both laughed. Her smile alone turned his heart inside out. And the thought of her ever being touched by another man made his head ache. Then it hit him, why keep fighting what his heart was feeling. Nick stopped laughing and stepped toward her. When she instantly stopped laughing as well, he knew she felt the undeniable attraction.

Before he could blink he had her in his arms, was kissing her. He'd kissed dozens of women before, all different shapes and sizes, but not one of them made his insides shake with so much emotion. Brenda's lips were soft and warm, he could feel her heart and soul through their kiss. She melted against him and he was lost. “Is it possible,” he asked against her lips, “that even though I've only been with you for twenty four hours, I've fallen completely in love with you?“

She pushed him away. “No! Of course you can't be in love with me. Nick, that's just crazy.”

Okay, even though he'd never told a woman he loved her before, he was pretty sure that was a bad response. “Why? Give me one good reason.”

“Because...because...”

“Gotta do better than that honey.” He grinned.

Nick watched as she paced the room. “Of course you don’t love me... because...because you don't know anything about me.”

“You're a data entry clerk at Action Mattress, you’re the middle born of five children, you appreciate classic television, you know how to play pinochle, and you know first aid for a sunburn. I think I know quite a lot about you.”

“That's just basic stuff, Nick, that doesn't mean anything.”

“You've never missed a day of work, which means you’re a conscientious person. If you can watch and enjoy a show like Colombo and not some dumb reality show, you're intelligent. And every time you touched me, with your hands covered in aloe, you took care in it, which means you’re gentle.” He stopped, a slow, sexy grin crossed his face. “Oh, and you have the ability to turn me on beyond measure. Shall I continue?”

She shook her head, and lowered her voice. “But...but we haven't even had sex yet.”

He smiled at her and raised his eyebrows. Tilting his head towards the bed, he asked, “Ya wanna?”

She stopped pacing, looked at the bed, then back at him. "What about your sunburn?"

Nick slowly crossed the room and gently kissed her neck. "Be gentle with me, sweetheart, and I think I can handle it."

Her body instantly relaxed as she gave in to him. When she sighed, he continued to rain kisses up and down her neck, up toward her ear. She sighed again. He must be doing something right, he thought.

He took her hand, walked her to the bed, and slowly lifted her dress over her head. He smiled when he saw her conservative tan bra and matching panties. "Brown is now my favorite color," he said gently pushing her onto the bed.

When Nick removed his own clothes he wasn't feeling any pain from the sunburn. His body was throbbing with lust instead of soreness. He joined her and began a trail of kisses from her pretty face to her cute little toes, removing her underclothes along the way.

Although kissing her soft, delicate skin provided an incredible sensation, he wanted to be inside her. Damn, not without a condom. He was on his knees in front of her. "Brenda, honey, we can't do this now."

"What? You can't kiss me like that and then change your mind. Get back to doing what you were doing right now!"

"I would love to, honey, but I don't have any condoms. I'm clean, I'm sure you are, too, but I don't want you to get pregnant until we're married."

Married? Okay, he was just really turned on. Brenda looked down at his impressive naked body and saw that, wow, he was really, really turned on. So that *married* comment must have just slipped out.

But she wanted this moment. Wanted this one shot at happiness, even if he walked out of her life tomorrow. She reached over to the nightstand drawer and took out a condom. "I bought some while you were out earlier." Her eyes lit with merriment as she threw one over to him and asked, "Extra large good enough for you?"

He caught it and began unwrapping the package. "You never cease to amaze me. Have I told you lately that I love you?"

"Yeah, but you're all talk, now get over here and prove it."

He covered himself and was beside her on the bed in a flash. With each gentle yet powerful thrust, he proved just how much he cared for her. Over and over again. "I love you," he said, and the soft tone of his voice combined with the sensation of him filling her so deeply made her believe it this time. Something about him was special. She'd never felt like this before with any other man. Had never considered going to bed with someone before getting to know them better.

It was crazy, but she was overcome with emotion for someone she barely knew. Somehow over the past twenty-four hours, between his humor and his caring, she found herself feeling the same way. "I love you, too," she replied just before he brought her to the edge and she climaxed with abandon.

Nick's finale soon followed and he collapsed on top of her. Afraid of crushing her, he quickly rolled off and onto his side.

"My wish was for something to happen on this vacation that would change my life forever," she confessed as they lay facing each other, their breathing finally calmed. "My wish came true, didn't it? Thank you for that. I'll always remember this—"

"I hope you think so, because you're going to call the boss later and tell her you quit."

She was stunned. "What? I can't do that. I know office relationships can be awkward..."

"Yeah, well, that too. But it's not why I want you to quit. I don't give a damn what they think in the office. I want you to open that dance school you told me about."

"But Nick..."

When he kissed away her protests, she realized no matter what excuse she came up with it wouldn't be good enough to satisfy him. With Nick by her side, she'd be able to do anything. Amazing—yesterday she would've been happy if they'd just ended up in bed together. But today she found that *just* anything with Nick would never be enough. She didn't know how she knew, but she did. With Nick's love and support she could do anything she dreamed...or wished for.

Visit Michelle's Website at
http://www.michellescaplen.com

Blue Moon Magic

by Ann Marie Bradley

"Omigod!"

A castle. Not just any castle, but *her* castle. Well, not hers, really, but the one that had haunted her dreams since she was a child. And now here it was in plain view. Sitting on the white sands of Key West, Florida. Claire Jacobs peered out the window of the taxi. Hotel Castle called to her. Built in 1886, the hotel had been fashioned after a European country castle, complete with round, ivy-covered towers and turrets. The taxi continued down the flagstone drive. Claire closed her eyes and pictured a grand horse-drawn carriage transporting her home to the castle in her dreams - and her prince.

Tired of being passed over for promotions and having senior partners take credit for her ideas at the interior design firm where she worked in New York, Claire had scanned the internet for jobs. When she'd come across the advertisement calling for someone to turn the more-than-one-hundred-year-old, run-down Hotel Castle into a twenty-first century luxury resort, she knew it was the job of her dreams and mailed her resumé. Rob Archer, owner of Hotel Castle, must have been impressed with her credentials, because he'd replied immediately. The offer of more money than she'd made in the past five years and the perfect job of a lifetime redecorating the wonderful old hotel had been impossible to turn down. Claire wanted this job, somehow knew it was right for her. Risking everything, she quit her job and accepted the position. Archer's attorney had sent a plane ticket and advance, so here she was. Anticipation stirred in her along with nagging doubts. Did she really have the ability to revamp and redecorate such a large building?

A doorman dressed in a Robin Hood wannabe green tunic and tights held the entrance door open for her and pointed out the manager. Claire stepped inside and stopped dead in her tracks as she surveyed the one-hundred-foot square lobby. “Ooooooo!” She spun in circles to take in the entire lobby. Spotting the magnificent tapestries that hung on the red brick walls, she smiled. But at the sight of the elaborate chandelier hanging from the ceiling, she exhaled an “Ahhhhh.” Never mind the carpet was faded. Never mind the upholstered chairs were worn—the hotel was perfect.

A deep, rich voice pulled her from her daydream. "Welcome to Hotel Castle, Miss Jacobs. We’ve been expecting you.” A man who looked to be in his mid-fifties extended his hand. “I’m Fred Miller, the manager.”

Claire cleared her throat to ease the embarrassment, sure her mouth had been hanging open. "Thank you.” She gripped his hand with a shaky grasp. "The hotel is breathtaking - just like a fairy-tale castle. I can’t explain it, but I feel I’m coming home.”

The manager smiled. "It affects most of our female visitors that way, the Cinderella syndrome. Lord Archer, Fifth Earl of Sundrey, had this place built exactly like his castle in Europe for his fiancée. They meant to live here, but she disappeared a week before they were to marry. When she didn’t return, he died shortly thereafter of a broken heart. It then fell to a distant relation and the new owner turned it into a hotel. Folks say Lord Archer haunts the place.” His face lit up in a wide, friendly grin.

"They never found her – the fiancée?”

"No. Lord Archer posted a hefty reward, even searched himself, but to no avail. It’s said grief overwhelmed him and he lost his will to live.”

"How sad.”

When his hand touched the bell on the elaborately carved and gilded desk, Claire jumped.

"I didn’t mean to frighten you. I’ll have the bellman take your bags to your room, and after you settle in and have dinner, I'll give you the two-dollar tour." He handed her a key. "Just call me Fred, by the way."

Claire sighed. "I'd hoped to meet Mr. Archer. Is he busy?"

"The attorney didn't tell you?" The manager frowned when she shook her head. "Mr. Archer is indisposed and won't be meeting with you." He reached under the counter and retrieved a large envelope. "He left these instructions for you. You're to have free reign over the place. Mr. Archer never puts in an appearance – well, only once in a blue moon."

"Oh? How disappointing." She glanced sideways at Fred as the bellman gathered her luggage on a cart and led the way to her room, across the great hall and past a magnificent marble staircase that curved toward the upper floors.

Inside her appointed room, Claire turned her attention to the spectacular queen-size four-poster bed. She kicked off her sandals and plopped on her back across the burgundy silk quilted comforter. Heaven. How could she improve on anything this lush? The room's vaulted ceiling was supported by inlaid stone columns and decorated with golden stars. She imagined what it must have been like when Lord Archer built it for his bride. Happy times and love lingered in the room. She felt it. She sighed as the calming, almost drug-like effects of her surroundings robbed her limbs of strength. Though still only late afternoon, the twinkling stars on the ceiling lulled her into a state of sleepiness. She wiggled under the covers and dozed off.

Hot. The dark-haired, handsome image of a man. His nearness kindled feelings of fire and like a narcotic gave her an euphoric feeling. Her heart beat with the pulse of the waves hitting the beach. His white shirt billowed open to the center of his chest. His gaze riveted on her face, then moved over her body slowly. Her skin tingled. The air around her electrified; her heart jolted and her pulse pounded. She tried to throttle the dizzying current racing through her as he stepped forward and cupped her face with his large hand. In one fluid motion she was in his arms, her curves molding to the contours of his lean body. He held her so tenderly her body ached for more, but...no, don't leave! What are you doing? Without a word, he turned away and walked across the beach.

She opened her eyes. Moonlight sifted through the windows, glistening on the golden ceiling stars and lighting the unfamiliar room. Disoriented, her gaze darted about until the shapes became familiar. Hotel Castle. She fell back on the pillow, wrapped in a serene quiet, and tried to remember the dream. He'd been so close, she'd felt the heat from his body. She touched a finger to her lips and they felt warm and moist from his kisses. Drugged with desire, she rose and crossed the room to the French doors. Footprints in the white sand drew her outside. Should she follow? Had he been real after all? The almost-full moon glinted on something in the sand. She bent and reached for the object. Her fingers curled around a smooth, cool ring. A man's ring. She turned it toward the moon's light and traced the unusual design with a finger. A ruby encircled with diamonds, with some sort of crest on each side. Funny, but it looked familiar somehow.

"If I find the owner of this ring, I'll find my prince." Claire giggled and looked up at the clear evening sky and its Blue Moon.

What had Aunt Lizy told her before she'd left? Oh yes, some nonsense about a Blue Moon appearing this month. "The second full moon in a month is magical, child. It only happens once every two years, so you must be certain to make a wish on it."

"What the hell? Maybe Aunt Lizy is right. So, moon, what am I supposed to say? If you were a star, I could say star light, star bright, first star I see tonight, wish I may, wish I might, have the wish I wish tonight." Claire stopped. "Of, for Pete's sake, I can't believe I'm doing this—talking to a moon! Oh well, before they drag me away and commit me, let's get this over with. Come on, moon, please let me find the owner of this ring and let him be my prince."

She kicked her foot in the sand. "Yeah, you dope, that'll happen as sure as the Blue Moon really is magical."

She tucked the ring into a pocket and went inside. She'd give it to Fred tomorrow. Surely a guest had lost it, but it was too late tonight to do anything. Funny, why hadn't someone wakened her? Fred had told her he'd take her on a tour of the hotel. Guess he changed his mind.

Putting on a tee-shirt and pajama bottoms, she placed the ring in the nightstand drawer before crawling back into bed. The digital clock clicked midnight and Claire yawned. Tomorrow. She'd turn the ring in tomorrow.

As she drifted to sleep, the dream began anew.

Her whole being sizzled with the waiting. When she saw him, her only emotion was relief. Slowly and seductively he walked closer, his steady gaze boring into her. Her body ached to be crushed within his embrace. Dreaming? No, real. It had to be. He came closer, his feet floating along the sand as if on a cloud.

He projected an energy and power that beckoned her to him and a quiver surged through her veins. He gathered her into his arms. His hands explored the hollow of her back; her trembling arms clung to him. His kisses teased her. His lips brushed against her as he spoke, his breath hot along her bare shoulder. She wrapped her arms around his neck, and when he claimed her lips with his, she returned his kiss. She twisted her fingers in his dark wavy hair and pulled him closer. Love for him so filled her, she thought she'd explode into a million tiny stars.

They met kiss for kiss, matching the urgency to be melded, a rending thirst to be joined, to be one.

"Ms. Jacobs?"

She jerked awake. Tangled in the thick comforter, she kicked her legs free and bolted upright. *Claire, ole girl, you're going mad.* Drawing up her knees, she scooted up in bed.

She heard a loud knock on her door and someone again called her name.

"Ms. Jacobs? You okay?"

Fred. "Yes, just a second." She jumped out of bed, threw on a robe and tied the belt around her waist. A quick glance at the clock told her she'd overslept. Nine o'clock. What a way to start a new job. She flung the door open.

"I'm sorry, Mr. Miller. I don't normally oversleep." She hesitated. "I really am sorry. I can be dressed in a jiffy."

He cleared his throat and looked up at the ceiling. "Quit apologizing, Ms. Jacobs. When you didn't come to dinner last night, I assumed you were beat and had gone to bed. And the name's Fred."

Claire tugged the robe tighter over her tingling breasts as heat from the remembered dream rushed to her cheeks.

"Actually, I took a walk on the beach...and found an expensive ring. Let me get it for you." She rushed across the room and opened the drawer to the nightstand. "Oh!" Her hand flew to her chest. "I don't understand. It's gone, but I know I put it in the drawer." Bending, she retrieved her slacks from the floor and checked the pockets. Nothing.

Fred cleared his throat again. "If you'll excuse me now, I'll meet you in the dining room in thirty minutes, if that's enough time for you to get dressed."

Claire hurried back to the door. "Of course. That's more than enough time. I'm sorry, I'm not usually this unprofessional."

"We're pretty casual around here. See you in thirty minutes." He started down the hall and Claire closed the door. She ran back to the empty drawer.

"I didn't imagine that ring—I know I didn't." She closed the drawer and grabbed her suitcase. She'd better hurry if she meant to be dressed and in the dining room on time.

Claire arrived with time to spare. After breakfast she told Fred, "If you don't mind, I'd like to acquaint myself with the whole establishment. Would you take me on the tour we talked about last night?"

At his nod, they set off down the timeworn, creaky corridors.

"Only a few rooms are currently occupied," he informed her. "I hope that will change after the restoration."

To Claire the cool air smelled of history. Beautiful chandeliers lit the rooms and hallways. She took notes in each room, commenting on pieces of furniture and questioning whether they would go or stay. The kitchen was large, with a vaulted ceiling supported by two massive pillars, and smelled of boiled herbs. "Oooooo," she squealed, "look at that free-standing stove! I've never seen one in the center of the room like that. No matter what renovations we make, we *have* to keep that! It's the life of the kitchen."

Suitably impressed with her ideas, Fred left her on her own in what he called the 'master' bedroom. The room Lord Archer was to bring his new bride to, and now the current owner's bedroom whenever he took it upon himself to be in residence.

In contrast to the other rooms, this one was sumptuously well preserved. Claire breathed deeply, smelling lemon oil and leather, with a lingering scent of fine pipe tobacco. Decorated in the Neo-Gothic style, the polished walls were paneled in dark wood, intricately carved. A massive stone fireplace covered nearly one whole wall. Claire imagined a magnificent fire on the hearth and the room warmed. The ceiling, unlike the one in her room, was all glass, letting in bright sunlight. She closed her eyes and envisioned stars in a midnight sky shining through the glass. The bigger-than-king-size bed drew her attention. It was covered with richly embroidered draperies and spreads and crowned by an elaborate woodcarving. A crest? She walked closer to run a hand across the wood and drew her hand back like she'd been burned. The crest! It was the same design as on the ring she'd found.

She shivered. An odd feeling of being watched by a strange presence crept up her spine. She pulled back the window curtains and stared at the beach below. Her mind wandered back to the dream and the mystery man on the beach. Had chance brought her here? Or had destiny? Would she find her prince? Could crazy Aunt Lizy be right and she'd find her true love in her twenty-eighth year on the night of the Blue Moon? "Yeah, like I believe all that crap, just because I was born under a *magical* blue moon."

She gathered up her notebook and headed back to her own room to work on designs. "Can't let superstitious nonsense cloud my work if I want to keep this job."

Claire worked on her designs all afternoon and on into early evening, stopping only long enough to grab a sandwich. The sun set and she lit candles all around the room. The flickering lights and musky scent helped put her in mind of olden times and life in a castle. Her pencil fairly flew across the pages, designing, *remembering. I've never been here before – not in this life.* She closed her sketchbook and stretched out across the bed.

Hours ticked by. She dozed fitfully, suspended in a dual state – asleep and awake simultaneously. Restless snatches of sleep in which her mind drifted from stars and a big round blue moon to prince charming and a ruby ring.

Only a few more weeks and she'd be a married woman. She accepted Lord Archer's hand and stepped down from the carriage, feeling pleased with herself. The eldest daughter of a sea captain, she'd been lucky to win the heart of Lord Robert Archer, Fifth Earl of Sundrey. Perhaps her aunt had been correct, she lived a charmed life since being born under the light of a blue moon.

A salty wind slashed her face and she grabbed her bonnet with one hand. Her rain-soaked cloak snapped behind her as Lord Archer held her close and led her through the swirling white sand to the front door of the castle. She paused at the entrance and squinted out toward the white-capped ocean waves. In the misty light between day and night, she closed her eyes and the water seemed to call to her.

The warmth and love of Lord Archer's arms pulled her back. She opened her eyes, but the sound of the wind played a haunting melody in her ears. "We'll be together always?"

He lifted her chin with a long finger. She felt the misty rain on her face, but he held her close, his body radiating warmth and strength. "Through all eternity, my love."

Claire tried the doorknob of the tower room. She paused, sensed a force on the other side that would disrupt her day as her dreams had her night. The knob wouldn't turn. Locked? Fred hadn't mentioned any rooms being locked except the few occupied ones and this wasn't one of them.

She hurried to the front desk, then waited impatiently while Fred registered a young couple.

"I need the key to the west tower, Fred."

She saw something flicker far back in his dark eyes. "There's no key. I've been here more years than I can count and no one's ever been in that tower."

"That's crazy. It looks structurally sound. Why is it locked?"

"Legend says it's where Lord Archer died. He locked himself in the tower after his Lady Claire – say, she had the same name as you." He shrugged. "Anyway, after she disappeared, Lord Archer locked himself in the tower and drank himself to death."

"So why has it been kept locked? Surely the new owners would have wanted it opened."

"Not for me to say." He busied himself with papers on the desk.

"Send for a locksmith. If I'm to restore the whole building, I want access to all of it."

Fred raised his eyes to hers. She thought he might object, but at the last minute he said, "Well, I do have orders to let you do as you want. Guess it'd be okay as long as you take responsibility."

"Of course I will. But I don't see the problem." She shifted her notebook to the other hand. "See if the locksmith can come out immediately. I'll be in the east wing. Call me when he arrives."

Claire poked around the east wing for nearly an hour before the locksmith arrived, then eagerly waited while he opened the lock on the west tower door. With a blast of cold air, the heavy oak door burst back on its hinges and slammed against the wall. An unearthly wind howled down the stairway. Claire shrank away from the sound, hesitated an instant, then lifted her chin and steeled herself to climb the spiral staircase. Dust motes danced on the sunlight spilling down from windows high above.

Isolation, vast and longing, reached out and touched her. In all her life she'd never felt such sadness. She shook off the feeling that something supernatural had reached out to her and studied the interior of the tower rooms, already planning improvements. Surely there was nothing abnormal about the area. She was tired, her strange dreams having kept her from a good night's sleep. Pressure to succeed and fatigue were just playing tricks on her nerves. That was it.

She fished her pencil from a pocket and sketched designs on the pad of paper she carried. The windows let in bright light, but she'd have iron sconces installed along the inside walls for evening hours. Black cast iron ones, of course, keeping with the castle's design.

She explored the tower rooms, making notes and sketching plans. Eager to find anything she could use in her designs, she crouched on the floor and dug through boxes and trunks. Out of the corner of her eye, she saw the sun glint on something in the corner, and she rose to investigate. Peeking out from behind a yellowed sheet she saw the edge of a gilded picture frame. Quickly she flung the cover off, coughing as years of collected dust filled her lungs.

She stared up at a life-size portrait of a sinfully handsome man with a noble, dark face. Black, wavy hair, combed in a style to tempt a woman's fingers. A small, close-cropped mustache above thick, well-shaped lips. Dark, rich brown eyes framed in lashes longer than any woman's, and thick brows that arched in a devilish curve. A short, jagged scar across his left cheek ...

The face of the man in her dreams! How could it be? She'd never been here. Never even heard of Hotel Castle until two weeks ago. But the man in the portrait was definitely the man in her dreams. He'd visited every night since her arrival—she'd never mistake his noble face.

She read the gold plate at the bottom of the frame with a sigh. "Robert Archer, Fifth Earl of Sundrey."

She became vaguely aware of a presence behind her and slowly turned. A light blue, misty glow gathered between her and the door. It expanded and glimmered with little specks of light. A shape began to form, fuzzy at first, then evolved into the figure of a man, from his dark good looks to well-muscled, long legs. He looked uncannily like the man in the portrait.

The light in the room suddenly seemed too bright. "Lord Archer..." Claire squinted and tried to see the man more clearly.

"It's me, my dear. God be praised, you've come home at last," she heard the man say before she fell into a lifeless faint.

Moments later she opened her eyes and sat up. She frowned and looked around the room. The apparition was still there, although he was more solid. "You!"

"I prayed you'd return." His voice choked with emotion. He reached toward her, but drew back when she jumped. "I've been so lonely without you, my love. Why did you leave me?"

Still a bit hazy, she blurted, "You can't be Lord Archer. You'd be – what, a hundred and fifty years old at least?"

"You jest," he blustered. "I'm not a day over thirty-five, the same age I was when you most unfortunately disappeared from my life."

She stared at him. "You're a ghost!"

"No. Not a ghost. Don't be afraid, my dearest. A shaman came to me after your disappearance. He promised, if I drank his potion, I would sleep, then find you by the light of the Blue Moon." He reached out to her again, but she shied away. "I'd begun to doubt him, but it's true. You've come back to me, my love."

Claire focused on the man before her. What kind of hokey joke was this? Something Fred concocted to scare her away? Who else could be behind it? But why would he want her to go? Suddenly she was sure it was all her imagination. Fred had mentioned Lord Archer's betrothed was named Claire, add that to the erotic dreams she'd been having, and of course Aunt Lizy's notion of true love under a magical blue moon. No wonder she was having visions. He had to be just a figment of her imagination. Anything else was ridiculous.

"I should not have rushed your love. I thought you felt for me what I did for you." He said it with such passion, she believed him for a second.

"Just wait a darn minute. You're pulling my leg, right?"

"Pulling your leg? I'm afraid I do not understand. I'm not touching you..."

"Joking. Kidding." She measured out her words slowly. "You know, making all this up."

"Please, Claire." She felt a feather-light touch as his hand stroked her cheek. "I assure you it's true."

Her heart lurched in her chest when she saw the ruby and diamond ring on his finger. The same one as in the portrait—the same one she'd found on the beach. She almost believed he was real. Good God, she was beginning to believe in ghosts or magical moons or whatever it was he claimed! She actually felt his heartache. Felt the love radiating from him. For her?

"But why have you stayed here all this time? Why not go to the light and find *your* Claire?"

"My soul is bound to this tower, but my spirit can roam the grounds. Each rise of the Blue Moon, I awaken and wait. I've tarried, dreamed, prayed you would find your way back to me. Yet each chance passed and you did not come. Until now." His form became yet more solid. "My darling, Claire, I have until the rise of the second full moon this month - the blue moon – to regain your love. And when I do, I will be once more alive and never let you from my side again."

She met his gaze straight on. "Well, that's certainly a different come-on."

"My lady love, your speech has become unfamiliar to me." His dark brows drew close.

Claire rolled her eyes. "Okay. This game has gone on long enough. I'll tell Fred you did a great job playing the part. Although I don't know why he concocted such a wild scheme in the first place." She started toward the door, but at the same time something pulled at her. A longing deep inside told her to stay. She shook it off. "I really have work to do."

A few minutes later she again found herself waiting for Fred to finish registering guests before she addressed him. She worried her lower lip with her teeth as she tried to think how to approach him. If he was the one behind the ruse, he'd be ready for her questions. She thought for a long moment, even paced the floor while waiting.

In the end, when Fred was once more alone, she just blurted it out. "Of all the nerve. Why the elaborate deception? Is it something you and Mr. Archer dreamed up to check my intelligence? Maybe put me in the mood for adding a romantic flare to the hotel?"

He frowned, but his voice was patient. "Is something wrong, Ms. Jacobs? Your room is not up to standard?"

"Don't play innocent with me." She felt her cheeks flame in anger. "Why the phony Lord Archer? Was the locked door part of the joke? If you're not satisfied with my work, there are easier ways to fire me."

"Fire you? I'm quite sure I don't know what you're talking about." He came around the desk and grasped her elbow. "Come to my office and we'll discuss this."

She jerked free of his hold. "I'm not going anywhere with you. Tell me what you know of Lord Archer."

"He was a soldier in the King's army and he wore his scars proudly. And he died a tragic, sad death."

He turned toward his office and she reluctantly followed him inside. Just like Lord Archer's bedroom, this room needed no improvement.

He pulled out a seat for her and sat opposite, behind his large oak desk. "Now, tell me what troubles you, Ms. Jacobs."

Though embarrassed, she started with the dreams and ended with Lord Archer's love-struck ghost. Fred listened quietly while she spoke.

"Perhaps the heat in the closed-off tower affected you?" He held up a hand when she opened her mouth to protest. "You've been working too hard. Go back to your room and I'll have some of our special herbal tea sent up. Rest a bit, then we'll check out what's in the tower. I'm sure you'll feel better after tea and rest."

Dismissed like a hysterical teen. How dare he! "Rest and tea be damned. I plan to go back to that tower and find the wires and mechanisms you used to pull off the prank. I'll..."

Fred picked up the phone and called housekeeping. After a short conversation, he turned to Claire. "I've sent for Brenda to take you back to your room. You're too shaky to go alone."

So that was it. A prisoner. Well, as soon as Brenda left her at her door, she'd sneak to the tower.

A few minutes later a grandmotherly woman dressed in a black uniform collected Claire from Fred's office and helped her to her room. Claire had to admit the woman was far from a jailer type. She was friendly and chatted while she drew back the covers, then ran water in the bathtub. "A good long soak and a nap will fix you up, my dear."

"I don't need a nap. I'm supposed to be working, not vacationing."

"Oh, I've heard Mr. Miller talking. He's pleased with your drawings. I even heard him talking to Mr. Archer on the phone. Said you were just the one they'd been looking for."

As Brenda started out the door, room service arrived with a white cloth covered cart. Pink tapered candles circled a bouquet of deep red roses on one side of the cart and a silver tea service on the other. The young man parked the cart near the bed, lit the candles, and hurried out before Claire fished in her purse for a tip.

She had to admit, it did look lovely. She gave in and poured herself a cup of tea, then sipped the hot brew slowly. The strong smell from the burning candles mixed with the sweet scent of roses and pungent taste of the herbal tea disoriented her. Maybe she *was* tired. She set down the cup and lay back on the bed.

She knew she was asleep, but had the harsh sense she was awake, walking along the beach. Someone followed her. She turned. "Stop. Go back." Why did he continue to follow?

"Claire, don't leave me. Wait." His voice, deep and sensual, sent shivers down her spine. The wind sighed and a cloud danced over the full moon. A rose petal path led to the open French doors and she followed. When she reached the bedroom, she heard music. Lord Archer stepped out of the shadows. When he reached her, he knelt and took her hand in his. She saw the full moon rising behind him.

"Come with me, Claire." His voice was deep, tender, almost a caress. His eyes searched her face. He rose and took her hand in his. "We must hurry."

The warmth of his flesh was intoxicating. "We must hurry where? Why?"

A beam of moonlight revealed an adoring look on his face. "We must be united while the moon is high. I love you,

Claire. I couldn't bear to lose you again after being this close."

"You think I'm the same woman you loved all those years ago? How could it be?" The idea intrigued her. A faint memory lingered around the edges of her mind. Could that be why she'd never found love with any other man? Had Aunt Lizy been right all along?

"I know you are, my darling lady. Fred promised me you'd return, and he's kept his promise." A flare of desire flowed into his eyes. Every time his gaze met hers, her heart turned over.

Confused, she started to walk away, but hesitated, torn by conflicting emotions. He smiled and sent her pulses racing

He took a step toward her. "You do remember, don't you?"

Something tugged at her mind. This man was touchable. Yet there was that microscopic glow around him. Was he a ghost? She glanced up at the moon. Tonight was his last chance. The wind whistled through the doors in a tormenting melody.

Fate pulling her forward, she could no longer deny herself his touch and wrapped her arms around his neck. He kissed her like she'd never been kissed before. She returned his kiss and knew she wanted more. She wound her fingers in his thick hair and whispered, "I love you, Robert."

"I love you too, my darling lady love." He began reciting the marriage vows and sealed them with a kiss before he slipped the ruby ring from his own finger to hers.

They clung to each other in desperation. He lifted her in his arms and carried her across the room where he gently laid her on the bed. She pulled him to her and began her own vows of love to him. She held him tight with a burning desire, afraid she'd lose him.

His breath was warm and moist and real against her face, and her heart raced. There was a bond between them.

With the moon rising higher in the sky, she was desperate to love him, to give him life. Excitement flamed in her and she pulled him closer still. She curled into the curve of his body, matching his urgency with her own powerful, unsated needs.

They loved in desperation - fighting time. Moving together as one, they joined in a burst of stars.

She woke in her bed, curled against her lover's side, astonished at the sense of fulfillment she felt. Bright sunlight shone in the open doors, lighting Lord Archer's face. Lord Archer? It hadn't been a dream? She recalled the ecstasy of being in his arms.

Lying beside her, he looked *so* real. Certainly not a ghost. No ghost could've made her feel like he did? She ran her hands over his body, assuring herself he was real.

"Promise to wake me every morning like this?" His smile widened in approval.

"Cross my heart."

"I can hardly believe we're together at last. After more than a century of waiting, you've come back to me." His arms drew her close, tightened around her and held her as if he'd never let her go. He pressed his lips against hers and sighed in contentment, then lay silent for a long moment, just holding her.

"There was a time when I didn't believe in magic," Claire confessed. "I was wrong. It does exist, but only if you believe. Especially the magic of love. It's the strongest sorcery of all, and it can work marvels. It conquered my fears. It saved your life."

"And it brought you home to me." Lord Archer bent his head and claimed her lips.

She pushed him away, panting. "I really must breathe." She giggled.

"I waited so long for your return, my dearest. You are my wife, you know. My forever wife." Putting a large hand to her waist, he drew her to him.

"Yes! I can't believe I almost didn't listen to my heart and memories. Thank God, Fred insisted I stay."

"Someone mention my name?" Fred peeked into the room. "Pardon my intrusion, but I believe a wedding celebration is in order. The priest is on the way and the cake is in the oven!"

Visit Michelle's website:
http://www.michellescaplen.com

Kissing Lessons

by Sherrie Holmes

She fell from the sky like a wing-shot angel.

One minute Viscount Selkirk was strolling along a wooded, sun-dappled lane at his country estate, whistling a bawdy tune and swinging his walking stick. The next minute he was flat on his back with a woman sprawled on top of him.

A large woman. A Rubenesque woman. A voluptuous woman in every sense of the word, from rounded hips and generous bosom, to kissable lips and plump, apple red cheeks. Big-eyed and open-mouthed, she stared down at him, her sable-brown hair wildly disarrayed and framing a face of uncommon beauty.

Had he the breath to speak, Selkirk would have uttered one of his witty bon mots. But he could no more muster the lungpower to speak than he could figure out where the devil the woman had come from. All he knew was that a shadow had passed over his head and he'd looked up, thinking a cloud had crossed in front of the sun. It had been a cloud all right—a cloud composed of frothy white petticoats, long legs encased in silk stockings secured with shocking red ribbons, and pink buttocks as bare as a newborn babe's. By the time he realized the apparition cartwheeling through the air toward him was a woman, instinct overruled self-preservation and he dropped his stick with a clatter to catch the female against his chest. The next thing he knew, he was flat on his back with the wind knocked out of him. Bowled over by a beauty. Pinned to the earth by a soft, warm body.

Dear God, he thought, *if I am dying, let me take her with me!*

She pushed up on her forearms, a look of astonishment on her face. "Oh, thank you, sir! Thank you!" Scrambling to a sitting position on his stomach, her knees straddled him on either side.

He opened his mouth to say *Think nothing of it, ma'am*, but all that came out was a strangled, "*Thnnnkkk*!" It was a puling weak sound, with a tinge of panic attached to it by dint of the fact he had no air in his lungs. In addition, the solid weight on his stomach prevented him from taking a deep breath.

His fallen angel was no slow top. She recognized his plight immediately. "Oh, sir, you have had the wind knocked out of you!" She grasped the hem of her skirt and began fanning his face energetically, unaware of the scandalous view she presented to her breathless and thoroughly speechless rescuer.

How he managed to lift one hand and clasp her wrist, he couldn't fathom. All he knew was that if he didn't reduce her to a state of maidenly modesty on the nonce, she would find herself on her back with *him* straddling *her*. He boasted impeccable manners and noble birth, but even with those hindrances he still was, after all, a man. A man with a luscious female sprawled atop him.

"Get off!" he bellowed, or at least attempted to. It came out sounding more like a feeble, "*Guff*!"

"I beg your pardon?" she said, leaning a little closer to hear him better.

That, at least, brought her rump up off his stomach. Unfortunately, it presented Selkirk with an eye-popping view of her generous décolletage. Afraid that if she leaned any closer he'd be suffocated by those heavenly mounds, he dragged into his lungs a fortifying quantity of air in a series of noisy and very unmanly gasps.

"Get off!" he wheezed.

Comprehension dawned. The angel said, "Oh!" and scrambled to her feet. "How rag-mannered of me!" she cried. "Here, take my hand and I shall help you up."

Selkirk gratefully accepted her offer and found himself hauled to his feet with alarming vigor. She began immediately to slap dust off his coat with enough force to send him staggering into the shrubbery.

She followed, hands brushing and patting. Selkirk batted her away, then grasped her by the shoulders and gave her a little shake. "Where, in the name of all that is holy, did you come from?" he demanded.

"I come from Meade House," she explained, "home of the late Baron Fairweather, my papa." She pointed to a large stone and timber house in the distance that, while imposing and grand, had a faint air of neglect about it. "Yonder lies the house of my father."

Selkirk dragged a hand down his face. "Ma'am, I did not ask where you *live*, I asked where you *came* from! As in dropping out of the sky!"

"Ahhh." Glowing with robust good health, she dimpled at him—one delightful depression beneath each pink cheek. "I came from the top of yon hill. Or rather, that is where I began. By the time I reached the bottom, my velocipede was going quite fast, you see, and then the front wheel struck a root and I catapulted into the air. It is fortunate you caught me, or heaven only knows what damage I might have sustained."

He stared at her in bewilderment. "What," he asked, "is a velocipede?"

"You do not know?" she said, a look of amazement on her face. "Wait here. I will show you!" Before he could reply, she bounded down a side trail and returned a moment later astride a two-wheeled contraption she propelled with her feet. She sat on a cushioned seat suspended between the front and back wheels by a rigid metal frame.

"It seems to have suffered no damage," she said, her tone clearly relieved. She dismounted and patted the handlebars affectionately. "Would you like to take it for a ride?"

Selkirk stared at the thing. In London people called it a hobby horse, not a velocipede. Whatever name one put to it, the contraption looked downright dangerous. "No, I most certainly would not like to take it for a ride. It looks untamed and vicious. The thing bucked you off. Keep it away from me. Does it bite?"

The woman gave him a startled look and then burst into delighted laughter. "Oh, sir, you are bamming me! Bite, indeed!"

He suppressed a smile. "You must admit, I have reason to be cautious after it flung you into the air."

"You do, sir. You most certainly do. But Millicent is perfectly harmless, I assure you."

"Millicent?"

"My velocipede."

"I see. And is Millicent's owner just as harmless?"

Her eyes twinkled. "Oh, no, sir, I am deadly! You must watch your step around Abigail Fairweather. I have been known to flatten innocent pedestrians without so much as a by-your-leave."

Selkirk grinned. He bowed and said, "Thank you for the advance notice, Miss Fairweather. It would not do for Lord Selkirk to be taken unawares by a demonic machine powered by an equally demonic woman. You realize, of course, that you are on Selkirk property?"

His comely trespasser blinked at him, her face devoid of expression. "I am?" An instant later her eyelashes dropped demurely over chocolate brown eyes and an alluring smile lit her face. "Are you going to turn me in?" she asked softly. "Because if you are, all is lost. I must meet Lord Selkirk. I simply must."

The viscount bowed again. "Then you are in luck, Miss Fairweather, for I know the viscount intimately. Allow me to introduce myself. I am David Neff, Lord Sel—"

"Lord Selkirk's gardener!" Abigail finished for him, hand pressed dramatically to her breast. "I can tell by the leaves and twigs in your hair. Oh, how fortuitous! I just knew my Blue Moon wish would come true."

"Blue Moon wish?"

"Yes. Did you not know, sir? Last night was a blue moon. I made a wish upon it. Mama told me it was silly, but I made the wish anyway."

"And your wish had something to do with Lord Selkirk?"

"It did." Her eyes glowed. "You are just the man to help me! You must know all about Lord Selkirk's habits. I hear he takes a constitutional every day. Perhaps you could arrange for me to meet him...accidentally, of course," she ended with a sly wink.

David was beginning to enjoy himself. He brushed the garden matter from his previously impeccable locks, suddenly glad for the comfortable old breeches and disreputable tweed coat that made him look like the gardener she thought him to be.

"His lordship is indeed a vigorous man, and he does enjoy his woodland rambles. What's more," he added with a wink of his own, "the viscount is new to the area, having come into his inheritance only recently. He has a strong desire to make the acquaintance of his neighbors, and will be staging a ball for that purpose in two weeks. I have it in my power to secure an invitation if you care to attend."

A calculating look appeared in her eyes, or so it seemed to David. In the next instant it was gone. "Famous!" she cried. "It is more than I could ever have hoped for. Thank you, Mr. Neff. Thank you." She grasped his hand and pumped it. "You must tell me everything about Lord Selkirk so I may be well informed and make a suitable impression on him."

My dear, thought David, *you have already made an enormous impression on him.*

She propped Millicent against a tree, then took David by the hand and pulled him over to a fallen log, urging him to sit with her. "Tell me all about him," she prompted.

She was still clasping his hand in her lap as she beamed up at him, her Gypsy-dark eyes alight with anticipation. He brushed his thumb slowly back and forth across the inside of her smooth, plump wrist.

"Tell me, Miss Fairweather, why are you so interested in the viscount?"

She was looking down at her hand, a distracted expression on her face. Her wrist was warm and soft beneath his caressing fingers. Her gaze lifted and she seemed to study him for a moment, and then her eyes suddenly danced. "I suppose it is safe to tell you," she said, dimples making another appearance. "I wish to make Viscount Selkirk's acquaintance because I plan on marrying him."

David had always been good at disguising his emotions when called for. He was known as a devilish opponent at cards and a shrewd player at the gaming tables. He had faced two duels with a nonchalance that unnerved his opponents.

When a highwayman stopped his carriage last year, David had cordially informed the thief he wasn't about to hand over his purse without a fight, and if the man cared to get down from his horse and give David a sporting chance, they could settle the matter like civilized gentlemen. If he lost, he told the highwayman, not only would he turn over his purse, he'd also throw in his carriage and horses. Fifteen minutes later the burly highwayman lay unconscious in the dirt.

David felt rather like that unfortunate highwayman. He had felled the thief with a sucker punch that laid him out flat. Her declaration had just dealt him her own sucker punch.

Well, this female might be awake on all suits, but he'd not cave in so easily. If she wanted a viscount for a husband, he would make her work for it.

Not that he planned on marrying her. Oh, no. He had other plans for the delectable young woman.

He glanced down at her. She was looking back at him with hope and a hint of devilry in her expression. Oh, yes, she was going to work hard for her supposed matrimonial prize. And if things went his way, this voluptuous, sloe-eyed minx would get more than she ever bargained for in the process.

David cleared his throat. "Ma'am, is the viscount aware of your plans to marry him?" She threw back her head and laughed merrily, exposing the white column of her throat and the generous swell of bosom nearly overflowing the top of her gown. David swallowed.

"No, Mr. Neff, he does not know of my plans, but I have every hope we shall make a good match. It is imperative I marry him. Mama and I...well, we have been in dire straits ever since Papa died, and I understand Lord Selkirk is fabulously wealthy. Oh, do not look so pokered up, Mr. Neff! Despite how mercenary it sounds, there is absolutely no doubt in my mind we shall rub along famously. I discovered his most pronounced traits are a wicked sense of humor and an unflappable nature, two features I possess in abundance.

Now, if you will just fill me in on the rest…" She let the sentence hang.

So, she was a damsel in distress? And she needed rescuing, did she? Interesting. It seemed he held all the cards.

His thumb continued to stroke her wrist. He found the sensation unbelievably erotic. "Are you passionate, Miss Fairweather? I assure you, Lord Selkirk is the most passionate of men." He shot her a hooded look and his fingers curled around her hand to caress the sensitive skin of her palm.

Her face colored and she snatched her hand away. David fought the urge to laugh out loud. Oh, he was going to have fun!

"Yes!" she replied in a high-pitched squeak, then cleared her throat and said in a more normal tone, "yes, I am passionate. About everything. About kittens and bright blue skies and tall trees and…and the smell of new mown hay, and walking barefoot in the grass and eating strawberries with fresh cream, and…and flying at breakneck speed down hills on a velocipede, and—"

"And you said you were as unflappable as Lord Selkirk, yet you snatched your hand away from me when I merely tickled your palm. Now you are babbling. If holding my hand puts you in such a pelter, what would you do if I were to kiss you? Have a fit of the vapors?"

Abigail leaped to her feet. "Oh!" she said, eyes flashing, "I would knock your block off! I would—" She suddenly clapped a hand to her mouth.

This time, David did laugh out loud. "Sit, my dear. I will not force my kisses on you. I must say your reaction surprises me. For one who is supposed to be imperturbable, you look rather flustered."

She plopped down on the log, her cheeks still pink. "Well, you startled me," she accused.

"Then you had best get over it, ma'am, for I can assure you, Lord Selkirk does not care for missish women. He likes bold, fearless women, women who let their passions show." He narrowed his eyes in speculation. "I believe you are afraid to kiss me."

She rose to the bait. "I am not afraid!" she huffed. "I am a good kisser and perfect for Viscount Selkirk and no one, not even his gardener, can tell me otherwise!"

"How experienced are you?"

She blinked. "Experienced?"

"Let me rephrase that. How many times have you been kissed?"

"Oh," she said airily after a brief hesitation, "dozens of times, *hundreds* of times!"

"Excluding kisses from your mother and father, how many times?"

Caught out, she flushed. "Well, it was only once, but it was a very good one."

David rubbed his upper lip, hiding a smile. "What did you do, coerce a footman into kissing you behind the stables so you would know what it felt like?"

Her look of mortification was all the answer he needed.

"He said I was a very good kisser!" she spouted, eyes flashing. "He said I was a natural!"

David couldn't remember when he'd had this much fun.

"One peck on the lips hardly qualifies you as a good kisser, ma'am. I suspect you know nothing of the art." He sighed dramatically. "Which is unfortunate, of course, because Lord Selkirk, from what I hear, is a first rate kisser. How can you hope to catch him in parson's mousetrap if you do not know how to kiss?

"Mr. Neff, I assure you, I am a good kisser." Her eyes slanted and she bestowed a slow, potent smile on him.

David felt it clear down to his toes. And other places. "Shall we put it to the test, then?" he said in a voice that didn't sound like his own.

She looked measuringly at him. "It would not be proper."

"Perhaps not exactly proper," David said, trying not to sound eager, "but it would certainly be to your benefit."

Her eyes narrowed in suspicion. "How so?"

"Well," he said, licking his lips, "as a gauge of your expertise. I can give you my, er, expert opinion. As it were." Lame. *Lame*! She would never fall for it.

Again, that penetrating look. "All right."

To his surprise, she leaned forward and her arms went

around his neck. Her body melted against him. She pressed her lips to his.

The world slowly disintegrated and fell away. Sound and light retreated. He couldn't breathe. Couldn't think. Could only feel, and what he felt was...illegal. Little stars burst behind his eyelids and he was in imminent danger of fainting from sheer, pounding excitement. Her fingers were threaded into the hair at the back of his head, her chest pushing him backwards so that he had to put his arms around her to keep from falling. It did no good because he fell anyway, right off the log and onto his back, with her sprawled on top of him, her arms still around his neck and her lips locked onto his.

She didn't seem to notice they had fallen, and David didn't much care. He was too busy returning her kisses with as much ardor as she, and having a hard time deciding where to put his hands because every place he put them, he encountered forbidden curves.

And oh, what curves!

He wondered if it were possible to expire from happiness.

It took him a while to realize his hands were not at her waist anymore and even longer to realize she had stretched his arms over his head and was pressing the backs of his hands into the ground. She was holding him down. By God, the wench was holding him down! His eyes flew open and he encountered a pair of dark, laughter-filled eyes staring back at him. Her lips curled up in a smug grin.

From that moment on, he was hers. She owned him, body and soul. Forget about making her his mistress. He was ready to marry her on the spot.

"Had enough?" she purred.

He looked up into smoldering eyes. "Take me, I am yours."

She shook her head, and her loose hair formed a cascade of chestnut ripples that tickled his chin and neck and made him want to bury his face in it.

"I cannot, Mr. Neff. In order to save Meade House, it is imperative I marry a rich man. If I do not, they will sell off our property and send Mama and me to the poor house."

"What if I were to tell you I am the viscount?" he said, despising the note of desperation in his voice.

Her dimples were back. "I would not believe you, sir, though I am beginning to wish you were. You are a prodigious good kisser."

"But I *am* the viscount!" he almost shrieked. "Really!"

"And I am Cleopatra." She patted his cheek. "Nice try, Mr. Neff." In one swift movement she was standing above him, offering her hand to him as before. "Turn around," she admonished. "Your back and hair are covered with leaves again." Brushing him down, she said, "I will count on your putting in a good word for me with Lord Selkirk." Her handshake was warm, firm.

Just like Abigail Fairweather.

Before releasing her hand, he brought it to his lips and pressed an ardent kiss to her wrist. "I will sing your praises to Lord Selkirk," he promised, and then added slyly, "though I believe you might want to improve on your kissing technique if you hope to snabble him."

"*What?!*" She looked thunderstruck.

And mortally offended.

"Make no mistake, ma'am, you are well versed in the art of osculation," David said, barely keeping a straight face. "The best I have ever encountered, in fact. But if you want to leg-shackle the viscount, you will have to make it impossible for him to resist you."

"I have done my research, Mr. Neff. He cannot help but fall in love with me."

Ahhh, the luscious little peach. He was half in love with her already.

"My dear, there is more to snaring a man than having similar tastes. That is all good and well, but you must make him pant after you."

"I made *you* pant."

Like a green schoolboy, David felt the heat of a flush creep up his neck. "I have it on good authority there are no less than fifteen other eligible young ladies in the neighborhood, Miss Fairweather. What do you have to recommend yourself over them? Can you play the pianoforte?"

"Tolerably."

"Sketch? Watercolor?"

"Not very well."

"Embroider?"

"Oh, pooh! There is more to life than stitchery."

"Dance? Waltz?"

"I have not learned how to waltz yet."

"Abigail Fairweather, what *are* you good at?"

She smiled brightly. "Kissing."

"Then you are in luck, because that will give you a leg up on your competition. I love to...er, Lord Selkirk loves to kiss more than anything else. Well, almost more than anything else."

"Really?"

"Really."

"Are you available to give me advanced kissing lessons, Mr. Neff?"

He closed his eyes in a momentary prayer of thanksgiving. *Him* give *her* lessons? She could give lessons to half the rakes in London!

"Oh, yes, ma'am," he said warmly. "I am available to give you advanced kissing lessons."

"Good!" She removed her velocipede from the tree where it leaned. "Then let us count today as our first lesson." "What time shall we meet tomorrow?"

She was serious! It was too good to be true. "How does one o'clock sound?"

"One o'clock it is. I will see you tomorrow, Mr. Neff." She mounted the hobby horse and pushed off with her feet.

David Neff, Viscount Selkirk, watched her delectable derrière until she disappeared from view around a bend in the trail. He picked up his walking stick and started off in the opposite direction.

"Abigail Fairweather," he said out loud, "your blue moon wish is about to come true. Within a month's time you will be wedded and bedded. I guarantee it."

Whistling and swinging his stick, he headed home.

Abigail Fairweather sidled her way through the throng of partygoers and made for the corridor at the far end of the room. Lord Selkirk's ball was in full swing. Though she had arrived only moments ago, the ball had been going on for hours. David Neff had told her to arrive precisely at eleven.

After two weeks of kissing lessons, David had pronounced her ready to sweep Lord Selkirk off his feet. He'd assured her that all it would take was one kiss and Selkirk would be hers.

David Neff was very sure of himself.

She and David had practiced kissing in the woods every day since their first encounter. He had taught her well—exceedingly well. Or perhaps she had taught him.

Hard to tell. One thing she knew for certain—they'd both enjoyed the experience immensely.

Today he'd actually broken off their kiss, put her away from him, and demanded she go home. She had protested their half hour wasn't up, but he told her gruffly that either she left *now* or he would not be responsible for his actions.

She had tried to keep from grinning as she rode away on Millicent. Now, Millicent was safely locked in the tool shed, and Abigail was making her way through a sumptuous home fit for a queen. Or the daughter of a baron.

Earlier this afternoon David had sent her a note telling her to arrive precisely at eleven o'clock. At eleven-fifteen she was to meet Lord Selkirk in his library. *Once you have kissed him*, the note had said, *you may expect an offer of marriage.*

She made her way down the hall, counting doors as she'd been instructed. The third door loomed on the right. The library. Taking a deep breath for courage, Abigail rapped lightly on the rich oak panel.

A masculine voice bade her enter.

The room was swathed in shadows, the only light coming from a cozy fire burning in the grate. A wingback chair was pulled up to the fireplace, its back to the door. The chair's occupant rested an elegantly shod foot on the hearth.

"The mysterious Miss Fairweather, I presume?"

He did not rise nor turn to look at her.

"Yes, my lord, it is I." She smoothed a hand down her skirt.

He stared into the fireplace. "I feel almost as if I know

you. Mr. Neff has told me so much about you. He calls you a delightful creature and says you are a superb kisser."

"Mr. Neff is a superb instructor."

"Is he? Well, I hold Mr. Neff's opinion in high regard, which is why I agreed to meet you. I would like to find out for myself how well you kiss."

He spoke so softly she could barely hear him. Or perhaps it was just the blood pounding in her head that made it difficult to hear.

"I cannot kiss you, sir."

He chuckled softly. "Cold feet, my love? Let me assure you my intentions are perfectly honorable. I plan on asking for your hand in marriage."

Abigail squared her shoulders. "How can you say such a thing, my lord? You do not even know me."

"*Au contraire*, my little turnip. Through Mr. Neff, I know you exceedingly well. Well enough to know I want to marry you."

"I will not marry you, sir, nor will I kiss you. That is what I came here to tell you."

He removed his foot from the hearth, though he did not turn around. He sat very still. "Come now, what possible objections can you have? Mr. Neff tells me there is no impediment to our marrying."

"There is one impediment, Lord Selkirk. I am in love with someone else."

"*The devil, you say*!" He surged from his chair and spun to face her. Silhouetted against the fire, she could only see his outline. He looked tall, imposing, and angry. He looked wonderfully masculine and wonderfully distraught.

"Who is he? I will tear him limb from limb! I will put a ball between his eyes! I will—"

"You will do none of those things, because the man loves me as much as I love him."

His shoulders sagged and he took a ragged breath. "Who is he?" he rasped.

Abigail paused, then licked her lips. "Your gardener, David Neff."

His head snapped up and he fumbled behind him to clutch the back of his chair for support. "You love him? *You love him*?"

She nodded, suddenly unable to speak. "With all my heart."

"Oh, this is rich!" Lord Selkirk said. "Abigail Fairweather, I love you. Will you marry me?" He walked toward her.

She pressed closer to the door. "I have already given you my answer," she said firmly. "I love Mr. Neff, and if I cannot have him, I will have no one, not even you."

He stopped in front of her, a silhouette backlit by the fire. "Not even me?" he asked gently, and placed a finger under her chin, tilting her head so he could kiss her. He dipped his head. It was a long, soul-deep kiss, one honed by hours and hours of diligent practice.

"Oh, David," she whispered.

It took a moment for it to sink in. David? "You called me David!"

"Would you prefer I call you 'my lord'?"

"You knew!"

Abigail beamed up at him.

"You little wretch! *You knew*!"

His face was still in shadow, but she saw the gleam reflected in his eyes.

She chuckled. "You really do love me?"

"Yes, you pea goose, I love you. Could you not tell?"

"Then why did you push me away earlier today? Why did you send me home?"

Even in the semidarkness of the room she could see his flush. He rubbed the side of his nose. "Because you inflamed my passions, my dear. I sent you home for your own safety." When he looked up again, a wicked smile graced his handsome face. "But once we are married, I will not have to send you home. I will send you to bed, instead."

She gasped.

"Just so," David said, and gathered her into his embrace. "I believe we owe a debt of gratitude to that blue moon of yours."

"Indeed we do." She put her arms around his neck. "I love you, Mr. Neff. I mean, Lord Selkirk. Oh, bother! What am I to call you?"

"Sweetest. Or darling. Or pookums. Tell me again that you love me."

"I love you, sweetest darling pookums."

He kissed her roughly, then softly, then languidly, branding her as his with each joining of their lips. He pulled back to look down at her and said, "Abigail Fairweather, for the last time, will you marry me?"

"I will, if you promise to kiss me every single day."

"I promise, you little minx. Now, let us seal the bargain with a kiss, shall we?"

Lord Selkirk's arms tightened possessively around Abigail. He pressed his lips to hers in the most ardent of kisses, and that was the last thing either of them knew for a very long time.

Muses in the Moonlight

by Patty Howell

Calli's long climb terminated atop the ridgeline and she'd barely broken a sweat. Although the day had been sweltering—after all it was July—a cool evening breeze whispered through the hardwoods and pines. The spot afforded an impressive view overlooking the valley where she'd been raised.

Once the place she'd called home, Allenvale, Pennsylvania, a small coal-mining town nestled into the Allegheny Mountains, had become an albatross...it presented too many unanswerable questions. Who were her parents? Where were they from? Why had they named her Calliope? Yet, most important...why hadn't they wanted her?

Education and changing locale hadn't settled her restless spirit. The Master's in Anthropology hadn't mattered one whit...it only opened the gate of her mind to more inquiry.

And Calliope? Her adoptive parents, whom she'd loved with all her heart, had told her the name had been printed in large block letters and tucked into the basket where she'd been found. Had her biological parents been patrons of mythology or had they been Allegheny Mountain people familiar with and lovers of the local folk music?

Her gaze shifted from the valley to the universe; her eyes roamed the cosmos seeking resolution to the barrage of mental provocations assailing her faculties. The stars were overshadowed by the huge moon that dominated the sky. It lay suspended from the heavens as though hanging from a puppeteer's strings. Was it beckoning, or was it ridiculing?

"Are you mocking me moon?" she yelled. Shocked at the loudness of her own voice, she chuckled to herself, thankful no one had heard her ranting. "They'd certainly think me a bit teched in the head." Her voice sounded subdued.

Calli jumped when a soft, deep voice replied, "Who would? And why would the moon make fun of you?"

She spun in the direction of the sound. A man rose from where he'd been crouched, leaning against a tree about fifteen feet away.

"How long have you been there?" Calli demanded.

"About an hour," the stranger replied as he walked toward her. The moon shining on his face reflected a kind smile, and sparkling white teeth between his parted lips.

It'd probably be a good time to take off down the mountain, she thought. These hills were as familiar as the back of her hand, having climbed them thousands of times as a young child and teenager. *And I'm faster than most things on two legs. So why are my feet fused to the ground*?

"You didn't answer my questions." His voice resonated a gentleness reminiscent of her daddy's.

She extended her hand awkwardly when he approached. "My name's Calli Winson. Who're you?"

He clasped her hand in his. "Jacob Isaacs. It's nice to meet you Calli Winson."

"Yeah, same here," she said—while thinking *I hope*.

The moon cast light onto his face illuminating its masculine features, especially his eyes. *Wise eyes*, she thought. The deeply calloused hand, still holding hers, conveyed a disciplined strength that radiated to the core of her being.

"So what are you doing here, Mr. Isaacs?" Calli withdrew her hand and immediately stuck it in her pocket, begrudging the loss of the warm imprint it had embedded in the pores of her palm.

She turned away and again stared at the moon.

"Actually, I come here frequently," he answered. "It's peaceful and conducive to prayer."

Calli glanced over her shoulder at him; a little scoff escaped her lips. "To pray? Is that something you're 'into'?" Immediately, a small stab pierced her heart. "I'm sorry," she quickly added. "I didn't mean that the way it sounded."

"It's all right," Jacob said gently. *Here indeed was a troubled, aching soul.*

He pointed upward. "If you look closely, you can see the Sea of Serenity flowing beside the moon's left eye."

"Are you some kind of moon aficionado?"

"No, not really. Merely awed and appreciative of all God's creation. Funny. Did you know you can buy a piece of the moon?"

"You're kidding, right?" Calli asked, facing him.

"Not at all. There's a place on the internet where you can purchase it. Only $31.25 an acre—the minimum you can acquire. For your money, you get an actual deed, a satellite photo, and geographic location." He chuckled.

Calli burst into laughter. "Does it include a map with directions?"

He smiled at her spontaneity. "I don't know about that. Did you climb all the way up?" he added, changing the subject.

"Yeah. I used to do it a lot as a kid. Some of the paths have changed, though it's mostly the same."

"It must've taken a while. It would've necessitated me leaving early this morning and packing a lunch," he said lightheartedly. "All that to say I drove. I'm parked in the overlook area. Would you like a ride down?"

"Yes. Thank you. I guess I did come up rather late in the day. However, this was the only time I had. I'm leaving tomorrow."

"I didn't think you looked familiar." Of course, she didn't—*I'd definitely have remembered,* he thought as he stared at her lovely face. "I believe I've met practically everybody in the valley over the last couple years. So, you're from out of town?"

"Yes," she said succinctly.

He casually took her elbow and led her toward the car. She's certainly a woman of few words, Jacob considered.

"What brought you back?" he asked as he opened the passenger door.

"Back?"

"You said you climbed this mountain as a kid, so I assume you lived in Allenvale at one time." Climbing in the driver's seat, he cranked the engine and swung out of the parking spot.

"Yes, I grew up here. My parents died ten years ago, and I returned to...to put flowers on their graves."

Jacob sensed there was much more to the reason, but didn't delve. "I'm sorry for your loss."

"Well, it was a long time ago, but it seemed like only yesterday when I placed those bouquets earlier. Returning has brought a flood of memories."

"I'm sure it has." Jacob expertly maneuvered the descending switchbacks. "Where do you live now and what do you do?"

"In Silver Spring, Maryland...outside Washington, D.C. I'm an anthropologist at the Smithsonian. How about you? What do you do in Allenvale?" Calli's curiosity piqued. He hadn't tried to dazzle her by extolling his achievements. By this time, the men she normally associated with would've inserted their entire curriculum vitae into the conversation.

"I'm a pastor at Allenvale Community Christian Church." He pulled onto the main highway into town.

She quirked a brow—her only comment, "You handled the mountain road with ease. I'm impressed."

"Well, as I said, I go up fairly often. I find it therapeutic to steal away and bask in the seclusion of the mountain's tranquility."

I can't believe my ears, she thought. "I understand that." It's the same reason she'd gone there so many years ago.

"So, Calli. Would you like to join me for a cup of coffee before heading home?"

"Coffee? No thanks. I'd be awake half the night. I'd love a glass of wine though. Oh! I guess you don't do wine, being a preacher."

"Ha! That's where you'd be mightily mistaken," Jacob guffawed. "Wine it is." He swung into the Moonlight Inn parking lot. "This seems appropriate for tonight." He turned off the engine and hopped out.

Calli opened her door just as Jacob laid his hand on the handle. "Oh! I didn't realize you were coming around," she said, swinging her legs out of the Jeep.

Allenvale had changed remarkably in ten years; Calli barely recognized the town where she'd grown up. Where most coal towns had dried up or stagnated, Allenvale had prospered, which surprised her. For a moment, she panicked, wondering if her attire—jeans—was okay until she noticed Jacob also wore jeans.

"Let us have two glasses of pinot noir, please" Jacob addressed the waitress once they'd been seated.

"How long have you lived here, Jacob? Do you like it? You said you're a pastor—you mean like a youth pastor?"

"A little over six years and yes, I do. I've grown quite attached to the town and the people. I'm the senior pastor, but there're actually several pastors and I view us as equals." Their drinks arrived. "Do you want anything to eat?"

"No, thank you. I had a late lunch."

Dismissing the waitress he returned his attention to Calli. "So, how come you left Allenvale?"

Why did I leave? "After my parents were killed in the car crash, I felt...detached." *And lonely.*

Jacob lifted his glass. "A toast. I pray you find what you came back for." He stared into her eyes.

Calli cast her eyes at her glass still on the table. How could he possibly know she'd been seeking something all these years? She barely knew herself. She'd tried to break it down to its lowest denominator many times—without success. It's as though this stranger pierced her soul and fathomed the long-buried desires of her heart. She picked up her wineglass and touched his without comment.

"You said you're leaving tomorrow. Why so soon?"

"Why did you say that?" Callie asked.

"I don't know. Returning after so many years, I'd think you'd want to reacquaint yourself with the town. See people you haven't seen—"

"No, not that. In your toast...why did you say you hoped I'd find what I came for?"

"When you yelled at the moon I caught in your voice a quiet desperation. As though the blue moon could reach down and bestow wishes. I was getting ready to leave when you arrived and I detected a sad heaviness in your spirit. And I now see a yearning in your eyes," he said gently.

"I didn't realize those things could be projected." Although skeptical, she didn't want to be unbelieving. But what could explain how he'd read her so well?

"Only you and God know if the things I perceived are real or not. If they are, even though we just met, please know I'll help in any way I can."

They finished their drinks and Jacob paid the check. "Are you staying close by or at one of the motels on the outskirts of town?"

"Actually, I'm at Tyndall's Bed & Breakfast. So much has changed. I mean, it's hard to reconcile the town I grew up in *has* a B&B," she said as they exited the restaurant.

"It's even changed a lot since I arrived. Tourism has boomed since the Civil War history buffs focused on the town. Though it's only two blocks, I'd be happy to give you a lift."

"No thanks. I think I'd just like to walk." She extended her hand. "It was a pleasure to meet you and thanks again for the wine. It topped the evening off."

Jacob watched her stroll away. *Wow! Be still my heart.* So work oriented over the years, he'd arrived at the ripe age of thirty-two without a hint of female companionship he'd always believed God would send.

He'd dated here and there...and been told on many occasions of his 'most desired bachelor' status. However eligible he might've been perceived, somehow his heart hadn't responded like he thought it should have. In the space of the last three hours, however, that had completely changed. *Calli Winson, I sure pray you don't leave tomorrow.*

The sun beaming through the open curtains awoke Calli. Exhausted when she'd arrived at the B&B last night, she'd washed her face and brushed her teeth before climbing into the big four-poster—literally climbed. The bedroom reminded her of something straight out of a historical tale. Everything looked ancient, especially the antique dresser with a washbasin and pitcher.

She leaned up on one elbow and peered out the window. The mountains rose majestically in the distance. It augured a perfectly clear day; one where she could stand at the peak of her favorite mountain and almost see tomorrow. But, the future wasn't her objective. She was searching for yesterday. *What a contradiction*, she thought—at work, I'm adept at reconstructing other civilizations; in my own life I'm an abysmal failure at doing so.

Sliding off the bed, she padded into the bathroom and stared in the mirror. Now girl, you have got to be honest with yourself. You didn't just hop into bed last night and go to sleep. And your thoughts weren't on getting up today and heading for the train station. Nor were they on finding out about your past. They were on the young preacher man.

While not the most handsome man she'd ever seen, Jacob Isaacs had rugged good looks. Surprisingly physically fit for a preacher, which occupation didn't fit with his calloused hands. Wonder why he isn't married with several kids? Well, stupid me. Maybe he is. We never talked about his family. She'd just assumed! What was the saying one of her professors had? Oh yeah! *Never assume, or you could make an 'ass' of 'u' and 'me.'* Inquire if you want to know for certain. Hmm...she'd best keep it in mind.

Calli ate breakfast in the dining room. "I'll be back for my things shortly," she told the owner. "I'm going for a walk."

Mrs. Tyndall called after her. "Whatever time you check out is fine, dear. There's no hurry since I don't have other guests arriving until the weekend."

Dressed in red linen cropped pants and a white, Tommy Hilfiger cotton tee, she headed toward the center of town. The train didn't leave until two.

A half hour later she swung around a corner on the fringe of the main drag and pulled up short. Across the street a large sign read: 'Allenvale Community Christian Church.' Next to the old, antebellum chapel, new construction was rising. Hammering emanated from within.

She crossed the street and approached the new

building—triple the size of the old church. She walked up steps, which appeared recently poured, and headed toward the source of the noise. Wandering through several rooms she came to the main church area. Jacob stood upon a ladder almost twenty feet in the air, pounding nails into crossbeams. So, this was the origin of his physique. He had on jeans and a tee shirt. Even from the distant vantage point, she saw the well-toned biceps. Her heart skipped several beats as she watched him wield the hammer.

She'd never been attracted to any lone aspect of a person—although she appreciated solitary attributes. But Jacob was one well-rounded individual: intelligent, sensitive, and physically attractive. No single man had ever appealed to her on such a scale.

"Hey," she yelled, not wanting to startle him. He hadn't heard her. She walked to the far side of the ladder and jumped up and down waving her arms.

Jacob couldn't get the pretty blonde with the beautiful eyes off his mind. He'd tossed during the night, a rare event. Usually when he hit the sack it was lights out. He seldom remembered dreaming.

Last night was a different story. Every few hours he'd awakened, Calli's image before him. He wanted to erase the sadness from those intense, blue eyes. Normally, he didn't hesitate to tell someone about the Lord. In her case, however, he sensed she'd think he was spouting platitudes. He'd seek a different way to approach her—and had no doubt he'd see her again.

Something caught his eye and he glanced down. Calli was a few feet away from the bottom of the ladder acting like the donkey in 'Shrek.' He broke out in laughter and had to grab the ladder to keep from toppling backward. Scrambling down he skipped the last few rungs and jumped in front of her.

"Hello." He grinned from ear to ear and wiped his face with a red and white handkerchief pulled from a rear pocket. "I figured you'd be on your way back to the big city by now. But I'm glad you aren't."

"Well, my train doesn't leave until two. I wanted to take a

walk around town and see the changes." She sauntered around the huge room, gazing at the newly finished work. "Who helps you with the building?"

He laughed. "Mostly my ineptitude. Church members pitch in when they can, usually on weekends." He glanced around. "Today there are two other guys working here somewhere." He didn't see his friends. "They must be taking a break or something."

"It's quite an undertaking to do this mostly by yourself."

"You want some coffee, or tea? Or maybe a soda?" he asked, wiping his face again.

"Sure. I could use something cold, thanks," Calli quickly accepted.

"Follow me." Jacob walked in the direction of the back of the new construction. He nimbly vaulted off the end of a concreted area about five feet to the ground, then turned and reached up to assist Calli. She sat on the edge and slid down into his opened arms. He held onto her long after she'd steadied from the jump.

Hitting the ground, a jolt shot through her; however, it wasn't from the impact of the earth beneath her feet. In fact, she barely knew she'd touched dirt. Falling into Jacob's arms rendered an electrical shock similar to one she'd received when a coworker who'd bought a home defibrillator for his mother wanted her to touch it to see what it felt like. One of the few unwise things she'd ever done. Come to think of it, it was called 'Heart Start'—a relevant term for what had just happened.

He released her, grabbed her hand and started across the lawn, pulling her along. She matched his stride. He ran into the rear entrance of the house adjacent to the church property. She recalled this had been an empty lot.

Jacob entered a kitchen and closed the door behind him. Then he turned and pulled her toward him. With one arm wrapped around her, he peered into her eyes. He tenderly caressed her cheek with the back of his fingers, tucking a strand of hair behind her ear.

She involuntarily quivered and closed her eyes. A feathery sensation coursed through her as though she'd been brushed by angel wings.

"You're a beautiful woman, Calli Winson," he uttered in a deep, throaty whisper. "Although that's not the only reason I couldn't stop thinking about you last night."

Calli's heart sang. *He thought about me last night.* If he were to let go, she'd sink to the floor. Words wouldn't form in her mouth because she was unable to part her lips. That is, until Jacob's lips parted them for her. It was the gentlest way she'd ever been kissed, and simultaneously earthshaking. She reached her arms up around him and held him tighter, moving into his hard, muscled body.

Reluctantly, Jacob relinquished her lips. "Lord, if I'm dreaming, please don't wake me."

Still atingle, Calli responded, "Me neither."

Jacob released her and she grabbed the counter to steady herself. He stepped to the refrigerator and pulled out a container. "Oh, I forgot...we also have fresh lemonade." He held it up for her approval. "Squeezed this morning," he coaxed. When she nodded, he put ice in two glasses and poured the opaque liquid, little bits of lemon sticking to the cubes as they floated to the top. He placed them on a bistro table in the corner and swept his arm toward one of the stools for her to take a seat. Sitting across from her, he took one of her hands in his.

"Calli, I think I'd better tell you..."

She abruptly pulled her hand away and sat straight. "Oh great! You're married!"

Unable to control the laughter that bubbled, he let it rip. "God, no!"

"You have something against marriage?" Calli retorted.

"No, Calli. Wait. We're getting on a wrong track here. What I want to say is no woman has ever affected me the way you have. I don't go around grabbing women and laying a kiss on them. Far from it. And, yes, I believe wholeheartedly in marriage. Until death do us part—the whole nine yards."

"So, why haven't you ever married? How old are you, thirty-five?"

"No. I'm thirty-two," Jacob replied, uncertain why she

was being so defensive. "And I just haven't met the right woman I want to spend the rest of my life with."

"Oh." She placed an elbow on the table, picked up the glass and took a big swallow of the cold liquid. She slipped off the stool. "Well, I'd better be heading out if I'm going to catch my train. Thanks for the lemonade," she said stiffly.

Jacob was off his stool in a flash. "Hey, what happened? Why did you pull away from me?"

She turned her back to him, tears welling in her eyes. She had no answer to either question. It's how she reacted to anyone who tried to get close, and it didn't matter how she examined it, she couldn't figure it out.

Gently, Jacob placed his hands on her shoulders and turned her around. "Why did you come to see me, Calli?"

"There's something I want to explain. I don't know why...I just feel the need for you to understand me."

"Please sit. Tell me what's on your heart."

His words penetrated to her innermost being. No one had ever shown a desire to know those secret places she guarded with such ferocity. Her parents had, of course; but by the time she was busting out of her teenage rebellious years, they were gone. How she missed them. She feared they never really knew how much she loved them.

"You asked why I didn't stay here, the place where I was raised, longer than a day. My memories here aren't happy ones."

Jacob leaned back in the stool, his eyes never leaving her face.

"I didn't find this out until I was seven. The kids at school seemed to take great delight in calling me names. They'd tell me I was dirty and other things I won't repeat. Yet, I'd look in the mirror and see blonde hair neatly cut, my body and clothes clean. Mom always dressed me well. So what made me different from them? Then I looked closer at the other children's parents and noticed the resemblances—a little boy would favor his dad, a girl her mother, or maybe a little of both. I looked nothing like my parents. I came home one day crying and Mom took me in her arms and asked what was wrong."

Calli stopped talking, left her seat and refilled her lemonade. After taking a long drink, it calmed the choking sob threatening to escape.

"'Why do I look so different from you and Daddy?' I cried. Thinking back on it now, I would do anything to retract those words. Although I didn't realize it at the time, my mom was a deeply compassionate person. She said to me, 'Calli, sweetheart, when people make fun and belittle others, it's usually to mask their own fears.' Then she hugged me and said we'd talk about it when Daddy got home."

Although Calli was sitting directly in front of Jacob, staring into his eyes, she'd stepped from the present into the past.

"When Daddy arrived from work, we sat in the living room. I was on Daddy's lap, Mom cuddled beside us. Then they told me how someone had left me at the IGA store in a basket. The police never found out who. Mom had been leaving the store after buying groceries. She said, 'I almost tripped over you, all snuggled down into a wicker basket. I looked up and down the street—no one was around. It was early in the morning and my car was the only one in the lot, except for the IGA employees. I sat my bags down and picked you up and went inside. The manager called the police. Your daddy and I volunteered to keep you until your parents were located. Needless to say, they never were. And by then we'd become attached to you. No, we'd fallen in love with you.' I knew they loved me. They were wonderful—I couldn't have asked for better parents. From then on though, I couldn't get over my biological parents having abandoned me. And Mom said the only clue inside the basket was a note with the word Calliope, printed in block letters—"

"Did you say Calliope?" Jacob asked, suddenly leaning forward in his chair.

"Yes. They thought it must have been my name and it's what they called me. One of the nine Muses is called Calliope and there's the local music referred to as Calliope. So, I've always wondered about my name."

"You said your parents were killed in an auto accident?"

Calli nodded. "Yeah. It was right before I turned eighteen, a week after I graduated high school. A logging truck had been on the highway and for some reason lost control and hit them head on. They were gone instantly. The logger flipped his eighteen-wheeler and was pinned in. They had to dig him out and he lost one of his legs in the process. He was never the same and not just because he was an amputee. During the investigation he was so pitiful. He told me, more than once, he wished he'd died instead of my parents. I didn't stay around long afterward. I moved, worked my way through college and stayed away from the things that had hurt me. But they still haunt me."

"I know the cemeteries around here fairly well, Calli. I don't recall any Winson's buried in any of them."

Calli walked to the door and twisted the knob. She turned to face him. "No, Jacob. It's because their names are Sara and Andrew Windsong; they're Native Americans." She slowly exited and quietly pulled the door closed.

Jacob wanted to run after her and ask why she'd changed her name. But it was unnecessary. He'd known too many people who'd tried to escape their past. Thank God Calli hadn't turned to alcohol, or drugs, or some other form of self-flagellation.

Cranking the Cherokee, Jacob immediately drove to the post office. "Is Marilyn here?" he asked Hank, the postal employee at the window.

"Yeah, Jacob. Wait a sec."

Marilyn Potts had been the Postmistress for the past five years. She'd arrived shortly after Jacob had moved to Allenvale and they'd become close friends. Her husband, whom she'd been married to for twenty-five years, had died a decade ago.

"Hiya, Jacob," her bubbly voice called as she rounded the corner. "What can I do for you?"

"Can we go into your office and talk?"

"Sure thing." She turned and flagged him her way.

He followed, closing the door behind him. "Marilyn, remember the letter you got from Pittsburgh several years ago? The one addressed to the Allenvale Postmaster and you said others had arrived previously simply addressed 'Calliope.'"

"Yeah, I sure do. Don't hardly forget something like that. Why? What's this about?"

"Bear with me a few minutes. Do you still have them?"

"Yep. You sit right there. I'll be back in a jiffy." Re-entering the office, she said, "Here they are." She handed several envelopes to Jacob.

"It's okay if I look at them?"

"Definitely. I've already told you about them and they're just dead letters at this point."

He removed the one on top—the one he was most interested in. Postmarked December, 2001, it was addressed in beautiful penmanship to: Postmaster, c/o Allenvale Post Office, Allenvale, Pennsylvania with the zip code. He glanced at Marilyn and turned the envelope over, removing the single sheet of paper. In the same handwriting was written:

Dear Postmaster,

I know this is a strange letter you're receiving. It's equally strange for me to be writing it. Approximately 25 years ago a baby was left in your town in a basket. I learned about what I'm going to relate approximately three years ago. I've sent several letters, hoping in a town as small as yours they'd find their way to the person to whom they were intended. Evidently they didn't. Now I'm writing to you, personally, in hope of discovering the whereabouts of my twin sister, Calliope Denton.

As I said, I only became privy to this information three years ago when I was located by my maternal aunt. I also had been left in a basket here in Pittsburgh, obviously a much larger city. Not that there's a good side to babies being left in baskets, but my being in Pittsburgh, where there are adoption records, led to my aunt being able to locate me.

If you know of a young woman approximately 25 years of age in your area named Calliope, I would appreciate you giving her this letter in hope she will contact me.

Thank you for your kind consideration.

It was signed—Cassandra (Denton) Hughes.

There was a Pittsburgh return address.

"Marilyn, didn't you tell me you inquired around town and then responded to the letter saying you hadn't been able to locate anyone named Calliope in Allenvale, and you didn't know of any Dentons?"

"Yep. I even asked the retired Postmaster. He didn't know of anyone named Calliope, nor any Dentons, either. Of course, the town was much smaller then. Well, not when he retired, but twenty-five years ago. It's tripled in size over the last ten years because of the pre-Civil War history and reconstruction. Are you going to clue me in on what's going on Jacob?"

"Not quite yet." Jacob pulled a pen and paper from his jacket and wrote Cassandra's name and address. "Hopefully, this lady will be able to solve the mystery." He replaced the letter in the envelope and handed it back.

He hopped into the Jeep and drove to the nearest gas station—topped the tank. Pittsburgh was two and a half hours away. He'd be able to get there and back before dark. If everything panned out as he thought, he hoped it would fulfill some of Calli's longings. If she went home—well, he'd have to find her in Maryland.

Pittsburgh was like any big city—too many people, too much traffic. He appreciated Allenvale all the more. Locating the address in a modest suburban area, he pulled his vehicle into the driveway. He walked up to the front stoop—a small roof protected a little red wagon and tricycle parked neatly side-by-side. Jacob rang the doorbell. He glanced around the yard and turned as he heard the door open. Calli stood there with a baby on one hip, a toddler tugging at her aproned skirt from behind.

"Can I help you?" she asked, a big smile curling her lightly glossed lips.

"Uh...you must be Cassandra," Jacob said, astonished at the identical likeness.

"Yes, I am." She tilted her head trying to draw a memory. "Do I know you?"

"No, Cassandra, you don't. My name is Jacob Isaacs—I'm from Allenvale, and I know your sister, Calli."

He had to reach a hand toward the baby as Cassandra

turned ashen. She brought the hand not holding the baby up to her mouth, which had formed into the shape of an O. Her eyes filled with tears. “Oh, thank you, Lord. Please, Mr. Isaacs, come in.”

She ran over and put the baby in a playpen and brushed her hands off, extending one heartily toward Jacob.

“Please have a seat and tell me how you know Calli. Is she well? Oh, my gosh. I don’t mean to be running on. And you’re not going to believe this. I was standing in my backyard last night and there was the biggest moon—I think it’s called a blue moon when it comes around twice in a month. Anyway, I prayed the same prayer I’ve spoken before. That God would show me how to find Calli. Listen to me just rattling on and not giving you a chance to talk. Please tell me everything about her.”

Jacob pulled up in front of Tyndall’s B&B around six that evening. He ran into the main room looking for Mrs. Tyndall. Much to his surprise, there sat Calli in the prettiest yellow sundress. His first thought *what a vision of loveliness*. She had on white high heels and was just staring at him as though willing him to appear in the doorway. Her legs were crossed—and *what lovely legs they are*, he thought since it was the first time he’d actually seen them—one leg swinging back and forth as though she’d been sitting there waiting for him for hours.

Which, he learned later, she had.

“What?” Jacob said. “You didn’t catch the two o’clock train?”

“Well, if you thought I’d left, what are you running in here for?” she taunted, a bright smile revealing glistening teeth between radiant, painted pink lips.

“I...uh...have something to tell you. No, I have something to show you,” he stuttered. “I think you’ll be happy about it. It may not answer all your questions, Calli, but I hope—in time—you’ll be at peace.”

“What the heck are you talking about Jacob Isaacs? I stayed in town and I’ve been waiting for hours. You come traipsing in here wanting to pull me off somewhere, without so much as being surprised I’m still here.” She stood and crossed her arms under her breasts.

"Calli, I'm ecstatic. It saves me a trip to Washington, D.C."

She looked more bewildered as he bent and kissed her lightly on the lips. Then he unhooked her arm and led her out the door to the Cherokee.

Traveling the short distance to his house, he pulled into his driveway and killed the ignition.

He swiveled and took her hands into his. "Calli, honey, I want you to take a deep breath before we go inside—"

Before he could finish, Cassandra came running out his front door. She pulled the car door open and practically yanked Calli out of the car hugging her and crying.

"Cassandra, wait...I haven't had a chance to explain," Jacob tried to intervene.

She wasn't paying attention. Years of searching had culminated in this joyful reunion. "Calli, I'm your sister. Your twin sister."

Calli was as stunned at the revelation as Cassandra had been when Jacob informed her he knew her sister. Both women were crying alligator-sized tears and jumping around hugging each other as if they hadn't seen each other for years...which, of course, they hadn't. In fact, they'd been nine months old the last time they'd laid eyes on each other.

Inside Jacob's house, Cassandra related to Calli as best she could about their separated years.

Still in shock, Calli paced the living room. "All right. So, what you're saying, is your Aunt Faith—I guess our Aunt Faith—was able to locate you. She told you our mother, Margaret Denton, had discovered shortly after we were born, that her father—our grandfather—had sexually abused both his daughters—Faith and Margaret."

"Yes," Cassandra said, shaking her head. "Totally disgusting."

"How did she not know this before?" Calli questioned.

Cassandra wrinkled her brow. "I don't understand it all, either. Something about repressed memories when traumatic events occur and then another traumatic event, in this instance, she found out she was dying, brings it to the surface."

Calli shook her head. "Okay, we'll find out more about it later. So Margaret—Mom—discovered she was terminally ill with less than a year to live. Her husband—our father—Jonathan Denton, a colonel in the military, was killed in a training accident right before we were born."

Again, Cassandra nodded.

"...And to make sure we'd never be abused by our grandfather"—Calli continued—"she decided to hide us somewhere he'd never find us. She couldn't involve Aunt Faith because...he would've coerced her into talking."

"Yeah," Cassandra said. "She took you to Allenvale and me to Pittsburgh, from Philadelphia, hoping it was far enough away. I guess we should thank God there wasn't an Amber Alert in those days or he might have found us."

"I suppose." Calli couldn't believe it. All of the haunting questions answered in the space of twenty-four hours. And a bonus of a twin sister, a brother-in-law, a nephew, a niece, and an aunt. And then there was...she turned to Jacob. "I've whined all these years about *my* life...our poor mother. What a wimp I've been. Jacob, how did you figure all this out?"

"Ah...inquiring minds want to know," he chided. "Before I answer that question, I have one of my own."

Taking several short steps he pulled Calli into his arms. "Calliope Denton Windsong Winson...I don't know how things can happen in such a short time span, but I know what I know. And the one thing I'm most certain about is...I love you."

Then he turned to Cassandra. "I'm an old-fashioned kind of guy and as Calli's closest living relative...well, I guess there is Aunt Faith, however, she's not here right now...I'd like to ask for your sister's hand in marriage. That is, if she'll have me."

Cassandra looked at Calli. "Isn't this kind of sudden?"

"I suppose it is," Calli agreed. "Yet, if I'm going to share that acre on the moon with him, I suppose I'll have to accept."

Jacob and Cassandra stared at her and said in unison,

"What acre on the moon?"

"The one I bought online today. I had it deeded to you and I certainly don't know the directions to get there."

Cassandra's eyes cut to her sister. "You're going to be in trouble, sister dear, if you head for a place you both don't know how to get to. Cause he'll never stop and ask directions!"

After Cassandra lavished kisses and hugs on her sister, and not too few on Jacob, she obtained a promise he would bring Calli to Pittsburgh tomorrow. Then she left to return home.

Jacob's hand snuggled Calli's waist as they waved goodbye. Cassandra tapped the horn in a quick bye-bye toot.

He pulled Calli inside and kissed her—deeply and intimately—then held her at arm's length, enjoying the image before him. "We can't let this lady get all dolled up with nowhere to go, now, can we?"

"It's unnecessary, Jacob. I'm happy just being with you."

"Oh, yes, it's definitely necessary. I'm hungry and your tummy's been growling for the last hour. Besides, I want to show my pretty lady off." He glanced at his watch. It was almost ten.

He stepped to the telephone and dialed. "Sam, this is Jacob...Yeah, hi. Listen I have a favor to ask..." He turned and whispered into the phone. Then he dialed another number.

"Let's go, beautiful one." He grabbed her elbow and led her out the door.

He stopped in front of The Hermitage Inn—an old, restored and renovated estate—the town's most prestigious restaurant. The maitre d' met them at the door and ushered them to a private area of the large dining room. There were only a few patrons at this late hour; all knew Jacob and spoke to him.

Once seated at a sumptuously appointed candle-lit table, the waiter immediately brought over a bottle of Beringer 2001 Private Reserve. "Compliments of the management." He opened the bottle for Jacob to sample.

"Everything else is in order Mr. Isaacs. Let us know when you're ready."

Jacob picked up his wineglass, but Calli intervened. "I want to do the toast this time, if it's okay."

"Of course, sweetheart."

Tears welled in Calli's eyes as she stared at the fiery red

liquid. Her mouth had gone dry and she tugged at her upper lip to stanch the flood of emotions.

"I don't know where to begin." A lone tear escaped, trickling down her cheek. "My entire life has been in pursuit of my origins. Since meeting you, Jacob, I've learned not to look backward, but forward. To believe in my hopes and dreams for the future and live for today. I thank you, Dear Jacob, for the good news you've brought and promise to reciprocate in love and devotion."

"I'll drink to that." He clinked his glass to hers. They gazed into each other's eyes as they sipped. Jacob's heart overflowed with joy as he knew it was only the beginning of the Good News he would share with this enchanting woman.

After the main course, the waiter served small, sweet strawberries in a twinkling, crystal compote—each bright red tip dipped in decadent dark-brown chocolate. Jacob retrieved one and brought it to Calli's lips. She bit into it and accidentally nipped the tips of his fingers. They laughed and Calli grabbed her mouth to capture the red juice flowing from the berry. Then she fed one to Jacob.

Calli had never been happier, and for the last time, she mourned the lost years. She vowed never again to be self-absorbed and instead to learn to be as giving as Jacob.

At the last strawberry, Calli insisted on feeding it to him. She lifted it from the dish and did a double-take. Under the succulent, juicy red fruit, a diamond ring glistened and sparkled from the dancing rays emitted by the candles. She dropped the berry as Jacob nimbly plucked the sphere between his fingers.

He moved from his seat and knelt beside her. "Calli, will you marry me?"

With unbridled ecstasy, her heart burst as she reached out amid tears and embraced him. "Oh yes, yes I will."

Visit Patty's website
http://www.pattyghowell.com

Blue Moon Reunion

by Gerri Bowen

Sir Edwyn cleared his throat preparing to speak. Piper listened whilst her gaze remained on the rising moon rather than on the besieging army sprawled below, outside Escewiche's walls. "My Aunt Elizabeth tells a story of how she once wished on a blue moon. But the tale is a cautionary one. She wished for her love to return to her. He did."

Piper looked at her seneschal. She'd heard this story afore. "...But he returned with another woman as his wife. Thus, be careful for what you wish."

Edwyn nodded. "But her wish did come true, My Lady, that is the point. Choose your words well."

"Is it?" Piper huffed softly and pulled her mantle tight against the brisk breeze buffeting them upon the battlements. "I thought the moral was we wish for what cannot be." She shrugged. "If I were to wish, obviously I would wish for those men to depart, never to return. Or any other besiegers." *But there would be other besiegers. Other men ready to take Escewiche. Ready to claim her as wife, willing or no.*

"Might you also wish for a man, My Lady? A strong warrior? With many knights of his own? Someone to..."

Piper's raised brow silenced the man. She rolled her eyes and looked out over the battlements. "A man. I have *had* a man, Sir Edwyn. Three, in fact. The first was Sir Robin, my *dearest* betrothed. Sir Robin who abandoned me, then had the unfortunate fate to get himself killed. Then his cousin, Sir Nigel. When he could not find me, he wed Robin's mother. When he did find me, he wed me to *another* cousin, Sir Unger. When Unger was killed and Robin's mother dead,

Nigel wed me." She turned to Edwyn. "Two years he kept me locked away. Two years! Yet you suggest I wish for a strong man? A warrior? To do what? Take what doesn't belong to him because I haven't the physical strength to best him on the field?"

"Not all men are like Sir Nigel and Sir Unger, My Lady. If you recall, it was the notion of treasure hidden in these walls that obsessed Sir Nigel, caused his madness. Robin was not like them. Our Robin was a true knight, the best of all men."

Robin. He *had* been her dearest love—long ago, when she still believed in love. Before he abandoned her. She raised her head to the moon. "I would wish for a man like Robin. But alive. In good health. Not a weakling, for I would despise him within the hour. Nor a tyrant, for he would be dead by nightfall. In all things, a man like Robin." *Except he won't abandon me.* She nodded. "I shall do it."

Edwyn expelled a breath. "Praise be. Be sure to include a right good amount of men under him, too. With food aplenty."

Sir Robin of Escewiche's wrists were chained together and his hands secured to his saddle. His guards kept him in the middle of their escort. He looked up at the full moon as he rode and wondered if his new cell would have a window. He thought not. Most didn't. Nor would he waste a wish for one. Nay, his wish—his *only* wish these past years—was for revenge against the one who had caused his imprisonment. His betrothed. Lady Piper of Auban. *The bitch.*

Robin stared at the moon, the second full moon for the month, and decided he had naught to lose by wishing. "I wish for my release anon. A rescue by allies. A speedy return to Escewiche. And Piper. Soon." No quicker had he uttered his wish, than the stars brightened, blinked rapidly and the moon turned blue. *Damnation. I should have wished for more.*

Piper rushed to the battlements to see for herself if the astonishing report was true. Aye, she could see a large swell of men advancing. Couldn't make out their banner.

"Praise be to God! The siege is broken!"

Even though Piper wanted to echo her seneschal's prayer, how did they know the troops advancing were friendly? "Can you make out..." She leaned forward and then whooped with joy. "Do you see? 'Tis the Auban banner! My brothers have come! They have come!"

She and Edwyn linked arms and danced until Piper recalled the men below would be leaving. There were a few things she wanted to tell them before they turned tail and ran. Looking to the far hill, she saw Sir Geoffrey and his men still camped—waiting to swoop in and claim Escewiche. Her eyes narrowed. Be damned, but she had a few things to say to that scoundrel as well. And say them she would, now her brothers had come.

She sounded a veritable shrew. Robin's helmet remained on his head, but he could hear. Where had she learned such words? Damnation, but she made *him* blush. Just as well he heard her true voice before she realized who rode with her brothers. 'Twas good Peter and Dunstan, her brothers, were there to hear her as well—haps they might now believe him. They'd laughed at his tale, refused to believe their sweet, innocent sister behind his imprisonment.

Looking like a witch, she shrieked and stalked about the battlements. Was she taller? Nay, thinner. He could believe the stories he was hearing. Snatches about the witch inside, how she was able to draw strange creatures to Escewiche, how she'd murdered Sir Nigel. The question of how the people inside had survived without food if not by her witchcraft.

Robin said naught, but listened. He wanted none to know he'd returned until the bitch faced him. Then he'd remove his helmet. Watch her face when she realized he was free from the imprisonment she'd set for him. And then he'd...Robin wasn't sure what he'd do. Strangling was his first choice. A knife to her black heart—if she had one—would satisfy just as well. He doubted her brothers would allow him such freedom, however. Not until they were convinced of her guilt.

His patience wore thin as he waited for the letter from the king to be read aloud, passed, discussed, and all agreed the besiegers no longer had reason to remain. Sir Robin of

Escewiche was not dead, the letter explained. He would travel here soon they were assured and would deal with the murdering witch inside when he returned.

Finally the gate was opened, the portcullis raised. Robin had to fight the urge to ride ahead and instead rode behind her brothers. He was grateful of his helmet, for the sight of his beloved home, a sight he never expected to see, unexpectedly raised water to his eyes. No doubt caused by the lump lodged in his throat.

Piper made her way to the bailey, Edwyn close, both running when they passed the last step. She absently noted how the bailey would seem to those newly admitted. But she'd like to know how she was supposed to have kept all inside alive if she hadn't reduced the inner and outer bailey to field and garden? God's bones, she'd all but whored herself to keep the people of Escewiche fed!

"Peter! Dun!" she cried as she launched herself at her brothers. "Where have you been? It was ages ere I sent for you!" She laughed, tears running down her cheeks. She didn't care. She laughed again. It was over!

Frenzied words and much laughter later, she learned neither had received the missives she'd sent. Peter had been forced to flee to Wales because of a trumped up charge of treason. Dunstan, too, had hidden himself at Penclyst, charged with a murder he'd not committed. Both, everyone was pleased to hear, were cleared of all charges. And in full favor of the king—for what that was worth at the moment.

"How did you know to come?" Piper asked, touching their faces as if to assure herself they were truly here.

Peter and Dunstan looked at one another and then looked behind them, to the man still wearing his helmet. They stepped to the side and the helmeted man stepped forward.

Robin saw Piper's lips part as she stared at him. Saw her draw back her golden hair from her face. *Bitch*. He kept reminding himself she was a perfidious bitch. So her joy at seeing her brothers appeared unfeigned. Haps she *was* gladdened to see them. She had been under siege, after all. But *what* in God's name had she done to his bailey?

He straightened and raised his hands to remove his helmet. Voices grew quieter. Slowly he removed his helmet, lifted it off and flung it away. His gaze swooped onto her face. He saw her eyes widen. Her face blanched. Her lips move soundlessly. Ah! She was shocked to see him! Yet the satisfaction he expected to feel wasn't there. Her words, when they came, were whispered.

"You're supposed to be dead."

The wish had brought him back to life.

That was her first thought. Her wish had brought him back to life!

But nay, she could see he was alive, was real. His dark hair and blue eyes were just as she remembered. She heard the murmurings grow to a swell as all in the bailey saw their master return to them alive. It was as if someone else had stepped forward and slapped their palm against his cheek. And uttered the words, *uncaring bastard*. Yet the second time her unruly hand made to swing itself at his face, her wrist was caught. That was when Piper knew she'd been the one to slap him. And then the twins descended.

"Robin! You've come to save us!"

Piper turned and glared at the two ungrateful brats. They ignored her and flung themselves onto their brother.

"Look at what she has done to us!" cried Emma.

"And we've been hidden with the *goats*!" Alice sniveled.

Disgusted, Piper rolled her eyes. So she'd cut their hair—it would regrow. She'd made them dress as boys—easily changed. And, she'd decreed their skin be rubbed with dirt and dung to disguise their sex and their beauty—now they could bathe. None had ever discerned their true identity, had they? She'd kept the twins safe and untouched as Lady Elizabeth, their mother, had requested, hadn't she?

Piper looked at Robin and stepped back from the look on his face. "I—"

"Say not a word, Lady Piper." He looked at the people gathered 'round. "It is I, Robin of Escewiche, returned to you. I am come to resume my rightful place. To see wrongs are righted. To punish those who have done wrong to mine own."

Piper allowed a small smile to play on her lips. Ah, she'd like to see Robin have a go at Sir Geoffrey. Her eyes widened slightly when she heard his last pronouncement. She was to *what?*

Peter and Dunstan protested loudly, but Robin had expected such. "You knew from the beginning I was aware of her treachery. Why now protest when I place her under guard?"

"You have no—" Peter began.

"You haven't heard—" Dunstan said.

"She is evil, Robin!" said Alice.

"She wants Sir Geoffrey for herself. And you know he was promised to me!" Emma whimpered, her lips quivering.

Robin held his sisters to his chest and stared narrow-eyed at Piper. *You're supposed to be dead.* Her first words had condemned her. "She will answer for each and every offence."

As the guard locked her in the cell, Piper had tried to smile at him. She'd tried to show she knew he had no choice but to follow Robin's orders. But God's bones, it was hard to smile when she felt her world crashing down on her. She'd tried for so long to protect Escewiche, and all those inside her walls. It hadn't been easy. Nor had it been a responsibility she'd asked for. God's bones, she'd come for the summer, to further her acquaintance with his family! Who would have thought when Robin rode out one day he'd never return? But she'd done what she thought was best. She'd kept most alive. How dare he gainsay her? Just because he appeared after she and everyone else thought him dead these three years... Appeared with no explanation and put her in a cell. A cell!

Piper looked around her prison and felt warm tears brim over her eyes. Well. She was due a good cry.

Robin smiled and raised his cup and laughed with good cheer. He was determined to be happy. He was free, he was back at Escewiche where he belonged. The bitch was locked away. Peter and Dunstan, he saw, did not smile or laugh. Edwyn sat and stared into his cup, or else stared at him, awaiting his chance to speak.

Emma and Alice sat on either side of him at the high table. They laughed with abandon and giggled over the plight of Lady Piper. He assumed they thought he would appreciate their humor. He didn't. As much as he wanted to find fault with the bitch...he couldn't smile over the fact she was sharing a dark cell with rats and vermin. Why was there a niggle of guilt over where she was? She'd brought it on herself.

She'd looked thin; gaunt. So did all his people. The extra food he brought wouldn't last long—these people were near starving. He was given to believe as each platter was thumped before him, each by a different servant, that Lady Piper managed to procure a goat and cow as needed, seeds for planting. How she stood firm in their daily allotment of food, even giving a portion of her share to new mothers—how she'd kept all from starving. It was *not* what he wanted to hear. He wanted to hear how selfish she'd been, not how noble.

Ah! Of course she would've wanted those at Escewiche to survive. If all died of starvation, who would serve her? She needed them alive—'twas all it was.

Except, Robin couldn't help but note, these people, *his* people, appeared to resent the fact she was imprisoned. He snorted softly to himself. They didn't know the truth about her. They'd change their minds once they heard of her treachery to their lord.

"Where have you been, Robin?" asked Emma. "Why did you stay away for so long?"

"Everyone said you were dead," said Alice.

Robin leaned back in his chair. Just the opening he needed. "Three years ago, on our way to London, my men and I were attacked. I was taken prisoner and held." Robin noted the silence his words produced.

"But who..." Alice began.

You're supposed to be dead. "I never learned who attacked us. I suspect I know why I was kept alive, hidden, and moved from cell to cell. What I do know is the identity of the one behind my capture—Lady Piper of Auban."

Piper sniffed and wiped her eyes with the palms of her hands. She felt better. A good, private cry always cleared her head. Now she could focus her attention on this latest disaster.

Why had he imprisoned her? Why hadn't she asked? God's bones, she'd been so shocked to see him, her mind went blank when she realized it was Robin come back. Then her foolish notion she'd wished him alive. She snorted loudly. She supposed she should have worded her wish differently. And ought not to have slapped him.

"Do you wish to come away with us now, Piper?"

She swung her head and focused on the direction of Terialis' voice. He was always quiet, stepping out from the Shadow. The cell was dark, but she could see the light that illuminated his body. If he allowed himself to be seen, most would call him elf, faery, or even angel. He was Dennene, as she herself was in small part Dennene. She sighed. "My brothers have come. I no longer have need for the Shadow."

Terialis gazed at her as he had when first she saw him after trying to escape Escewiche by entering the Shadow; his face blank, his eyes full of acceptance. He'd found her, brought her back from the terror of her first entry into that in-between world. Since then he'd assisted her, although Piper thought it was more like keeping watch on her, to make sure she didn't enter the Shadow alone. She smiled, but his expression didn't change. It never did—'twas said the Dennene had no emotions.

She lifted her hand onto his arm. "I thank you for all you have done for me, for all of Escewiche, that we survived. And you have kept me sane."

"Why do your brothers allow you to remain in a cell?"

Piper withdrew her hand and turned her face away. Leave it to a Dennene to ask a question one didn't want to answer, or could not. "I know not."

The tumult caused by his words died slowly. Peter and Dunstan had risen, as had Edwyn, to glare at him. All in the hall ceased shouting at one another, and now edged toward him, determined to speak their piece. It was clear he'd struck a nerve. Also obvious none believed him. Well, his sisters hooted with glee before repeating to him all the evil things Lady Piper had done to them.

"Silence!" shouted Sir Edwyn at the twins.

The hall grew quiet as Edwyn stood before Robin, his face flushed, his finger shaking at his sisters. "For shame! Nigh three years Lady Piper protected you two churlish girls. Hidden the two of you as boys, kept your identity from those who would have used you immodestly. *She* took on burden of those who invaded, after..." and here he swung to shake his finger at Robin, "after your body was brought back for burial!"

Robin's midsection felt as if he'd been hit hard. There had been a body? He shook his head. "Nay, 'twas Lady Piper—"

Edwyn continued as though Robin hadn't spoken. "None knew where you'd gone, or why. A month after you'd left, your body was returned by your cousin, Sir Nigel. After a month, you can imagine the state of the body. We saw and recognized your clothes, and were quick to bury you. As for Sir Nigel, who by his own words *miraculously* survived, once he entered Escewiche the man never left until he was carried out, dead, some months ago.

"Sir Nigel demanded Lady Piper wed him. He didn't care about her, he wanted Escewiche and the treasure he felt certain was hidden within these walls. She hid where he and his men couldn't find her. So Sir Nigel took your mother to wife instead. When Lady Piper was found she was forced to wed Sir Unger. Soon after, your mother was found dead at the foot of the stairs. Less than a sennight later Sir Unger was dead and Lady Piper was wed to Sir Nigel."

Edwyn leaned closer. "For near two years he kept Lady Piper locked away. In the beginning he beat her, to force her to tell him where the treasure was hidden. She said naught. We knew she'd never tell what she knew." He looked around the hall, pride showing plainly on his face. "We devised a plan to make Sir Nigel believe ghosts were haunting the walls, disturbed by his searches. We may also have put about Lady Piper was a witch. Sir Nigel believed us, for he stopped beating her. Although that may also have been due to the fact he became violently ill after each time he struck her.

When he finally died, his men were anxious to leave Escewiche."

Stunned, Robin sat silently, staring at Escewiche's seneschal, his fingers drumming the table. "None knew I traveled to London?" He shook his own head. Nay, Nigel was supposed to have returned to Escewiche to inform all where Robin had headed. Of course, he'd always suspected Nigel's part in the attack—he'd just assumed Piper was behind it as well. He shifted uneasily in his chair. To find Piper had been wronged as well as he... Robin didn't know if he could give up his sense of outrage, his anger at her.

"All believed I was dead?"

"Lady Piper took it hard, My Lord." Edwyn nodded. "We feared...she was young and delicate if you recall, and we feared..."

Robin remembered Piper as she'd been. An innocent, with soft curves and rosy, plump lips. Quiet, modest, with hazel eyes he never tired of studying. Very different from the shrieking shrew he'd seen earlier. But she had survived. And so had he.

"She doesn't deserve to be locked away, My Lord," said Edwyn.

"She tried to steal my betrothed away from me!" Emma declared.

Robin's brows arched and he looked at Edwyn.

"Sir Geoffrey," said Edwyn, with obvious distaste, "refused to aid us when we were besieged, unless concessions were granted him."

"Concessions?" Robin's eyes narrowed.

Edwyn stood tall. "Lady Piper refused. He came back with a counter offer. She accepted."

She accepted? "What was the counter offer?"

"I'm not aware of their entire agreement, but Sir Geoffrey would come to our aid only if it looked as if the besieging army would overcome us."

"You see?" said Emma. "If she would have allowed me to wed him, Sir Geoffrey would have gladly rendered assistance to Escewiche!"

Robin looked at his sister. Granted, she needed to bathe, clothe herself as a lady, and her hair was short, but still...other than their dowry, Emma and Alice would need a few more years before a man would find something to appreciate about them. Robin doubted Geoffrey's interest went beyond Escewiche. If the man had come to their aid, he wouldn't have departed, either. So, Piper had again come to their rescue.

Damnation. He'd wronged her. He'd have to apologize. Damnation.

"What about the treasure Sir Nigel was after?" asked Peter.

"He never found it," said Edwyn. "Lady Piper hid it well."

Robin's eyes widened. "Lady Piper *hid* it? She knew where it was?"

Edwyn nodded. "Told her first thing when they said you were dead. Thought it best."

"There *was* treasure?" asked Dunstan. "But you always said Piper was...your treasure."

Robin's brows snapped together, and he wondered if Dunstan might actually faint away; the man's face was white. "What's wrong?"

Dunstan looked as if trying to smile. "Well, bugger me blue, but I...I might have said something to your cousin Nigel about...your treasure here. But I meant Piper."

"Speaking of my sister," said Peter, "when will you release her?"

Robin knew it was time. *Damnation.* Never, in all the scenarios he'd created in his mind these three years past, had he expected he would have to apologize to her.

Piper shielded her eyes against the bright fire of the torch, and knew it was Robin come to her before she saw him. She'd reasoned out that her act of slapping him instead of welcoming him with smiles was why she was locked away. *Men!* She'd had enough of their emotional outbursts, illogical thoughts, not to mention their bullying. However, she hadn't expected it from Robin. 'Twas obvious he was a man no different from the rest. One had to be careful what one said around men—one never knew what would enrage them. Due to past experience, and no desire to sleep with the vermin, she knew what needed to be done. She rose to her feet and addressed his chest.

"I pray you forgive me for my earlier transgression, My Lord. I should have met you with a warmer welcome and...smiles." She moved her lips to what she hoped bore some resemblance to a smile. "My presence here is surely as distasteful to you as my being here is to me. Escewiche now has her lord, and all is well. I pray you not hold my brothers accountable for my...thoughtless actions, and allow us to be gone as soon as may be. Before dawn would suit."

Her lips refused to do more than bare her teeth—but she didn't care. She'd groveled sufficiently, hadn't she? Be damned to him if he expected more. She raised her chin and kept her gaze on his arm.

Silence didn't bother her. She found men needed these minutes to chase after thought so as to put them in order to make their simple sentences. Some never bothered, but bellowed the first vapid thing that sprang to mind.

"You would leave Escewiche?"

Piper kept her eyes from rolling. "I believe I just—"

"Wait. Did you know I was told 'twas you who was behind my imprisonment?"

Astonished, Piper's gaze jumped to Robin's face. "You were imprisoned? All that time?"

Robin hadn't known what he would say to her. Didn't know how she would receive him.

She had changed.

No longer the sweet, biddable girl he remembered. But then, hadn't his perception of her changed after he thought she'd caused his imprisonment? She had changed. Piper was now a woman. A strong woman. What some might call a shrew. He smiled at her, and his smile increased when her nostrils flared and her lips thinned. But she'd kept Escewiche from those who would have taken her. Kept his sisters safe. Fed his people. His eyes roamed her too thin body, rested on her nose. Saw her put her hand to cover it.

"It was broken," she said.

Robin's smile faded. It was time they spoke. Time she knew what had happened, what he had thought about her. And time for him to hear what she had gone through, too.

Piper listened to Robin's tale and then told her own.

He'd laughed when he heard she'd been told he'd gone to London to visit his mistress. He'd objected when she'd punched his jaw, but allowed that, aye, if true, would be worth such punishment.

She'd gaped at his mild response, but was quick to close her mouth and agree.

Both believed his head injury saved his life. Whoever originated the plan to capture him for information about the hidden treasure had decided to keep him alive when Piper couldn't be found. Piper was inordinately pleased when she learned he'd told his captors, when conscious, that Piper was his treasure. She didn't even mind that his words had caused all her misery.

"You are my treasure, Piper," said Robin. "Please don't leave Escewiche. Recall, if you will, when I departed you were my betrothed." He smiled. "You are a strong, fearless--"

"Nay, I am craven. I tried to escape, run from here." She shook her head and settled her gaze on the floor.

"But you did return. You saved—"

"I returned when reminded that my...my heritage does not allow one to run from duty." She remembered the disdain in Terialis' voice when he said it was her human blood that caused her to flee. Dennene blood, he informed her, was strong—Dennene never retreated from enemies. "I returned, aye, but I did not *want* to."

He took her hands in his and smiled. "Yet you did. I would wed you."

Piper's eyes brimmed over and she blinked her tears away. She shook her head. "I am no longer she, the girl you knew. I have been wed. Twice." She shook her head again. How could she explain her feelings of being defiled? Could not go to him as a bride. She doubted she could welcome his or any man's embrace without retching.

"Piper! I care not you have—"

"Nay!" She turned her head away when she saw him staring at her nose. Ah, God but she felt unclean. "Look elsewhere for a suitable bride."

"That is your final word?"

Piper nodded. "I will return to Auban with my brothers."

"The way I see it," said Robin, "we needs overwhelm her with our plans and lay waste to her doubts." He looked to her brothers and Edwyn to echo their agreement.

After he'd returned with Piper to the hall, he saw how well received she was. It fueled his determination to have her as wife. Piper had since retired to her chamber.

"Peter is head of the family," said Dunstan. "He'll order her to wed you."

Robin shook his head. "I don't want her ordered to wed me. I want her to agree to wed me."

Dunstan frowned. "The difference?" he asked as he looked at his brother.

Peter pursed his lips. "If Piper is opposed to—"

Robin grabbed Peter's arm as he leaned forward. "Piper is a woman. Women form the notion they must be virgins, untouched and innocent or they are unacceptable to a man. I want Piper."

"Why? Why when you were so quick to condemn her, to lock her in a cell and punish her." Peter held Robin's gaze. He leaned forward. "She would forgive you."

Robin shook his head. How to explain? "I have no desire to wed another. Piper... She is a woman, not an innocent to be sheltered, slowly exposed to life's harshness. I left her a child and have come back to a woman. A woman who cared for my people, my home, even though she thought poorly of me. A woman who survived because it is in her nature to do naught but survive. A woman I would do aught to consent to wed me. She has captured my heart. She is half of my soul."

Edwyn cleared his throat and frowned at the three men. "It would seem serious thought needs be given Sir Robin's plight."

Stilled by his words, Piper backed away and kept in the shadow of the hall. She hadn't meant to eavesdrop. Well, she had, once she heard what was being discussed, but she hadn't expected to hear Robin's declaration. He wanted her! She smiled and fanned herself with her hand. Then her smile faded. Was it true...or did Robin feign his desire for her because he knew she'd turn him down? Was it all just to show her brothers he wouldn't back out of his proposal? She smiled. What would Robin do if she *did* accept him? She giggled and then stopped. She'd not giggled in years. No reason.

"You accept me?"

Piper strove to keep her expression clear. "Aye, Robin. I accept you." She looked at Peter, ready to explain to her brother why Robin was backing out of their betrothal after such an impressive proposal. Instead she found herself grabbed around her waist and swung around until she was dizzy. And then there were congratulations from her brothers and Edwyn and the people of Escewiche. And then she was kissed.

She'd received wet and mushy touches of lips on her mouth and parts of her body she chose not to remember. But she'd never been kissed. Not as Robin kissed her now. When his lips touched hers, there was an answer from her lips, her entire body. She grinned at the thought she might turn wanton; not a bad thing, that. What with her mouth open, Robin stuck in his tongue.

It was, Piper thought, best that men held women tightly, else when their knees turned to water, the women would fall. With all that thought going on, Piper managed to stick her tongue inside Robin's mouth. She was pleased when he growled and made noises and pulled her closer. Not pleased when Peter pulled her away.

"She's accepted. Wait for the wedding," said Peter.

Not now brother. Piper curtailed her immediate reaction to punch his nose. But, he was her brother and thought he was looking out for her. Best not hurt him.

She looked at Robin and her lips curved upward. Be damned if he wasn't more attractive to her now than three years ago. Her eyes widened when she listened to her own thought. That was what he'd meant. He found her more attractive now. It was why he wanted to wed her. Just as she found him more attractive. *He wanted to wed her. Robin wanted to wed her*. Her lips curved high.

"When can we wed, My Lord?"

Visit Gerri's website
http://www.gerribowen.com

A Wish Times Three

by Jeanne Van Arsdall

Kathleen assumed she was out of her mind. The deadline for her new book loomed and she'd agreed to babysit her niece—for an entire month. Her sister and brother-in-law had persuaded her it would mean the *difference in their careers* if she'd tend Siena while they gallivanted around England on a 'working vacation.'

Siena, was sweet—but when would she have time to get any writing done? A seven-year-old couldn't look after herself. This would be a twenty-four seven commitment.

Take today for example. Busy writing, she'd gotten her rhythm going, was deep into a scene, when the intrusive alarm blared. Otherwise, two-thirty would've come and gone. Instead, she was sitting in her car at Siena's school waiting for her. *What would Siena have done if she'd forgotten?* This afternoon she'd make sure Siena memorized her phone number—in case of such emergency.

"Hey, Aunt Kath," Siena squealed, running down the sidewalk. She climbed in. "Your car is prettier than anybody's in the whole world! I want a yellow one like this when I get big."

"You do, huh?" Kathleen didn't have the heart to tell her this was *not* her first choice in color—sunshine on wheels. "I'm glad you like it. If it still runs, I'll give it to you when you're old enough to drive."

"Honest?"

"You bet. Now, tell me about your day."

"Oh, something really important happened—but not today. Just partly today."

"Ummm...sounds interesting. Tell me." Kathleen smiled, thinking how important little things are to children.

"Well, my teacher, Mrs. Williams had a baby. On Saturday or Sunday, I think. Anyway she's in the hospital and we wrote a note concrad...con..."

"Congratulating?" Kathleen suggested.

"Yes, ma'am. Congratulating her—because she has a baby boy."

"Siena, what a nice thing for your class to do. Who helped write it?"

"Our new teacher. He's not just a teacher though. Our principal said he's a doctor, too. Why would a doctor want to be a teacher?"

"I'm not sure, honey," Kathleen said, parking in front of the yogurt shoppe.

Kathleen wondered about the new instructor. "Did your teacher say what kind of doctor he is?"

"Yes, it's a really big word. He digs up bones and things, something like that."

"Did he say an archeologist?" Kathleen asked, hiding a smile.

"That's it! But why does he dig bones? Does he use old bones on people when they go to the hospital?"

"No, sweetie, he's not that kind of doctor." Kathleen understood how this might confuse a second grader. She wondered why 'the doctor' hadn't explained himself more thoroughly. "This type of doctor doesn't work in a hospital caring for sick people. He goes all over the world and works at places called a 'dig.' He digs up the ground searching for dishes or tools or even food people ate years ago. This helps explain what happened in those people's lives."

"Why?"

"That, my dear, you can ask your teacher tomorrow."

"Great idea, Aunt Kath. He asked if we had any questions, but we didn't know anything to ask."

"What's his name?"

"Dr. Kevin Collins. He said to call him 'Dr. Kevin,' and we did. Our whole class yelled, **Hello, Dr. Kevin,** really loud. He laughed and said we had good lungs. What did he mean?"

"It means you have lots of breath and can yell really loud. But, he probably prefers you speak normally when you're in the classroom."

While they waited for yogurt Kathleen's mind wandered. She remembered a man at the entry where the children waited for rides. Several children had spoken to him, so she hadn't thought anything of it. She'd lived in Stone Mountain, Georgia all her life, and knew most of its residents, but she'd not seen him before. She'd never have forgotten *that* face. He was the epitome of the alpha-male heroes in most of her books.

Traveling home, Kathleen asked, "Was your new teacher standing in front of the school when I picked you up?"

"Yes, ma'am. He's very tall, with dark hair like daddy. Did you see him?"

"I think so. And you're correct, he looks very nice." Kathleen couldn't say what she thought. He was a hunk and belonged in one of her books. She might have to take her sister's advice and stop working so much—get out more. Throw on some make-up and look presentable. It was so easy to work all day in her jammies. But, the *jammie route* had axed her socializing. Not that she'd done any since Roger's death.

She remembered the accident like yesterday. The quick trip to pick up his special sourdough bread—the one he insisted he needed for sandwiches. She'd bought two different kinds of bread because their regular grocery was out of sourdough. Why couldn't he have tried one of those? And how could she still be angry with her husband three years later? *Because I loved him so much, that's how. Because I miss him every day. Because his death changed my life forever.*

"Aunt Kath, are you okay?"

"I was only thinking, honey. I'm fine. We'd better get inside so you can do your homework, then you can play until dinner's ready. How's that for a deal? Maybe you'll grow up to be a doctor."

"Yeah, but I want to be a real doctor, not a bone-digger doctor."

Kathleen laughed. "Siena, don't say that to Dr. Kevin,

okay? It might hurt his feelings if he thought you didn't like what he does."

"Oh, I wouldn't do that, Aunt Kath."

Siena began her homework and left Kathleen to sort through old memories. If truthful, she *had* looked twice at 'Dr. Kevin' today. Was her heart finally on the mend? For three years, she'd longed for the comfort of strong arms around her. She missed the snuggling—and making love. It had been safer to bury her feelings and fill her time with writing. Maybe she was ready to share her life with someone again.

Much later, Siena said, "Aunt Kath, I'm hungry."

Kathleen looked at her watch. "My heavens, it's six o'clock. I lost track of time. I'm sorry, honey. How about we go out for dinner tonight?"

"Can...I mean, may we eat at the Japanese Steak House?"

Kathleen rumpled her niece's hair. "Sounds good. I'll dress and we'll go watch them cook our dinner."

Siena ran to the car, fastened her seat belt and talked a mile a minute. "I love to eat at Nagano's. Especially when he makes a lot of fire. It's called a volcano and fire shoots up really high. You have to sit way back so the fire won't burn you. Mama, Daddy and I eat there all the time!"

Traffic was light to the neighboring town of Lilburn. In the restaurant, the hostess approached. "Well, hello, Miss Siena. Who's this with you tonight?"

"My Aunt Kath. I'm staying with her while Mama and Daddy are on vacation. They're in England—a long way from here."

"It certainly is. And what a nice aunt you have to take you out for dinner. Would you like to sit at Mr. Mark's table tonight?"

"Yes, please."

They went through the entire meal, including dessert, with Siena providing a running commentary on every detail—entertaining everyone at the table.

Leaving, Siena nearly bumped into some local teachers and 'the Dr. Kevin.' As they greeted each other, one person asked Kathleen if she'd met him.

"No, I haven't."

Promptly introduced, they shook hands. Siena said, "I already told her your name. And that Mrs. Williams has a little boy!" Everyone laughed.

"We'd better be going, Siena. It's very nice to meet you, Dr. Collins."

His eyes met and held hers. "My pleasure."

Kathleen arose early, dressed in a capri outfit, and applied makeup. She dropped Siena off at school, then visited Helen Williams, a long time friend, at the hospital. After seeing the baby, Kathleen said goodbye, but Helen stopped her.

"I've found a man for you, Kathleen."

"What?"

"Now, don't bite my head off. I know you've not been looking, but you've heard the saying 'good things come to *she* who waits.' Well, I think your wait is over."

"Helen, you're talking in riddles."

"Have you met my substitute yet? Dr. Collins."

"As a matter of fact, I met him last night. And before you jump to wild conclusions, he was with several teachers at Nagano's Steak House. Siena and I were leaving as they arrived."

"Well, what did you think?"

"He seemed nice enough." *And drop dead gorgeous, invading my dreams.*

"He *is* nice, and he's got a good head on his shoulders. That's more than you can say for today's yoyos. Plus he must be sitting fine financially. I heard he bought the old McIntyre place west of Lilburn. There's 300 acres or more on that spread."

"You're a regular walking encyclopedia. What'd you do, go through his personnel file line by line?"

A sheepish look crossed her friend's face. "Actually, I did. But, for your information, the principal requested it."

"Did his file also say he was financially set and had bought the McIntyre Farm?"

"Well...not exactly. I heard that from very good sources. Anyway, the man's definitely easy on the eyes. I'd planned to invite you both for dinner last weekend, but our little bouncer decided to make his debut a few days early."

Kathleen laughed. "Thank goodness for early arrivals. Listen, I'm sure Dr. Collins is a nice man, Helen, but I don't know if I'm ready. I'm comfortable the way I am."

Helen sighed heavily. "Kathleen, how long have we been friends—ten, fifteen years?" At Kathleen's nod, she continued. "It earns me the right to say this. You can't hide out writing stories about other people's love and happiness for the rest of your life. You've got to find your own sooner or later. It's been over three years since Roger died. That's long enough—too long, if you ask me. He loved you...he'd want you to be happy. Think about it, okay?"

"Yeah, yeah, I'll think about it. Only don't go matching me up. I mean it, Helen." Kathleen shook her pointer finger and exited the room.

She rehashed the conversation on the way to get Siena. She hadn't been totally truthful with Helen. True, her writing brought her satisfaction, but something was definitely missing. And it wasn't difficult to determine what it was.

Siena handed her a note from Dr. Kevin when she picked her up. "He wants to meet with you."

"Me?"

"He wants to talk to all the kids' parents. I told him, again, my parents are on vacation, so he said you could come. When can you go, Aunt Kath?"

"We'll see. I'll contact him and set up an appointment."

Siena scrunched her nose. "Are we going for yogurt today?"

"How about we skip it this time? I had so many errands, I didn't get to the grocery store. What if we buy strawberries and make strawberry shortcake tonight?"

"That's even better. Can...may I pick out the strawberries?"

"I was hoping you'd help."

Siena insisted on steering the cart. She rounded the corner to the produce section too quickly and collided into...Dr. Kevin's cart.

"Well, fancy meeting you ladies." He grinned.

"I'm so sorry," Kathleen stammered.

"No problem. I should've had better control of my vehicle."

"We're going to get some strawberries for dessert," Siena said.

"That sounds tasty, Siena."

"Can I go pick them out, Aunt Kath?"

"Sure—stay where I can see you though."

"Okay," she called and hurried off.

Suddenly, Kathleen became mute. Finally, she stammered, "I got your note...about meeting...about Siena."

"Good. So when...what works best for you?"

"Most anytime's okay. Your schedule is probably more difficult than mine, so you choose."

He stared at her, seemingly unable to pull his eyes away. Finally, he said, "Tomorrow. How about we meet tomorrow?"

"Sure. Siena has ballet after school. I could meet you then." For one crazy minute, Kathleen felt like they were planning an illicit rendezvous.

"Perfect." It appeared he wanted to say more, but closed his mouth at the last minute.

Siena bounded back with two packs of strawberries. "What else are we having, Aunt Kath?"

"Lasagna, a green salad and garlic bread."

"Would that be *homemade lasagna*?" the doctor asked.

"Why, yes. It's one of my specialties."

"It's one of my favorites." His eyes locked with hers.

"Really?" *What's happening here?*

"Really," he said, holding her with his gaze.

Siena's head whipped back and forth following the conversation. "Why don't you come eat with us?" she piped. "Aunt Kath always makes a really big dish full, don't you?"

"Uh...yes, I do, but..."

"I hate to invite myself, but it sounds better than my cooking."

Kathleen's eyes shifted between the man who'd invited himself to dinner and Siena. "Oh, no, it's fine, really. We're on Somerset...124 Somerset. How about six-thirty?"

"Sounds wonderful. Can I bring anything? Wine?" He looked at the berries. "You already have dessert planned."

"Wine would be nice, thank you."

"I assume red goes with lasagna—would you prefer Merlot, Cab or Shiraz?"

"Actually, I love Shiraz...if you do." She shrugged, not wanting to presume.

"It's another of my favorites—just like lasagna and great company."

"Well then. We'll see you around six-thirty." Kathleen took Siena's hand, paid for the berries and left while she could still stand.

Driving home she second-guessed herself. Had she actually invited a man—whom she hardly knew—to dinner? She hadn't spoken that many words to any man since Roger's death, much less contemplated inviting him for dinner; but deep down she *was* looking forward to it.

"Are you angry Dr. Kevin's coming for dinner, Aunt Kath?"

"No, honey. I just don't entertain much anymore. But, it's okay."

"You mean 'cause you're sad about Uncle Roger?"

"Exactly. When someone you love dies, it's hard to remember you still have to go on doing things and trying to be happy. Maybe it's a good thing you invited Dr. Kevin."

"I think so. We can talk about blue moons. He's teaching us about them. Do you know what a Blue Moon is?"

"It's a rare occurrence. That's where the saying 'once in a blue moon' comes from, I believe."

"Some people say if you wish on one your wish will come true. Do you believe that?"

"Well, honey, I don't know if it's the Blue Moon or not. Maybe we're blessed when we wish for something with all our heart, then it comes true."

"Dr. Kevin told us there's going to be a Blue Moon at the end of this month, and I'm going to make a wish on it. Did you know about that?"

Kathleen smiled. "No, I didn't."

The lasagna was almost ready when the doorbell chimed. Kathleen opened the door to a beautiful bouquet of flowers covering Kevin's face. She laughed. "Are you in there somewhere?"

"Hi, beautiful."

"Uh, thank you." His comment shocked her, but she liked it.

"Are you going to ask me in?"

"Of course..." She stepped aside and motioned him in.

"Ummm, the lasagna smells heavenly. I can't wait to taste it."

"I hope you like it. Since it's such a favorite of yours, I'm a little intimidated."

"Please, don't be." He handed her the bottle of wine. "Anything smelling that good has to be delicious."

She arranged the flowers in a vase. "These really are lovely." She looked over her shoulder. "There's a corkscrew in that drawer," she said, nodding toward a cupboard. "Would you please open the wine so it can breathe?"

"Sure. And what is my prize student preparing over here?" He leaned down to inspect the bread.

"Garlic bread. It stinks, but tastes good, and Aunt Kath says it's good for you."

Kathleen nodded at her niece, then turned toward Kevin. "When you're ready, Kevin." *How nicely his name rolled off her tongue.*

"Excuse me?"

"Oh, I'm sorry—I meant the wine glasses. They're over there in the third cabinet to the right. Do you mind getting them?" Kathleen stammered.

Kevin poured the wine, then juice for Siena. "What shall we drink to?" He lifted his glass.

"How about our Blue Moon wish?" piped Siena.

"Perfect. Have you two thought of your wishes yet?"

"I have, I have," squealed Siena.

"I'm afraid not," admitted Kathleen. "How about you?"

"Without a doubt," he answered softly, caressing her with his eyes. He touched his glass to theirs. "Here's to all our Blue Moon wishes coming true."

After dinner, in the family room, Kevin explained the Blue Moon theory. Fascinated, Kathleen failed to notice it was past Siena's bedtime, until she heard her yawn. Siena bid Dr. Kevin goodnight. In her room, Siena said, "See, I told you he was nice."

"You're right." Kathleen tucked her in, pulled the door closed and rejoined Kevin. The chair she'd vacated moments earlier held a stack of books as did the other chairs. "What's this?"

"Oh, those seats are taken. The only seat available is here beside me."

"Is that so?" A tingle raced down her spine.

"Please."

"How creative you are, Kevin." She sat beside him.

He stared deep into her eyes. "Powerful matters require strong measures."

"And is this powerful?"

"Very," he said, gently taking her hand. "I don't know how to say this, except to come out and say it. I believe in saying what I mean, and I mean what I say. I've never met anyone I've felt this way about, and certainly not this quickly. I'm attracted to you, Kathleen, and I think I'm feeling some response from you. I hope I'm right about that. I'd like for us to spend some time together and get to know each other if you share my feelings."

Wow! I certainly didn't expect this. Her heart pounded and she squirmed.

"Well, say something." He lifted her hand to his lips, kissed it. "I didn't mean to rush you. To be perfectly honest, I had no intention of saying this tonight. It's just that I can't take my eyes off you. You're so beautiful...you're gracious, kind and loving. All the traits that make you perfect... for me."

"Thank you, of course, but you're correct...I wasn't expecting this—not in my wildest dreams. I'm flattered, but I haven't had a relationship in three years. Not since my husband...died."

"I understand. I'm not asking for any decisions tonight, just think about it. But would you answer one question?" He leaned in and brushed his lips across hers, soft and tender.

She closed her eyes and drifted off to some faraway place. It stirred emotions long buried. She didn't want to open her eyes, and when she did, he was waiting.

"Tell me you didn't feel anything special and I'll leave, no questions asked."

"No... I mean, yes, I did feel something...wonderful. But I'm not sure about—"

He interrupted. "Maybe this will help." This time his kiss was serious—sensuous—and her knees turned to jelly and would have buckled, had she not been sitting.

"Well? Does that prove anything?"

"What it proves, doctor," she said mischievously, "is you're one fine kisser."

"Is that all?" he asked, disappointed.

She inched closer. "No, I felt the fireworks, too, but I still want to take things slowly—need to take them slowly."

"That's fine with me. I'm not going anywhere." He rose, grinning from ear to ear. "It's getting late though. I've got an early appointment tomorrow, so I'm going to say goodnight. I'm also leaving so I keep my word and take things slowly. In case you haven't noticed, I'm having difficulty keeping my hands off you."

Kathleen walked him to the door. He started out, then turned and took her in his arms. He kissed her cheek, her neck, then her mouth. This time his message was loud and clear. And *this time* she sent him one right back.

"What about tomorrow? Do we still have a meeting after school?" she asked, encircled in his arms.

"Yes, I have something to show you. Don't worry about Siena, she's doing fine. I was merely trying to get an appointment with *you*."

"You sneak."

"I enjoyed our evening together, Kathleen. I hope we'll have many more. Work on your wish and I'll see you tomorrow." He kissed her lightly and left.

She closed the door and leaned against it, recalling his last kiss. He was correct about one thing. When he'd held her close, she could tell he was having a hard time with *something*.

Awaking the next morning, she realized she felt content and happy. And alive!

Her bed was strewn with four outfits. She had to decide on one or be late for her appointment, or should she say date. She was reminded of high school when she, and every other girl, filled an entire note page with their boyfriend's name. Sometimes it would be just his name, sometimes both. She'd said several times this morning, "Kevin and Kathleen, Kathleen and Kevin." It had a pleasant ring. *Stop it! After all, I'm the one who wants to go slowly.*

She arranged for Siena to play at a friend's house after ballet. As she approached the school parking lot she saw him. Leaning against a sidewall, his legs were crossed at the ankles and he sported designer sunglasses. What a looker! Any woman would glance twice at him. It was amazing someone hadn't snatched him up long ago.

When she parked, he headed in her direction. He opened her car door, took her hand, pulled her to him, and kissed her. It happened so quickly and naturally, she responded. He led her to his car.

"Where're we going?" she asked.

"It's a surprise. I'd like your opinion on something."

"What kind of something?"

He cocked his head toward her. "You'll see. If I told you, it wouldn't be a surprise. It's only a short ride."

Kathleen settled back into the comfortable seat, curiosity chewing at her.

"I'm glad you came. I was afraid you felt rushed last night and wouldn't show today. I *am* serious, Kathleen, but I'll go at your pace."

She flashed him a smile. "Thanks, Kevin." A flood of relief and passion swept over her. The man was a keeper her heart said.

He leaned his arm across the seats and rubbed a lock of her hair between his fingers. "Your hair's like silk. I kept thinking last night how good it would feel to run my hands through these inviting curls."

Kathleen shivered with anticipation. The blood rushed to her face as she searched for an appropriate response. *Has it been so long I've forgotten how to flirt?* Finally, she stammered, "It's too curly."

"No, it's perfect. I hope you won't change it."

Before she could respond, he pulled in front of a big, beautiful home. "The old McIntyre Farm," she exclaimed.

"It's the Kevin Collins Farm now. How do you like it?"

"It's fabulous. I can't believe it's the same house. You've restored it beautifully." She stared at the home in disbelief. "Have you completed the interior work as well?"

"Pretty much, but that's where I could use your opinion. I'm not good with accessories and I really don't want a professional decorator. I don't like that 'perfect decorator look.' So what do you say, want to take a peek?"

He got out, then opened her door. "I'd love to."

"I don't know how I'll handle all these steps when I get old." He laughed. "But for now they're good exercise."

Kathleen stared, open mouthed. The paint was perfect, the repair work excellent and the home was warm and inviting. "I simply can't believe the difference. I love it!"

"That's exactly what I hoped. Would you be willing to help me?"

"Absolutely," she said without hesitation.

Kevin led her through each room, explaining what he'd done. When he got to the master bedroom, he stopped. "I realize this is quite masculine, but at the time that was my focus. If I were to redecorate this room today, I'd probably have a different slant on things."

She looked around. "It's perfect for you."

"Yes, it is. But I'm hoping in the not-too-distant future it might need to be redecorated." He kissed her palm, then closed her fingers one by one. "Now anytime you need a kiss, you'll have one close by. But..." He bent and kissed her cheek, her earlobe, her neck before whispering, "...for now you've got the real thing."

Kathleen heard someone moan. *Was it her?*

Kevin took her mouth, ravishing it with his tongue. Her eyes closed and she gave in to sensations she'd nearly forgotten. She returned his hunger and sought more.

"Kathleen," he whispered, "if we don't stop soon...is this what you want?"

Speaking her name returned her senses. "No. I can't—not yet." In anguish, she tore herself from him. "I'm sorry, Kevin, I'm just not ready. I mean...I am, but I'm not."

"That's all right, honey. It's okay. I promised we'd move at your pace. When you're ready, we'll move forward." They left the master suite, circling back to the front of the house to the car.

Kathleen attempted apologizing.

"It's unnecessary. Honestly. Let's talk about the house. What do you think it needs? We could discuss it over a bite to eat. What do you think?"

Siena was eating at her friend's home, but Kathleen wanted—no, needed—time alone. "May I have a rain check?"

"As many as you need." At her door he lifted her chin with his finger. "Don't fret, sweetheart. We have a lifetime ahead of us."

His kiss was passionate and stirred her to her toes. Her heart ached for him, wanted him desperately, but her mind screamed 'Stop!'

Leaning back, he smiled, then kissed her cheek. "I'll call you tomorrow, okay?"

"Of course." She watched him drive away.

Inside, she was saddened—as though she'd lost something valuable. *Why can't I be like normal people? Why am I so afraid to fall in love again?* She entered her room and fell hard onto her bed. The tears she'd held back for years broke loose. Exhausted and spent, she finally drifted off to sleep.

The phone startled her. "Aunt Kath, I'm ready to come home." Siena's chirpy voice roused her.

"I'll be right there." On the way to the car, guilt bombarded her—she'd forgotten her niece.

Siena chatted nonstop all the way home, detailing her afternoon. Kathleen got her to bed then sorted through her own eventful day.

The next morning, Kathleen tried to work on her manuscript after dropping Siena at school, but her mind was like a sponge—floating and soaking up thoughts of Kevin. She determined to respond differently the next time they were together. For now, she decided to include an intensely romantic scene in her writing. *Would it make it easier to add one to her life?* She worked an hour and suddenly had a great idea. Selecting the 'Find' option, she searched for her hero's name and replaced it with 'Kevin,' then did the same with the female counterpart, replacing it with 'Kathleen.' By the time she'd reread the scene her cheeks were flaming and sexual desire rekindled. Maybe there was hope for her after all.

Traveling to get Siena, she remembered Kevin had said he'd call her today but she'd heard nothing. He was probably waiting until after school. If she saw him, surely he'd come over and chat...or would he? *Maybe he thinks I'm too shy. I'm not, but what am I? Scared? But why?*

She wanted to love and be loved.

Kathleen gathered Siena and scanned the schoolyard for Kevin, but to no avail. Disappointment rode home with her. *Probably scared him off for good. Well, if he doesn't want me, I'm not going to chase him.* Maybe she could call—he might be ill. Fearing the latter, she asked, "Siena, was Dr. Kevin at school today?"

"Oh, yes ma'am, and he told us more about the Blue Moon."

Well, that takes care of illness.

Kathleen sent Siena to do her homework, saying, "I'll be working in my office." She pulled her chair up to the computer. Aggravated with herself, she glanced at the phone while her computer booted. The message light blinked. Her heart raced and tiny pricks of excitement chased up and down her spine. After a few deep breaths, she played the message.

"Hi. Sorry I'm so late. We had an incident after school and I had to referee. Anyway, can we get together tonight...if you don't have other plans? We could cook at my place or yours—or eat out. Anything is fine. Call me. I can't wait to see you—bye for now."

Kathleen replayed it three times. Her cousin had offered to keep Siena for a sleepover, so tonight would be the night. *There, the first part of my 'resolve to be bolder' is working. Now for the more pressing call.*

Fingers shaking, she dialed Kevin's number. "Hi, it's Kathleen."

"Yeah, I had that one figured out." He laughed. "How are you?"

"Great. I got some writing done." She didn't tell him he was the inspiration. "How about you?"

"Good, except I miss you. How about tonight? I'd like to see you."

"I'd like to see you, too. In fact, my cousin has Siena."

"Great. Do you want to eat out or cook in? I'm anxious to try my new grill if you're game, and I bought groceries. Want me to come pick you up?"

"No. I'll drive—no need for you to make two trips. What time?"

"It's already four, so whenever you're ready. The sooner the better."

His voice carried a husky, hungry sound. Kathleen wondered if hers did. If not, she was a better actress than she thought.

Kevin was sitting on the porch when she arrived. "I'm glad you could make it." He pulled her close, kissed her, and stared into her eyes. He started to speak, then stopped, turned and led her up the steps.

The house was filled with Celtic music—peaceful and inviting. "I love your choice in music."

"It's some of my favorite. It pleases me when I find things we both enjoy. Have you noticed we have a lot in common? And, I hope you like steak—I've got a couple of beauties ready for the grill."

"Another thing in common." She followed him into the kitchen.

"Wine?" He held up a glass. He poured and passed one to her. "To us." He pinned her with his eyes.

Maintaining eye contact, she whispered, "To us."

"Would you like to see my garden?"

"I'd love to...I didn't know you had a garden."

"I've always kept one. I love flowers. I've worked with them and now I'm finally pretty good. I killed my share in the beginning though." During the stroll, he pointed out different species—some she'd never heard of.

"I'm impressed."

He wrapped his arm around her shoulder as they returned to the house. "Good, that's my goal."

Returning to the kitchen she realized the vase of flowers on the counter was from his garden. She leaned and inhaled the sweet fragrance. *What a nice touch—he keeps surprising me.*

"Can I help?"

"How are you with salads? I have everything imaginable in the fridge."

"I make a mean salad. I'll even whip up a special dressing."

Kevin prepared baked rosemary potatoes. "They're pretty good, if I do say so myself."

When she finished she caught Kevin watching and couldn't resist a trial of her new-found courage. Sticking a finger in the dressing, she placed it between pursed lips, slowly withdrawing it. "Umm...that's delicious."

Instantly, he was by her side. "Let me taste." He took *her* finger, dunked it into the dressing and put it in *his* mouth. He suckled it gently then rubbed it back and forth across his lips, all the while flicking his tongue over and under it. He slid it from his lips, continued layering kisses up her arm, her shoulder, then her neck. Working his way to her mouth, his lips smothered hers with pent up hunger. Burying his hands in her hair, he pulled her closer, kissing her passionately.

Fireworks exploded in her head and heat stirred in her central core. Faraway, she heard him whisper her name, but she was too consumed to answer. Inhibitions melted away.

Kevin emitted a ragged sigh. "I'm not hungry for steaks anymore." He lifted her, carried her to his room.

She clung to him. "Kevin, it's been a long time."

"And for me. No passion—no sweetness. Until you."

He gently laid her on the bed, kicked off his shoes and removed hers. He leaned over and resumed his sizzling kiss. He rolled from the bed, pulling his shirt off in one swift motion. The remaining clothes followed in hot pursuit. Their mutual goal became the removal of every piece of clothing that stood as a barrier between them.

His glance caressed her soft, smooth body. To him, she was perfect. He nuzzled her neck and along her shoulder, slowly and deliberately traveling to her firm, round breasts, marveling at how well they fit his hands. Gently nibbling, he took a nipple into his mouth. His body ached with desire as he continued to touch every inch of her.

Kathleen arched, giving herself to him. She slipped deeper and deeper, drowning in passion and desire... steaming like a hot volcano. Love and newly birthed desire pooled like molten lava in her core. Old emotions and fears bubbled and exploded, leaving her free and seeking.

Their wild, raging storm continued, tossing them to and fro on the cresting waves, with passion and raw desire taking them to their final crashing surge of pure rapture.

"I love you with all my heart, Kathleen."

Lying snuggled in his arms, she was no longer afraid of love—now she accepted it and returned it. "I love you, too, Kevin."

He twisted and kissed her. "Well, I don't know about you, but I've worked up quite an appetite. Think you could handle one of those steaks now?"

She laughed. "Yeah. I thought it was supposed to be the other way around. Something about the way to a man's heart being his stomach. I think maybe we took a detour."

"You have my permission to take that detour any time. Meanwhile, I'm going to light the fire."

"You've already done that." She sat with her arms around her knees.

Kevin laughed and winked, then sobered. "How have I ever gotten along without you?" Turning, he walked out the door.

In the kitchen, she realized how comfortable she was in his house. She poured them another glass of wine and joined Kevin outside.

After dinner, he said, "I wish you didn't have to go." He kissed her sweetly. "Call me when you get home. I want to make sure you're safe."

"It's not that far, Kevin," she said, playfully.

"I know, I know, humor me. Okay?"

"All right, I'll call." He leaned in the window, taking her face in his hands, and kissed her. This time hungrily. "You'd better leave before I pull you back out for round two."

She grinned. "Is that a threat?"

"No. I mean every word of it."

"I guess I'd better go, but could I have—"

"Yes, my love, you can have a rain check."

Kathleen talked to Kevin every day. Days flew by since they'd met. When she could get a babysitter, they were alone. He filled her thoughts and began to fill her manuscript. Writing love scenes had become incredibly easy. The grief that had filled her heart had vanished.

She was on her way to meet him for some big surprise. She wasn't sure who the surprise was for, her or Siena—he'd been so hush-hush about it. She walked into Siena's classroom.

Kevin stood by the window, his back to her. He'd been looking at something in his hand.

"Penny for your thoughts."

He turned and quickly stuck the item in his pants pocket. "Oh, no. These thoughts are worth far more than mere pennies. In fact, they're priceless."

He walked over, took her hands and kissed her cheek. He crossed the room, examined the hallway and closed the door. Taking her in his arms he kissed her passionately. "I've been dying for this. I keep thinking of all the things I'd love to do to you. I can't keep you off my mind, Kathleen, nor do I want to."

"Wow, what a welcome! Could I have an encore?" she teased.

"I aim to please, lady." His tender kiss left her breathless.

"I hope you'll always kiss me like this."

"Always? I like that word." He was about to continue when the late bell rang loudly throughout the school.

Startled, she flexed and he tightened his arms around her. "Was the bell for us to separate and go to our respective corners?"

"No, Miss Funny Face, we're never separating. Come...let me show you some of Siena's work."

"Was that my surprise?"

"No. We're having dinner, then taking a drive. I'm going to show you and Siena something you've never seen before. It's very special. That's all I'll tell you. And now, we have to leave and get Siena."

Kevin double-parked in front of the dance studio while Kathleen went inside. He pulled the ring box out of his pocket and looked at it again. He'd known her less than a month, and didn't do things impetuously, but he knew what he wanted. He prayed it wasn't too soon for her. But tonight there was the Blue Moon. He knew what he'd wish for and hoped she would also. He closed the lid and stuffed the box into his pocket. "I could use some good Irish luck tonight," he whispered.

Kathleen and Siena joined Kevin in the car. "Hey, Dr. Kevin. I'm all ready to go."

"It's too early to eat, so I thought we'd ride to my farm and take a look around. I think you'll like it out there. How about it?"

"Okay."

When he drove up to the front gate, Siena exclaimed, "Wow, this is a big house!"

"I'm glad you like it. Come on, I'll show you around."

Siena squealed with delight at the cows and horses, especially the baby ones. Kevin showed her how to pitch hay, and she got as much on herself as she fed to the animals.

"I guess we'd better go eat," Kevin said. "We need to be back here around seven for my surprise." He looked at Siena and winked.

Siena looked like she would burst with excitement. "And you can't ask any questions, Aunt Kath, 'cause it's something Dr. Kevin and I talked about at school today."

"What's going on, you two?"

"Never mind, sweet...uh, Kathleen. We've got everything covered, right, Siena?"

"Right, Dr. Kevin."

After it was sufficiently dark outside, he put an arm around Kathleen's shoulder and drew her close, took Siena's hand and led them to the back porch.

"Now look up," he told them.

"Oh, my goodness, I've never seen a more beautiful moon in my entire life. It's almost like you can see right through it. Siena, do you see it, honey?"

"Yes. I told you, Aunt Kath, I told you it was really true."

Kevin turned Kathleen around and looked into her eyes. "I wanted to be with you when you first saw it. Now, it's time to make our wishes."

They each turned toward the moon and stared for a minute, making their private wish. "Now, if you want to, you can tell your wish. Unlike some wishes, it's supposed to come true either way."

Surprising both of them, Siena announced she didn't want to tell hers, so Kevin went first. Taking Kathleen's hands, his eyes met and held hers. "I wish Kathleen McDowell will love me as much as I love her, and that she'll marry me and live on this farm."

Kathleen's eyes brimmed with tears. She squeezed his hands and looked up into his eyes. "I've been heartbroken and lonely for years. But, Kevin, you've brought love and joy back into my heart and my life. I think I fell in love with you the first time I saw you. You've made me want to live again and I've been happier than I can describe since I met you. You might not believe this, but my wish was almost the same—that we share our love and our lives."

"In that case," he said, reaching into his pocket, "will you become my wife, live with me here, and be my love forever?" The diamond sparkled by the light of the moon.

Siena squealed, jumping up and down. "That was my wish! That was my wish! Oh, Aunt Kath, I wished that, too!"

Both adults laughed. Kathleen looked back at Kevin, tears coursing down her cheeks. She brushed them away with the back of her hand. "Becoming your wife will make me the happiest woman in the world."

He took her in his arms, helped brush her tears away and kissed her—a long, sweet kiss, full of promise and love.

Pulling away, Kevin leaned down, picked up Siena and put his free arm around Kathleen's shoulder. All three looked up at the moon. "So what do you make of that, girls? Looks like we all made the same wish on the beautiful Blue Moon!"

Visit Jeanne's website
http://www.jeannevanarsdall.com

Moondance

by Kemberlee Shortland

"Love that's true happens only once in a blue moon"

Three Sisters, Dingle Peninsula, Ireland

"What do you suppose is wrong with me?" Blánaid tugged her jumper closer about her body trying to conserve warmth.

Ronan had certainly chosen a chilly enough evening to watch the sunset. He'd driven them out to the Three Sisters headland and they'd climbed to the top of the Middle Peak. To the left was Binn Hanraí, Henry's Peak, to the right was Binn Diarmada, Dermot's Peak and below them nothing but jagged cliff-face.

It was beyond Blánaid's comprehension why the Three Sisters had men's names on two of her peaks. Right now, the only things she knew were that she was freezing her bum off, and that if she were here with a lover, she could snuggle against him for some warmth. The North Atlantic winds were blowing right up the legs of her trousers. She tucked her legs under her, but it did little to alleviate the goosebumps.

"What do you mean?" asked Ronan, glancing at her. The breeze caught his sandy colored hair and whipped it around his face for a moment before leaving it in a wild state that gave him a handsomely roguish appeal.

She swallowed hard at his intense gaze. "Just what I said. There must be something wrong with me. It's Saturday evening and we're sitting here watching the sunset together."

"And what's wrong with that?"

"What's wrong is I should be sitting here with a lover and a bottle of wine between us instead of a friend and a flask of tea."

"Are you saying you don't love me, then?"

Blánaid lifted an eyebrow in response to his question, but her unease continued to grow. Even in the fading light she saw curiosity in his hazel green eyes. His gaze was penetrating, as if he were trying to look into her thoughts. Things had always been easy between them, but something seemed different now and she couldn't quite put her finger on it.

She shifted nervously and faced the horizon again. It was awash with amber, gold and russet with streaks of clouds in lavender and peach. Silver starlight began to shimmer along the edges. The sea echoed the glow along the path of the setting sun, rippling as if on fire. Night was approaching quickly on a deep azure velvet sky from the eastern horizon beyond Ballyferriter Village. The moon was out, but not quite full, giving it a lopsided appearance.

The perfect night for lovers, yet Blánaid saw none of it. Instead, all she could think about was her unseasonably dry dating spell.

"What I'm saying is that it's been months since anyone has asked me out. You haven't dated either if I'm guessing right."

Ronan cleared his throat. "Yes, well..."

"And now, if we want to take pleasure in something as simple as a sunset, we have to come out here together."

"Are you saying you don't want to be here with me?"

"Are you telling me you wouldn't rather be sitting here with a woman you love rather than me?"

Ronan didn't reply immediately, forcing her to finally look back at him. The words seemed trapped on his tongue. When she opened her mouth to speak, he finally said, "I wouldn't rather be here with anyone else."

Blánaid couldn't have been more stunned.

Ronan gathered her hand in his. It was warm and strong, and instantly alleviated some of the chill seeping into her bones. Something else warmed inside her and she found herself looking into his eyes—really looking. She shivered again, but this time not from the cold. His tender gaze hinted there was more on his mind than he was letting on.

Unnerved, Blánaid slipped her hand from his and crossed her arms in front of her, tucking her fingers under her arms to keep them warm. She looked back to the horizon.

"You don't believe me?" asked Ronan.

Blánaid chuffed to herself. "It's not that I don't believe you, Ronan. It's just that...well, I'm sure if you had the choice, you'd rather be here with someone special."

Blánaid shivered noticeably. If he'd been thinking of the weather rather than getting her alone, he would have remembered to at least bring a lap blanket. What bothered Ronan as much as her discomfort was that he couldn't bring himself to tell her how he really felt about her.

If he were a real man, he'd confess that he was in love with her and had been for some time now. Like, since the moment he'd first seen her almost a year ago when he'd moved to Dingle. He'd made friends with Blánaid almost instantly.

As he got to know her better, he'd thought he might have a chance with her. Then a few months back he'd overheard her talking to their friend Siobhán about the kind of man she wanted in her life and knew he could never live up to her expectations. She was looking for Mr. Perfect. He'd gotten it from the horse's mouth, so to speak.

He believed the man Blánaid was looking for couldn't possibly exist. Bits and pieces of him, maybe, but not the whole package. So he'd settled for being her friend and hoped his actions alone would prove his feelings to her and she'd change her outlook toward him. He was her shoulder to cry on, a partner to go out with. He was always there for her whenever she needed him—day or night, no matter the hour.

But it wasn't working. Not for him. Not anymore. He'd either have to confess his true feelings or walk away from her altogether. His love for her was tearing him apart.

The silence seemed to drag on. Her last statement echoed through his head.

Finally, he looked at her. She had the traditional Irish features—creamy porcelain skin, curling auburn hair that framed her heart-shaped face, and full rosebud lips. Her beauty was the kind that didn't require make-up. Not even around her eyes. Thick, dark lashes made her emerald eyes sparkle.

Her cheeks bloomed with color from the chilly air and the breeze tossed curls around her face. Impulsively, he reached and brushed the hair away from her temple. His heart squeezed in his chest at the sadness in her eyes.

"Come here." He slipped his hand under her hair. His thumb brushed her neck as he reached for her shoulder to pull her to him. She came easily, as she always did when she was sad. He pulled the side of his jacket around her and enfolded her in his embrace. She rested her head on his shoulder, but didn't say anything. He wondered if she could hear his heart pounding like a bodhrán in his chest. The wind calmed the moment Blánaid settled in his arms. Everything seemed right with her beside him. Why didn't she feel it, too?

"Blán," he started, his voice barely audible over the sound of the waves below them.

Before he voiced what was on his mind, Blánaid straightened slightly and said, "When I was young, my father and I used to watch the sunset sometimes. He was a fisherman and would take me out in his curragh to the Blasket Islands. We'd sail around the tiny islands going from place to place pulling up mussel lines, cutting seaweed and fishing for things feeding around the rocks. Before heading back to the dock at Dunquin, we'd watch the sunset."

"That's a wonderful memory," he said. Her father had passed away almost five years ago and he knew she missed him terribly. He'd been out fishing with a mate and a squall had come in unexpectedly. The boat capsized and both men had been lost. It was weeks later that Blánaid's father had been found washed up on one of the islands. If not for the pattern of his cream jumper, he wouldn't have been identified.

"Of all the silly stories he used to tell me, it was the one about the setting sun I remember the most."

"I don't think I remember any old Irish tales about the sun."

Blánaid chuckled lightly. Her body trembled against his, flaming the fire already building inside him. He had the urge to pull her onto his lap, but let her continue. "I don't think it's an Irish one."

"Tell me, then," he prompted.

"See the sun, how it's lowering toward the horizon. Listen." At that moment, everything around them stilled. The breeze ceased. The sound of the waves breaking below calmed. Even the blood pounding in his ears dissipated.

Then, the lower edge of the sun touched the horizon. "Hear it? The sizzle? That's the sound of the sun setting into the sea."

Sure enough, there was a distinct crackling that seemed to grow louder the further into the sea the sun went.

Blánaid turned her rosy face upward. Her sparkling eyes had lost some of their sadness. He could tell her memory had lightened her heart a little.

"Amazing, isn't it?" she asked.

For a moment, Ronan was speechless as he gazed at her. Her gentle smile crinkled the corners of her eyes.

She was amazing.

He was lost.

He leaned closer and pressed his lips to hers.

Ronan always thought shooting stars and electricity blazing a path to his groin were things in romantic novels. But in that moment he was a convert. There was a whole fireworks warehouse going off behind his eyelids, and an inferno flashed through his veins to lodge in his lower belly.

Kissing Blánaid was a state of ecstasy he never knew existed. Holding her here, now, in this place and kissing her—it all seemed perfect. The more he kissed her the more he wanted to kiss her.

Ronan slid his other arm around her waist and pulled her closer. His heart regained its rapid pulse against his ribcage and his body vibrated with pent up desire. He slanted his lips over hers, tasting the sweet tea they'd shared and her own natural flavor.

He breathed heavily in an effort to control himself. The combination of perfume, warm skin and salty sea breeze assaulted his nostrils.

Blánaid's name echoed through him as he devoured her with his kiss. Her hands were all over him—clutching and grabbing at him. Her whimpers filtered through his ears and inflamed him all the more.

Then it dawned on him. She wasn't clutching and grabbing at him. She was fighting him. She was pushing at him and trying to pull out of his arms.

The realization was like a slap of ice water washing over him. He released her instantly. She sprang away from him as if he were fire and she'd gotten too close. Alarm etched across her face; tears streamed down her cheeks. She took giant gulps of air as she inched away from him.

Reality of what he'd done swept over him.

"Blánaid..." he started, but what could he say? By the look on her face 'I love you' wouldn't have been appropriate. And he wouldn't apologize. He meant every kiss he'd given her.

"Blánaid..." he tried again. He ran his shaky fingers through his windswept hair. "I—"

"D...don't say anything."

"Do you want me to apologize?"

Blánaid's spine stiffened noticeably and her gaze turned serious, but the tears still shimmered on her cheeks.

She rose. She was leaving.

Ronan lifted himself to his knees and was nearly pushed back down by the gust that swept up the cliff face.

"Stop," she warned.

"Blánaid—"

"Leave me alone," she cautioned, turning from him. "Let me be!"

"Blánaid!" he called after her, but she was gone.

Blánaid ran down the rise until she came to the road. She didn't stop running until she reached the outskirts of Ballyferriter Village.

At the edge of town, she stopped at a high stone wall

edged with red fuchsia. She hadn't looked back while she ran, but she didn't hear Ronan behind her either. She'd just kept running because she didn't know what else to do.

She sank down into the grass at the edge of the stone wall and rubbed her palms over her face. Ronan's kisses still burned on her lips and her heart pounded more from the feelings he'd awakened than the run.

What had he done to her?

It wasn't as if she hadn't enjoyed the kiss. In the beginning, she let him kiss her. If she were being honest with herself, she'd melted into him.

Then the realization of what was happening hit her. Ronan was kissing her. And she panicked.

Ronan, she sighed.

He was her closest friend next to Siobhán. She'd never thought of him any other way. Everything changed the moment his lips touched hers and anything she thought she wanted for her future became obsolete.

Blánaid's mind spun like a whirlwind. What was she going to do?

Ronan kissed her!

Her breath caught in her throat. How could he have done this to her? He'd changed everything.

She couldn't think. And she couldn't sit here in the dark in the cool, damp grass. Ronan had driven them to Three Sisters so she didn't even have a way to get back to Dingle. She pulled her mobile out of her pocket and called someone she knew would help her sort out her feelings. Siobhán.

Blánaid sat with Siobhán in Murphy's Pub in Dingle.

Siobhán was a great friend. Blánaid had known her since childhood and was the only other friend she counted on in an emergency—Ronan being the first. Now that he'd changed their relationship, Siobhán was the only one she could turn to for advice.

Siobhán had driven to Ballyferriter to collect her and take her back to Dingle. The least Blánaid could do to repay her friend for putting her out was to buy her a drink—or in this case, several.

"Are you ready to tell me why you were stranded in the

wilds of Ballyferriter?" asked Siobhán.

"Maybe after another one of these," she replied, presenting an empty tumbler in her fingers.

"You've already had three. Must have been bad." Siobhán held up two fingers in the bartender's direction. When he nodded to indicate he'd seen her, she returned to the subject at hand. "You know, when I collected you, I thought you were just cold. Now that you've warmed up, I must say you're absolutely glowing."

Blánaid lifted an eyebrow in her friend's direction. "It's the Jameson."

"No, girl, I know what you look like with a few jars in you. This is different."

The bartender delivered their drinks then Siobhán turned her attention back to Blánaid.

"What?"

"Out with it. What were you doing in Ballyferriter without your car?"

Blánaid knew she'd have to tell her sooner or later, so she might as well get it over with. "Ronan took me out to Three Sisters to watch the sunset."

"Ooh, romantic."

"He's just a friend," she reminded Siobhán.

"You two have a fight? Ronan doesn't seem the kind of lad to leave a girl stranded."

Blánaid took a deep breath and told Siobhán everything. When she finished, her friend sat back, just looking at her. The only indication that she was awake was the smirk on her face and her laughing eyes.

"Well? Say something."

"It's about damn time." Siobhán chuckled.

"What do you mean 'It's about damn time'?" There was something in her friend's voice that made her uneasy.

"Are you sure you want to hear this?"

"You think?" Blánaid rolled her eyes skyward. "If you know something I don't, please tell me because I swear I don't know what to do."

Siobhán leaned forward and gazed into her eyes. "How do you feel about Ronan?"

Blánaid shrugged. "We're friends. I like him. He's a nice

guy."

"Sean's a nice guy and he's your friend. Do you feel the same for Sean as you do Ronan?" Siobhán asked.

She crossed her arms in front of her and looked into her tumbler, wishing there was more in the glass than just an ice cube.

She thought she had everything figured out. She thought she knew where her life was going. She never planned for...this.

Friends were friends. Friends were the people you turned to when you had a fight with your boyfriend, or they dumped you. You loved them, but you weren't supposed to be *in* love with them.

"He's just a friend," she finally said, as if repeating the statement would force her heart to obey her mind.

Siobhán lifted an eyebrow, but didn't say anything.

"Honestly?"

Siobhán nodded enthusiastically, urging Blánaid to continue.

"Honestly, I never thought about how I feel about Ronan. He's always just been a friend. He's not my—"

"Type?" Siobhán finished for her. "Blánaid, 'types' are like old wives' tales. They don't really exist. They're just excuses we use to brush off guys we're not interested in. You'll have to do better than that."

"Well, I can't," she snapped.

Siobhán sat back again and refolded her arms in front of her. "I thought you were being honest with me."

"I am!"

People turned to stare because of her outburst. Blánaid took a long, deep breath to calm herself and sank into her seat.

"Oh, for the love of God," Siobhán exclaimed under her breath. "Ronan loves you."

Blánaid was shocked by her friend's statement. But when the thought of Ronan's kiss flashed through her mind for the thousandth time since she'd run from him, she had to wonder how she really did feel about him. He had to care more about her than he was letting on to kiss her as he had.

Blánaid remembered sitting here with Siobhán only a

few weeks ago. They'd been sharing a few jars and talking about men, not unlike now. Then they'd been dreaming, of course, in their slightly inebriated state, and really exaggerating what the ultimate male would be like for each of them. Blánaid knew their descriptions were purely fantasy, but they'd had fun.

This was serious, though.

Could Ronan really love her? If he did, how did she feel about him?

Her heart leapt at the thought of his kiss and how she'd responded so quickly to him. She hadn't kissed many men in her life, but she'd never reacted to them like she'd reacted to Ronan. Could she love him? Was she *in* love with him and just didn't know it?

Siobhán sat forward again. "Has Ronan ever said or done anything you could have missed that might be a clue to his feelings for you? Besides kissing you tonight?"

Blánaid thought for a moment. They did spend a lot of time together. Since neither of them had been dating, they would go out together—for the company she'd thought. Even if she'd asked him to go with her to the pictures he'd still taken her out for a meal beforehand, and he always paid. And more times than not, he brought her flowers. Sometimes it was a handful of blooms he'd bought in a shop in town, and sometimes it was a simple wild rose he'd snipped from a roadside plant growing along the stone walls.

Nights like tonight, he shared the warmth of his coat. Or he comforted her when she was melancholy, or held her up while they were laughing themselves silly.

When her car was on the blink, he took her to work and picked her up at the end of her shift. If she needed company on a drive up to Killarney, he went with her, "for the craic," he'd say. That was a lie. The only entertainment he wanted was the pleasure of her company.

"A few months ago," she said to Siobhán, "not long after Ronan moved here, we were going to drive to Killarney to the pictures. I'd just closed the café and was waiting for him up by Murphy's Ice Cream Shop. I've always hated working in the winter because it gets dark so fast. Four o'clock and it's lights out, you know?"

Siobhán nodded.

"Ronan was running late. I probably should have waited in the café, but I knew he'd be there at any minute and we didn't want to miss the start of the movie. I walked up to Murphy's and was going to meet him coming down Green Street.

"A man came around the corner. He was drunk, and well...if Ronan hadn't arrived just then, I don't know what would have happened."

"You never told me about that."

"I never told anyone. I just wanted to forget it, and Ronan never mentioned it again either. He held me while I cried, said all the right things and made me feel better. He whispered encouragement and promised he'd protect me forever. At the time, I'd thought it was just stuff you said to someone who'd just narrowly missed danger...but now?"

"Now you think it might have been a sign?" Siobhán suggested.

Blánaid nodded. "Yeah. Everything he's ever done for me makes sense now—putting himself out for me, going out of the way to make me happy...saving my honor."

"Sounds like love to me," said Siobhán.

"What I don't understand is why he hasn't said anything to me." She looked into Siobhán's eyes, hoping for an answer, but none was forthcoming. "You know what I don't understand?"

Siobhán shook her head. "What?"

"I don't understand why no one's asked me out. I'm not full of myself, if that's what you're thinking, but I used to get asked out occasionally. Not anymore."

"You really don't know, do you?"

"Know what? Tell me, Siobhán. I started tonight thinking something was wrong with me. If you know what's happening...I'll buy you another drink," Blánaid promised.

"I'm sure we've both had enough."

"Tell me what you know. Please."

"You're blind, Blánaid. You have to be if you can't see what everyone else around you does. Ronan loves you. We all know it. No one is asking you out because everyone thinks you two are sparking."

Blánaid let out a very unladylike snort. "Yeah, we're sparking all right. Just not the way you think."

Siobhán took Blánaid's hand. "The point here is that everyone sees you two together and we keep waiting for you to open your eyes. None of the lads will ask you out because they see how it is with Ronan. No one wants to be 'the other man,' even if you don't see how he feels for you. Didn't you ever consider it odd how he's not dating either?"

"I thought it was ironic, all right, but didn't think it was strange. We all go through dry spells."

"It's no dry spell he's been on. He hoped the more time you spent together the sooner you'd realize how he felt about you. Something must have happened tonight that made him take the next step."

Blánaid nodded. "It was perfect up there. Everything was perfect. Except me."

"And now?"

"Now I need to find a way to make it up to him."

"Do you love him?"

For a moment, Blánaid didn't say anything. Then, "Yes, I think I do. Maybe it's wrong to put all the blame on him. I saw the signs, but I ignored them. I don't date the lads we hang out with as a rule so I considered everything he did for me an act of friendship. He was new here. I thought he was just making friends.

"I can't deny that I find him really handsome, but I never dated friends so I wasn't looking any further than that. Just like I don't date any of the lads I work with in the café. It's just too uncomfortable after a breakup."

"Kind of limits the dating options though, doesn't it?"

Blánaid laughed lightly. "It does."

"So what are you going to do now?"

"Now, I make it up to Ronan." Blánaid gave her friend a big wink.

Ronan stood on the Middle Peak facing the sea, watching the setting sun. The evening was nearly as perfect as it had been a few nights ago. Only Blánaid wasn't with him—yet.

He was waiting for her.

Just standing here, in the spot where he'd last held her,

brought every memory of that evening back. How could he have gotten it so wrong? Kissing her had seemed right. He didn't understand how a kiss could have led to this. She could have slapped him, but she didn't. She could have shouted at him, but she didn't do that either. She just ran from him. He'd wanted to go after her, but something told him to let her go. She didn't look angry—just frightened.

No, not frightened...confused maybe. Undoubtedly, his actions had given her something new to think about.

It was exhausting trying to come up with new ways to tell her he loved her without actually saying the words. He wanted her to realize it herself. He wasn't perfect, certainly not the kind of man she told Siobhán she wanted, but he loved her more than any other man ever would. If it took another few days for her to realize her feelings for him, he'd wait.

He'd begun to think he'd scared her off. She'd made it clear she wanted to be left alone that night, and he'd obeyed her wishes. He hoped she would contact him when she was ready. And she had. Fortunately, it had only been three days. The wait had slowly been killing him.

She'd sent a text to his mobile. It simply read: *it's a marvelous night for a moondance—meet me on the middle.*

He wondered what she was on about. The message was cryptic. Did she want to go dancing?

And what did she mean about meeting him in the middle? Was this some kind of compromise? The typo was confusing. He reread the message and realized that maybe she hadn't made a typo. Maybe she didn't want him to meet her *in* the middle but back *on* the Middle Peak.

Well, he would find out soon enough. He only hoped tonight would go better than the last time.

"Ronan." Her voice was so faint he'd almost missed it. He thought it was a memory echoing on the evening breeze. Then he felt her presence behind him and turned to look at her.

"Blánaid."

She stood on the crest of the peak. The breeze whipped her hair and her skirt flagged around her legs. She was made more beautiful by the last of the sun's glow warming her skin. She boldly stood her ground.

He let his gaze take all of her in and noticed she carried a bottle of wine in one hand and pair of glasses in the other.

Blánaid moved toward him slowly. “I thought this would be appropriate.” She smiled softly, holding up the bottle as she moved forward.

He stepped forward to meet her halfway. Her smile went right to his heart and hope bloomed in him.

“It’s a marvelous night for a moondance,” she sang softly. “All the stars up above in your eyes. A fantabulous night to make romance, ‘neath the cover of October skies.”

Ronan choked on his chuckle. He didn’t think he could grin more than he was. He really loved this woman and now it was obvious the feeling was mutual. He didn’t know what had happened over the last few days, and he didn’t care. His only thought was that she was here before him now...and singing a Van Morrison tune.

They stopped inches from each other. Their gazes never wavered.

“October is months away, love. Please tell me I won’t have to wait that long.”

Once the shock had worn off, he took the wine bottle and glasses and set them in the grass. Blánaid wound her arms around his shoulders as he rose.

“Blánaid,” he started, sliding his palms along her neck and threading his fingers through the hair at her temples.

She placed a finger on his lips. “Shhh, kiss me.”

He tested her reaction with a single soft kiss. When she didn’t pull away he kissed her again. Her body relaxed into his and she met him kiss for kiss. He slanted his lips over hers and made love to her mouth, stealing his tongue between her lips to tease with hers.

Ronan nipped her lower lip and traced the line of her jaw from chin to temple. She tasted lightly of sea spray and clean skin. Her delicate flavor, the natural scent of her skin and the feel of her body against his caused a riot of his senses. Her whimper of pleasure enflamed him. Need pooled warmly in his belly, and lower still.

His body vibrated with desire. But, if he didn’t rein in his control, there was a strong chance he and Blánaid would never have the chance to talk. With great reluctance, he ended the kiss and leaned away from her.

"So, is it true love?" he asked with a graveled voice.

Blánaid's eyes fluttered open and found his gaze. Smiling, she said, "I could get used to this."

"Me, too." When she leaned into him for another kiss, he asked, "Shouldn't we talk first?"

"About what? We both know what a fool I've been. Anyway, there's time enough for talk. There's something I want to show you, first. Sit with me?"

For a moment, neither moved, then Blánaid stepped out of his arms and took the heat with her. A gust came up the cliffside and chilled him. "I brought a blanket this time."

"Grand. You spread it on the grass and I'll open the wine."

A moment later, they were seated on the blanket holding a glass of red wine. Ronan reached over and took her hand. The warmth of it took away the chill seeping into her. She really shouldn't have worn a skirt, but she'd wanted to look nice when she saw him again.

It felt so natural kissing Ronan and she wondered what it would be like when they made love. But before she could think of that she had something special to show him. It would prove to him that she really loved him.

"Before I offer a toast, I want to apologize." She gazed into his eyes and hoped he saw her sincerity. "I was a fool, Ronan, and I'm sorry. I should have seen the signs. If my eyes had been open, I would have."

He shook his head gently. "You don't owe me any apologies. I should have just said how I felt, but I'd overheard you and Siobhán a few weeks ago at Murphy's and..."

"Say no more. I remember the night. Let me just say we were well into our jars and talking a load of shite. I know the kind of man we were talking about doesn't exist. But if he did," she said, reaching up to stroke his jaw, "he'd be exactly like you."

"Blán," he sighed. He took her hand and kissed her palm.

She put her finger to his lips. "You talk too much,

Ronan." Holding up her glass, she toasted, "To us, and the blue moon."

Ronan clinked his glass with hers then surprised her by wrapping his arm through hers, drawing her close. They sipped the wine, gazing into each other's eyes. Blánaid's heart beat so fast she was dizzy with longing.

Was this what it was like to be in love? If so, she wanted more.

She leaned into him with the intention of more mind-bending kisses, but Ronan edged away slightly.

"Is something wrong?"

Ronan shook his head. "You said you had something to show me."

She grinned and nodded. The sun had finished setting and the evening sky had darkened, but the Three Sisters headland was awash in light. Blánaid took Ronan's glass and set it and hers in the grass. She gazed into his eyes momentarily, then reached up and stroked her fingertips gently over his lids. "Close your eyes."

She grasped him by the shoulders, pulled him toward her and then down onto the blanket. His lips parted, as if expecting her kiss. When it didn't come, he asked, "Can I open my eyes now?"

"Just a moment." When she'd settled down beside him, she wove her fingers with his. "Okay, open them."

Blánaid heard the sharp intake of Ronan's breath. "Wow!"

She turned to face him. His face glowed with blue light and deep black shadows. Wonder shimmered in his eyes and in his smile as he looked into the sky.

Just above them hung the full moon. Not just any full moon, but a blue moon—the second full moon in one month.

"Amazing, isn't it." Blánaid turned her gaze back to the sky.

Ronan rolled toward her and gazed down at her. "You're amazing."

She reached up to stroke his jaw. "I have it on good authority that love that's true happens only once in a blue moon."

"Is it true love?"

"Could be, but I won't know for sure until you kiss me."

Ronan leaned down and her heart leapt into her throat. She placed her palm against his shoulder to stop him and gazed at him. This was the start of a new life for them and she wanted to remember this moment forever. She took in every rise and plane of his face, the tender look in his gaze, the beat of his heart against her breast, the touch of his hand on her ribs.

His muscles bunched beneath her touch when he shifted. The heat of his skin radiated through her hand, up her arm and continued through her body until the sea breeze coming up the cliff became nonexistent. The only indication of the ambient temperature was the exhaled vapors that hung in the moonlight like sea mist.

Blánaid smoothed a path up his chest, along his neck and threaded her fingers in his thick hair. He had the kind of hair that looked coarse so its softness was a surprise. She toyed with strands at his nape until he groaned.

"Blán?" whispered Ronan. The soft, tender timbre in his voice drew her gaze. There was such love in his eyes. She knew the look now. She didn't know how she could have mistaken it for anything else all these months.

Blánaid stroked his lower lip with her thumb and answered the unspoken question. "Ronan, how do you like your eggs in the morning?"

He was noticeably stunned by the question, but the instant he realized what she was suggesting, a Cheshire cat grin spread across his face. He leaned in, brushed his lips against her cheek and whispered, "I like mine with a kiss."

She chuckled. She'd waited a lifetime for Ronan, but it had taken the magic of a cerulean blue, full moon to make her realize that everything she'd ever dreamed of was right beside her the whole time.

"I think it can be arranged." Blánaid closed the gap between their lips and showed him just how much she loved him.

Visit Kemberlee's website
http://www.kemberlee.com

Beneath The Velvet Blue Moon

by Candace Gold

"Which star do you want to wish on, Nadine?" Father asked as we leaned against the railing, gazing up at the brilliant star-studded summer sky.

I pointed to the brightest and we each made a wish.

Sometimes when there were two full moons in one month—a Blue Moon—which happened approximately every two and a half years, we made special wishes. All my wishes were special to me, for I always wished for a handsome prince to come and sweep me off my feet. However, I was willing to wait until I grew up.

The summer of my nineteenth year, my wish came true. That was when I met Michael Greene. Michael was everything I'd dreamed my prince would be and we spent those sun-kissed days together. I have to admit, though, we met in a most unconventional way.

On the second day of our vacation, my parents, both English professors, were fast at work on the novel they were co-authoring. Basically, that left me pretty much on my own. I grabbed my beach bag and scribbled a note telling them I'd gone to the small beach on the other side of the lake. Chances were I'd be back before they even read the note, anyway. I only liked to bask, not bake, in the sun. Being a redhead with fair skin, my freckles didn't need new relatives.

I found a nice spot not too far from the water and spread out my blanket. Then I took my book from the bag, stretched out on my stomach, and began to read. Suddenly, out of nowhere, something hit the sand a few inches from my nose.

"What the...!"

"I'm so sorry," a deep male voice said as a hand reached out to help me to a sitting position.

I couldn't actually see him because I had sand in my eyes, not to mention the ton that found its way into the top of my bathing suit.

"Stay right there—don't move. I'll be right back," he said.

I tried to shake some of the sand off me in the few moments he was gone. He returned with wet towels and gently began to wipe the sand off my face. I opened my eyes to find myself gazing into beautiful eyes.

"Better, huh?" he asked.

"Much." I took the towel from him and wiped the sand from my shoulders and chest. Now that I could see again, I took in the rest of him, from the tussled full head of blue-black hair hanging over his forehead, the straight nose and dimpled chin, to his muscled arms and chest. In my wildest dreams, I couldn't have conjured up a more handsome guy.

He grabbed the offending missile—a volley ball—and apologized again. "Look, it was an accident. I'm really okay."

Before he could reply, another guy with bronzed skin and windblown hair trotted over. "Hey, you coming back to play?"

My handsome stranger wrinkled his nose and shook his head. "Nah. Play without me," he replied, tossing the ball to the other guy.

"Catch you later," the guy said as he ran off with the ball.

"I'd like to make it up to you. Can I buy you a drink or something to eat at the snack bar?"

"My mother told me never to go off with strangers," I teased.

He smacked his forehead. "Forgive me for not introducing myself. I'm Michael Greene," he said, extending his hand.

I shook his hand and said, "I'm Nadine Stone."

He grinned, his green eyes twinkling. "Now that we're no longer strangers, how about getting something to eat at the snack bar?"

"I really should clean up first."

"No. I don't want to waste a moment."

"I'll only be a few minutes," I protested.

"You might disappear before I can learn everything there is to know about you."

"All right, you win," I said and walked with him to the snack bar.

He bought franks, French fries and soda for us to eat under the umbrella at one of the small tables. I hadn't realized how hungry I was and quickly took a bite. I must have gotten some mustard on my nose, because Michael smiled as he took a napkin and wiped it off. A strange vision passed in front of me of my own child asking Michael what he remembers most about me. I can hear the reply now. "Forever wiping off your mother's face. It always seems to get in the way of things."

"Tell me, who are you, Nadine Stone?" he asked, bringing me back to the present where I vowed to be neater.

"Nobody special. I'm starting my sophomore year in college this September."

"Have any idea what you want to do when you finish?" he asked before taking another healthy bite of his frank. He must have been just as hungry as I.

"I'm not sure. Maybe teaching, maybe research. What about you?"

"I'm finishing my senior year. Architecture's my thing. It was probably those Lincoln Logs my parents bought me when I was a kid."

I chuckled. "You must have designed luxury cabins."

"Not quite. I guess it's in my genes. My dad's an architect, too."

"Well, if genes count, then I'll end up a teacher. Both my parents are English professors. They're hard at work, as we speak, writing the great American novel this summer."

"Together?" he asked looking skeptical.

I nodded. "They're pretty close."

"I hope they remain that way after the summer is over," Michael said.

I smiled, understanding fully what he meant. I wanted to be alone with him, too.

"So you'll be here the entire summer, Nadine?"

"Yes. How about you?"

"Two of my buddies from school rented a cabin for the summer with me. Sort of our last fling before plunging into the real world."

I wanted to know everything there was to know about Michael. As we sat talking, I suddenly became conscious of the rhythm of my heart. It seemed to be beating at a dangerously fast rate. I feared if it beat any faster it would crash right through me. If he could have this effect on me by only talking, I found myself wondering what would happen if he kissed me? Was there such a thing as love at first sight? I'd never given it much thought until that day, for I'd already fallen in love with Michael Greene.

Being with Michael every day made all ordinary things, like hiking and biking magical. Of course, my parents weren't totally unaware of what was going on, nor were they completely thrilled. My mother felt she needed to caution me. Knowing I was with Michael every day caused her parental radar to go off the screen. Instead of just coming out and saying what she actually meant, she used figures of speech and euphemisms. I found it somewhat amusing that she seemed so uncomfortable.

I was halfway out of the cabin one morning when she stopped me. "Nadine, I'd like to talk with you a moment."

I turned around and faced her.

"Are you on your way to meet Michael?"

"We're going bike riding around the trails. Why?"

"You'll be careful, of course."

"I'm *always* careful, Mom. And the bike is sturdy."

She had such a look of frustration on her face. "*We're* concerned about you."

"Don't—"

"Seeing someone everyday...well..."

"Stop worrying. I'm a *big* girl now."

"*That's* why we're worrying."

Obviously, my mother was speaking for my father as well, hence, the use of the pronoun *we*. I knew exactly what they were thinking and worded my reply carefully.

"You and Dad brought me up right. I can tell the difference between what's right and what's wrong. You've instilled in me the smarts needed to make rational choices.

So why are you doubting yourselves, now?"

She pursed her lips in thought as she mulled over what I'd said. I'd taken the worrisome wind from her sails and she gave me a less harried, anemic smile. Then I blew her sails into a tailspin when I half-teased, "I love him, Mom. And I'm going to marry him. See ya later."

I left my poor mother standing there wondering whether or not she should chain me to my bed. I might have been kidding with her then, but in my heart I meant every word. I'd meant what I said about being grown up. I knew what I felt for Michael had to be love. I'd never felt this way about any guy before. The very thought of him had the power to lift my spirits and make my heart soar. I may have spent nearly every summer of my life at Lake Flint, but with Michael I felt as if I were seeing it for the first time. I suddenly became aware of the quiet beauty of the place. I discovered more to do and see than merely hanging out at the lake or beach.

One beautiful summer's night in early August, Michael and I walked along the lake holding hands. We stopped by the rail where my father and I had made our wishes when I was a child. A gentle breeze ruffled his hair as he smiled down at me. I smiled back at him. He drew me close and covered my mouth with his. Then he turned to look at the full moon.

"Look, Nadine, it's a Blue Moon."

"My father told me that anything you wished for under a Blue Moon always came true," I said.

"Always?" he asked with the mischievous little smile I found adorable.

"That's what he said."

"Then let's make wishes." His eyes were like emeralds, twinkling in the moonlight.

We closed our eyes and made wishes. I wished to be with Michael forever. Since you couldn't tell anyone your wish or it wouldn't come true, I didn't know what he'd wished for, but by the look on his face I had a pretty good idea.

"Promise, Nadine...promise me on that Blue Moon that you'll meet me here next year."

"I promise," I said.

Then, under that magnificent moon, we sealed our

pledge to meet with a kiss. If I could have put that moment into a bottle and saved it forever, I would have. I had been granted my childhood wish. My handsome prince stood there before me. And no matter what, I knew with all my heart I would always love Michael.

We swapped telephone numbers. I'd keyed his into my cell phone. We'd stay in touch while we both went back to school. And perhaps, if time permitted, get together during the holidays.

That night of promise turned out to be the last night we'd spend together. The next morning, my grandmother called my mother with terrible news. My grandfather had been rushed to the hospital. He'd had a heart attack. I'd hastily said goodbye to Michael. The tears in my eyes were for Michael, but my concern was for my grandfather.

We drove directly to the airport and booked a flight to Arizona. From the airport, we went straight to the hospital. My grandfather was already in the operating room when we got there. We found my grandmother sitting in the waiting room, her eyes red and swollen from crying. My mother tried to comfort her, but ended up adding her own tears to the mix. It took another two hours before the doctor came to speak with us.

"Mrs. Carlson, if he gets through the night, he's going to be all right."

A collective sigh of relief could be heard after he gave us this prognosis. He then proceeded to explain what he'd done in the operating room. My grandfather was a feisty old man. Even though Grandpa wasn't out of the woods just yet, we were given hope. I knew that if anyone was going to pull through a quadruple bypass it would be him. We were allowed to peek in on him before we all went to my grandparents' place to spend the night.

The following morning we returned to the hospital to see him. He was fully awake and though his voice was dry and gravelly, he managed to bark orders to the nurses. Though his skin still bore a gray cast, we knew he was on the mend. And that's what counted.

My parents and I remained in Arizona with my grandmother until my grandfather was able to go home. It wasn't long before he was his usual cantankerous self. He was very political and extremely opinionated. He was forever writing scorching letters to the local newspapers. I guess, no one ever told him it could be dangerous to discuss politics. To tell the truth, when my grandmother had told my mother that Grandpa was in the hospital, I actually thought that somebody had shot him.

We returned to New York in time for the beginning of the new semester. That's about the time I realized I couldn't find my cell phone. For me it was a category five disaster. It contained every important telephone number—including Michael's.

My father found me in my room ransacking all my bags, dumping everything out, as I frantically searched for my phone.

"What's going on, Nadine? This place looks like it was hit by a bomb."

I must've had a panic-stricken expression on my face when I looked up because his demeanor changed quickly to one of concern.

"What's wrong, honey?"

The pent up tears began to stream down my cheeks. "I think I lost my cell phone."

"Don't worry. I'll call the carrier and discontinue your service. We'll get you another phone."

"You don't understand..." I whined as more tears welled in my eyes.

"Honey, we'll replace it. Losing your cell phone should be the worst thing that ever happens to you."

"It is."

"You're right, I don't understand," he said running his fingers through his hair.

"It was my phone book. Michael's number was in it. And now it's gone..."

As if a curtain of uncertainty had just lifted from his eyes, my father took me in his arms and held me as I sobbed on his shoulder. I could tell we were both on the same page now.

"Sweetheart, he'll find a way to get in touch with you."

My father contacted the carrier and let them know I'd

lost my phone. I purchased another a few days later. I thought about what my father said. If Michael was going to find a way to contact me, he'd have to be very creative. I now had a new cell phone number and hadn't given him my home number, which is unlisted. My parents didn't want a ton of calls from students.

I tried to get in touch with Michael, but hit a dead end. I was beside myself. How do you meet the man of your dreams only to lose him? The last resort would have to be the summer. Would Michael still keep his promise and come? I never got the chance to find out.

A few weeks before Christmas, my parents were killed instantly in an auto accident caused by a drunk who'd run a red light. We'd started the day as usual having breakfast together. Had I known it would be the last time I'd ever see them alive, I would've said all the things I should've told them and held them close. However, I'm no seer and can hardly deal with the present than be able to read the future. I've been told nothing is instant, not even pudding. Well, they were wrong. I was an instant orphan. An only child, I didn't even have siblings with whom to share my grief. All I had were my grandparents who flew out to be with me.

It's difficult for me to retell what actually happened from the moment the police came to my door with the news about my mother and father to the days following their funeral, because I was in some kind of suspended animation. I knew I wasn't taking their deaths well. In truth, I didn't care. I didn't want to feel. I wanted to believe it was all some stupid nightmare I'd awake from and they'd be still alive.

My grandparents put my house on the market and whisked me back to Arizona with them. During this time I was a caterpillar living in a cocoon of my own making. My grandparents tried everything they could to bring me out of it, but I resisted. It was easier to sulk and feel sorry for myself. Then I met one of their neighbors, Charlotte White.

Charlotte was somewhat younger than my grandparents. I guessed her age to be around fifty-seven. She had a pleasant, round face, permanently lined from always smiling. The gray streaks in her hair were becoming and she wore her age well. However, it was the inner beauty that made her special. Whether or not our meeting at the pool was planned by my grandmother or pure chance, I'll never know. I'm truly glad we had the opportunity to talk.

When my parents' lives were snuffed out like a candle, I had trouble dealing with it because of the way I'd always viewed things. I've never considered myself a deep thinker. Solving the world's problems I left to my grandfather and others. But, I always believed things happened for the best. It's my version of looking at the glass being half-full as opposed to half-empty. I'd tried to find the silver lining or good in everything. I had a great deal of help in doing so from my father who was a born optimist if ever there was one.

However, I couldn't find any good in the death of my parents. My entire world had come undone. There was no longer any rhyme or reason to my life. And like my world, I simply came apart at the seams. Until my meeting with Charlotte.

She had lived in Los Angeles, a single mother trying to bring up three kids. Her husband, a construction worker, had died in a freak accident leaving no insurance money. This forced Charlotte to work two jobs in order to keep a roof over her family's head and food on the table. She found it difficult, but had no choice. Her oldest son joined a gang and was killed. The middle child got hooked on drugs, while her youngest was killed in a drive-by shooting. Her world imploded. As she put it, "I didn't just hit bottom, I lived there. I crawled into a bottle of vodka and grew gills."

Looking at her the day we met, I couldn't believe she was the same person she'd just described. She'd had more than her share of tragedy and loss in her life to last three lifetimes and yet she'd pulled herself together and moved on with her life. What was my excuse?

"Don't look so amazed. I found my answer in the Lord. With Jesus' help, I found the strength to stop drinking and help my Jared kick his habit."

No, I didn't find my answer or salvation in religion. Instead, following my conversation with Charlotte, I took a hard look at myself in the mirror. I didn't like what I saw. I'm certain my parents weren't happy with me, either. They were probably furious with me for feeling so sorry for myself. Knowing my dad, he'd want me to get on with my life.

I enrolled in the local college and soon decided to become a paralegal. I'd begun a new chapter in my life; one I knew would please my parents. And no, I never forgot Michael. He would always remain in a special part of my heart.

I landed a job at a prominent law firm in Phoenix. There were five partners, fifteen lawyers and three paralegals, including me. At twenty-two, I was the youngest of the paralegals. The other two women were in their late thirties. They took me under their wings telling me which lawyers to be wary of and which to definitely avoid.

There was one lawyer, in particular, who seemed to be off their radar—Josh Thompson. I met him at my first office Christmas party, which I hadn't wanted to attend at first. Since Michael, I hadn't really dated much and found I didn't care one way or the other. Molly, one of the other paralegals practically twisted my arm.

"Coming to the office Christmas party, Nadine?" she asked during lunch one day.

"No."

"Why not?"

"Don't want to," I replied quickly.

She came back at me immediately. "You never go out. What kind of life is that?"

"Mine. And I like it just fine, thank you very much."

She rolled her eyes at me. "Well, it's about time you started dating again. A pretty girl like you...damn! A nun gets more action."

My face grew hot at her implication, but I managed to say, "I like the way things are."

"How could you? It's as if you're watching the world go by from the other side of the window."

Despite Molly's butting into my personal life, I truly liked her. She'd been a good friend to me from the first day I'd started with Thompson, Brown, St. Charles, Gould and Woodward. She was always there when I needed help and advice. She also knew about Michael. I'd hoped she'd respect my feelings on the matter of dating and my desire not to get involved with another man.

"Just come to keep me company," she said.

With all she'd done for me, it seemed the least I could do, so I gave in and said, "All right."

"Great." She hugged me, nearly sucking all the air from my lungs. All I wanted was for her to release me so I could breathe again.

When Molly and I walked into the employee lounge where the party was being held, the room was already filled with people, buzzing with the cacophony of a dozen different conversations. My gut instinct was to turn around and run. Unfortunately, Molly sensed this and took hold of my arm. "Let's go to the bar and get something to drink. After all, this *is* a party."

We got our drinks and moved off to the side. The room became more crowded and we somehow got separated. This was the last thing I'd wanted to happen. I backed my way into a corner where I'd feel safer. I didn't mind being alone. However, I soon discovered I wasn't.

A male voice behind me said, "I see you love crowds nearly as much as I do."

I turned to face a tall, pleasant-looking man in a navy blue pinstriped suit. For a split second, he reminded me of Michael, with his dark good looks. The smiling eyes I looked into were blue, not green.

"Is this your first office Christmas party?" he asked.

I nodded.

"Thought so. I'm Josh Thompson, not to be confused with the partner. Couldn't even get him to adopt me."

I laughed, already liking this man.

"I'm Nadine Stone and probably even lower than you on the food chain."

"Why, you have the distinguished look of a lawyer," he replied.

Smiling, I told him I was only a paralegal.

"Don't sell yourself short. Without your work, the cogs of this fine institution wouldn't get oiled."

"Thanks for being nice."

"My fair lady, nice doesn't come into the picture. I was merely being honest. Come, let's refresh our drinks and go sit somewhere and talk. We have a great deal of catching up to do."

Josh and I talked the afternoon away and had dinner together. He was a nice guy and I enjoyed his company. We shared many things in common, especially heartbreak. He was coming out of a relationship that had gone sour after a year-and-a-half. He'd thought she was everything he wanted until he discovered she led a secret life. A sales rep for a large pharmaceutical company, she traveled a great deal. Josh had no idea she had lovers in different states. He discovered this by accident.

"She'd mentioned she had a convention in Las Vegas. Since it was her birthday and I'd never been to Vegas, I decided to go surprise her. Only, I was the one who was surprised."

"What happened?" I asked, leaning closer.

"Well, I was told by the front desk clerk she wasn't in her room. I figured she might've gone out to dinner and decided to have a drink while I waited for her to return. I walked into one of the bars and nearly freaked."

"She was there?"

"Oh, she was there all right. She was in the corner giving some man a lap dance."

"Did you confront her?"

"Not just then. I had a couple of drinks while I tried to calm down. I didn't want to commit murder in front of all those witnesses. I waited until they left and followed them up to her room. Now I was certain."

"So you banged on her door and..."

"Nope. I had a better idea."

This was like a suspense novel. I was hooked and couldn't wait to hear what Josh had done.

"I went home and waited for her to return. She had no idea I knew about Vegas. I'd used my cell phone to take pictures of her with this guy and blew up the pictures. I hung them up over my bed. You should have seen her face when she saw them."

"Just like one of those MasterCard commercials, priceless?"

"Exactly. She couldn't deny it. Spitefully, she told me about the other men. How I didn't strangle her, right then and there, is a miracle."

I knew that woman had hurt Josh badly, for even now as he retold the story, I could detect pain in his eyes. I found myself telling him about Michael. In a way we were kindred spirits and became close friends, often having dinner or getting together on the weekends.

In the blink of an eye, two years had flown by. Josh and I grew closer. My grandparents loved him and envisioned us getting married. I loved Josh, but it wasn't the same kind of love I'd had for Michael. It could only be characterized as a comfortable relationship, with no bells ringing or whistles going off. If I married him, I knew I'd never want for anything. He'd be a good husband, faithful and loving. However, as good as it sounded, I felt something was missing.

Josh and I talked about the possibility of marriage, only it was always just that, talk. We didn't go beyond. Perhaps he sensed my hesitancy or was uncertain himself. However, as time wore on, I knew we were heading down that path.

As August approached, Josh found himself wondering where his life was heading and shared these thoughts with me.

"It's time I settled down and began to raise a family. Want to help?"

"Are you asking me to marry you?"

"Yeah, if you'll have me."

I didn't answer right away.

"Are you still unsure?"

"Maybe."

"Not a problem."

I was confused. "What are you getting at?"

"I'm going to be tied up with a pretty big case. Why don't you take a vacation and go cool off somewhere and think about us," he suggested.

I realized it wasn't fair for me to go on indefinitely as we were. Either I wanted to marry him or not. Absence made the heart grow fonder, didn't it? I kissed him goodbye and took a flight back to Lake Flint. I hadn't been there in years. The change of scenery would do me good.

I closed the book I'd tried to read and stared out the window. My mind drifted back to that last magical summer I'd spent with Michael. I'd accepted the fact a long time ago that I'd never see him again. And yet, I knew I'd never truly gotten over him any more than I'd forgotten him. So many times during the passing years I thought of him and often wondered where he was and if he'd thought of me. Perhaps going back now I'd be able to close that chapter of my life and be able to marry Josh.

At the airport I rented a car and drove to the lake. I was lucky to get a cabin for the week. As I drove toward the resort, I noticed changes along the highway. There were more restaurants and strip malls, leaving hardly any open land. The signs of progress, I mused. I rounded the lake. It looked smaller than I'd remembered. The cabins looked older and could've used a fresh coat of paint. Children were playing on the swings at the small playground and several seasonal fishermen were fishing from small boats. In my mind's eye, I saw myself riding bikes with Michael around the lake.

Stop it! I scolded myself. I came to think about Josh, not Michael. I went to my cabin and unpacked my things. I could almost hear my parents moving about in the other room. Tears welled in my eyes. I still missed them. I blinked away the tears and left the cabin to get something to eat. The manager of the restaurant had gotten older. He still reminded me of Vincent Price, but not in a creepy way. I was surprised when he remembered me.

I had a grilled cheese sandwich and coffee and read a local newspaper. Families came in for a bite and I wondered if the kids knew how lucky they were to have a family. One thing I'd learned the last several years was life is so very precious. It's the one commodity you can't replace. I finished my sandwich and returned to the cabin. It had been an early flight and I was exhausted.

After dinner, I strolled to the lake and leaned against the railing—the wishing railing. It was a beautiful night. The sky was blanketed with twinkling stars, reminding me of the times my father and I would wish on a star together. I realized as the full moon rose in the sky that it was a blue one. Dad had insisted all wishes made on a Blue Moon were special and always came true. Even though I no longer believed it, I decided to make a wish anyway. I'd intended to wish that Josh and I would have a long and happy marriage, but instead of saying Josh, I said Michael. I laughed at my own Freudian slip.

Suddenly from behind me a voice said, "I'd never forgotten that laugh."

My heart began to beat in triple time as I turned to face the man whose infectious smile I'd never forgotten, either.

"Michael?"

"You're more beautiful than I remembered," he said moving closer.

"Am I really seeing you, or have I conjured you up?" I asked.

He chuckled. "I'm really here, Nadine. I knew if I waited long enough, you'd return, too."

Tears welled in my eyes as I touched his face. He took my hand and brought it to his lips.

"I couldn't reach you during that year and thought I'd see you in the summer..." he began.

As the tears slipped from my eyes, he kissed each and every one of them.

"My parents were killed and I lost your phone number. I'm so sorry."

"You're here now. Nothing else matters," he said as he kissed my trembling lips.

When we broke apart, all I could manage to say was, "Oh, Michael, Michael..." before his lips recaptured mine, once more. "I never thought I'd ever see you again," I whispered. "I can't believe you're actually here with me now."

"I love you, Nadine. I always have and I always will. This time, I'm not letting you get away."

Michael scooped me up into his arms and carried me into his cabin. We made sweet love and like magic, the years and distance melted away as we were transported back to the golden summer we first met.

I now knew what was missing from the relationship I'd had with Josh. It was the fire and passion I found with Michael. I also knew I would return to Phoenix with a different answer from the one he expected. I didn't want to hurt him, but my life belonged in New York with Michael. It had been ordained. After all, wishes made under the magic of a Blue Moon always came true.

Visit Candace's website
http://www.candacegold.com

Devil in Spurs

by DeborahAnne MacGillivray

The road was a ribbon of moonlight, over the purple moor,
And the highwayman came riding–
Riding–
~ Alfred Noyes

Desdein Deshaunt's spurs dug into the horse's side, goading the animal onward. *Faster. Faster.* Devil take him, he abhorred running fine-blooded horseflesh until foam lathered its neck. Grimacing, he swallowed the crumbs of conscience. Warrior's Heart was a mount worthy of royalty, only fate left him no choice. This night he must push his steed to the very limit.

His brother's life depended upon it.

He leaned forward in the saddle, willing the magnificent black stallion to sprout wings and fly through the pitch-black night. With rising dread, he glanced up at the moon, his heart slamming against his ribs when he saw how high it sat in the sky.

A Blue Moon.

Folklore said if one wished upon a *Blue Moon* an enchantment would be granted. He stopped believing in hocus-pocus parlor-magic back before he left Eaton and went to live with *grand-mère* in France. Even so, circumstances warranted desperate measures.

When man needed help, he called upon God. When no answer came, he turned to the Devil. Desdein knew his soul was black as the stallion he rode, that he cared little about anything in life these past years. But he did care for Jeremy. He'd see him set free—or die trying. If he could just rescue his brother, there was a ship setting sail at dawn, bound for the Americas.

He'd give his life's blood to see Jeremy safely onboard.

Make a wish? If he had one wish, he prayed to catch the coach up ahead before it reached Kildorne Manor.

If he'd ridden hard on the heels of Lady Ashlyn Findlater, this night's work would have been a simple matter. Forced to hide his real identity, he played the *ton* buffoon, so all eyes had been upon him at the small country ball. His quick departure would've raised eyebrows.

Quite absurdly, he was in great demand these days. His rapier wit, droll humor and deadly lampooning of those about him saw Desdein at the top of all invitation lists for fêtes of the nobility. One didn't dare give the *cut direct* to the Marquis de Fournier. Though the title was real, it was worthless, coming through his *grand-mère,* who never had any blunt. Less since they escaped the *Reign of Terror*. Being a *ton* fop was just another mask he used to move through life these days.

By day, he was a gentleman horse breeder, but each night he donned the plumed apparel of a *ton* peacock and became the rapier-wit Marquis de Fournier at the most lavish balls of English nobility. Men feared him. Women wanted him. There wasn't a female—married or virgin—who'd deny him—except for Ashlyn Findlater.

Her image shimmered in his mind, the dark blonde hair, the huge grey eyes that always seemed to hold a sadness few bothered to notice. He dismissed the vision, though those eyes lingered, haunting him. They had drifted into his dreams more than once these past weeks.

The *Mad Marquis* they called him. What no one knew, under the moon's pale rays he was a highwayman. They whispered in dread he was the *Devil in Spurs* and the sobriquet stuck.

He hadn't taken to the roads for enjoyment or gain. His path was one of vengeance, pure and simple. Twenty years ago, the Earl Whitmore and Viscount Kildorne had robbed his father of nearly all in a game of Whist—*so they said*—then killed him in a duel to make certain no claims of malfeasance could be lodged. Desdein swore upon his father's grave he'd one day crush the bastards. After Father's death, Mother slipped into decline, gave up on living until she, too, lay in the cold grave. At sixteen, Desdein had been left with a worthless French title and much younger brother to see into manhood.

Since their return from France, everything had been rubbing along nicely. He robbed from the rich—men who stole from and killed his father. Gave to the poor—the very poor—he and his brother. That is until Jeremy—drunk as a lord and too cocky by half—decided to take a hand in poking Kildorne. The lackwit rashly followed the viscount home last night and stopped his carriage, pretending he was the *Devil in Spurs*. Unaware there were men in the coach with Kildorne, he suddenly found himself arrested for misdeeds his older brother had committed.

Kildorne, now the magistrate for the area, pledged he'd send Jeremy to Newgate come morn to be hanged. He swore it was because of the robberies, but Desdein feared the viscount somehow had discovered Jeremy was John Deshaunt's son. Desdein's only hope was to save Jeremy, by hook or by crook, and get him on the ship by dawn. Then he'd deal with Whitmore and Kildorne. In his own time and on a ground of his choosing.

Masquerading as the Marquis de Fournier, neither man had any idea he was Desdein Deshaunt, the son of the man they'd murdered nearly twenty years ago. A man set upon revenge.

The key to stopping Kildorne rode ahead in an elegant black coach with gold trim. Nothing but the best for the daughter of Edward Findlater, Viscount Kildorne. He grimaced as his mount failed to overtake the swift vehicle.

Lady Ashlyn Findlater was a riddle. He'd spotted her lurking around the edge of ballrooms, watching him these past weeks. The sly country mouse unnerved him, made him think she saw through his foppish mask. Her witchy grey eyes seemed to see past the façade he conjured. It was demme unfashionable for a woman—especially one firmly on the shelf and never had a season—to show she had a mind. Clearly, Lady Ashlyn needed a husband to take her in hand, keep her fat with babes and living in the country away from this nest of noble vipers.

A strange knot formed in his belly at the image of Ashlyn Findlater carrying a child. Another man's child. His groin bucked, saying the harridan had appeal. That startled him. He'd never warmed for a *healthy* lass before. Oddly, his blood buzzed from this unexpected bit of nonsense. Gritting his jaw, he dismissed her image from his mind.

The horse's neck inched forward as he spotted the coach up ahead through the trees, the light of the moon shining down upon it. He smiled. He doubted the *Blue Moon* could grant wishes, but it sure made hunting his prey easier. Reining up, he decided to cut through the wood and come out ahead of the Findlater party before they crossed Ravens Creek Bridge.

Perfect spot to stop them.

He matched the speed of the carriage, then finally pulled just ahead. Warrior's Heart vaulted the ancient stone wall, then clattered across the creek and emerged at the middle of the road, blocking the bridge's entrance.

He reined the stallion in the centre, turned and walked him slowly forward. His free hand skimmed over his pistols, at ready, but figured there would be little call for them. He noticed as Lady Ashlyn and her aunt decamped the Clevengers' route that there were no outriders for protection, just the spindly old coachman. Damn fool Kildorne obviously didn't take good care of his beautiful daughter.

It only made his night's work easier. He cocked his pistol and leveled it at the balding driver as the coach rattled around the bend.

Ashlyn leaned out the coach window, ignoring Aunt Dora tugging on her gown, trying to haul her back inside. Words on the proper deportment for a lady of her station went in one ear and out the other.

"You hang out the window like some Irish boghopper," Dora railed, giving the gown another stiff yank. "Damn your father, leaving your entry into society until this late date."

"Do stop, Auntie," she chided playfully. "You are Irish. You should not insult the land of your birth or its people."

"Aye, sure Irish, I am. And a boghopper, too. So I know

perfectly well how they act. Like you are now."

Ashlyn smiled. "There is a *Blue Moon* out tonight and it's beautiful."

Her aunt sat back on the cushion with a resigned thud. "I despair. You shall never learn the value of proper deportment."

Ashlyn didn't want to hurt her aunt's feelings. Aunt Dora tried hard to help her fit in. Only, she was so *tired* of being told what was proper—and especially what was *not*. Life was *dreadfully dull*. She hadn't been welcomed by the *ton's* cliques. Hated corsets. Refused to play their frivolous games or hide her intelligence, however unfashionable that might be.

She cringed. Her father clearly had her on the marriage mart, 'for sale' to the highest bidder. It was beyond understanding why they didn't just line up the eligible females and trot them around the room, let men check their teeth like they did horses at *Tattersalls*. Ashlyn felt out-of-step. At twenty-six, she was too old for a season. Father insisted he was trying to make things up to her. She didn't believe him. Once he got it through his maggoty brain she wasn't what men wanted for a titled wife, she figured he'd ship her back to Chattam Lane Hall. Well, she wouldn't mind. She was good at managing, making do on damn little—money or emotions. She accepted she was a bluestocking, not the proper rave, not an *incomparable*. Not even an *original*.

She was poor Ashlyn. No one ever wanted her.

Father had schooled her tonight on whom to favor, which titled sons would be a suitable match. Stuff and nonsense. The jugheaded man actually talked of the Duke of Devonfield as being a good catch. She didn't want a Duke for a husband. Nor an Earl or a Marquis. Father deemed the Marquis de Fournier his choice above all others. Her sire was impressed with the power the man wielded, the connections that would come with having him for a son-in-law.

Haunting lavender eyes flashed before her mind. Especially not a *Mad Marquis*. He'd never want her. Even if he did, she'd shoot him before the week was out. The supercilious sop. She'd seen him look down his nose at her as if he sniffed something odious. She wasn't sure why that hurt. She laughed at the *ton* and their foolish airs, but for some reason, the *King of the Buffoons'* disdain pierced her self-worth as none other. At odd instances, when those pale lilac eyes met hers, she felt a bond, a connection, like he, too, harbored scorn for the shallow people around them. Then he'd arch a brow, lift his quizzing glass haughtily and look down that aristocratic nose at her. It was all she could do to keep from kicking him in the seat of his satin-clad arse!

Oh, what she wouldn't give for a dashing warrior to sweep her off her feet. Maybe ravish her, too, though she wasn't entirely sure what ravishing involved. She knew Aunt Dora fanned herself with her hanky when the word was spoken, so surely it couldn't be all bad.

"Whatever is happening?" Dora's curiosity was aroused as why they'd slowed to a crawl.

"I cannot see. I popped out the wrong side."

She started to scootch back in, but the *Blue Moon* peeked out from the clouds, capturing her enrapt attention. It was huge! And it was beautiful and blue. Most *Blue Moons* were really white, but this one was a true blue. Her maid said on the night of a *Blue Moon* charms could be cast and enchantments woven. The huge, luminous ball surely called faeries out to dance.

"Oh, I wish something wonderful would happen to me. If not something wonderful, may I please be ravished just once before I am too old to enjoy it!"

"Ashlyn, you shameless hussy!" her aunt hissed.

The carriage rolled to a standstill, but she couldn't see anything other than the back of the driver's bald head. She heard John Coachman—whose real name was Horace—talking to someone, but the words were low, murmured. Curiosity biting, she pushed inside, intent on finding out what was occurring, when the opposite door swung open and a man leaned in.

He motioned with his gun. "You, Lady Ashlyn, come with me."

"Ashlyn is my charge. I guard her with my life," Aunt Dora declared in thespian fashion. Her mouth formed an O as the muzzle of a pistol pressed to her nose. Almost going cross-eyed, she tried to stare down the barrel.

"I take it you see my point, Madam."

Dora blinked in umbrage. "No, I see your gun, sir. This is nothing short of rude."

Ashlyn wondered if all *Blue Moon* wishes were granted so promptly. Could one make more than one wish?

Patting her aunt's arm to reassure her, Ashlyn took measure of the man on the other end of the gun. She had only the moonlight to distinguish by, just enough to make her think she wanted to see more.

His hair was dark, midnight under the moon's glow. A swatch of black material covered his eyes and nose, holes cut for them, and was fastened at the back of his head. Dressed in black and in the heavy black cape, he was little more than a phantom.

A phantom with a sensual voice that sent a shiver up Ashlyn's spine.

"I have no coinage, no valuables, you despicable varmint. I shan't give you my wedding ring. 'Tis all I have left of my poor George." Dora sniffed, then waved her kerchief in dismissal. "So off with you. We have nothing for your likes."

Ashlyn rolled her eyes. 'Uncle George' only existed in her aunt's imagination. She hated being an *old maid* and thought it better to have a dashing husband who died fighting for Wellington in Spain. In true widowly fashion, she spent her time *pining away,* for no man would ever measure up to her saintly George.

"Madam, I sorrow for your *loss*, but I am not here to rob you, especially not of anything as *cherished* as your wedding ring."

An odd note of humor in his deep voice gave Ashlyn pause. She tilted her head to study him. He sounded if he knew George Fitzgerald only existed in Dora's pretend world. Squinting, she tried to see the eyes behind the mask. She *knew* that voice. It haunted her. Something about it made her think of...

Dora fell back on the cushion, fanning herself. "Oh, mercy! My niece is a virgin. You shall ruin her. The Marquis de Fournier shan't offer for Ashlyn's hand if she has been spoiled."

"Thank God." Ashlyn turned her face aside. "Not that he'd ever want me."

The masked man's head snapped around. "Pardon?"

Their eyes locked, their minds meeting. She *knew* those eyes. It was almost *there*, shimmering out of reach, precisely where she recognized him from. In the eerie light of the *Blue Moon* they appeared a light grey. They were bedeviling, holding her until she felt air swell in her chest, unable to expel it. Incisive thoughts flickered in those ghostly depths, but she couldn't read the emotions or understand why they held such hypnotic sway over her. Why they caused her heart to slam against her ribs.

"If you must have your wicked ways with a female, then I sacrifice myself," Dora proclaimed in histrionics.

The highwayman trained the gun on Dora once more. "Keep your distance, Madam. The only sacrifice would be mine."

Ashlyn giggled discreetly as Dora spluttered in outrage. "Well, I never—"

"On that I have little doubt." With a wicked smile, he grabbed Ashlyn's upper arm and pulled. "As I said, you come with me."

Ashlyn grabbed the edge of the door and stiffened her elbow to stop him dragging her from the carriage. "Wait!"

"Resign yourself, you *are* coming with me." Resolve threaded his statement.

Ashlyn nearly growled through gritted teeth. He was strong. Very strong. And determined. "I realize you are a highwayman and all, but must you be so precipitous? I merely ask that you wait."

"Do not force me to shoot your aunt," he threatened, renewing his effort to haul her out.

Ashlyn used her foot to brace against the inside of the coach. "You...shall...not... shoot...anyone—"

"Shall I gun down your coachman to prove I mean what I say?"

"Oh, gor!" Horace fell on his bony knees, hands steepled in supplication. "Please, Mr. Devil in Spurs, do not murder me." He groveled at the highwayman's boots.

"Get up, man. Have some pride." The poor man looked quite exasperated.

Horace kept repeating his plea, inching closer. The highwayman gave one strong tug and dragged Ashlyn out the carriage door as two things happened in the same breath. The spindly coachman, in the guise of begging for his life, wrapped his arms around the robber's knee and held on, and Dora latched onto the arm he used to control Ashlyn. Her aunt fell forward and began to gnaw at the man's wrist to break his hold.

"Damnation, woman, you want me to club you down?" He shoulder butted Dora to get her to remove her teeth from his flesh while shaking his leg to force Horace to let go. "Bloody hell!"

He lifted the pistol with his left hand and discharged it into the air. Instantly, both Dora and Horace fell back, mouths agape, eyes wide.

Ashlyn frowned as he released his hold on her. She was quite willing to go with him and be ravished—maybe more than once if she liked it—but she wasn't going anywhere without her basket.

He waved the weapon at Horace. "Over there by the horses, they are spooked. Calm them or you and *this mastiff—*" he leveled the pistol at her aunt, "shall walk back to Kildorne. And you—as I said before—Lady Ashlyn, are coming with me."

"No." She leapt toward the carriage. "I am not going without Cyril."

"Who the *bloody hell* is Cyril?" He dragged her back, swinging her in a circle to face him. "Lady, you are not worth the effort."

Ashlyn couldn't move. Pain spread through her until she couldn't hurt any worse than if he'd doubled up his fist and slammed it into her stomach. Her mouth quivered as she tried to find a witty retort to show him his words held no sway over her. Extraordinarily, they did. She wasn't sure why a stranger wielded such power to cut her so deeply.

But was he a stranger? Again, a sense he was familiar brushed against her mind.

"Not worth the effort? Most likely. I have been told the

same thing, many times before, so your words hold little sting." She sucked in a deep breath to steady herself. "I merely wanted Cyril."

She leaned into the carriage and snagged the basket's handle. He snatched it from her and stepped the coach light to see inside. "Is it alive?"

Ashlyn jerked the basket back. "Of course he is."

He tilted his head as if he doubted her. "*That*, I presume, is Cyril."

Ashlyn lifted the old cat from the basket and cradled him to her chest. "If I am to go with you...Cyril comes, too."

"That is the most pathetic excuse for a moggie I have ever seen."

She tilted her chin in defiance, ruining the stance by trembling. Scared for the first time since he'd stopped the vehicle, she shuddered, clutching the tabby cat to her. "He comes."

He frowned at her in dismissal, then motioned with a second pistol for Horace to mount the coach. "You, woman, inside the carriage before I shoot you where you stand."

"Sire, your deportment is horribly lacking." Aunt Dora huffed, then stepped before Ashlyn. "Ashlyn is my charge. I shall not abandon her."

He pointed the weapon at her aunt's chest. "Fine. I have no time to argue."

Ashlyn kissed the kitty's head. "Auntie, do run along. Cyril and I shall be fine."

His smile flashed winningly in the moonlight. "Yes, Auntie, do run along—and take Cyril with you."

"Cyril goes with me." Ashlyn stomped her foot.

He cocked his head at her show of temper as if assessing her, surprised by her spirit. "I shall shoot him, but I am not taking him with us."

"Over my dead body."

At the break in her voice, his tone softened. "We have a hard ride ahead. Your kitty would not be happy. Leave him where he will be comfortable and cared for."

Tears welled in her throat. She clutched the precious cat tighter. Her only friend, at times. "Then go ahead and shoot us both. He shan't be cared for. If I am not there, *my father* will see he starves or order him drowned. I'd rather you kill us both now."

The cat in her arms purred reassuringly, as if to remind Ashlyn they'd been through a lot worse. What did it matter if the most exciting thing to happen in her life was to be shot down like a dog in the middle of the road by a highwayman? There were worse ways to die...like loneliness

He exhaled his irritation. "Can you hold him? Or does he have to be in the basket."

"I can hold him," Ashlyn assured, the tightness in her chest easing.

The man remained motionless as if making up his mind. He gave a faint nod.

"Where are you taking Ashlyn?" Her aunt demanded as he slammed the carriage door.

He took aim at Horace. "Drive...drive like the Devil is after you."

"Mr. *Devil in Spurs...*" Horace hesitated. "You ain't gonna hurt Lady Ashlyn? She's a good 'un, not like the rest of you nobility."

The highwayman cocked the trigger. "What do you know of my heritage?"

"Quality speaks. Lady Ashlyn is the only one in neigh on fifty years who ever bothered to learn my name was Horace instead of John Coachman."

"Drive on, Horace Coachman."

"Only if you give your word of honor you shan't harm the lass. She has had enough sorrow heaped upon her young shoulders."

White teeth flashed. "You accept the word of a highwayman?"

"The word of the *Devil in Spurs,* aye. A modern day Robin Hood, they say he is."

"I am no Robin of Loxley. Off with you, man." He slapped the flank of one of the horses; the coach lurched, then settled to a swift pace.

Ashlyn clutched Cyril to her chest, needing the warmth from his small body. The night was cool, but she figured the trembling was from fear. Not from standing before a devil in spurs, but the unknown.

What did he want from her? No one had ever sought her for anything before. Her father had only taken interest in her of late because he decided to use her, sell her to the highest bidder. So what could this man expect in plucking her from the carriage?

Blue moonlight broke through the passing clouds, almost shining down upon him in a halo. Stirred by the rising breeze, his mantle pulled back slightly on his shoulders, rippling and swaying with a sentient force. Her eyes traveled down to the black jackboots, which lovingly hugged his muscular thighs, to the gold spurs gleaming, then slowly up the strong, virile frame. His inky hair lay in stubborn waves, so thick she itched to touch them, discover if the curls were that soft.

Even with the mask covering part of his face and dressed all in black, he made Ashlyn's breath catch, stirring to life something in her that left her lightheaded. It wasn't quite alarm. This emotion was a drug that stilled rising apprehension within. Bathed in the sweet rays of the moonlight, he was surely conjured from her darkest heart, all that her whispered words to a *Blue Moon* could summon.

A fire started at the pit of her belly and spread downward, the radiant heat taking off the edge of the night chill. She wanted to touch this strong man, make sure he was warm, that his heart beat in his chest. Reassure herself he was man and not phantom.

He slowly came toward her, sliding the pistols under his belt. "Give me the cat." He held out his beautiful hand.

Jolted from the bit of moonlight reverie, she stepped back from him. "No. You'll hurt him. If you kill him, then shoot me, too."

"You are mad." He laughed derisively.

She tilted her chin. "Cyril is my friend."

His sensual mouth pursed as he seemed to silently count to ten. "Stop trembling. I promise not to shoot you or your kitty. You need your hands free to mount." He whistled shrilly, then his black stallion pranced up, shaking its head. "Give me...*Cyril*...while you get on."

"What a beautiful horse." Ashlyn looked at the finely arched neck and the broad back of the animal. "I've never ridden a horse. I am not sure how..."

"Damn *rouleaux*," he muttered about the trim on the hem of her gown limiting her movements. "You have to ride side saddle."

Grasping her about the waist, he easily swung her up to sit crosswise on the horse, still clutching Cyril to her chest. He rearranged her cloak so it was tucked under her legs. Lightening shot through her blood, as she'd never been touched by a man before.

Actually, no one touched her, outside of Cook when she was growing up. Mum had been too weak, bedridden most of Ashlyn's early life. She rarely saw Father in the years after Mother's death. The servants—what few Father maintained at Chattam Lane—took care of her, but none ever hugged or touched her.

His hand remained on her thigh for an instant before he looked up. In the blue luminosity, his pale eyes stared into hers with thoughts she couldn't fathom.

Then with a swirl of his heavy mantle, he swung into the saddle behind her. His strong hands took her waist and settled her securely across his thighs, enfolding the heavy cape around her. Instantly, warmth from his body rolled over her, spread through her, banishing the night's chill.

Ashlyn sat shivering, hardly able to breathe. The highwayman had his arm about her. She couldn't see it, since Cyril rested against her chest, but his hand was firmly on her waist. Each exhale pushed against his palm.

She'd often wondered what it would feel like to have a man touch her. And while it wasn't a caress of a lover, it still made her feel strange inside. Scared. Yet, not precisely panic or fear.

He urged her closer. Nervous, she tried to keep her spine stiff, but his radiance lured her. Never had she felt such body heat. Her shoulder rested against his chest. Melting slowly against him, she basked in his fire. Her eyelids slowly lowered. She was tired. So tired.

Father had played cards late last night. On nights he had men in the house and they gambled and drank, she dared not sleep, fearful one would try to slip into her room. She'd sat holding Cyril until dawn, clutching a loaded pistol.

So tired, she sighed...*so very tired.*

Scatty female had gone to sleep. She and that moth-eaten cat seemed quite content wrapped in his cape. Had they no sense a'tall? A masked man kidnaps her—and her kitty—and the two of them sleep like babes in his arms.

Jacob rushed out as he neared the cottage. He valet started to take the reins, but hesitated when he saw the sleeping woman and the cat. "Well, if that ain't trusting, your lordship."

"If you value your life, say no more." Desdein shifted, trying to figure how to dismount without waking her. "Take the cat."

Jacob's brow lowered. "Do I have to? Pretty decrepit looking."

Cyril is my friend. Why did he hear her words and think she really meant to say Cyril is my *only* friend. One she was willing to die for.

He wondered if anyone ever cared for him like that. Jeremy adored him, but he figured if pushed to the limit his brother wouldn't make that choice. Had Mother or Father cared for their eldest son that strongly? He doubted it. Oh, Father had been proud of his first-born, but Desdein was unsure if he *loved* him. Mother had lived only for her husband.

Suddenly, Desdein felt very alone in the world and envied that damn cat. He'd do what he must to set things right for Jeremy, but then he needed to take a harsh look at his life. If he survived the dawning. He wasn't a young man any more. At thirty-six, he should have a wife and sons of his own. Longing suddenly wracked his body. He *wanted* a son. Wanted that child to grow up knowing he was loved.

Jacob shook his head. "She ain't letting go of the cat."

"Hold the horse steady." He turned so he could land on two feet, still cradling her and the stupid cat.

He carried her inside the cozy hunting box and gently placed her on the bed in the darkened room. The cat let out with a raspy meow, stretched and then cuddled back down against his mistress.

Desdein pulled off her shoes and unfolded the blanket

over her. He noticed the shadows tingeing under her eyes. Reaching out, he lightly brushed the back of his hand against her cheek. A pressure built in his chest, regret he had to use Ashlyn in this manner. Inhaling to exorcise shards of scruples, he went to the outer quarters.

Putting a chunk of wood into the fireplace, Jacob looked up at Desdein in question.

Desdein glared at him as he removed his cape. Why did he have to have a valet determined to play his conscience? "Stop looking at me in that manner or I shall turn you out."

"We go back too far, you and I."

"Yes, we do. That's why you shall do my bidding without question."

"Take off that bloody mask. You'll give her a fright."

"Best I keep it on until she is ransomed."

He crossed to the table and took up the quill, scratching out a note to send to Ashlyn's father. He looked at the ring on his index finger. His father's seal. Taking up the taper, he dripped it on the flap to close it, then pressed the ring into the black wax. The time had come to let Kildorne know a ghost had arisen to haunt him.

"Take this to your contact." He tossed him a gold coin. "See he delivers it this night. I shall return the Lady Ashlyn unharmed to her adoring father as soon as Jeremy is set free. If he tarries past sunrise, I will return her *well used*. If he still has not met my terms by sunset, I shall kill her and leave her body on his doorstep."

Jacob looked down at the missive in his hand, then into Desdein's eyes. "You ain't going to really do those things to the lass, are you?"

Desdein didn't hesitate. "I shall do what it takes to see this matter at end. Now go. Time wastes."

Jacob nodded sadly and shuffled out the door.

Desdein stood staring into the fire, contemplating his actions. He felt a presence, then glanced down at his feet. That mangy cat curled around his ankle, rubbing. Irritated, for reasons he couldn't enumerate, he did his best to pretend the cat wasn't scratching his chin against his boot.

Cyril didn't take a hint.

Exhaling disgust, he leaned over to pet the cat. The beast began a raspy noise, which he took to be purring. “Worthless puss.”

As he looked up, his eyes were drawn to the dim bedroom. Ashlyn lay on her side and was wide awake. From the unblinking stare, he knew she’d heard him say he’d kill her if Jeremy wasn’t released.

Those grey eyes always seemed to have the ability to strip away the mask he wore, to reach into him. Why he’d kept his distance from her at the balls. Somehow, he’d always felt her stare and would look up to find Ashlyn watching him with hungry eyes. Those times, when their eyes locked, he’d found it hard to look away.

Once again, she held him spellbound with their witch’s power. He couldn’t even draw air.

The cat jumped up on his hind legs, trying to gain Desdein’s attention. Silly thing nearly fell over he was so wobbly. Giving his head a shake, he picked up the feline and laid him across his arm. Running his other hand down the kitty’s spine, he strode into the room.

“I believe this is yours,” he said, but didn’t return the cat to her arms, just stood stroking him as he studied her.

She sat up, pulling the blanket around her like a ruana as if cold. “I am sorry.”

Perplexed, his brow lifted. “For what, *demoiselle*?”

“You think to ransom me for someone called Jeremy?” At length, she smiled sadly. “It shan’t work. I hold little value for my father.”

Desdein’s breathing slowed as a mix of emotions hit him. He assumed she lied, most people would under the circumstances. Her eyes said otherwise. A predator’s stillness spread through him. Fear unfurled as he worried he’d miscalculated. Deeply. A blunder that could cost Jeremy his life.

What father wouldn’t go to any lengths to protect his precious daughter? He wouldn’t have thought even Kildorne could be that low. He was getting a sense that Lady Ashlyn was a sad lass and not aware of her true value.

“My father married my mother under mistaken impressions. He thought she had a lot of money, would gain him entry into the *ton*. Oh, she had the bloodlines, ancient ones, and Chattam Lane Hall was impressive—if one didn't look too closely. Mother was frail, a country lass. When she fell ill, Father grew distant. Drank a lot. Often, he would go away for long spells. She died when I was eleven. This spring, I presume he decided I might be of use on the marriage mart. My reputation shall be in tatters once word of the kidnapping becomes *on dit*. I shall have no value. So your ploy of using me to get something from him shan't gain you anything."

She looked down at the blanket, her finger tracing the lines of the tartan. Desdein's heart tightened at the sight. Ashlyn seemed so lost, so alone. Legs weak, he leaned his shoulder against the door for support.

"If...if..." The long lashes lifted over fearful eyes. "I...I ask a boon. I know you owe me naught, and possibly resent me since I cannot aid your quest...if...when you kill me..." She stopped and went back to tracing the lines of the *plaide*. Finally on a heave of her chest, she continued. "Will you care for Cyril? If you will not do that, please...kill him when you kill me."

Desdein wasn't sure what to make of this strange woman. "You are going to sit there and let me kill you? Are you a coward?"

She tilted her chin up at the insult, swallowing hard. "I am no coward, Sir, but adept at facing facts. I have no weapon to fight you. You are stronger than I, faster, so I cannot outrun you. If you want me dead, there will be little I can do to stop you. I merely wish to make sure Cyril shan't suffer. I would not like my last thought to be of him cold...hungry."

He sat on the edge of the bed, tired, in need of a few hours sleep, but this gentle soul's acceptance of her death troubled him. She was no coward. She'd fought him with amazing strength when she struggled to get the cat. She wasn't stupid, but there was a childlike innocence within her the *ton* hadn't spoiled yet. So why this acceptance of death?

"Why would," he stopped stroking the cat and lifted her chin with his crooked index finger, "a lovely young woman such as yourself accept death? I saw spirit in you tonight.

You fought to keep this worthless feline with you. I have no doubt if I said I was going to shoot him right now, you would likely claw my eyes out. Why fight for this bag of bones, but not for yourself?"

She shrugged, tried to smile but failed. "I am tired. My life has been such a struggle. Making do. No one there to care. Still, I was happy with Cyril. Then my father decided I could be turned into the proper lady a rich titled husband could want. Several nights a week his friends come. They drink and play cards until the wee hours of the morning. I sit with a gun in my lap, fearful of falling asleep. Several made crude suggestions so I knew what they would do if given the chance. Should you send me back, what would my life be like? Father will have no use for me. His *friends* will view me as prey. I am soiled goods now, even if you do not ravish me...Desdein de Fournier."

"Desdein Deshaunt," he corrected, dropping his hand. "De Fournier was *grand-mère's* name. I lived with her in France after...my parents died."

Ashlyn observed the violet eyes, enchanted by their power, as he put down Cyril and untied the mask. She'd never seen the *Mad Marquis* up this close. "You are beautiful."

There was a slightly mocking glint to his eyes, as a crooked half-smile curved the well-formed lips. Ashlyn blinked, trying to fight the spell. Despite, she couldn't help but wonder how it would feel to be kissed by those lips. Silly wish, perhaps spurred by the *Blue Moon*.

"Beautiful? Women are beautiful. Men merely handsome."

She shook her head. "You are beautiful." She nearly jerked when she caught herself leaning into him, almost tasting that kiss.

The *Mad Marquis* would never want to kiss *her*. She turned away to hide the pain that surely showed upon her face. She was so tired of being alone, tired of living with disappointment and fear.

"What is it?" he asked.

"I am weary. Not much rest last night. May Cyril and I sleep before you kill us?"

"Oh, for godsake, sleep. We shall talk about me committing murder on you two later."

Ashlyn cuddled Cyril to her stomach and huddled under the blanket, shaking. She was scared, despite what she'd told him. No one accepted death, but she was limited in what she could do in life. Women didn't have choices. A woman of her station, the best she could hope for was a good marriage. She had no control of her small inheritance, no money, no place to go. Now, the chance of an offer for a decent man was moot.

Her wants weren't many—a safe, warm place for Cyril and her to live. In the odd moment, she secretly wished for a man to care about her. One to make her feel safe, even loved.

His weight shifted on the bed, causing her to jerk. Peeking over her shoulder, she saw he slid behind her. With a quick flick of the blanket, he scooted his body against hers. Her heart jumped, slamming with strong thuds against her ribs.

"What...what are you doing?"

He lay on his back, staring up at the ceiling. "You, I and that pathetic excuse for a cat are napping until dawn."

Ashlyn had never slept with anyone but Cyril. "With me?"

Desdein raised up on his elbow and glared. "Oh, that's not proper, eh? Since I am going to ravish you and kill you, and other such horrendous things, what does it matter if we both close our eyes until light?" Yawning he laid back. "It is much easier to murder when there is light to see by."

Ashlyn feared he laughed at her, but then the *Mad Marquis* had, more than once, looked down that aristocratic nose as if she'd crawled out from under a rock.

"I never said you would ravish me." She swallowed the tightness in her throat.

"I know the Marquis de Fournier deems me unworthy enough to polish your jackboots."

His brow furrowed in perplexity. "Since I am weary, mayhap this makes no sense to me. Only, it sounds like you are disappointed because you assume I shan't ravish you."

"Don't be silly," she huffed.

He chuckled. "You believe I will kill you—and that cat.

Such deeds are in keeping with your expectations of me, yet you have no fear I would *ravish* you?"

Her chin quivered. She felt it. Tilting it up, she shrugged indifference, though she felt anything but that inside. His aloof dismissal of her as not worthy of the *ton's* acceptance had hurt. Somehow, in that setting his disdain had been hard enough to swallow. However, this very approachable version of Desdein de Fournier—Deshaunt—left the rejection all the more piercing.

"I would never presume such self-value to think the Marquis de Fournier would ever lower himself to ravish one he obviously finds distaste with. So, yes, you might kill me, but no, I would expect only your disdain at the idea of anything else."

He shifted so quickly it startled her. One moment he was quiet behind her, the next he was over her, pinning her to the bed with his hard body. Shocked, she started to ask what he was doing, when his mouth closed over hers. Then she knew! The *Mad Marquis* was kissing her!

So many things came at her all at once. His taste, the warmth of his lips. The heaviness of his body pressing down on hers. His heat seared through her, warming her to the tips of her toes. She tried to breathe, but that only filled her mind with hints of male sweat, leather and the soap he'd used, leaving her dizzy.

He lifted his head, watching her face. "You have never been kissed?"

Ashlyn faintly shook her head.

A strangled cry came from against her side. "Oh, Cyril. You crush him!"

He moved his leg so the cat could crawl out from under the blanket. "So sorry, Cyril."

The cat staggered a few steps, then crumpled. Desdein leaned toward the feline, checking to see if he breathed. He said, in his most droll fashion, "I think he's dead. If he croaked, I am chucking him out. I shall share my bed with a live cat, but I draw the line at sharing it with a dead one."

She sat up and cradled the limp creature to her breasts. Nice breasts, too, he noted; he rather envied the ruddy beast.

"He just wore himself out. Poor dear tires easily days."

He carefully lifted the tail, so limp he really questioned her assessment of Cyril's ability to breathe. "Poor thing is about to stick his spoon in the wall." Desdein was sorry he mentioned the stupid cat dying, for she clutched him all the tighter.

Rubbing her cheek to the furry head, she sneaked a tearful glance at him. "There is no need to be cruel. I know I shan't have him for much longer."

Desdein sighed, feeling like a knave. "How long has Cyril been your friend?"

"I was eight when I found him. It was deep winter and I kept hearing a kitten crying. At first it sounded like it came from within the wall. Then I figured out he was under the house. I went out and found him, hiding in a break in the foundation. Hungry, thirsty and scared to death. There were no other kittens about, no mum kitty, so I don't know where he came from. You might say he was my Christmas present. Never had one before."

"You were not allowed a cat before?"

Her grey eyes reflected sorrow. They held his with a power that seemed to reach into him, affect him, change him. With such love and tenderness, she rubbed her cheek against the cat. "No...never had a Christmas present before."

Desdien's head snapped back, shocked by her statement. "Why ever not?"

She swallowed, then shrugged as if it didn't matter. "Mother was sick, bedridden for most of my childhood. Some days she barely knew what day it was. Father was often in his cups or off in London gambling for weeks at a time. Christmas came and went. More important things to spend money upon. Food, medicines for Mother."

So Cyril had been her friend for eighteen years. A pressure welled in his throat and the muscles tightened as he considered Ashlyn's friend's days were few. Who would be her companion then? "Let me fetch him something to eat. He is likely hungry."

"I would appreciate it. It gets harder and harder to keep his weight up."

He bit back commenting on Cyril's numbered days and

scooted off the bed, wishing he'd never kidnapped Ashlyn Findlater.

Wishing he'd done it years ago instead.

Ashlyn curled on her side, staring into the flames, as she stroked the cat. After a meal of milk, oatmeal—and whisky—he was quite content. The oatmeal had been Ashlyn's suggestion since he needed to keep from getting any more decrepit than he already was.

As Desdein stood mixing it to a good consistency, he chuckled to himself. The *Mad Marquis* making gruel for a cat. The *ton* would have a hearty laugh if they ever learned about that. Then he noticed the bottle of Highland Whisky. Maybe the silly beast had aches and pains from being old, so he slipped a wee dram into it and didn't mention it to Ashlyn. She seemed surprised Cyril cleaned his plate. The moggie rested on the bed, enjoying the pets, and actually looked content, eyes bright.

From across the room, Desdein sat in the chair, watching her, wishing she'd run those strong hands over his body. Heat crawled over his skin and licked at the base of his brain, then spiraled downward to his groin with a pulsing hunger he found hard to dismiss. In order to ignore the rising compulsion to stalk over and cover her, taking her with smooth and sure strokes, he sought distraction in provoking her.

"Have you a last wish?" His teeth gnashed at his foolish prodding for her eyes widened in alarm. He wasn't really a cruel bastard, but it gnawed at his mind this woman was dispirited. His intuition said she wouldn't accept death as peacefully as she presumed. There was a banked fire in this lady, just waiting for the embers to be stirred. "No, I am not plotting to murder you—*just now.* I merely thought to get the preliminaries out of the way."

She glared at him. "You are different without the affectations of the *Mad Marquis*, yet you find it hard to drop the mask, do you not?"

Putting his hands on his hips, he slowly stood. "Meaning precisely, little mouse?"

She frowned at the sobriquet, but let it pass. "You belittle people, make them feel small, worthless."

"The *ton* must have its amusements." He gave a mock bow as if a performer. He sat on the edge of the bed and regarded her. How could she make him feel shallow, empty with so few words? "I was never cruel to you."

She glanced at the cat, then buried her face against his neck.

Had he hurt her? Too often, he felt the many masks he wore beginning to take over, to where it was harder to recall who Desdein Deshaunt was. He reached out and lifted her chin, forcing her to look him in the eyes. "Was I?"

A tear glittered in her eyes. "You kissed me."

"And that is cruel?" His thumb stroked the corner of her mouth, watching her lip quiver. "Such sadness in those eyes. Why would you think a kiss was my way of hurting you?"

"Why did you kiss me?"

"It seemed logical at that moment. That still doesn't explain why you assumed I meant it as cruelty."

"Had you kissed me because you wanted to, it would have been nice. But you only kissed me to prove a point."

"*Nice?*" Desdein growled the word. "You arrogant little mouse."

"Mouse!"

He pointed a finger at her. "See you even squeak like one."

"I am not a mouse!"

"The mouse insists she is no mouse. Shall we find out just what you are?" The spurs had set in his mind. There was no pulling back.

He leaned to her, his mouth closing over hers, slowly teaching her the way to kiss. She was quickly swept up in the building sensations. He felt her release the cat, then grasp his upper arms as if she needed to hold on to steady herself.

His body burned, fire slithered under his skin, spreaded down his spine and slammed into his groin with a power he'd never felt. Gently he placed his hand on her waist urging her closer. Her taste sped through his system and hit his brain with the effect of fine whisky, making him dizzy with the need to take her. That fine edge of losing control rose within his mind, so he forced himself to pull back.

Nearly his undoing, she leaned into him, following.

The side of his mouth tugged up into a smile. "Eager little mouse." He slowly ran his thumb over her lower lip as his eyes studied Ashlyn. "Now that you have had your kiss, I shall stop being cruel to you and you can go to sleep. I fear it's going to be a long night."

"Will you lie down with Cyril and me again?" came the soft question, as she slid down under the blanket. "You were so warm. It felt...nice."

"I forbid you to ever use the word *nice* again." He tried to sound threatening, but feared it wasn't reflected in his face or tone.

She shifted, covering both her and the cat with the blanket, then peeked out. "If I say nice again what will do you? You are already going to murder me, so that does limit your threats."

"I could beat you."

She took a couple of breaths, the grey eyes stripping his soul. "You could. You are very strong. Only, I do not think you would ever raise a hand to a woman in anger. Why I think you won't kill Cyril or me."

He frowned, wondering what else she saw within his black heart. Uncomfortable with her directness, he snapped, "Go to sleep, little mouse, before I think of other means of torture for you. Your constant prattle gives me a megrim."

"To torture something is to be cruel, is it not?" A glint flashed in those eyes, showing a mischievous spirit that had been missing before. "Will you kiss me again?"

"Methinks you are too interested in kisses for a virginal miss." He leaned forward, but pulled back when he realized he'd placed his hand on upon her hip. Glancing toward it, he noticed the roundness, wondering how it would feel to have his palm on her warm flesh instead of the rough tartan blanket.

She propped her head upon her hand. "I asked, but you never answered. Why did you kiss me?"

Cyril's head popped from under the blanket, evidently requiring a great effort, for he promptly rolled over in a drunken faint.

"Is he strangling?"

"He's purring."

"It sounds like he's gasping for air. I think I should shoot him. Put him out of his misery."

"Stop threatening to shoot Cyril. You do that just to tweak me. You play at being perverse, Desdein Deshaunt. You wear the mask of a highwayman, but methinks it's not for gaining of coin or jewels. And the *Mad Marquis* is yet another of your pantomimes. Who kissed me? The Devil in Spurs, the Mad Marquis or Desdein Deshaunt?"

"Very well, I shan't murder you—or that pathetic creature you call a cat." He swatted her hip, causing her to yelp. "That does not mean I cannot beat you. Go to sleep, Ashlyn Findlater, or..." He nearly flinched. Why had he added the *or* on the end?

"Threatening me, Desdein?"

She smiled. The bloody wench smiled! One of those virginal come-hither smiles that sent a man's blood to boiling, asking things from him she shouldn't. He'd never spent time chasing virgins, they were so bloody boring, but he had a feeling Ashlyn would never bore him.

Like a crack of lightning, Desdein knew this was the woman he could spend his life with. She could give him fine, strong sons, maybe a daughter with her eyes. They could be happy together. Desdein saw tomorrow, and all the tomorrows thereafter in those grey eyes.

He also knew it was naught but mist under a *Blue Moon*. He wasn't sure if he truly believed in fate. Deep inside he knew one thing—come morn, Jeremy would be free and on that ship or by damn, he'd die trying. Might die in any case. Nothing mattered but his brother's safety. He'd promised Mother on her deathbed that he'd always take care of his Jeremy. Comprehending this, he had nothing to offer this gentle lass, no dreams of maybes, if onlys or castles in the air to conjure.

His heart had a strange pressure, like a cramp seized it and it couldn't beat properly.

Now he faced a new problem with Ashlyn. He'd ruined her reputation. No gentleman would want a wife who'd been carried off by the *Devil in Spurs*. Poor lass would be sent to the country, once more to live a solitary life, soon not even to have even Cyril. No man would look at her and see the fine intelligence, the quality breeding, the pure soul. A heart aching for love.

Unable to bear looking at her lovely face, he started to turn away, but she caught his sleeve.

"Who, Desdein?"

The mask slipped back into place—too easily. The condescending tone of the supercilious fop answered for him. "Who kissed you? Why the *Mad Marquis*, of course.

He will have something to recant to all the *ton*. That he kissed a country mouse, and the silly goose called it torture."

Her smile faded. Her full lip quivered. "No...I called you cruel. I was right."

Jaw setting, he glared at her with icy arrogance. "Yes, I live for it."

Desdein turned and strode back into the other room to the fire to warm the chill spreading in his body. He didn't look back, knew if he did it'd be a mistake. Not even when he heard her quiet sob. Should he turn back he'd have kissed every tear he'd brought to those solemn eyes. Then he would, indeed, be cruel.

Not to her. To himself.

For touching a dream that could never be.

Ashlyn awoke with a sense of unease. Immediately she feared it was Cyril. Often she broke her slumber, fearful her small friend had drawn his last breath without her getting to hold him one last time or tell him how much she loved him and would miss his gentle company.

She reached out and felt the warmth of his body, then tension eased in her somewhat. Still, there was disquiet within her. Something was wrong.

She slid off the bed, her eyes went to the other room, seeking Desdein, saw he was in a chair before the fire.

He was slumped in the chair, a half-empty decanter on the floor within reach. His arm hung over the chair arm, the long fingers gripping a single piece of paper. As she neared, she thought he was asleep, but when her body blocked the fire from his face, he looked up.

Weary, the dark of his beard showing, he looked very

rumpled, very accessible. For once the masks were down. His long legs, sprawled wide, were still encased in the tight riding breeches, the jackboots, fitting like a glove to mid-thigh.

Being a bold, sinful lass, she knelt between his knees and put her hands on the leather covered thighs. He watched her, the lavender eyes bloodshot from lack of sleep and the drink. She wanted to ask him what was wrong, but could only stare at the beautiful face of Desdein Deshaunt. She'd always thought him handsome at the few parties they'd both attended. He was a graceful, elegant man who played at being a fop. But she'd noticed how his clothes fit his body, how there was solid muscle under the silks and velvets.

There was a throb in her body, like a heartbeat, but slower, stronger, moving through her, driving her. As she watched him, the inner plaint strengthened.

"Desdein, what is wrong?"

His lower arm lifted, holding the piece of paper. "Your father's reply."

She shivered with a chill though the fire burned brightly, warmed her back. There was no need to read it. She knew what her father's response would be, had warned Desdein her sire would never trade her for his brother.

"What shall you do?" she whispered.

He leaned forward so they were almost touching foreheads. "Do you wish to know what it says?"

She swallowed. There was a hard edge to Desdein's measured words. His mood was dangerous and she'd be stupid not to recognize it. His feral stillness set her heart to slamming against her ribs, as she stared at the sensual lips she so wanted to kiss again. And again.

"I told you I had no value to him. I am sorry. I wish I could make it up to you."

"How would you make it up to me, Ashlyn? What would you do?"

"Whatever you want." She tried to smile, but the words hurt. "I told you I am not worth much to anyone."

Releasing the letter, it fluttered to the floor. "Do you know what you offer me?"

"No. I know volumes about ancient history, or how to do

accounts for an estate. I did not have a tutor. Could not afford one. I learned what I know by reading."

"Then let me be your tutor."

He took her mouth with a roughness that was startling. It shocked her, but she quickly accepted the wildness within him. His arms pulled her against his body, her breasts pressing to his chest. She felt like a leaf caught in a storm, unable to do anything but let the wind carry her along into the maelstrom.

He reached down, then rose, sweeping her into his strong arms, cradling her. She stared into the lavender eyes, realizing they had a bluish tint up close.

Just like her Blue Moon wish.

Desdein was her *Blue Moon* wish come true.

He should have never touched her. There was too much frustration, anger, blind rage boiling within him. Too many things to consider. He had to save Jeremy, but he couldn't use Ashlyn in this manner. He owed her that. There was only one thing left to trade—himself.

He looked at the paper on the floor, barely making out Kildorne's words, shakily scrawled across the cream-colored velum.

For God sake, please don't harm her. I shall do anything you want. Name it.

He'd been selfish not to show Ashlyn that she'd more value to her father than she knew. But he'd wanted Ashlyn. Wanted to carry her sweet memory with him when he faced Kildorne. Maybe carry it to the grave.

Desdein sighed, then thought of the second missive he'd sent to Kildorne, telling him to protect his daughter, bring Jeremy to Hallowden Hill at dawnbreak and he would trade the Devil in Spurs for his brother. The reply came, agreeing. He'd hold Kildorne until Jeremy could be sped upon his way. Then damn his soul, Kildorne and he could die together.

Only what to do about Ashlyn? He had sat before the fire trying to drown his fury in the Scotch. She'd be ruined in the *ton's* eyes, even though he'd done naught more than kiss her. They'd brand her fallen. He recalled her speaking of being tired, from sitting up at night with a pistol to protect her honor. His kidnapping her had sentenced her to endless nights of such terror.

His hand had clenched around the paper that held Kildorne's reply to his second offer and tossed it into the fire.

No matter. He'd know he left her unsullied, the one pure, honest thing he'd ever touched in his life. He would've spared her innocence, though he burned with every fiber of his being, wanting her as he'd never wanted anything in his whole life. In Ashlyn's arms was Salvation, the power to heal his troubled soul. But for once, he was going to do what was honorable.

Maybe on nights of the *Blue Moon* she would gaze out her window and think of him, of her first kiss from a man known as the *Devil in Spurs*.

Only, she came to him, put those strong, beautiful hands upon his thighs and said she'd do anything. Sealing her fate.

He'd die come dawn, so he wanted these last few hours with her. He wanted her burned into his memory.

Pausing by the bed, Desdein kissed her, softly, sweetly, reverently at first. As he broke it, intending to put her down, Ashlyn's raspy sigh of hunger let loose the demons within him. His mouth took hers, letting her feel the power of his need, almost fearing he'd shock her. Being a virgin, Ashlyn deserved tenderness, but he wanted her with a forced that rocked him. It empowered him, yet in the same breath left him helpless against the driving energy, pushing him to take. Claim. Brand.

Setting her on her feet, he trembled—not from holding her weight, from reining in the frantic craving that twisted his guts. As he unfastened the back of her gown with the care of a lady's maid, he suffered the need to bury himself in her body. Make them one. Ashlyn held no comprehension how much it cost him not to rip the clothing from her lush body.

He left her the chemise; so thin, so sheer it inflamed his desire more than protected her from his gaze. Utterly dumbfounded, he paused to stare at her beauty, the rounded hips, the full breasts. Unable to stand not touching her, he fell to his knees before Ashlyn, intent on worshipping her. His hand seized her waist, yanking her to arch to him so his mouth could latch upon one breast through the gauzy material. Her hands clutched his upper arms, her fingers biting the muscles. He drew hard on the soft breast, sucking with a rhythm that brought mewls to her throat. He kept it up, pushing her higher and higher, her hips pressing against his stomach in age old mating instincts. Her open responses made it harder for him to keep control.

"Oh, Desdein, is this ravishing?"

His mouth released the hold oh her nipple to reply. He lifted her onto the bed, as he began to undress. "It is indeed."

"Can a man ravish a woman more than once in a night?" she asked in seriousness.

His smile was predatory. "He can...should he enjoy it."

"Will you...*enjoy* ravishing me, Desdein?"

As he pulled off his shirt, the sly minx leaned to him and her mouth latched onto his hard male nipple, her actions mimicking his. He sucked in a sharp breath to steady himself as his groin nearly exploded with the wildfire she set off in him. "Enjoy? Hmm, ah...yes...I think that is a distinct possibility. Enough! I cannot think with you doing that."

He pushed her back on the bed, dancing on one foot then the other as he pulled off the jackboots. Ashlyn laughed and lay back on the bed, watching him with hungry eyes until he finally was naked. Putting a knee on the bed, he slid over her careful to keep his weight on his elbows.

"Why are you laughing, you scatty woman?" He slid one of his legs between hers, pushing them apart, smiling at her lack of resistance.

She loosely wrapped her arms about his neck. "I think Aunt Dora's comments on ravishment to be grossly misconstrued."

"Shall I teach you the right of it, my pet?"

Her radiant countenance, bathed in shadow and firelight, turned solemn. Her grey eyes stared into his, so open, so needing him. "Teach me, Desdein."

"For you, lass, I would slay dragons and duel wizards." He liked the sheer material of the chemise, gossamer, as if it was made of faeries wings, so he left it on. As if feasting, he took her other breast in his mouth, using his tongue, his teeth, drawing on it until she writhed and keened in need.

She came apart in his arms, barely understanding her body's responses to him.

Barely felt the virgin's pain as he entered her.

Ashlyn jerked awake and tried to focus. Sore in places she didn't know a woman could be sore, she smiled, recalling her night with Desdein. If Aunt Dora knew how much she enjoyed being *ravished*, poor dear would faint and need smelling salts.

Blindly, she yawned and stretched, looking for Desdein. She wanted to touch him, run her hands over his strong body. Her lover. Those two words had a special, secret ring to them.

Cyril sat on the end of the bed, his tail snapping, unhappy for some reason.

Apprehension crept up her spine as she felt the bed was cold where he'd lain beside her. She looked about for her dress, then spied Desdein's black breeches and shirt, and quickly dressed in them. They were much warmer, and it felt rather free wearing men's clothing. Easier to put on, requiring no maid. Except for the waist, they were a decent fit, but by tightening the belt she solved that problem.

She pulled up short when she saw Desdein's valet building the fire. "Where is your master?"

"Gone."

Why did that word provoke such fear in her? "Gone where?"

"He arranged a trade with your lord father."

"Trade? What? My father shan't want a daughter who has been soiled."

He shrugged, handing her the paper. "Mebbe, you underestimate your father. Maybe Deshaunt ain't trading you. He figured the *Devil in Spurs* would do the trick. Sought to spare you."

Ashlyn's eyes skimmed her father's words, startled by

the emotion they conveyed. In spite, she could spare little time to wonder at him. She paled when Jacob revealed Desdein's intentions. "He cannot! Yes, the blasted man would. Oh, drat. How long ago did he leave? Where did he go?"

She dashed to the door, then remembered Cyril. In a dither, she hunted for his basket, recalled they hadn't bought it, then searched for her shoes, but could only locate one. Shaking, she was doing her best not to cry, but she feared she'd be too late. Blasted man might do something stupid, like give himself up or shoot her father and get shot himself. Of course, with her father it would be an accident since the man couldn't hit the broad side of the barn.

"Here now, you cannot go barefooted." The valet came back into the room with a pair of boots. "They were Master Jeremy's when he was but a lad. They might fit."

"Thank you." She sat down and tugged one on, pleased by how well they fit. "Where did he go?"

"The master said not to tell you, but I figure you are the only one to stop him getting himself killed. Hallowden Hill. There is a ship anchored in Hallowden Bay. The master hopes to see his brother onboard and at sea by first light."

"How long ago did he leave?"

"Not long."

"Can you fetch me a horse?" She bit her lip. "I forgot. I cannot ride."

"I have a carriage awaiting you. The marquis said I should take you and the cat to Crayford Hall. He left papers naming you as the new owner."

"How kind of him, but if he thinks he is going to get away from me that easily, the man has pudding for brains."

The sour faced valet smiled. "Sounds like, miss, you care for the Marquis."

"I hate his bloody guts." She scooped up the cat. "Come, Cyril, we have to go catch a devil."

The sun was up, for the good it did. Fog rolled in at daybreak and was so thick Desdein could hardly see a few feet ahead of him. He'd dismounted and waited. Two loaded pistols were tucked behind his belt, against his back, another was in his hand.

Warrior's Heart murmured deep in his throat, then jerked against the reins, alerting him that the black coach slowly eased forward, inching its way through the fog. The driver, Horace, reined to halt at the top of the hill when he saw Desdein. Heart slamming against his ribs, he wasn't sure he breathed until the door to the carriage opened and Kildorne finally stepped down. The man glanced back inside the coach, then back to Desdein, surprise in his eyes.

The Viscount held up both hands to show he carried no weapon, then started forward. "Marquis de Fournier, I...did not expect you to be here. I meet that highwayman...*Devil in Spurs* they call him." His eyes rested on the pistol in Desdein's hand.

Desdein lacked time for pleasantries. "Did you bring him?"

"Then I take it *you* are the highwayman?"

Desdein sketched a mock bow. "At your service, Viscount.

"Where is my daughter?"

"Where is my brother?" He raised the pistol and trained it on Kildorne.

The elder man lifted his lower arm and made a flick with his wrist. Horace tied off the reins, then stepped down. Going to the door, he leaned in and pulled Jeremy out, hands tied before him. He looked a little mussed, but none the worse for wear. Since hearing of his arrest, Desdein feared they might have beaten him...or worse.

As his brother took a step, Desdein heard a carriage racing up behind him, driving too fast in the fog. He figured there could only be one person foolish enough to have Jacob clattering about in this mist at breakneck speed. *Ashlyn*.

His heart swelled she cared enough to come, yet it would've been much easier if the matter were over before she'd awoken. Her father's eyes tracked the carriage, as it rattled to a stop behind him. The door flew open and Ashlyn leapt out, even before it came to a full rest.

"Jacob, I shall turn you out without references for bringing her."

"Yes, your lordship. Better than her beating me with the

horsewhip, as she threatened." Jacob's nonplussed tone said he hadn't really feared that. The meddling valet had brought her hoping she'd stop him. "Of course, if you are tossed in Newgate you shan't need a valet and your references would have dubious value."

The corner of his mouth twitched, seeing Ashlyn wore his clothes. She ran to him, putting her left hand on his back, and asked breathlessly, "Desdein, what are you doing? What is this about Newgate?"

Just as he opened his mouth to explain, Cyril staggered out of the carriage and came to wind around his feet. "Ashlyn, gather Cyril before he exhausts himself and then get back into the coach. Jacob, take her to Crayford Hall as per my instructions."

"No, Desdein," she refused, placing a hand on his upper arm.

Jacob just shrugged.

Desdein glanced at her beautiful face, pale but determined. Ashlyn hadn't batted an eyelash that he held a pistol on her father, nor had she spared his brother a glance. Her focus was on him. He smiled. It felt good to have someone worry about him. Sad it came too late in his life. Maybe had he found Ashlyn years before, he'd be comfortably settled with her, too wrapped up in making babes with her to let vengeance claim his whole life.

"'Tis a good thing I did not ask you to marry me. I would likely have to beat you every day just to get you to obey me."

She sighed. "Most likely, and on Sunday you might try to murder Cyril and me, as well."

"Trust me?"

She swallowed her fear. "I trust you not to beat me or murder me. Or Cyril."

"Then let me do what I must without interfering. Yes, Desdein?" he prompted.

She hesitated so long he feared she'd refuse, finally she said, "Yes, Desdein."

"Stay behind me while I handle this." He looked to her father, noticing the man intently watched the byplay between then. Rather than loathing, he saw calculation and possibly a spark of hope. That puzzled him. Did the man hope to use Ashlyn against him?

"Send Jeremy toward me." His voice rang out in the hushed fog that eddied about them.

Jeremy glanced toward Kildorne, who nodded, so his brother started forward.

As he neared, his blue eyes rested on Ashlyn, then traveled the length of her body. He arched a brow as he returned his gaze to Desdein.

"Well, it seems big brother rescues me yet again." Jeremy grinned, then noticed Cyril curled around Desdein's leg. "I suppose *that* comes with her?"

Desdein tossed Jeremy the reins of Warrior's Heart. "Get on him and ride. There is a ship waiting in the bay. It shall carry you to the Colonies. Money and clothes are in the bag." He turned to Ashlyn. "Untie his hands so he can leave."

"Damned if I shall be packed off to leave you alone—"

"I must deal with this, Jeremy, in my own way." He glared at his brother, but saw it had no effect.

This seemed so easy in the planning. In his mind he'd set Jeremy on his way, then he'd challenge Kildorne to a duel, face the man as his father once had. Then kill Edward Findlater. Fate full circle. He figured Kildorne's man would shoot him for the effort, but what did he really have to live for? He was thirty-six, wasting his life playing games of revenge, courting death—for each time he rode out as the *Devil in Spurs*, it might be the night that cost him his life. Jeremy would soon marry, start his own family. He'd be alone.

Nevertheless, as he stood facing Kildorne, he felt that mangy cat curved around his ankle, purring in his asthmatic wheeze, Ashlyn's hand at the small of his back, her fingers flexed on the muscles of his upper arm.

Suddenly, he wasn't alone. Suddenly, he no longer had nothing to lose.

Only he couldn't back off from his vengeance. He owed his father whom he'd loved.

"You present me with a problem, Marquis. You said you'd trade yourself for Jeremy. I kept my end of the bargain." Her father moved forward, holding his hand out for Desdein's weapon.

As Desdein passed the pistol, both Jeremy and Ashlyn pulled the guns out that he'd tucked in the belt at his back. His jaw set. Everyone was muddling his plans!

"Father, give him the gun back. Now. I cannot ride a horse, but you know I am a crack shot."

Ashlyn held the gun aimed at her father. Not shaking, the woman was resolute, determination etched in the tilt of her stubborn chin. When there was no move to comply, the reckless wench actually stepped before him as a shield.

"You defend a criminal...a highwayman?" Kildorne queried.

"Yes, Father, I would. With my life."

Desdein batted his eyes, to blink away the forming tears. Knowing if he hadn't loved Ashlyn before, her words would've stolen his heart in that instant. His lady was worth a king's ransom—worth life itself. There was a strange stillness in him, regretting he couldn't have seen her value weeks, months ago, when there was still time to turn back from the course he'd set before them.

"Ashlyn, give me the gun."

She must've noticed his odd tone, a tone of finality, for confusion flooded her eyes. "You should take the gold and board the ship, Desdein. Go free. I...I would follow you...if you would but have me. I would not care where we go as long as I was at your side."

The corner of his mouth twitched in a sad smile. "You and Cyril?"

She licked her lips nervously. "Of course Cyril comes with me."

Cyril looked up at Desdein and meowed as if saying yes, he would come. "Stupid, worthless cat. I need to shoot you."

He leaned to Ashlyn and brushed his lips against hers, a kiss so gentle, so sweet he could die for it. With his left hand he took a firm grip on her wrist, then pried her fingers from around the pistol's grip. "Jeremy," he said and then gave a faint jerk of his head, signaling his brother to take control of Ashlyn and move her out of harm's way.

His brother came around, taking hold of Ashlyn's shoulders, pulling her back. "Come, Lady Ashlyn, leave Desdein to do what he must."

She jerked away and threw her arms around him. "Please, Desdein, don't go with him. We can go anywhere. I love you."

He glowered at his brother, who tried to pull her away. Desdein caressed her cheek with the back of his hand. "I am not going with him, My Love. It ends here...now."

Her father, watching Jeremy drag Ashlyn to the coach, finally allowed the words to register. He seemed befuddled, then a trace of fear spread over his countenance.

"See here, I did as you said. Release my daughter, de Fournier—" He stepped backward as Desdein moved toward him.

"My name is not de Fournier."

"I...I don't...understand..."

Desdein kept walking him back toward the other coach. "Oh, I am the Marquis de Fournier, a title through my *grand-mère,* distaff side. But my family name is Deshaunt—"

"Deshaunt!" The name rattled the man, his skin turning sallow.

Desdein stopped halfway between the two vehicles. "Yes, John Deshaunt's son. The man you murdered."

"It wasn't mu...murder. It...wa...was a duel."

"Just like the one we shall have now."

"Duel..." The man shook his head vigorously. "I...I am not fighting a duel."

"Shall I shoot you where you stand?"

He saw Horace chuckle silently atop the Kildorne coach, obviously thinking back on his previous threats to shoot him and Dora, so Desdein glared at him.

"Your...fa...father was killed in a fair duel—"

Desdein shrugged. "This one will be fair. Turn your back and I turn mine. Horace count to ten."

The bald head nodded. "Aye, Sir."

"On ten we turn and fire."

"And if I refuse?" The man clutched the gun by the barrel as if he'd never held it before.

"Then the *Devil in Spurs* will shoot you where you stand, your lordship." Horace appeared to be enjoying this a tad too much.

The viscount slowly turned and put his back to Desdein.

He felt the trembling as they stood shoulder to shoulder.

"One!" Horace called out.

Desdein should have faced the other direction. As the coachman called out, each step took him closer to Ashlyn. Tears streamed down her face as she silently watched him, her eyes pleading. Something brushed the side of his boot and he looked down to see Cyril tottering along beside him.

He saw her mouthing the words, *I love you. Do not do this, My Love.*

Warmth filled his heart. He wasn't alone anymore—someone loved him.

Suddenly ravens took flight passing overhead, their cacophony discordant within the fog's stillness. Ravens. Birds of death in Celtic lore. They carried souls to the otherworld.

He looked at Ashlyn's grey eyes. Should he soon draw his last breath, the last thing he wanted to see, to carry with him, would be her beautiful face. Only, he'd rather see it each morn as the sun rose. Kiss her by the flicker of firelight. Gaze upon her lovely countenance as she slumbered in the shadowed night.

Sometimes life is as simple as that.

Distantly he heard *ten* called, but he could only stare at Ashlyn. *One last look.* He sucked in a breath and turned to tell Kildorne he was calling quits to this. It served no purpose. The dead were dead. Killing Kildorne wouldn't bring his parents back. Though Ashlyn harbored little love for the man, he was her father, murdering him wasn't the way to start their life together.

Desdein dropped his arm, the gun pointing to the ground and stared at the man, trembling so hard his knees nearly knocked together. Kildorne lifted the gun and tried to point it, his arm quivering so he couldn't keep the gun still. Worse, the silly man closed his right eye tight, as if struggling to see. Then he switched and closed the left trying to focus with the right. Finally, he closed both and pulled the trigger.

The ball whizzed past, striking a tree far to his right. Desdein wanted to throw back his head and laugh. The man wasn't just scared—he was little better than half-blind! He looked to Ashlyn in question. "He always like that?"

She nodded. “He cannot see things at a distance.”

Desdein drank in her tear-stained face, thinking how he loved her. But he had to finish this before he could tell her, show her. She strained against Jeremy’s hold, but his brother’s grip held fast. Wicked wench, she tried to kick back with her booted foot, but his brother deftly dodged.

He lifted his finger to his lips, a gesture to hush her, then slowly walked back to the trembling man. “I believe I still have a shot to take.”

The man fell to his knees, hands folded before him in prayer. Eyes skyward, he beseeched, “Oh, Lord, I am a sinner, and if it is Your will that I die for those sins, then so be it. But I will not die with the untruth still spoken.”

“What untruth?” Desdein demanded, stopping before the kneeling man.

The man swallowed and looked Desdein in the eyes. “I did not fire the shot that felled your sire.”

“You cannot see in the distance?”

He nodded.

“Then who?”

“The Earl Whitmore. Of course, he was not the earl then. His father was alive, threatening to disinherit him if he brought any more shame upon the Whitmore name. The old man was on his deathbed. Whitmore and your father fought. Whitmore turned on a count of eight and fired.”

“And you lied,” Desdein accused through gritted teeth.

He nodded. “He paid me. Half his fortune upon his father’s death. I needed the money...Ashlyn’s mother...”

Desdein’s head jerked around to his horse, taking a step. But the man lunged, catching his arm. “No, do not think it. God has judged him. Word came, night before last he was set upon by footpads in London and was beaten senseless.”

“He lives?” Desdein growled.

“Aye, the man does, likely not long. The physician says he will never have his wits again—if he recovers.” Kildorne looked toward his daughter. “Ashlyn has been wronged by me. I am not wicked, just selfish. I was poor when I married Ashlyn’s mother. When she grew ill, it was hard keeping Chattam Lane so it didn’t fall down around our heads. It was hard to watch the woman I loved die a little each day before my eyes. I drowned my sorrow, my worthlessness in the drink, stayed away when the pain became too much. I stayed away too often. One day, I awoke to Ashlyn's hatred and no words to heal the breach between us. I was weak. Sometimes I just wanted to die so much that I failed in my duty to my daughter. Do not fail her, as well, Desdein Deshaunt."

Ashlyn finally stomped on Jeremy's foot, causing him to release her. She ran to Desdein and threw herself into his arms, sobbing.

He chuckled, then wrapped his arms around her, holding her against him. His lady in breeches. "I have never hugged a woman in trousers before." He looked past Ashlyn to her father. "Looks like you shall get the Marquis de Fournier as a son-in-law after all."

Kildorne smiled. "If my daughter shall have you."

He pulled her arms from around his chest where she nearly squeezed the breath from him and eased her back. "Will you have me, Ashlyn?"

His bride-to-be doubled up her fist and belted him in the stomach. Not expecting it, the blow caused him to bend forward. As he gasped, he looked down at the silly cat. "I think that was a yes, Cyril."

"Perhaps we should retire to Kildorne Manor." The viscount suggested tentatively, "We have much to set right. Your brother's name to clear—surely naught more than a young man's drunken joke gone awry? After all, no one would believe such of the Marquis de Fournier's younger brother. *They wouldn't dare.* Then we much concoct the demise of a phantom called the Devil in Spurs and, I presume, a marriage to arrange? And a longer apology on the ill deeds of a time when I little cared for life. I think with your love of my daughter you might comprehend." The older man's eyes watched his daughter with a mixture of pride and pain. "She is so the image of her mother."

Ashlyn reached out and touched her father's arm. "I...I never understood you loved her."

He nodded, fighting the tears. "There are many things I never permitted you to see. Maybe now you know love, you will have an ear and compassion to hear me." Kildorne forced a smile. "See, daughter, I still know a thing or two. I said the Marquis de Fournier was my choice for your husband above all others."

She smiled at Desdein, linking fingers with his. "Aye, that you did. He might be a devil in spurs, but he's my devil and I plan to keep him. Eh, Cyril?"

The cat looked up at them and meowed.

Other books available by Deborah MacGillivray:
A Restless Knight
The Invasion of Falgannon Isle

And...
Coming soon,
DeborahAnne's solo anthology,
CAT O' NINE TALES

Visit DeborahAnne at her website,
http://www.deborahmacgillivray.co.uk

You've read the 'enchantment', now we invite you to join us for the 'magic.' We hope you'll look for the companion book in the Once In a Blue Moon Series:

BLUE MOON MAGIC

Available now from Highland Press:

HIGHLAND WISHES
NO LAW AGAINST LOVE
BLUE MOON MAGIC
BLUE MOON ENCHANTMENT

Upcoming:

DANCE EN L'AIR
IN SUNSHINE OR IN SHADOW
THE CRYSTAL HEART
REBEL HEART
CHRISTMAS WISHES
HOLIDAY IN THE HEART
RECIPE FOR LOVE
FAERY SPECIAL ROMANCES
CAT O' NINE TALES
ALMOST TAKEN
PRETEND I'M YOURS

Check our website frequently for future Highland Press releases.

http://www.highlandpress.org

Cover design by DeborahAnne MacGillivray
Copyright 2006